A Southern Woman

A Southern Woman

Elena Yates Eulo

St. Martin's Press
New York

Design by Dawn Niles

Library of Congress Cataloging-in-Publication Data

Eulo, Elena Yates.
    A southern woman / Elena Yates Eulo.
       p. cm.   93986
    "A Thomas Dunne Book."
    ISBN 0-312-08751-9
    1. Tennessee—History—Civil War, 1861–1865—Fiction. I. Title.
PS3555.U54C68 1993
813'.54—dc20   92-43883
                                                CIP

First Edition: March 1993

10 9 8 7 6 5 4 3 2 1

For Bob and Claudine Yates, Jack and Topsy Morgan, and Elizabeth (Ezzie) Fishback . . . because little girls have heroes, too.

Acknowledgments

I thank Alice Marlis Noble, Robert L. Fenton, Maureen Baron, Winfield Scot Gibson, and Michael and Barbara Shimkin for their generous help and encouragement during the writing of this novel.

Especially, I am grateful to Mildred Marmur and Reagan Arthur. They made the journey easier and more pleasant.

Ama said: *"We tell our stories in order to live. . . ."*

A Southern Woman

One

$\mathcal{I}$ am Elizabeth Allen Crocker, born 1844 in Frisbin, Tennessee, child of the Roger Allens, one out of nine. My husband, Joe Crocker, he fought for the Yankees in the war. At the time, I didn't know why he done that. I reckoned just to be contrary. Because Joe didn't have no high ideals or nothing. And I knew he didn't like the Nigroes because he was always cussing them and saying how much he hated them, so I didn't think it was that. Anyhow, he fought for the North and it changed my life.

First off, I should say I was born with a melancholy. Just a sadness in a dark place inside me. I never asked myself no questions about it. I think a lot of people have feelings like that and never ask why. But when Joe Crocker went away to fight and I was left alone in Frisbin with nobody talking to me no more, not even Mama, unless they said hurting things like some of the young ones did and some of the older ones too, then it was harder not to think about things. Things like being alive and dying and how small we are. Like the point of my needle or the wing of an insect. But that kind of wondering could stop the world. At least for me. So I stayed alone then, with just the baby inside me and the melancholy growing stronger, and nothing about life seemed real any longer except for the lonesomeness.

On April nineteenth in '61 my pains started up real bad, and I walked two and a half miles to Mattie Simpson's house, on account of she birthed most of the babies close around, especially since Doc James left for the war. It was all known ground to me. The same path to Gallagher's orchard where us children went for peaches. The same way Papa went when he drove the wagon to Chisholm Valley with us piled in the back with the potatoes and corn. Bouncing up and down and singing "Bessie Jenner Was Her Name!" and Papa laughing up front. Sometimes he'd sing too, roaring out the words and slapping down the reins on the horses' backs. Seemed to me like I couldn't of lost them all. They just couldn't of turned their backs on me over somebody else's war. Not all of them. I kept walking and remembering and sometimes I had to stop because my pain was too bad to keep going. Then I'd start again.

I passed by Bluebottle Creek and by Wilbert Barr's where we got a pup once, then up the hill to Mattie's place, gray, flimsy, and neat as a pin. Even the yard looked like she'd swept it with a broom and I remembered how folks always said in the fall the trees were afraid to drop their leaves all over Mattie's lawn. Up the walk, blooming with flowers on both sides.

When I knocked, there was a tight feeling inside my chest. Scared is what I was. Like a wild rabbit in a trap.

Mattie's husband, Earl, come to the door and he'd been drinking. Earl couldn't go fight. He was old and he had a bad heart, Mattie said. So he stayed at home and rocked and drank what whiskey he could come by. He had a big soft belly and his voice sounded like he was wheezing, just a thin whisper or a whine. "What you want, Yankee slut?" he whispered. He used his big body to block the doorway, so's not to let Mattie see me. "Go on. Git!"

I felt tears coming down all over my face and I didn't know if I was crying because of the baby coming or from something else. There wasn't no use to say nothing to Earl, not if he could see me standing there like that and say what he done, and I turned 'round to go away. But I didn't have no place in the world to go. Anyhow I knew there weren't no time left.

"Move out, Earl, or come in, either one you'd druther," a voice said, and Mattie come poking her way past Earl with a washmop, hauling a pail of dirty water in her other hand. She gave me a squint and pitched out the bucket. I had hold of the porch rail, bent double. "Earl, why didn't you call me?" she said, leaning the mop in a corner. "How close are the pains, Liz Ann?"

But I didn't say nothing, just dropped to my knees and screamed because I was in hard labor and scared and hurting worse than I ever thought I could hurt.

"I ain't havin' you birthin' no Yankee bastard, Mattie," whispered Earl, soft as a mama croons to her baby.

"Hush," Mattie said. "I don't care about Yankees no more'n you, but that don't count when there's doctorin' to be done. I seen her three days ago at the store and never spoke a word, but that don't add up to a hill a beans right now. Now does it, Earl?" Mattie squatted down next to me, and her eyes were warm. "Pain passed on, youngun? Can you walk inside if I help you?"

She put her arm 'round my waist and I could feel the strength of her. I never had thought of Mattie as a strong woman before, just an old woman, waddling fat, with long breasts hanging down to her stomach. I leaned against her because I was weak and because it was good to have a human body to lean on again.

Earl never said nothing else. He didn't have the strength to stand by his principles, even if they were evil principles. He just grunted and went away somewheres.

That hour and a half till Melissa Sue come was full of a kind of pain I'd never known before. But after I got used to it, I didn't much care about the suffering. I heard a woman say once that she'd never been able to love her babies 'cause they'd hurt her so bad to have them. But I didn't feel like that a bit. When the baby was in me all that time I never really believed there was a baby there. That pain in me was like joy, because all of a sudden, I knew there was life there. Life that was a part of me. When it was the sharpest, right before Melissa Sue come, it was the best joy and I was screaming and laughing right

3

together. "It's a spirited youngun," I said, watching Mattie knot up a pillowcase. It was for me to bite down on, now that the baby was so close to coming.

"I got to say it for you, child," Mattie said. "You take to this natural as anythin' I ever seen. You got courage and pluck."

"I'm not going to be alone no more, Mattie," I said, feeling another pain coming on. "I'll have my baby to sing to and play with and talk to and—and I'll never be alone no more."

Then the pain was bad and I was listening to Mattie real careful. She had my legs straddled out and I hated that because it made me feel helpless, like I was going to be torn apart right up the middle. But Mattie had to know what was best and I tried not to pull my knees back together. Sweat run into my eyes and burnt them till I couldn't see and I wanted Mama so bad.

"Mama," I whispered, but Mattie was yelling now.

"Push, Liz Ann. I can see the baby's head. You got to push now. It's comin'! I got my hands on it. You got to push harder."

I screamed till I couldn't hear her and kept on pushing. Seemed like there were two of me. One screaming for all she was worth and one calm and looking down over the bed, wishing the other one would keep still. But I couldn't keep still. I yelled as hard as I could and I knew for sure I was bursting and tearing on the inside. Mattie's voice yelling, "Push, Liz Ann. Right now! Push!" and me bearing down as hard as I could and then all of a sudden, the baby shooting out between my legs, right into Mattie's hands. Melissa Sue come out squalling.

"You've popped it!" Mattie laughed, holding up my baby for me to look at, and I was afraid because of all the blood and the way the baby was crying so hard.

"Is she supposed to cry like that?" I asked, forgetting about birthing and pain and only thinking about my baby.

"She's got good lungs." Mattie chuckled. "Just listen to that gal yell. She don't want to get no paddlin'. I'm goin' to give her a swat though, just for superstition."

I watched as she laid a lively hand to Melissa Sue's bottom. "She all right, Mattie? She got all her toes and all?"

4

"She's got it all. Goin' to be a real nice-lookin' woman, like her ma."

Mattie was busy cleaning Melissa Sue up and it all felt so homely and nice, like my mama was there or something. She cleaned me too and took away the afterbirth and I felt so comfortable and taken care of and emptied out. I laid real still and I could feel my eyes closing. "Mattie, I can't stay awake. You take care of Melissa for me, all right?"

"Why, course, honey. I'm a old hand at baby-tending. You go on to sleep now. You earned it."

"Well, but this is a very special baby," I said. "A happiness baby. So, you see, she's got to have real good care. She's paid for, too. I brung you a dollar. It's in my shoe."

"Thank you, child. With farm taxes and all, there's not many can pay nowadays." Mattie gave a little *hmph* down in her throat.

"And don't worry. You don't have to talk to me in public places or nothing. I understand all about that. And . . ." My eyes were dropping closed. "Melissa . . . isn't no Yankee. She's . . ." I could feel my lips smiling. ". . . She's . . . just plain baby."

Two

That spring was the prettiest season I ever saw in Tennessee. The grass was green on the hills and the sun was so bright it brought tears to my eyes. The mountains that rose on all sides of our town were thick with budding trees and their rocky cliffs were melted free of winter snow and shining like white bone under the sun.

Somewheres else, further north I guessed, for I never got no news of the war, men were taking lives and giving up their own. I wondered what happened to Joe and if he'd ever be coming back—and if he did, whether life would ever be like it used to be—but I never put no feeling into the wondering. It was like Joe Crocker was a stranger and the Civil War . . . well, even though our town flew the Stars and Bars, the war didn't have nothing to do with me.

Sometimes I imagined that Mama would come knocking on my door, all smiling and wanting to see her granddaughter, but she didn't, neither she nor Jessie Lee nor even Nellie. Nellie was my favorite sister and I kept thinking she'd surely come. But then women can't do what the men order them not to. I never thought much about Papa and the boys anymore, I guess 'cause of some of the things they'd said to me after Joe left. They were soldiers for the South now, all of them. I wondered if Papa and the boys were fighting in a battle now and were they all right?

"God bless Papa," I whispered, my lips barely moving.

6

"And Gary and Buster and Harry and Buddy and Steve and Will."

I looked out over the land, because that's the way I thought of them. Men whose lives were in the earth. Farmers plowing their fields and taking crops in harvesttime. I stared out over the land and forgot them. Because they were faithful to the earth but they didn't care about me no more.

So the days turned into a hot blistering summer with hardly any rain at all. Most of the crops burnt up and all this time the only one I set my affections on and prayed about was my baby. And when I held Melissa Sue up to my breast and gave her my own nourishment I could understand how women said they lived for their children.

Yet sometimes I was scared, too. In broad daylight my teeth would start to chattering. Can I take care of you proper, Melissa? I kept wondering. And who will take care of me, so that I can take care of you? And who will be family to you, child of mine? And what church will baptize you? Oh, child, what will become of us?

Outside of Mama and Papa, there weren't no Allens in Frisbin. Pa'd moved us up from Georgia when Buster was three months old. Good cheap land. Not seventy miles from the old homestead, and yet I never remembered an Allen visiting us, or us them. And Joe's family must hate me as much as they hate him, I thought, or Mary Crocker would of come for us. How can a mother hate her own child, I wondered, and I kissed the top of Melissa's head and promised her I'd love her forever. No matter what, Melissa. You hear me? No matter what!

Finally it was fall with all the leaves heaped up on the ground. The trees turned in on themselves, saving their strength to get through the winter, and the people I seen when I went for supplies wore lines in their faces.

The nights were dark and cold, and so still you jumped to hear creatures rustling in the leaves or a wolf howling up in the hills. Possums were on my roof, and listening to them run over my head was like hearing my own brain chasing after itself. No matter how hard I'd try to calm myself, to sleep, thoughts kept coming into my head and I didn't know if it was me making them up or whether they were alive and coming to me on their own. Ruby. Ruby like the jewel. Nigger Ruby, Papa called her. I wondered how come he had to remind her all the time she was a Nigro. I used to wonder if she was ever able to forget she was colored. Was it the first thought in her mind when she woke up in the morning and the last thing she thought about in her bed at night?

I asked her once when I was too little to know better and she looked at me for a minute before she said anything. Then she knelt down and looked me in the eye and said, "Why I be wantin' to forget, Liz Ann?" with such dignity and pride shining out at me that I was ashamed for asking the question.

"Ruby *is* a jewel and that's the truth," Mama would say, putting her arm 'round her like she was a child. "I wouldn't know what to do without my Ruby. No. And that's a fact. Ain't that the truth now, Ruby?"

Ruby always laughed with the kind of Nigro laugh that she knowed Mama liked to hear, and answered, "You too good to me, Miz Allen, you just too good."

"And don't we treat you just like one of the family? Now tell the truth now, Ruby."

"Miz Allen, now that the gospel. I a happy nigger." And she'd fix her black eyes on Papa with another laugh 'cause she knowed how he liked to hear her call herself a nigger, and I wondered if it was only me that thought her eyes were playing with him and that Ruby was having her own private joke on us all. I loved Ruby and I reckon the rest did, too. I heard Mama say many times she loved Ruby much as it was humanly possible to love a Nigro.

Ruby ran away at the start of the war, before Joe and the others had gone, so I wondered if she really had loved any of us back. I reckon she did. Just as much as it was humanly possible for a Nigro to love white folks.

It was because of Ruby and our two field Nigroes that we

got our social standing. I never would of understood if Mama hadn't explained it to me how that made us better than the people who lived the next farm over. They had about the same-size piece of land as we had, and their house wasn't much different either. But Mama didn't visit Mrs. Louden and we didn't play with her children because they weren't slave owners. We weren't rich or nothing, Mama said, but we were genteel and we had to be careful to keep proper company and to marry as well as we could. That's why Mama said I should marry Joe Crocker. His father had two house Nigroes and four to help with the crops and in time Joe would amount to something. That's what she said.

I stared at my ceiling and saw Joe's face there in the shadows. Every girl in Frisbin had wanted him, so Mama said I should take him quick when he asked me. He was a fine-looking man with his own spread and a cabin, so it was only natural him wanting a wife.

It was on a Friday night he asked me. We'd been for a buggy ride after one of Mama's special fried-chicken dinners, and on the way home he stopped the horse. Seemed to me, my heart half stopped, too.

"Liz Ann," he said, "you're a strong-looking woman and your mama says you're a right tolerable cook. That right?"

"Ay, Mr. Crocker, that I am."

He threw back his handsome head and give out with a laugh. "Reckon you can take your orders from a husband like a good girl and raise me up a batch of younguns to help me in my old age?"

"I reckon I can, Mr. Crocker." My voice sounded scared and he put out his hand and covered mine.

"Now Liz Ann," he said, "I betcha you could do yourself a lot worse than me. Don't you 'magine?"

His brown eyes looked into mine and I felt the strangest feeling like my heart jumped inside me, so I figured that was a pretty good reason to marry Joe Crocker. But nobody ever told me exactly what a married woman has to put up with, and how men act with their wives at night. It wasn't the pain and it wasn't how degraded I felt or how he acted while he was doing it, like I wasn't there, almost like he didn't enjoy what he was doing or want to remember it. It was the fact that after the first night, the first time he done it to me, never again did he look into my eyes like he done when he was asking me to marry him.

"I don't hate Joe Crocker," I whispered against the back of my hand, and then I wondered how come I said that. "It's all right, Liz Ann. All right. Maybe it'll be a long war."

And it *was* going to be a long war, too, from the look of things. More of the men were gone now and it was getting hard to get flour or sugar. No coffee at all, although they said the cities still had plenty of everything. Sometimes I'd get news of the war by going into a shop and pretending to look at something, maybe just stare at a bolt of material, and listening to the ladies talk. They were scared, like me. They watched the mountains and wondered how close the fighting was, just like me. They were more patriotic, though. They said they didn't care about supplies, not even coffee. Supplies were for the fighting men. I wondered if any of them were getting as hungry as me. Because my money was gone, and what few crops of mine that survived until harvesttime were dug out of the ground at night before I could get to them. The beans went to the Prewitts. The rest to who knew who. The Prewitts didn't sneak around. Probably, they wanted me to recognize them.

Then it was December and raw cold and I didn't have no store left and the cow died of milk fever or maybe somebody poisoned her. For a week, I hadn't been eating right and I was afraid my milk would dry up or that I wasn't giving my baby nourishment. It got to where Melissa cried all the time and people always said that when babies cry a lot, it's because they're hungry. And even though I'd been pretending to myself that I had enough to eat, I felt the hunger inside of me, too, and that hunger was fear. Fear for Melissa Sue.

So it come to where I guess I always knew it would come, to going home to Mama. I had done the best I knowed how, with no man to take care of me and no friends and no family and now I had to go explain to my mother exactly how it was and, looking deep into my heart, I knew I wasn't sorry to go. I sang a lullaby to Melissa Sue whiles I was dressing her in the clothes that used to be mine when I was a baby, the same nameless song that Mama used to sing whiles she was rocking me.

Don't cry, Melissa. It worries Mother so. It makes me worry that maybe I waited too late to take you home. But now everything's going to be all right. Your grandmama's going to doctor you up and nobody on earth knows more about doctoring babies than she does. You'll see.

I knew Mama would take us. I knew it. There was this warm feeling right in the pit of my stomach, and my heart beat like a drum, marching us home. So why was I praying over and over again, "Please, God, please dear God," to a God I wasn't sure was there? Was there a God, and if there was, would he still be there in Frisbin, Tennessee or would he be with the soldiers? Don't us women count too, God? And what about our babies? Melissa Sue cried and I cried, too. Can you hear that, Lord? Just a woman and a girl-child both crying. *Don't let my baby die, Lord, or I'll hate you forever. Hate you!* Then I stopped that kind of thinking. Maybe I put a curse on my baby with wicked thoughts like that. Forgive me, Lord, for my evil.

There wasn't no sound anywheres when I went up the path and knocked on the old door. My home. How can you love a house? It's just made out of wood. Please, Lord, make Mama want us. Then my sister Nellie come and answered the door. Her face was thin and her eyes were red 'round the lids. I just walked up to her and put my right arm 'round her shoulders. I was holding Melissa Sue in my left. What is it in a human body that lets you know not to hug it? Nellie didn't pull away or nothing, least not so's I could tell. But something inside her did. I backed up and we stood there like two strangers who don't know each other well enough to be comfortable together. Nellie kept looking over her shoulder into the house, like she wished somebody else had answered the door.

"Can I come in, Nellie? Please," I said, half froze, Melissa sagging against my arm.

"You ought not to come here, Liz Ann. It'll worry Mama." She shut her mouth and swallowed hard. Nellie always had the prettiest softest mouth. Her upper lip curved in the middle like a heart and it was full and womanly with a dimple in the right corner. Her hair was thicker than mine and curly and it always shined from brushing. Her eyes were blue, like mine, only mine were darker and bigger.

Nellie and I used to stare in the looking glass and try to decide who was the prettiest. She thought I was and I guess most people agreed with her because I was called the handsomest girl in the family. Papa even said I was the handsomest girl in the county. Nellie said my skin was pretty and my eyes were bluer than any eyes she'd ever seen and my nose was good. But I told her I thought she was prettier than me, and I meant it. That's why I hated seeing her now, so thin and sick-looking. Her hair dull and her eyes staring.

"Come on in, anyway," Nellie said, coughing against her arm. "Let's get it over with." She jerked her head for me to come in. "Go on in the parlor. I'll get Mama."

She went away to the back of the house and I carried Melissa into the parlor. It was funny how everything I looked at hurt me. Mama's glass dogs that I always loved so much. A bright wool coverlet over the back of the rocker that I'd knitted myself. Mama's whatnot shelves. China cups and a blue-and-white-painted pitcher. Even the rug on the floor and the curtain at the window. It all hurt. Everything looked dark and gray and I had a thought in my head that since we'd all been separated from each other, life had sat still inside the house. There were voices, and then I heard someone laugh, and Mama said, "Hush."

Then Nellie come back with Mama and Jessie Lee. Jessie Lee walked beside Mama, a smirk across her mouth, and it was the first time I ever noticed how like Mama she was. If ever anybody was born in someone's image, it was Jessie Lee, the spitting image of Mama.

Mama stopped inside the door to light the lamp, because it was so dim, like we were in shadows. The light shined on her face and that reminded me how she used to stand over my bed at night and tuck the covers 'round me. Then she'd kiss me and blow out the light. Mama's hair looked grayer and it wasn't so neat as it used to be. She had it twisted up on top of her head and pieces of it were loose and hanging. Mama was a square-faced woman with narrow turned-inside lips, and she didn't smile much because she was ashamed of her missing tooth in the front.

The four of us sat down and looked at each other. Mama was in the hardest chair with Jessie Lee beside her in the company chair. Because of its wide back and curved arms, it was the prettiest chair in the house and Mama would always offer it to the company. Nellie was on the sofa with me, but all the way over as far as she could sit. Jessie Lee's lips kept looking like she wanted to laugh but didn't dare. She lifted her handkerchief twice and I knew what for. It was to smile into.

"Mama, how are you?" I listened to my voice to see if it was steady, but it wasn't, not as much as I'd hoped.

"Oh, right tolerable, Elizabeth Ann. And you?" Mama were sitting straight as a rod in her chair already, but she got even stiffer.

"Oh, I've been fine. I've been taking real good care of myself, just like you taught me to. I've been cooking and sewing and keeping the cabin real neat, just like a pin."

"Keepin' it straight for your *husband*, I reckon, when he comes back," Jessie Lee said, then shut her mouth when Mama looked hateful at her.

Nobody said nothing for a minute and I could hear Nellie breathing raspy and loud. The house was damp and cold. The windows steamed over. "You ought to have a fire, Nellie," I said. "It's cold." I looked, but I didn't see no firewood.

"There isn't no kindlin' chopped," Mama said in a short way. "The niggers all run off."

I wondered how come my sisters hadn't chopped no wood. I was about to ask, but the strangeness between the four of us unsettled me and Melissa Sue must of felt it because she started to cry. I rocked her and my arms felt calmer, because my love was stronger than the trembling inside me.

Finally Mama halfways looked at Melissa Sue. "So he left you a Yankee baby, did he? Well, I reckoned he'd come to a shameful pass. Weren't never no good and I told your pa so at the time."

"But, Mama, you *liked* Joe. You said—"

"Shut your mouth quick. I always knew he was no-good trash, struttin' round like he owned the town. Ain't no better judge of character than me, and your pa always said it. Your poor pa. That trash of your'n could be killin' your own pa, or one of the boys, putting a *bullet* right between their eyes, right this here minute, but you don't care nothin' about that."

"Mama . . . I haven't been eating right. The baby ain't getting her nourishment. Mama, she's starving."

And then Jessie Lee laughed.

"Please, Mama," I said. My words did not move her.

A death-silence fell down then, and it was the end of my family. Good-bye forever, Jessie Lee. I looked into her eyes and seen her for what she was. Say something, Mama. No? Then good-bye forever, Mama. I didn't look into her eyes. I didn't want to see what was there. Nellie wouldn't look at me. She just kept wringing her hands in her lap. Good-bye, dear Nellie.

They watched me out the door, Melissa Sue screaming in my arms, and I could feel their eyes behind the curtain watching me down the stone path and down the steps clear up over the hill. And when I was away from their eyes, I was for a moment very calm, like water gets calm after a sea storm's over. Like the earth lays still after nature finishes stirring things up.

But sometimes nature kills things. That's where hollow logs come from after a tree blows down. Or dried-up crops after a drought. Maybe I'd be like that, hollow inside, all the loving burnt out . . . if my baby died. She'd stopped her crying and I imagined to myself that she was giving up. I stared into her thin little face and thought it was already too late. No, it couldn't be. I was just making trouble inside my brain, thinking something like that. But the thought was there, that she was dying, and I couldn't seem to get rid of it.

She really is going to die, I thought, and it was real to me. Realer than the world 'round me. I could see her slipping away from me and I started running down the road, as fast as I could run. I had to save my baby. Oh, God, she's going to starve to death. And I can't stop her. Melissa Sue Crocker is dying.

I stopped running finally, because I couldn't run no more. She was going away from me, dying by inches. I sat down by a big rock. How do you kill a baby, so it dies quick and doesn't linger? I picked up the rock and thought about hitting her in the soft part of her head. Would that kill her quick? But no, God, I couldn't do that. It would hurt her, I knew it would. Anyways, then how would I kill myself? I couldn't live, not for a minute longer than my baby. I set the rock down slow and I didn't get up.

There was the sound of horses coming, but I never even wondered who it was. When the carriage drove by, I didn't look up, just pulled my shawl closer 'round the two of us. I heard the voices, though. Soft women's voices drifting through the cold, damp air. Then the sound of horses being pulled up.

Someone calling my name. I barely lifted up my eyes and lowered them quick, feeling ashamed of myself, sitting beside the road, poor as trash. It was Ama Hadley from the big house. The Hadleys were the richest family in Frisbin, but they were plainspeaking good people. Mr. Hadley was silver-haired and always smiling and Ama Hadley was a gentlewoman who never talked down to a soul and always acted like everybody she met was her equal, no matter how poor or ordinary the person would be. They used to come to church ever Sunday until one day, Mrs. Hadley asked the preacher if she couldn't bring her Nigroes to worship. "You could of blowed me over when she said that," the good Reverend had said later, retelling the story. "Niggers in the white church. 'Mrs. Hadley,' I said, 'you're a good woman. But that kind of thing never has been done and never will be done. Now I hope you understand.' That's what I told her," said the Reverend, proud of his good judgment.

Knowing Reverend Harper, I was sure he certainly did hope that Ama Hadley would understand. He wouldn't of wanted to lose the Hadleys' big church donation. He *had* lost it though, because Mrs. Hadley never had come again, and neither had Mr. Hadley. Folks said Mr. Hadley thought his missus was an angel and whatever she decided about things was all right. He had even freed all his Nigroes when she said to do it, giving them papers to show they were free men and women.

Ama Hadley's maid was riding with her today, sitting beside her wrapped in a blanket. I heard her voice, tender, soft, and I knew she was talking about me. "Oh, Miz Ama, the pore little thing just sittin' there like the whole world done run out on her."

"Maybe it has, Jinny." A full skirt rustled down from the seat and a soft hand laid down on my shoulder. "It's Ama Hadley, Elizabeth." I looked up at her and she seemed like she must be out of some other world. There were lots to separate us—my thin wore-out clothes and the starving baby in my arms, and her fine carriage and elegant clothes. She took off her cloak and put it on me. That's just how quick people can get close, if they're the right people. "Elizabeth, are you in trouble?"

I stared up at her face and she smiled like we were meeting in proper society. Nobody hadn't smiled at me like that for a long time. And smiles never meant so much neither back in the days when everybody talked and everybody smiled. I heard Mrs. Hadley and her maid talking between themselves, but I couldn't make out what they were saying.

As cold as it was, sweat rolled down my back and behind my knees and all down my face. Where do people go when they die? Somewhere where babies don't starve and people don't hate you 'cause of something your husband done. How long will you live, Melissa Sue, before you go to that place?

"Elizabeth, can you hear me? You're going home with me." I could feel her arm 'round my back, holding me. Other arms reached out to take my baby, but I held on to Melissa tight. "No, Jinny, you let her keep her baby. She won't let it fall." And

16

then, somehow, they had us up on the seat next to Mrs. Hadley, with Jinny in the back, and the horses were going again.

"Is that baby's life in danger, Jinny?" Mrs. Hadley's voice was commonplace, like she was asking about whether to plant taters or corn. I wondered how come it didn't scare me to hear her say that. No, it was a relief to hear it said, like they knew Melissa Sue was sick and were trying to save her.

Jinny leant over my shoulder and took a good look at the baby, and I let her. "Let me see that Lamb Bone," she crooned. "That a li'l gal Lamb Bone or a li'l boy Lamb Bone? Come on, honey, you let ole Jinny see." She wasn't a bit old actually, but plump and ageless. She reached down 'mongst the shawl and pulled up Melissa's little skirt. She give a good-spirited cackle. "Law, if it ain't a li'l gal. I ought to knowed from the *charm* o' the face. Looky there that honey-pie face and you see for yourself. This here a real li'l lady, yessum."

Jinny started making over her and cooing and before I knowed what she was doing, she pulled Melissa Sue clean out of my arms and had her nestled up right next to her breast. I didn't mind. It seemed like she was in real good hands and it was the first time I could rest in a long time. "Yessum, this here ole Jinny li'l Lamb Bone. We gots put us some fat on them li'l bone, yeah, we have now." She gave Melissa Sue a rocking that wasn't none too gentle at the start, but seemed like it shook some life into her, 'cause she stirred up and commenced crying. Then Jinny changed and got tender with her and went into some kind of low deep humming that wasn't no song I ever heard.

Mrs. Hadley had been busy driving her horses, and driving them like she knew what she was doing. Now she give a laugh. "Well, the healing's begun now. You leave her with Jinny. She knows things about nature you can't read in a book."

"Mrs. Hadley . . . do you think my . . . my baby . . ."

She looked back at Melissa, then at me. "Well," she said thoughtful-like, "I'm inclined to believe she'll be all right." She give a little nod to herself like the whole thing was settled.

17

I was hungry to hear words about hope. "But why do you think so, though?"

"Because I don't believe in coincidence." We reached a bumpy stretch of ground and the horses lost their speed.

"Coincidence? I don't understand."

"Well, just for debate . . ." Her eyes sparkled, and she was enjoying herself, I could tell. "Let's say I'll give you so much toward the argument of coincidence. Let's say I believe that things accidentally came together in such a way that a beautiful green world came to be and that upon the face of this world, whatever phenomenon had to happen in order to create life as we know it just happened. And that brains were accidentally endowed with such potential that they could develop into wondrous thinking machines"—she clucked absentminded-like to her horses—"and that eyes accidentally occurred to observe the accidental beauties of the world and that accidentally nourishing food just happened to be also (and most fortunately) delicious to the taste of our accidental taste buds and that—"

"Whoa, Mrs. Hadley, my head's spinning."

She laughed fit to kill. "Well, that's good for it. Stir things up a bit. But we're talking about accidents. I'm just trying to explain how I don't think that it was anything but meant to be that we'd be here at the exact moment you're needing a good friend and a good baby doctor (couldn't be a better one than Jinny). What I'm saying, Elizabeth, is that I believe your baby will live because I don't believe that the patient would have been delivered into the arms of the master doctor unless she was meant to be saved. Of course, Elizabeth," she said, matter-of-fact-like, "I could be and am very often wrong."

She smiled as she said it, looking sideways at me in the gray winter light, and I thought I never seen such a lady, kind, peaceful, lovely like a caring woman is lovely. It give me an ache inside me just to look at her. I don't know why. She slapped the reins against the horses' backs, but it wasn't like she was whipping them. It was too easy for that, more like she was talking to them, reminding them to get on. "Elizabeth," she went on, "you did get my message in the spring, didn't you?"

I got red, 'cause I did get a letter from her, away back before Melissa Sue was born or anything. It was left on my cabin door one day when I was out and it said how she understood how I was having a hard time and how I was welcome and she *urged* me to come to her and let her help.

"Yes, ma'am, I got it—long time ago," I said. "But I didn't want to be no nuisance to you and things weren't so hard yet. I had supplies and some money Joe left me 'fore he . . . 'fore he went to the war. I meant to get word to you thanking you for your offering to help when nobody else did, but I . . . I was all alone and I got real sad—so's I couldn't think right anymore. I'm not saying that for pity, Mrs. Hadley. I'm just saying it so maybe you'll know I *was* thankful to you and maybe you'll forgive me for not saying so sooner."

Mrs. Hadley's fingers touched under my chin and she drew up my face. Her eyes met mine. "How old are you, honey?"

"Seventeen," I said, but couldn't say no more 'cause tears washed in a flood down my face till I wondered where they were all coming from. I could feel her sympathizing and just when my eyes were drying up to where I could barely see, I looked across at her and for some reason both of us started laughing. I laughed so hard I finally got to gagging and had to stop. "What was that all about?" I wondered out loud.

"You need healing too, Elizabeth." She wiped the laugh tears out of her own eyes, not looking a bit surprised or ashamed at showing such unladylike emotion before someone she didn't know real close. "You needed to cry and you needed to laugh. Never fight emotion—try to understand it—go along with it."

"Oh, now, Mrs. Hadley, I can't be acting like a fool now. Bad enough, everyone despising me for being a Yankee, which I *ain't,* Mrs. Hadley, on no account. But now they'll be calling me a crazy woman, if I start laughing and crying right out in the streets for no reason of any account." I pictured me laughing and crying out in the road and prim old Mrs. Yager watching me from behind her lace curtains pulled just so and it started me laughing all over again. But it didn't last long this time. "Well, maybe I'm getting cured." I smiled at Mrs. Hadley.

"I suppose it was a more appropriate response," she agreed. "That's because you got rid of all that emotion. You were equalized—you'd gotten rid of all those stored-up tears and all that unlaughed laughter."

"Huh! You mean, I didn't have nothing else left over inside me. Well, that's real interesting." I never heard nobody talk like she talked.

"You're a fine patient, Elizabeth. You've got spirit and sensitivity and a good mind. And I like your sense of humor. The prognosis is excellent—for both of you." She nodded over at Melissa Sue in Jinny's arms and I jumped a little. I'd plain forgot my baby for a minute.

"I forgot her, Mrs. Hadley. How could I forget her when she's sick?"

"Best thing you could do for her. You were worried half to death over her and it was fairly well killing her. See how much brighter she looks, now that somebody's got hold of her that thinks she's got a chance?"

Melissa Sue did look better. "And she hasn't even ate yet," I whispered, watching her.

Jinny cradled her, protective-like. "We just take li'l baby-chile to Beulah and her give you a real good meal, ain't that right, sugar? Beulah give you *pork chop*"—she jabbed at Melissa Sue's nose with a happy finger, laughing all the time—"and you get a fresh-bake *wheat cake* with lots of 'lasses"—another jab of her finger and another laugh—"and some black-eye *pea* . . ."

"What's she talking about, Mrs. Hadley? Why, Melissa's just barely eight months old."

Mrs. Hadley and Jinny both had a laugh at me. "Beulah's a nursing mama, Elizabeth, and I guess she'll have plenty of milk for two."

Jinny whooped out again, like she had enjoyed a good joke. But not like she was poking fun or making me uncomfortable. It was like I was already a member of their family. All of a sudden I felt peaceful and tired and, listening to Jinny's rich voice humming its healing chant to my baby, I felt ready to nod off to sleep right there in the middle of the day.

Before I did, I remembered to give thanks. Dear God, thank You. You sent us a friend to save us. I know it was You done it—'cause I don't believe in coincidence!

Three

*A*ma Hadley said the war wasn't real to the people of Frisbin yet. Oh, she said they felt the inconvenience of it, the men living away from home and the tax on farms and the Confederate army requisitioning the crops. But the true meaning of war would occur to them when the blood began to flow and when the graves were dug.

And the war wasn't real there either at Ama's place that she called Symphony Oaks, 'cause when the wind blew it made music in the trees.

Inside the house it was musical, too. There were four women besides me, Ama and Jinny and Delilah and Beulah, and they all liked to sing. Beulah, the nursing mama, and Delilah had the best voices. They could sing in harmony something wonderful, almost as if they'd sung together their whole lives. Odd thing was they'd been slaves on Georgia plantations that weren't far from each other, but they'd never met until they'd been bought then freed by Ama.

Beulah was a soft big woman, very black, with smooth skin and a mouth that would of been beautiful excepting she hardly ever smiled. She was a silent woman, but strong and smart. Delilah was the youngest, about the same age as me I'd guess, though she didn't know her own age. She said almost no slave did, and it was true that none of the three black women in the house knew the date they were born, or the year. Delilah was always smiling and laughing while she swept and dusted the beautiful rooms of tall dark furniture, sometimes stooping down to stare at the daguerrotype of Ama's husband taken in full uniform, his saber strapped 'round his waist. The picture fascinated Delilah and she said she wanted one of herself and Sinclair, the man she meant to marry after the war. Sinclair had belonged to a Tennessee farmer, but had been hired out by his owner to work for wages at Lee and Gordon's Mill just south of us. He had run off from the mill towards the beginning of the war, in too much of a hurry to come for Delilah—at least she believed so.

"But someday," Delilah said, "he be comin' back for me. Lord, that man love me half to death. And I never been had by no man. Sinclair love that 'bout me too. On my plantation, I the only gal there didn't get had. Only young one, anyhow. Them men come for me, I said, Kill me or be killed, that the only way. So come on, try. I rather be dead. They come close, I haul off and slap the livin' daylights out them. And not one ever had me! I right proud myself over that. Sinclair so proud 'bout it he wouldn't even take me hisself. He say, 'I want a wife never been had.' Oh, I tell you, Sinclair just love that 'bout me."

Nobody used the word "nigger" at Symphony Oaks. If they had, it would of killed something between us, same as using a gun. With us, it were just five women, different from each other in our own ways, and two girl babies, both of them beautiful.

Sometimes there in the house with Ama and the others, I could almost forget the war and what it meant to be Joe Crocker's wife. But when Ama's friends and neighbors stopped by to visit, then I saw it there in their faces and in the way they wouldn't really look at me. If only the rest of the world would go away, I'd think, watching them come up the walk.

But what I learned quick, and what the visiting folks found out too, was that no matter how they might feel about me, they had to act civil. If they sat in Ama's parlor, they had to sit with me. If they talked to Ama, they had to talk to me. Course, people already knew Ama had her odd ways. For instance, it was no unusual thing at Symphony Oaks for a white woman to share a sofa with the black women, because Ama was their friend and protector, too.

Excepting, of course, for Beulah. She was different from the rest of us. She was a friend, but she wouldn't be protected.

"I ain't no child," Beulah told me, full of her dignity, when I asked her about it. Then she set her jaw and stared off into her own fierce private world. "And I ain't gon' share no sofa with no white woman."

"I'm white," I said. "Ama's white. You sit with us."

Her brown snapping eyes turned on me. She said, "If I ever think—" And her throat swelled like a bullfrog as she breathed out her nose in a long loud breath. "If I ever think of either you as a white woman—then I never sit down with you again. No'm," she said, waving her hand to cut me off when I tried to speak. "And I never share no talk with you and never be nothin' to you 'cept a black woman. As white as you gettin', that how black I gettin'. And you be nothin' to me. You hear me now? Nothin'."

I tugged on her hand, trying to make that terrible look go away. "I ain't *never* going to be white," I promised her. "Not ever."

And after a while, Beulah nodded and smiled some and the look went off her face.

Things will be all right now between Beulah and me, I told myself. They had to be. Please, God—make everything all right.

But by the end of January, I could see that folks had stopped coming to Symphony Oaks. They'd swallowed sitting and sewing with the colored, but they weren't about to sit with no Yankee.

So I knew the time had come to go. The only trouble was I couldn't stand to leave that nice safe place, to go back into the aloneness of my cabin, back to wait for Joe Crocker.

I looked out the window at the long row of trees leading away from the house and I thought about the other women who

24

were waiting for their husbands and wondered if they really knew who they were waiting for, or cared. But of course they were waiting for more than just a man. They were waiting for the old way of life to come back home. Maybe, I told Melissa, we'd go away somewheres when her daddy come home. Maybe up North to live with the other Yankees. I wonder what Yankees are like, Melissa Sue. Heathens, I reckon. But Ama said there were lots of Yankees right here in Tennessee. She said in a war like this one it was going to be hard to know who to shoot at, that friends were going to fight friends and brothers brothers. If that be true, I wondered how come Joe was the only Yankee in Frisbin. Even Mr. Hadley was a major in the Confederate army. Though Ama would of rather him sign for the North, that was one time he'd made up his own mind.

"As for me," Ama said, "my sympathies are all for the North. I'm Yankee to the bone."

"Ain't that funny," I said. "Because I'm—"

"A Confederate?" she asked when I stopped, her eyebrows raised like she couldn't believe it.

"I always thought I was," I said, not sure any longer just what I was.

Ama put her arm round my shoulder. "Believe me," she said, squeezing me, "you're no rebel, though they'd have you believe you are. This whole town's been hoodwinked, walking around calling themselves citizens of the Confederacy. In a pig's eye, they are. The only *citizens of the Confederacy* are the planters with their mansions and hundreds of slaves whom they keep in drafty cabins and make sleep on dirt floors. Half the time without even a cover to put over themselves or anything to call a pillow under their heads. They call them property, they call them niggers. They use the whip to force their laws, and keep them half starved and ignorant to make them submissive. This war isn't about anyone who lives in Frisbin; it's only the dreams in their corrupt souls that make them think it is. The dreams of owning the mansions and the black property that makes it all possible. The truth is there's hardly a person who lives in our town who wouldn't be looked on as trash by the

25

lions of the Confederacy. But they just don't see it. And you can't get anybody to see what they won't," Ama finished with a shake of her head.

Still, even with her views, I could tell the Frisbin people were under Ama's spell, like me. And I knew they would forgive Ama her ways, forgive her for almost anything but me, just for the pure joy of her company, the life force that ran so strong in her that it could bring the dullest soul to life. It was only me that was taking away her neighbors, taking away her friends.

"I'll be going home tomorrow," I said on the last day of January.

Ama looked at me for a horrible long moment and then said I wasn't to go away from her. Not till the war was over or Joe was to come for me.

"But Ama," I said, "haven't you noticed how nobody comes here anymore? Don't you know it's because of me?" I felt tears burning my eyes. "They aren't going to sit down with no Yankee. Now don't tell me again that you're one, because the truth is, they don't look at you like that. Not with the major fighting for the South. It's only me. And if I leave, they'll come back, so—" My throat closed and I stopped.

Ama looked at me with eyes that were neither sad nor serious. She smiled and said, "Now you listen to me, Elizabeth, for this is how it is. Good riddance to those people, the ones you speak of. Be off with them! They won't break my heart. But if you leave me, well . . ."

Deep inside, I knew maybe what Ama said might not be enough for Beulah, that Beulah's pride might insist on her leaving, but it was enough for me. If that meant Beulah was better than me and stronger than me, that was all right, too. All I could feel was rejoicing in my heart and I could feel the others feeling the same thing when they heard. I baked a cherry pie for dinner and we had sweet potatoes, corn, and roast beef. Then we had a glass of wine in the parlor and I felt the glow inside me.

"Ama," I said, and stopped. I didn't have no gift for words, like her.

26

She smiled over at me like she knew what I was wanting to say. "You're happy, aren't you?"

"Yes'm. Happier than I been in a long long time. I wish I could tell you how thankful I am, but there ain't no words, that *I* know anyways, that can say it."

"You've just said it. Now, please, Elizabeth, I know how you're going to want to be thanking me all the time, but I'd really appreciate it if you'd just restrain all that gratitude. I'm just as grateful to you for staying, as you are to me for asking. You keep away my loneliness and I'll keep away yours. How's that? And we'll call ourselves even, if that's all right." She smiled again and leaned back in her chair.

There was a peaceable silence between us as we sat there by the fire sipping on our wine. I could hear Delilah and Jinny in the kitchen, squabbling over whether to serve the pie by itself or to bring out the pudding and the sauce alongside. I heard Jinny say "war" and Delilah say "celebration." Silence, then Jinny said, "Long's us celebratin', I get the cream."

"Ama," I said, feeling light-headed. "I'd do anything for you. Anything at all. Why, I'd walk up to a cannon's mouth or straight through hell if it was for you."

She looked odd. "That's tempting fate. Seems like every time a mortal makes a declaration, something steps in to make them prove it. I remember I once declared something similar to what you said. Something about my willingness to go through the fires of damnation to prove something or other. And within the week, sure enough, there I was busy walking straight through hell. Right where I'd sworn I was ready to march.

"Another time I told God I was ready to accept His holy will. I wouldn't grieve, I told Him, no matter what earthly affliction He sent. My dog died the next day. After that, I got positively superstitious about the whole thing and resolved not to improve my character a whit. The theory being that since God only sends what you can bear, the best idea is not to be able to bear too much." She laughed, but I felt a shiver go up my spine. Like a premonition of something to come.

* * *

On February twentieth, with a freezing rain coming down and the wind moaning around us, come a knocking on the door. A black man, desperate and shy all at once, fell to the ground holding onto Ama's skirt and told her his story. He was a runaway slave, he said. He belonged to the Jackson family and they was after him on horses.

"If they catch me," he said, "they gon' kill me. That all I got to say." He bowed his head and waited.

My heart beat all over my body, that's how scared I was. I thought, That man, he's just kneeling there on the floor, waiting to see if he lives or he dies. But they're coming. If we hide him and they find him, what then?

Ama's hand was on his head. Her teeth chewed her lip while time passed. Beulah come up beside her. She said, "You 'speck them folks . . ."

"The Jacksons," Ama said. "From the other side of Lee and Gordon's Mill. I've heard of them."

"You 'speck they hear 'bout that man us help? Man name Nat?"

"Another runaway," Ama said to me even before I could ask who Nat had been.

"Did he make it?" I whispered.

Ama's head moved from side to side. There was something in her eyes that kept me from asking what happened. But I knew how come Beulah asked about Nat. It meant that there be folks who knew Ama had helped hide runaway slaves.

"Did anyone see you?" she asked the poor man, who was still on his knees before her, and he said that he'd been seen by an old man who'd passed by him in a carriage on his way home. A place about half a mile up the road. The old man had shouted at him and he'd taken off running even faster.

"Old Man Higgins," Ama said on a long sigh.

I didn't need her to tell me about Old Man Higgins. He owned the second-biggest acreage in Frisbin, and the most slaves, till they run away. He was also one of the meanest old men to ever walk the earth.

I thought, If we hide him, they're going to find him. They're going to find him for sure.

But the man, he was crying. Not begging, not talking. Just crying because he felt worse than I felt in the road that day. Because he was looking at worse than death. Worse than anything I ever wanted to think about.

"Elizabeth," Ama said, her face white as a lily but determined, "we'll hide him in the shed, on the top shelf, behind the tools and the old carriage top. Hurry now, Delilah, give him a drink, but just one." She said to take off my shoes, and she took off her shoes, too, and then she got burlap and covered up our hair.

It were me and Ama that took him out to the shed, and while I held up the lantern, poor Moses, for that was his name, scrambled up to the top rafter and hid hisself where he wouldn't never be found unless it be someone knew wheres to look.

"Don't be afraid, my friend," Ama said soft-like. "God is with you. Now, not a word, not a movement, until we come for you. Don't answer to a voice unless it's mine, no matter who comes, no matter what they say. Trust me. You won't be betrayed."

And he cried out, "Thank you, Missus. God bless you, Missus!" as we left him there in the dark. Outside the wind blew out our light straightaway. Ama bent low over the ground, the frozen drizzle still coming down on our bodies.

"Well, I'll be damned!" she said in a ladylike whisper. "Even with all this rain, the ground's cold enough to hold some imprint."

So shivering, with the water coming down on us from the sky and more blowing from the trees, we dragged branches behind us, covering up as many tracks as we could see.

"As to the rest"—Ama shuddered—"we'll have to trust God to wash them away."

Jinny and Beulah met us on the back porch with buckets of

29

water and helped us wash ourselves and threw our hair wrappings under the house. Even with the burlap, our hair was wet some.

"Now, Elizabeth," said Ama, "get out of all those wet clothes. Every stitch, don't hesitate. Beulah, roll them in strips and plug up that attic window. Put some water on the floor right under it, so they'll think we're trying to plug up a leak. We can't have them finding wet clothes." Ama's shaking fingers were already tearing away her own dress fastenings and I was convinced to do just exactly as she said, no matter what she said. It was ice cold and it felt odd to be naked out in the night with people 'round, but I were too scared and cold to be embarrassed about it. It seemed like it couldn't be happening, but it was. This is real, I reminded myself as Jinny wrapped me in a blanket and Delilah gave a last wipe of the towel 'round my legs.

"Hurry, Elizabeth," said Ama, with her hand on the door. "Dry clothes at once. Stoke up the fire for us, Jinny, and we need a glass of brandy."

So we hurried. Dear God, we hurried. Delilah and Jinny brushed and fanned at our hair till it was dry, and Beulah scrubbed away all trace of mud and water from the house. And we were ready in time with not thirty seconds to spare, sitting at our fire with knitting, when we heard the horses. Ama nodded at me with the same kind of look on her face I imagine men at war might wear looking at each other just before a battle.

"Show them in, Jinny," she said, calm as you ever saw. *Show them in,* even though it was like saying "Show the devil in." In a minute or two Jinny come with two men, an old one and one that wasn't nothing more than a boy.

"Apologies, ma'am," said the handsome old man with a bow. Curt Jackson was his name, he said. "I'm right sorry to bother you on such a night and to bring our mud inside," he went on. "But the fact is we seem fair certain to have tracked one of our niggers here."

"Oh, really," Ama said in a voice I never heard her use before. Like she was a cut above the average. "Well, believe me, sir, I stand at your service. Jinny!" in a commanding tone.

30

"Yes'm," Jinny said, cringing like she thought Ama was going to lay into her.

"Get the other niggahs at once and then prepare the table. Are you alone?" When she heard there were four more men, she ordered hot coffee and brandy for the men and hot milk for the boy. "Step lively now!" and she clapped her hands to scurry Jinny out of the room. "Please, sir, get the rest of your men. No, never mind the mud. Such a night for you to be out." She was arranging chairs before the fire and chatting like it was a party. "What's your name, son?" she asked the boy in a quieter voice when the old man had left the room. "I don't believe we know each other."

"No, ma'am," the boy said. "We're from Bedford. I'm Gray Jackson and that there's my grandfather." He looked scared. "Ma'am . . ." Almost whispering.

"Yes?" Ama bent close to him.

"What—what do they do to niggers when they catch them?"

"I don't know, Gray." Ama looked him in the eyes and she didn't smile. And there were silence with us.

The others come in and warmed theirselves by the fire and had their coffee and brandy and filled up on beef and cake. The three Nigroes were lined up before them and they flung questions and took care to use the word "nigger" a lot. Fair insulting they were, and one of the men run his hand down on Delilah's bottom whiles he was talking to her. Ama's face turned whiter than ever, but she kept her look civil. Delilah never said one word or moved, even when the man had his hand on her bottom. I knowed then that we were in the deepest kind of trouble, because there were men here who didn't have no mercy in them. I never let myself think about the man Moses who was shivering out there in the far shed.

The man who had his hand on Delilah's bottom squeezed it.

"Please, sir," Ama said to old Mr. Jackson, "no coarse treatment. Remember, sir, that Elizabeth and I are ladies and

31

present in your company. If your man insists on that sort of thing, I'll have to ask him to go into another room."

"Beau!" said Mr. Jackson with anger to the man who done that to Delilah. "I don't stand for that. Get your hands off that black wench and keep 'em off or I'll knock the living daylights out of you."

Beau was his overseer, he said, and the three others were neighbor men, two of them ready to leave for the army. The other had lost the lottery to his three brothers and had to stay home and take care of the property whiles they went away to fight.

The questions went on, and Ama herself took the three Nigroes to task and declared as how Nigroes couldn't be trusted to tell the truth anyhow. Finally though, everyone seemed sure enough that the runaway couldn't have come by our house.

"But would you mind, ma'am," Mr. Jackson said, smooth as oil, after Beau give him a look, "if my men took a quick search through your home. The beggar could of sneaked in and you wouldn't know a thing. I'm worried about your safety, you understand."

"Please." Ama shivered. "I hadn't thought of such a thing. Please, gentlemen, look closely, or I won't be able to sleep a wink tonight. Why, Elizabeth, think of it. We could have been murdered right in our beds while we slept. How came such a thing to happen?" she went on as Mr. Jackson's men left to search.

"Ma'am, it's a hard thing to manage the black cusses anymore, 'scuse me, ma'am. These niggers have all got it in their heads they're the same as the white man." And he give a genteel chuckle.

Ama shook her head like she was confounded. "What's all this leading to, Mr. Jackson? That's what I'd like to know. Pretty soon, they'll be having us white folk serving the coffee and harvesting the crops."

I seen the young boy's eyes fastened on Ama's face like they didn't understand something, and then he turned to look at me, but I stared at my knitting. Those were wise eyes for such a young lad.

"Ah, it's hard times, Mrs. Hadley," said the old gentleman. "You say your husband is away at the war?"

Ama handed him over the daguerreotype of Stuart Hadley in his gray Confederate uniform. "I had a letter from him last week. I've heard it said, Mr. Jackson, that the war's as good as won, and I must say the major certainly sounds optimistic."

"No doubt about the outcome of this war, Mrs. Hadley. When you're on the side of right, God provides. I expect to hear the news any day." He ate a mouthful of cake and licked his lips. "That's about the best apple cake I believe I ever ate. Yes, we'll be taking the victory 'most any time, you can depend on it. My son and his boys are all fighting, except for the lad." He rubbed young Gray's hair till it stood up all over, and it was clear that he loved him.

I looked sideways at the boy, thinking how handsome he was. Made out of sharp clear colors. Black hair and white skin. With skin that light, he must be a thinker and a reader. Not an outdoorsman. He had a strong-cut chin, a straight nose, and full black eyelashes 'round his green eyes. Anyone would say what a beautiful face. But it was more than that. There was something really fine in that face.

"Gray's too young yet to leave home," said Mr. Jackson, still with his hand on the boy. "Least, if he did, I reckon his mama's heart would break. So this old horse, yours truly, had to take up the duties of a young one again. But I'm mighty afraid, Mrs. Hadley, truth to tell, that I'm too old and decrepit for the job. Still, I've never shirked my share of the work. Never did and never will. No, never will, Mrs. Hadley, and if I drop dead tomorrow, it'll be in harness."

The old man stiffened up proud-like and then sighed. "It isn't easy. No, it isn't easy"—with a shake of his head. "But I've got to keep up a strong appearance or there won't be anything left to hand over when my son comes back to his farm. That's why I'm fair fit to be tied unless I get that darky back. I got to use him for a bloody example of what happens to my run-aways."

"And what will you do to him, Mr. Jackson?" Ama asked, pouring him more coffee.

"You wouldn't want to know that, Mrs. Hadley. No, you wouldn't, now. I'm not soft like some others. On the other hand, I don't get carried away. You've probably heard of blacks that was whipped to death." Mr. Jackson stirred two level spoonfuls of sugar into his coffee. "Well, ma'am, those are expensive whippings. Generally speaking, we try to be a little more careful of our property than that. Not to say some of them don't wish they were dead—the worst ones, that is. Now, this Moses . . . he's going to wish he was dead."

Even Ama couldn't think of nothing to say to that, and we sat there with very little talking between us, waiting for the men to finish going over the house. The search was long, but finally it was over and they all said as how there couldn't be nobody there.

"No, there isn't a flea in this house that isn't accounted for, Curt," said one of the men to Mr. Jackson, and Ama allowed as how there weren't no fleas in her house, accounted for or otherwise, and everybody laughed. "But I sure don't understand it, though," the man went on. "Just appeared to me like he *had* to be here. You know what that Mr. Higgins said . . ."

"Check . . . outside buildings," come low words from somebody, but I couldn't hear the whole thing nor tell who said it.

"No tracks 'round anywheres outside. I checked when we first come in, bein' as how we got the report of him headed straight this way." This from the man called Beau. His head wagged thoughtful-like toward Ama. "And nobody 'pears to me to been out in the weather so's to hide him."

Mr. Jackson glared at him, angry at the slant Beau put to his words, like one of us white women would hide a Nigro.

"None of the niggers, I mean," Beau said, explaining his-self. "No, I'd guess we lost him. They can be tricky as coons. That's how they got the nickname."

34

Mr. Jackson exploded. "Lost him? *Lost him,* you say? Now you haven't worked for me long, Beau, so you don't know exactly how I feel about things. But I'll tell you this. We'll find that nigger if I have to comb every square inch of the country." He recovered hisself to turn back to Ama and give a little bow. "We'll be leaving you, ma'am, and we give you heartiest thanks for your hospitality."

We saw them to the front porch and they were saying their last good-byes when I saw Mr. Jackson's eyes on the closest outbuilding where the corn was kept stored. Ama saw him looking and said something about how he must be sure to stop in again if he was to find himself back in Frisbin and he said he'd be sure to do that, but his mind wasn't on it. He was still looking at the corn bin.

"Beau, are you sure about all those outbuildings?" he asked, rubbing his chin with his forefinger.

"There ain't no tracks," insisted Beau, standing on his word.

"Well, what about the rain? It could of washed them away. Course the ground's cold. . . . Still, I believe to myself we ought to have a quick look. That man Higgins struck me as a reliable sort of man. If he said he was headed straight this way, I'm inclined to believe him."

As he stared into the black night, I had a flash of two old men talking together, one telling the other about a black man on the loose, the other pointing the way to Ama's. Both understanding the other. Both raised to have a certain outlook on runaways.

"He ain't here, and anyhow it's late," said one of the neighbor men who had come with Mr. Jackson. "Besides, I've got a tickle in my throat. I believe I better head on back."

"Well . . ." Mr. Jackson put his hand on the porch rail. "Maybe you can take the boy back with you, Wayne. I'm going on looking for the buck. Beau and me are liable to be out the rest of the night. What do you say we ride on north, Beau? I knew I should of brought those dogs. . . ." He seemed to of forgot about searching the sheds, and they were finally leaving us.

But then, just when I was thinking that Moses was saved, that they'd never be finding him, the shed door banged open and there was the sound of a running man sloshing his way through the mud. There weren't a doubt in nobody's mind who that man was, and I felt Ama's nails cutting into my arm, the first sign she'd made to me since the men come.

Then they were jumping on their horses, laughing like boys having fun. Gray stayed back with Ama and me, but his grandfather ordered him on his horse.

"No, sir. I don't want to go," he murmured, drawing back.

"This is the best part, boy!" cried the old man, prancing around on his fine-looking horse. "Now mount up. I don't want you to miss it." His breath was uneven from the excitement. But the boy would not go, and finally the old man rode off alone towards the others, shouting and waving his hat in his hand.

Straining our eyes through the dark, we saw a man on foot, running through the shadows, the men galloping after him and then circling him like they were trapping a wild animal.

"Dear God," said Ama in a hushed voice.

"But, Ama, why? How come him to do such a thing? He were *safe*. You promised him you wouldn't betray him."

"I guess, Elizabeth, he'd believed as long as he could. He didn't have much reason to have faith in white folks."

"I knew it," said the boy Gray.

"What did you know?" asked Ama.

"I knew you were different. Your voice and your words sounded different from the way you looked. And I was right." Gray's young face were bright for a minute. "I'm glad you tried to help him," he said, "and I won't say nothin'. I promise."

Ama nodded, then turned to look out across the yard again. We could hear the yells of the men, and seemed to me I never heard anybody having so much fun. When they come back, Moses was tied up behind Beau's horse and running and falling and running, trying to keep up. Ama made her way through the light rain and got to Mr. Jackson.

"You know sir"—and she looked up at him in his saddle, a triumphant glorified gentleman—"I do believe you must have

36

been born on a horse. My, you certainly can ride." A soft admiring laugh. "I was thinking . . ." She glanced at Moses, on his knees before the laughing Beau, begging for mercy. "That's a right strong-looking niggah. I wish— But of course, you had mentioned you mean to make an example out of him. Oh, dear, that's too bad."

Mr. Jackson was reared up in his saddle. "Why, what's on your mind, Mrs. Hadley? You'd best go in. You're wet to the skin."

"Am I?" She laughed again. "It was the excitement. I never saw anything like that. But perhaps, we could talk for a minute on the porch. My, it's coming down now, isn't it?" And the heavens opened up.

Pretty soon, the entire party were gathered back on the porch, with the sobbing black man lashed upside down and hung from a tree branch in the rain.

Ama seemed not to notice him and not to hear his screams for mercy, but I couldn't help looking at him ever once in a while. Every time he'd yell, the men would bend up double laughing. Mr. Jackson was laughing loudest and enjoying a high time, but finally, he withdrew himself from his men, who were having another glass of brandy, and turned to Ama.

"Now, ma'am, you were saying?"

Ama was smiling like she was a hostess and Mr. Jackson was her honored guest. He couldn't know that the lines 'round her lips weren't there before and that she was two shades whiter than I'd ever seen her.

"Oh, yes!" she said, turning to him like she was just 'minded of the subject. "I was about to say, I surely do need a good hand around here. I'd be glad to buy him from you, if . . . But I don't suppose, though, he'll be much good after you finish with him. Maybe I'd best not." And she seemed ready to give up on the idea.

Mr. Jackson said, slow-like, "Well, he's got to be punished. Make no mistake about that. If he's not, he'll never be any good again. Won't be able to trust him. But perhaps, ma'am, since you've been so good to us tonight, and it would save us hauling him back . . . maybe we could arrive at a fair dealing. We'll take care of the whipping; that's not a job for a woman. As to his condition, just throw him in one of your sheds for a week— these bucks heal up wonderful in no time. I'm not the man to destroy good property."

Ama jumped in. "That's the sweetest thing I ever heard. Just hear, Elizabeth. He's going to let me buy the niggah. Why, I can't thank you enough. I surely can't. Let's go right inside and set terms."

But he wouldn't, and there was a queer light in his eyes that bothered me. He wouldn't set no terms till after he'd had his way with the nigger, he said. No, he wouldn't feel right whipping somebody else's property. Probably wouldn't be able to give him his fair punishment. He turned around and looked at Moses, who was still hanging upside down in the apple tree, still begging for mercy. A bird would as well beg for mercy from a duck hunter, I thought, and I wished I could keep from wishing over and over again like I been ever since Moses went running: Why couldn't those men of left just ten minutes sooner, God? Five minutes? Why didn't you send them away just five minutes before Moses lost his faith? This wishing I could turn time backward was the worst part of it all. It been so terrible to see salvation out there just out of reach, like the apple just in front of the horse that makes the horse go. The horse couldn't reach his apple, God, and we couldn't reach salvation.

"Beau," said Mr. Jackson, "is that a buck I see hanging upside down out of that there tree? First time I ever saw an apple tree growing niggers. Cut him down," he added in a voice gone dead casual.

A crack of lightning shot through the sky and for a minute, I wondered whether God wasn't going to kill all of them. Gray thought so, too; it was in his eyes, in the shiver that run clear through his body. And I thought looking at his fine face that he wasn't made out of the same kind of material as his granddaddy. He had a look I felt on my own face, of somebody who has to watch something terrible happening and knows he can't stop it.

In a minute Moses was unlashed and brought to the porch,

where he flung hisself to the ground and caught hold of the old man's boots. "Please, Marse Jackson. I never meant you all no harm, sir. I was just a-wanting my *free*dom—"

At the word "freedom," almost moaned out, Mr. Jackson pulled back his boot and kicked Moses in the mouth so vicious that blood poured out directly and he gagged. I wondered if he'd swallowed a tooth or if he was gagging on the blood. He was bent forward wiping his mouth out and wiping his face too with his shirt, when Beau come up behind him and kicked him in the back, sending him sprawled out on his face.

The man roared with laughter. "Now, there's a buck"— Beau sniggered—"that don't know whether he's comin' or goin'."

There was a sick feeling back in my throat, but Ama's cold hand was gripping mine and I wouldn't leave her. I thought of my words about going through hell for her, and maybe this was hell. Young Gray shrunk back from the others and come to us.

"Can't we go inside, Mrs. Hadley?" he begged. "I can't bear to watch. I can't."

She put her other hand on his shoulder, joining the three of us. "But you will watch, Gray, so that you will understand this evil, this sickness, and so that you will not tolerate it in your own life."

Mr. Jackson ordered us inside, but he was so engrossed in the business at hand, he didn't seem to notice that we didn't go. Seemed to me like years were passing away, like it wouldn't never be over. It was Beau's hand holding the whip, but I thought, looking at Mr. Jackson, that it was his power bringing it down on Moses' back, and with ever lash and ever scream from the Nigro, Mr. Jackson seemed to raise up straighter and prouder. I'd heard about whipping before, like when Mama used to say to Ruby playful-like, "Ruby, you do that again and I'll whip you. I'll whip you good." And Mama and Ruby'd both laugh, and of course Ruby never got whipped. I think Papa whipped Sam once. Sam was one of Papa's field Nigroes and he was mean and hard to handle and Papa said he'd finally had to whip him to settle him down. But, dear God, surely Papa'd never whipped him like that. The black skin was fair cut away from Moses' back and there was just the blood, a river of blood, and Beau was still bringing down the whip he called Black Lightning. The black man was screaming and screaming without stopping even when Beau took to resting his arm. Ever time the whip come down, the screaming just got worse, until seemed so that ever part of that man was screaming, every pore of his body.

Gray had his face hid against Ama's dress and his arms 'round her waist. Every time another slash was cut into that human property, Gray screamed too. Not a loud scream like Moses' but a hopeless scream that echoed more inside him than out into the night. A crying out that showed he hated and despised what was happening.

"Hush now, baby," said Ama, running her hand through his hair. She had tears in her eyes, too, but some power from God, I guess, kept them from running down her face. "Elizabeth, he's seen enough. More than enough. God forgive me, I never thought it could be this bad or I wouldn't have had him see it. Take him inside."

"Can't we do something to stop this?" I asked.

"If we try to stop them, they'll kill him. Take the boy inside."

"Oh, Ama, please come with us," I begged. "Please, please, come with us." I watched her cold face turn back to the black man, her lips doing silent talking. What they were saying, I didn't know. I guessed it were prayers. "Ama!"

"Yes, Elizabeth," she said, watching Black Lightning.

"Come with us."

"No, I can't do that. Go on now."

"But why won't you? Why won't you come away? What good do it do? Oh, Ama, what good do it do?"

"If there is one blow, Elizabeth, that won't be struck because a woman is here to watch it, then I stay for that." And she closed her mouth as again Black Lightning flashed through the air and another scream burst through the guts of the man Moses.

"Gray, come on," I said. I'd take him to Jinny and then I'd come back here, back to hell.

Gray was crying, the tears covering his face fast as he wiped them off. We turned to go, but then all of a sudden, in back of us, there was a change, a quietening.

"Beau, hold up there!" Mr. Jackson was preened up like a proud strutting bird. He looked like he'd been doing something noble, shining with a sweat that seemed like it must come from honest work. Actually, he hadn't struck a lick—he was too old to do justice to a whip. He come up to Gray and me and turned the boy by the shoulder till they were face to face. "What's the matter, son? A little strong for you?" He led the men in a laugh that filled up the night 'round the black man, who never quit screaming, even now. "Well, that's normal, son. I remember my first nigger-whipping, and it was hard on me, and that wasn't nothing compared to this one. It's all right, boy. It'll make a man out of you."

Gray drew back out of his hands. "Is that what you are, sir? A man?"

The young eyes stared into the old ones and I held my breath, thinking the boy would be struck down at the words. But he wasn't. Maybe Mr. Jackson was thinking of that first whipping that was hard on him. Anyway, finally he said, "Get the branding iron, Beau, and that's all of it."

Beau straddled back to hit Moses one more time, but the old man yelled, "Goddammit, man, I said *that's all of it!*" and Beau let his arm fall back to his side and headed for the saddle-bag on his horse.

"A brand, sir?" Ama stepped over to Mr. Jackson, and I thought I could see the lines of her body trembling. "I declare, my property is beginning to look in poor shape," she said.

"Not your property yet, I believe, Mrs. Hadley," he said dangerous-like.

"No. No, of course not. But what on earth would you be using a branding iron for?"

He let up some. "Brands him as a runaway, ma'am. Came up with it myself." A bit of color come back into his hawk face.

41

"It's in the form of a . . ." His lips puckered up. "Well, I don't rightly know if I should . . . Well, ma'am . . ." He leaned over and whispered, with a wink: "It's in the form of a . . . jackass, ma'am!" And the men roared with laughter, and he looked proud and roared too.

Beau come back with the iron. "Thank you, Beau," said the old man, wiping his eyes where he'd laughed tears. "Now, ma'am, if we can just use your fire . . ." He made a move toward the house, but Ama stepped in front of him at the door.

"You can't," she said.

"What?" He halfways laughed, like he'd misunderstood her.

"I said you can't. You can't use my fire."

The smile went away from his face. Finally he drawled out, real slow and studied, "Are you telling me I can't brand my own nigger?"

"I'm sure I can't stop you. I'm simply telling you that you can't use my fire to heat the iron."

"As you wish." He made her the same bow that he was so fond of using, and turned away. "Boys, make a fire."

"Nothin' to make one of," said one of the men. "Everything's full of water."

"I see." All of a sudden, nobody were talking no more and some were edging toward their horses.

Moses lay still on the porch, finally quietened down, only groaning deep inside himself, and Mr. Jackson turned to look at him. The old man's eyes had a far-off stare to them, like he was remembering something he'd learned a long time ago. "I never did like a nigger," he said, walking in a slow circle round Moses.

I was scared bad, worse than I was ever scared in my life.

The old man stopped walking and stood still as a stone an inch from Moses' head. He stood there and nobody said a word.

My heart was beating so loud, seemed to me everybody must be hearing it.

At last he moved, leaning down, panting from the bending of his body, because he was such an old man. He reached out and took hold of the black fuzz on Moses' head and jerked it up with all his strength, until Moses' head was right level to his own. Eye to eye they looked at each other and something silent passed between them, something deeper than words. Then, never moving back a inch, the old man gathered his saliva into his mouth and spit in Moses' face. The spit ran down his cheek like a tear. "No, sir," said Mr. Jackson, "I never did like a nigger."

He dropped Moses' face back onto the porch and then he took the heel of his boot and slow and deliberate he began to grind it into the back that was bare of any skin to protect it. Moses opened up his mouth and give what sounded like a mortal scream, worse than anything I ever heard or imagined, and I thought, This time he's dead. Ama run to Mr. Jackson and tried to pull him away, but Beau and one of the men held her back, though she was fighting them. Finally, Mr. Jackson removed his heel and finished with another hard kick. Then, taking a spotless white handkerchief from his pocket, he wiped his face and his hands.

"And what are you doing, Mr. Jackson?" asked Ama. "Are you trying to wipe off that man's blood?"

He didn't look at her at all, just went to his horse. "You can keep this nigger, Mrs. Hadley, no charge. He'll be dead by morning. Come on, Gray. Hard ride ahead." He was breathing heavy, almost panting, like the sound Joe Crocker made when he'd taken his man pleasure.

Gray put his arms 'round us. He wasn't crying no more. He was beyond crying. He wouldn't ever be no child again. "I won't forget," he said, then he run for his horse. The men rode off, not saying nothing, not looking at each other.

Deep in the night I looked at Ama's white hands holding Moses' black ones and I thought that if I was a painter I'd paint those hands. Then Moses was throwing up again and Ama tended to him herself, holding his head, cleaning him with warm water. Then settling him back on his stomach, his face turned toward us.

"You're free, Moses," Ama said. "You're free now."

His eyes closed. We couldn't tell if he'd heard.

43

The only sound in the room was breathing and ever once in a while the window shutter flapping back and forth in the wind. Now Moses was quiet, too quiet. I was afraid, 'cause he never gave a sign of life. For over four hours, Ama and I sat together watching him with Jinny coming in and out with things and Delilah and Beulah crying in the hall. Then finally he opened his eyes, looking better, like he was coming out of a bad sickness and was going to be all right. He smiled like he knew us, and with thanksgiving in his voice he said, "I'm safe." Then he died. It was hard to believe he was dead just when he'd seemed so much better.

Ama moved 'round him like a spirit woman. Closing his eyes. Washing his face again and his arms. Straightening the covers on the bed. Crossing his hands across his breast. Then she went down on her knees beside the bed and folded her hands, praying. I did the same and so did the other women. There was the sound of skirt material rustling as they come through the door. The joints of Jinny's legs popped as she went down on her knees next to me. Beulah started humming and Delilah picked up the sound. Their two voices blended beautiful together. And I thought about what Moses had said. "I'm safe." How can anybody be safe when they're dying? But it was peaceful in the room, and sure enough it didn't seem so bad. He died free and with friends and we buried him close to the house.

Four

*S*eems to me that a person's life is made out of long stretches of time that don't mean nothing and a few days here and there that do. The first is like being asleep with your eyes open and the second is seeing life clearer than you did before and doing surprising things. Like Moses had lived as a slave all his life, and then one day he opened his eyes. Then he risked his life to change things. Maybe that's why none of us would ever forget Moses while we kept on living our lives, because we'd known him during his most surprising hours. The hours that said the most about who he was in his heart. I always thought of Moses when the air were the sharpest and the cleanest and the wind was blowing my hair.

February turned into March and the lists of the war casualties started coming. Once when we drove the wagon into Frisbin we saw a man handing out newspapers, but Ama kept driving. Past the dead silence and the sudden crying out of a woman already dressed in black. Ama kept driving and she never looked back like I was doing. She said bad news would find its own way home.

So we waited, but no word come to our house even though three of us five women had husbands at war—Major Hadley, Joe, and Beulah's Henry. There wasn't no word either from Delilah's beau, Sinclair, but we didn't know if he was with the troops or not. Jinny had nobody to worry about. She'd lost her husband and children in a fire long time ago.

Beulah's Henry was an army cook on the Federal side, cooking for a special unit of men who went around busting up Confederate rails. Since Henry didn't know how to write and Beulah hadn't seen him for a year, she was worried whether he was even alive.

"I hopin' they take care my man." Beulah frowned. "You know the white don't see hungry, don't see sick. Don't see nothin' when it the black."

"Henry's with a unit of Federal soldiers," Ama said. "They're fighting to free the slaves. Not punish them."

Beulah snorted. "They fightin' to keep they country."

"To the contrary. They could easily have kept their country if they'd allowed the planters to keep their slaves."

"Better business up North," Beulah said, "let the black work for dollar a week. Then charge the dollar for food and bed. Plus, the war probably close the plantations. Do away with competition. Work out fine."

"Let's have coffee and continue this conversation," Ama said, throwing her dust cloth aside. "I'm willing to learn my politics at your knee, Beulah."

"Politic," Beulah said, "is a rat nest."

"Poetical," Ama said.

Pretty soon winter was over and spring come with the sun shining down like rays through white clouds and the oaks making music with their leaves. Then the first letter come to our house. Full of thanksgiving it was for the warm weather. It was from Beulah's Henry, written for him by a white Federal soldier, and she kissed it like it was Henry hisself she was kissing.

"My man can't stand that cold weather," Beulah said, laughing, wiping away the tears that flowed down both cheeks. "If I know him, he done spend the winter roll up in a log somewheres."

Then more letters, dozens of them on one day. Older letters, mailed months ago and delivered all at once. But there wasn't no word from Joe Crocker, and I saw the others looking at me and I knew what they were thinking. I was thinking myself that maybe Joe was on a Northern dead list. But of course he wasn't a writing kind of man. I only heard from him once since he left, just letting me know where he was if I needed him. It was a short letter with no feeling to it till the end when he wrote, "Sometimes I recollect your face, Liz Ann, and it makes me want to come home. Be sure and let me know what the baby is. Love to the both of you. Joe." When I got to that part, I ran my hand over it and it felt hot.

For days and weeks, I dreamt about Joe and I thought how maybe his eyes would look into mine again and my heart would shake inside me. I wrote to him near ever day for a while, but there never was no answer, even after I wrote about Melissa Sue, and after a while, I forget when, I put his letter away. But I watched Ama reading her mail and I wondered how come I had a husband who didn't send letters. If he didn't send letters, he must not be thinking of me, I thought. Only some kind of fool would think anything else. And if he wasn't thinking of me, he didn't love me. But why would a man marry a woman he didn't love? Especially a fine-looking man like Joe who could of had a woman he *did* love. This I couldn't understand.

Every night in our house where only women lived, we ate cake and had tea or coffee and talked. And one evening when Delilah was going on and on about Sinclair, about saving herself for him and not being hardly able to wait to see him again on account of loving him so much, I blurted out, "Marriage isn't always so wonderful, you know. Why, sometimes you might even think your husband don't love you or something."

The room fell still that instant and every eye was on my face. If I could of stuffed the words back inside my mouth, I would of done, but it was too late to do anything but pretend it was some other woman's husband I meant. But even as I opened my mouth to say something like that, I read a certain knowledge on every face and in every eye and gave up on the idea of lying. Besides, they knew I didn't get letters.

47

After a few minutes of silence, us looking at each other, Delilah said in a small timid voice, "How it feel when he lovin' you in bed? Feel like he love you more then?"

"Feels like he loves me less then," I said. "Makes me feel like he's disgusted with what we're doing. It makes me disgusted, too. 'Shamed."

Jinny wagged her black head at me. "Something wrong," she said, " 'bout the way you doing it, then."

"Course now," Beulah said, "we got to remember it could be the white. White don't half understand they body."

"How come loving feels right to me then?" Ama demanded. "I'm white."

"It still feels good to you?" I said. "After all these years? I don't mean to say you're old."

"Fifty-five," Ama said. "And Stuart is fifty-seven. The way it feels is that we're touching each other's souls."

"That what I mean," Beulah said, " 'bout the white not understandin' they body. You got to mention soul all time. Keep thinkin' all time like that, you ain't gon' feel much down where it count."

"I use to feel that stuff 'bout my man," Jinny said, tears falling on her sewing. "Spirit stuff. And down there too. I miss body, but soul too. Both way count."

Beulah swallowed a mouthful of cake and snorted. "Just that moment, you know what I means? When it really happen' and you let go down there? What you scream? 'Oh sweetenin', stroke my soul just hard as you can'?"

Everyone laughed, even Jinny, who knuckled away her tears and sat there smiling.

"Let me ask you somethin', Beulah," Delilah said, slipping an extra spoonful of sugar in her tea. By now all the tension in the room was gone, and Delilah's grin was wicked as she fixed her gaze on Beulah. "How you feel"—she giggled—"first time Henry seen you without no clothes on you back?"

"Feel little fat." Beulah shrugged. "But my Henry like that, so it fine."

48

"My man love that," Jinny said. "He always like big breast and all."

"Now see, that part bother me," Delilah said. "Me havin' small breast. Still, got nice little waist. Pretty nice big hips."

"You all right." Beulah nodded. "Just fine. The hip put you over with the man, even without breast. And you don't got no stomach hangin' out so you and Sinclair can't see over it. Can't tell what goin' on down there when the stomach get in the way. But anyhow, it nice to see each other body. Touchin' better when you see everthin'. Umm!"

Everybody laughed fit to kill. I never heard no ladies talking about taking off their clothes before their husbands. Law, I never did do it, much less talk about it. Joe never saw me without my nightgown and I never saw him. When we done it, it was night and underneath the covers. I thought about that and then I had the thought that I'd never even seen my own body naked. I'd seen parts, of course, but not the whole thing.

"Love between a man and a woman," Ama said, "is one of the most mysterious things in the world. It seems we're almost desperate to find it. Blessed beyond words if we do. Restless and empty if we don't."

"I think the rich and beautiful people always find it," I said. "And the rest of us take what we can get."

"Not always true." Ama smiled. "I know a young man— well, Cole should be almost thirty now—"

"From Frisbin?" I asked.

"From Virginia," she said. "Very aristocratic family. Very social people. Colonel MacPherson, the major's fondest boyhood friend, is the young man's father, and his mother, Hannah, was dear to me before she died. In any case, Cole MacPherson is the young man's name and he never married, never had a serious interest in a woman that I know of. Hannah told me he grew tired of the whole social scene in Richmond, belles and all, and lost himself in an academic life. Brilliant lawyer. One of these crusaders for human causes. The colonel has said if Cole didn't come from money, he wouldn't have a dollar, for the poorest clients draw the boy like a magnet." Ama stopped talking for a minute to chew on her lip, but Delilah plucked at my sleeve.

"He been here, that man," she said. "Most handsomest man I ever seen."

"For white," Beulah said.

"For any color," Jinny said. "He handsome if he green."

"But what about him?" I asked.

"Some woman killed herself over him," Ama said. "A client. If you knew Virginia society, you'd understand what a scandal it made, especially since the girl was not of his class, but Cole didn't give a snap of the fingers for that. He actually went to the young woman's funeral." Ama smiled some, halfways between sad and proud. "Here she was from the kind of poor family that Cole specializes in helping, and everything under the sun being whispered around Richmond. Including that the poor girl was expecting a child. But Cole came right out and defended the young woman's character as if he were standing in a court-room. He said that nothing at all had ever happened between them. Except one had loved. And one hadn't. But ever since that happened"—she frowned—"there's been something in Cole's face that . . ."

"Maybe he really did love her," I said.

"Cole's not a liar," Ama said, shaking her head. "He sounded almost apologetic, in fact, that he hadn't loved her. I think he would have liked to say that he did. For her sake, you know. But the boy's so damned honest."

"Imagine killing yourself because a man don't love you," I said, slicing a sliver of cake.

"Well, women have always been like that over Cole," Ama said. "But this young woman was so unlike the belles he'd grown tired of. Knowing him, you would have thought she'd have been exactly the sort he'd fall madly in love with."

"Some can't love," Jinny said. "And if you can't, it like bein' dead inside."

"That man eye don't look dead to me," Delilah said. "Look like he in pain."

"Look dead to me," Beulah said. "He a cold one, no use denyin'. I bet he can't love no woman with his body neither. Can't get his thing hard 'nough."

"I would prefer," Ama said, rather stiff-like, "that we not talk like that. Not about Cole. I only mentioned him because he's not only rich, but handsome, and he never found love, Elizabeth. In fact, he's a young man who— Well, I think he's bedeviled by emptiness." Ama sighed, then turned her attention to pouring one last cup of tea and straightening the tray, and talk turned to weather and war.

Only I sat there thinking that somehow it was good to know the rich had their problems too, and feeling guilty for thinking it.

That night when I got undressed, I put my lamp on the chest and stood before the looking glass naked. Maybe it was because it was dark and the lamp glow made it prettier, but my body was real nice to look at. Full breasts. Little waist. Nice legs and hips. Skin shining white. I stood there turning 'round and 'round trying to see from all different sides. It was right strange how almost eighteen years could have gone by and this was the first time I saw myself like God made me.

After a while I touched myself down where Beulah said the feeling counts. Little tingles. Rubbed harder, bigger tingles. I felt like something was supposed to happen, but what? After a few minutes, the tingles went away and I quit touching. One of these days, I thought, when Joe comes home, maybe . . .

But just thinking about Joe brought on a solemn feeling. Remembering him on top of me didn't have to do with tingles. It had to do with somebody in a hurry. He alone up there on top, me alone down there under him.

Living with him was like living alone.

I put on my cotton nightgown and climbed in bed, but I didn't feel sleepy. I laid there with my eyes open, thinking about life at Symphony Oaks. Cool breezes and dark polished wood and women's soft voices. And two babies to love. Both babies so different and so alike. Beulah's Daisy was a year and a half and *running*. Melissa not quite a year and tottering after Daisy.

51

Daisy with brown snapping eyes and a face like Beulah's, except laughing and smiling all the time. Melissa Sue with soft blue eyes, dreamy as the sky, and a solemn, very white face. Daisy bold as brass and into trouble, turning the churn upside down. Melissa quiet and good, almost too good, but watching Daisy do all her mischief, dipping her finger in the cream. How they were alike were in sweetness and light. Love for each other. They could of been sisters. In a way, they *were* sisters.

And yet the one bad feeling I suffered in silence was the way I sometimes saw Beulah looking at me when I was holding Melissa Sue and she was holding Daisy. Sometimes it seemed like Beulah almost hated me. It even seemed that maybe she hated Melissa Sue, too. But that couldn't be, I told myself. That had to be something I made up.

I looked over at Melissa in her crib next to my bed. The moonlight was shining on her face like a blessing. Ama and Jinny had made a special trip to the cabin for that crib, so's Melissa could sleep in the same bed I'd slept in as a baby.

She made a face in her sleep and I put my hand on her. I still couldn't get over how beautiful she was. Especially now in the moonlight. With her soft brown hair in wet curls around her face where she'd sweated in her sleep and her little turned-up nose and her long eyelashes. Having Melissa made my life make sense like it never did before. I thought about how unlucky men were. They couldn't never understand what it was to bring life into the world. It was like helping God do a miracle. Melissa's mouth curled up fiercer till she looked like she was growling, then she yawned instead and fell deeper asleep. I put my finger against her hand and stroked it. Beulah can't hate you, I thought. Nobody could hate you.

But looking at Melissa's white skin in the moonlight, I all of a sudden thought how Beulah must feel to think of white folks treating Daisy bad, 'cause of her black skin. But the color of Daisy's skin was rich and beautiful, smooth and soft as brown satin. Just to look at her was to know beauty comes in all shades and different kinds of things are beautiful.

Ama said anything gave pleasure to look at it was pretty.

"Even my old mother's face," she said. "Lined and no teeth left in her head, right before she died. Beautiful."

A picture of my mama come to me before I could stop it, and it wasn't beautiful to me. I stared at Melissa for a long time and she must of felt me staring. Because all at once her eyelids flickered and then opened wide to see me standing over her in the night.

"Everything's all right," I whispered. "Mama's just checking on you. It's all right."

Her gaze stayed fixed on me, her lips opening in one of her grave little smiles, and in those unblinking seconds that passed between us in the night, it seemed to me I could see my own eyes looking back at me.

Five

I heard a saying that the smell of trouble comes before it on the wind. So too war, I guess, and for us, it was Shiloh. In early April, two local men were killed there. One was Wade Burris, son of the Ronald Burris family from up in the hills, and the other was Chester Logan, a man I actually knew, for he'd worked planting and harvesting for Papa, a man with short bowed legs that trotted rather than walked, and huge hands that picked at double speed.

Fought 'round the Pittsburgh Landing area, hundreds of miles from us, Shiloh was anyhow a southern Tennessee battle, and the bloodiest one so far. Twenty thousand dead or wounded. Beyond grief for the dead, what gripped me was a sudden terrible belief that the war could creep up on us any time now, maybe any day, and explode in our faces. Before Shiloh, I'd took comfort in believing that most of the fighting happened in faraway fields, probably land that had been set aside for war. But at least, please God, out of the way of ordinary civilians. I'd been so sure that south Tennessee was safe, it being almost a part of Georgia. Now that feeling was gone from me and I was afraid. It was almost like I'd seen "the elephant," or by other words, seen battle. Or at least I *believed* in the elephant now. Believed that it was a huge wild beast that could go where it liked, maybe even into our giant mountains, or come crashing down the slopes of Missionary Ridge and Lookout Mountain and charge across our valley. Killing farmer and soldier alike. Killing women and children as no more than casual accidents along the way.

First reports from the telegraph claimed victory for the Confederates. But by the time newspapers came out, Beauregard had lost to Grant after all. Though who could really claim to win anything, I thought, when the papers screamed blood and pain and bodies swole to twice their size laying in the rain waiting to be buried. In the same papers, right next to the descriptions of bodies with no heads or legs, there was President Davis calling for new soldiers. And below that Grant saying that now only total conquest of the South could save the Union.

"I don't know about this war stuff," I whispered to Delilah, and she said: "Don't think 'bout it. Think somethin' else."

But in our house, whether we were supposed to think about it or not, we went around in a daze, me and Delilah and Jinny, with tears in our eyes. Beulah was so drained of any kind of expression you couldn't tell what she was thinking.

Only Ama was the same. But not really the same—busier, more determined than ever. More filled with energy, but with a pinched look between her eyes, her lips thinner and pressed together. The days were warmer now, and she'd hired five men from town to plow and plant fields of corn and beans, most of the crops already requisitioned for the troops in Vicksburg. She never seemed to stop working and it was not uncommon to see her walking across a cornfield wearing an old dress with a sunbonnet crammed down on her head, the strings untied and dangling on both sides of her face. A sack of seed corn slung 'round her neck like a yoke.

With her for our example, the rest of us worked through our fears too, cooking for the workers, lugging sacks and baskets and jars of water, tending to children and animals, but always with an eye to the mountains all 'round us that rose to meet the blue sky.

"Get to us," Jinny said, "got to cross them mountains. They never gon' do somethin' like that, never do it."

55

"Oh, no, never," I said with my teeth so closed I was talking through them.

"Hell, what you talkin' 'bout," Beulah said, disgusted with both of us. "You act like a mountain bigger than a army. They want to, they cross a mountain fifty time bigger. Hundred time bigger. And you! You no bigger than a bug to them! They squash you, go on. Never even notice."

Delilah started crying then, her shoulders shaking, tears falling so thick down her face, that Beulah sucked in her breath and stopped talking. She never liked to make Delilah unhappy. There was some kind of bond between them, almost like Delilah be her oldest child. "Well," she said, "them hills pretty big, after all. Who know what happen. Can't say them soldiers come no more than won't come. Y'all stop cryin' now, sugar. They come, Beulah take care of you like a mama bug."

I lifted my eyes to the rocky steep cliffs where copperheads sunned theirselves on the highest rocks and where wolves and mountain lions roamed and the forests grew so thick you couldn't see between the trees. They can't never march over all that, through all that, I thought.

But maybe, though. Maybe they could. Because who really knew what the elephant could do?

Already, more and more neighbors come scavenging for food and begging at Ama's door. Though our supplies still held, we had no coffee or sugar and were right down to the bottom of the flour barrel. We had some of most but less of everything, and somebody stole twenty chickens in the night, but still we counted ourselves luckier than most. And our fields were brown with new-plowed dirt.

On the twentieth day of April, the day after Melissa Sue turned one, Ama got a telegram that Cole MacPherson was stopping by on his way to Georgia. Right away, I remembered the story Ama had told of him, how the woman had killed herself over him, and how Beulah said he was dead inside. I went with Ama to Chickamauga Station to fetch him from the train, and for that day at least, the war wasn't so heavy on my mind.

Instead, I was curious over what Cole MacPherson would be like, this man Ama had called bedeviled with emptiness. The picture in my head was of a thin fair-haired man with white skin, his eyes somehow tortured, somehow dead at the same time. Handsome in a stiff, prim kind of way.

"I guess we should of dressed more, him being used to society and all," I said to Ama. She'd worked all morning and barely stopped to wash and change into one of her plainest dresses, just grabbing the first thing she put her hand on, and I was in my blue gingham, pretty on me, but not like the dresses Cole MacPherson must be used to seeing on the Richmond matrons and belles.

"Cole's known me far too many years to expect a bird in fine feathers," Ama scoffed.

"Just out of respect, though."

"I respect him too much to bother putting on a show for him," she said. "These are war times. Times to work in, not dress in."

Then the train was pulling in and before I knew it, a man was stepping off the train, his hat in one hand and his bag in the other, wearing a fine gray suit of clothes and a black silk cravat at his throat over a beautiful white linen shirt front. So much for not dressing, I thought.

Next thing I saw were his eyes. They were like no eyes I ever saw. Hazel with little flecks of gold in them. Deep as oceans. If they were dead or cold, who was to know, that's how deep they were. Just on eyes alone, you could understand why women killed theirselves over him, but of course that had nothing to do with me. As a married woman, as far as Cole Mac-Pherson was concerned, I was good as dead anyhow.

But it was a treat just to look. Thick straight brows over those eyes. Beautiful skin, almost tan, not white like I'd expected, and dark hair, curling some 'round the temples. Straight nose. He stood tall and slim, but not downright skinny like I'd pictured, with broad square shoulders. Good hands, with beautiful long fingers and shiny perfect nails. Not farmer's hands, but the hands of a man who worked with his mind and used his hands to handle books and papers and to write letters.

"This must be Elizabeth," he said, setting down his bag and taking my hand in both of his. His hands were warm, not cool, his eyes were curious and set on mine, not dead at all, and crazy little shivers ran clear through me.

"Of course, this is Elizabeth," Ama smiled.

I could scarce say hello, or pay any mind to what he said after that. It had suddenly come to me that I was actually in the presence of a real Southern gentleman, like the ones I'd read about. Like the ones Ama said led the whole South into war. The ones who dressed in a certain way, rode horses in a certain way, smoked Cuban cigars and moved through fine society easier than I'd ever walked the streets of Frisbin. Our town didn't have men like him. Men with all the rough edges filed smooth. Yet there appeared something reckless under his skin, something bolder than the men who lived up in the mountains and wrestled mountain lions with their bare hands.

"You wouldn't recognize Richmond," he told Ama later that night, all of us sitting together in front of the fire after dinner. Cole was holding a big brandy snifter, swilling the brandy around. Ama had sherry and the rest of us women were drinking dandelion-root coffee we'd made ourselves after being without coffee beans for months.

"The hotels in Richmond are full?" Ama asked, fixing her needlepoint onto a frame and examining it under the light to make sure the cloth was tight.

"Full to exploding." Cole shrugged. "And the boarding-houses at capacity and fistfights in the streets, if you can believe it. It's a free-for-all. I blame Davis and Stephens and the entire Congress for not staying in Montgomery where they belong."

"How's your own work coming? Are you having trouble getting your cases through court?"

"What court?" he said. "There is no court, in a manner of speaking. It's all a mess. My clients rot in jail. Or they do without the money that is owed them. Or endure the harassments that have befallen them. And, of course, the government has yet to even create a Supreme Court. The senators are too afraid His Majesty Jeff Davis will pack the bench with his cohorts."

"Have you really met President Davis?" I said in a low timid voice, and the way he turned his eyes on me made me aware my mouth was hanging open like I was some kind of child staring at a tray of fresh-pulled taffy. I shut my mouth and he smiled, a little at first then full out, as though I'd dragged the smile from him with both hands.

"I know him," he said as if I'd just reminded him that the man was really president of the whole Confederacy and not one of the commoners out having fistfights in the Richmond streets. "It's just as well you've never met the great leader of our celebrated Cause," he went on, still smiling. "He has a reputation for bad first impressions. And you must have heard of his famous temper. No? Surely, you have. Why, even his wife has termed him a nervous dyspeptic. And his own vice president compares him to a military dictator in one breath and to an old blind deaf dog in the other. In a nutshell, he's cold and arrogant, and there are those who say that without his imperious leadership, the rebellion would die inside of a day."

"Are you a rebel, Cole?" Ama murmured, squinting over at him, her glass in hand, her needlepoint in her lap with needle laying on top of it. Though every inch a lady, tonight she could almost of been another man, she was so relaxed and interested in the Richmond news. She'd even used the word "rebel," almost a profanity in the South.

"I'm nothing," Cole said. "I'm a lawyer."

"Have you never thought of enlisting in the army?" Ama asked.

"With conscription, I may not have to enlist," Cole said, laughing a little. Though he wasn't looking at me, he must of seen the question on my face because he turned to me to say that the army was at the point of conscripting soldiers from the South. Drafting them, he said, against violent protests from enlisted gentlemen who swore the draft would rip the heart out of the movement. Who could fight if ordered to fight? "Still,"

59

Cole went on, after he and Ama had gone back and forth on that question for a while, "what else is Lee to do? Just think of his predicament. All his gentlemen soldiers who did him the favor of enlisting for one whole year find themselves at the end of their service. And though there's a whole war left to fight, the bloodiest, most uncomfortable part still to come, for the food supplies are dwindling and there are shortages of everything from shoes to weapons, these gentlemen are prepared to march straight for home regardless of Robert E. Lee. Yes, at this point, Lee will take any man he can get, any way he can get him, even if he has to order him to the field at riflepoint."

Lord, I thought, the man's talking seems to bring Richmond right into the room. Lee himself into the room. And all of a sudden I could see past the soldier holding the gun and understand the politics that put him on the battlefield.

Cole told us about documents coming out along with conscription that were sure to be unpopular enough to put a price on the heads of Davis and the whole Congress. Especially the twenty-slave law, which exempted anyone who owned or oversaw twenty slaves or more from service.

"You must be joking," I said.

Cole laughed. "The twenty-slave law's sure to be a favorite among the farmers who are too poor to own any slaves themselves, and must now go out and fight for the right of slave ownership for their richer counterparts who are going to be sitting out the war, thanks to friends in Congress.

"As a matter of fact," he said, "there are so many exemptions, the poorest farmers are about the only group I can think of who won't be able to cut through the red tape. And the few wealthy who don't find a legal loophole will be able to hire substitutes to do their stints. That's legal too! Yes, I'm afraid our boys in gray will be a poor man's army, and half starved at that."

Ama said, "I still think you'd cut a fine figure in a blue uniform."

But Cole said that as little inclination as he found to fight for the rebellion, neither could he really see himself going over to the Federals. "I'm afraid I'm Virginia to the core," he said. "Which shows you that patriotism has more to do with geography than ethics. Although one of these days, I just may kill my father by throwing in my lot with Abe, after all. Do you think the colonel would ever forgive me, Ama?"

"Not for a second," Ama said, getting to her feet and taking a poker to the fire. Sparks shot against the half-drawn fire screen as she jabbed a burning log. "But then he hasn't forgiven you for not giving him any grandchildren, either, and he's still speaking to you, isn't he? By the way, are there many attractive young women in Richmond these days?"

Cole grinned. "Belles, not women. They don't become real women until they get married. And yes, there are acres of them, each one more beautiful than the last, each with a waist of about three inches and a skirt wider than a fair-sized outbuilding. I really don't know why I'm not married. The belles are absolutely irresistible and I don't have another male friend who's escaped matrimony."

My eyes were on my embroidery. I could see another world in my head, full of beautiful women in ball dresses dancing with men like Cole MacPherson, while I sat here in my narrow dress of plain cotton, wishing that my husband had signed up with the Confederates so's I could have my family back, my town back. But at least I had Ama and the women. This brought me a good deal of cheer and I looked up all of a sudden, glancing over at Ama and surprising Cole staring at me with a frown on his face, his eyebrows drawed together something fierce.

Talk drifted into Shiloh then, and then income tax and finally the battles out in Albuquerque and Santa Fe in the New Mexico Territory. Somehow it seemed strange to think the Civil War was going on in places that weren't even states, places so far away, it were like they were in another country. Cole said he'd always wanted to take a trip west, but with the rails slow to civilians these war days, he might wait a year or two.

To me, sitting there looking at Cole MacPherson and listening to him talk, he was big as the war, glamorous as the Southern civilization so close to us and yet so removed from our way of living. But the wonder of Cole was how comfortable we all were around him, even Jinny and Delilah, who were quiet and shy 'round most folks—and, most surprising, Beulah, who were actually sitting with a white visitor tonight, a tolerable pleasant look on her broad face.

So this is what Southern society sounds like, I thought. And looks like. And sits like, kind of lounging in his chair and yet somehow with a straight back.

It was only when Ama left to take Cole to his bedroom that I had the thought that to most folks, it would be considered indecent, him staying here in a houseful of women without so much as one other man on the premises. But then these were war times, so maybe nobody would think much of anything. In my mind, I could see Cole walking across the floor toward the bed I'd helped Delilah make, loosening his collar with one hand, maybe looking out the window and thinking how empty the fields looked, compared to the excitement of the city streets. I could see his suit hanging in the wardrobe. Him laying on his pillow, breathing the deep peace of sleep. Dreaming of belles and Jefferson Davis and clients with causes.

With Cole in the house, life seemed more interesting, us hanging 'round his chair hearing tales of the capital. How many people shared how many rooms, with extra beds shoved into rooms, strangers sleeping side by side. Sitting close while he read out loud from his *Southern Illustrated News* about Belle Boyd, the famous Confederate woman spy. Even serving him food took on special interest, us trying to cook as well as Richmond and serve as well as Richmond. Him laughing and saying how Richmond couldn't come close to Beulah's roast mutton.

So we were all glad when he decided to stay on for a week, taking long walks across the fields and sitting nights in the major's chair and reading beautiful bound volumes of books I'd never seen off the shelves, looking up to smile when one of us would slip a cup of tea on the side table next to his elbow.

Fact is, I thought, the house was going to seem downright

empty when Cole left. For the vacant look I'd heard about were gone from his eyes, and he smiled and laughed and went 'round with his collar open and his face turned to the sun, getting a flush to his skin that made him look even more handsome. Like a lost god or something, wandering around on lonesome hilly acres and coming back with armfuls of early wildflowers.

I bet he does have a girl in Richmond after all, I found myself thinking. Because from the first second I saw him step off the train, even before he saw us standing there, he already had that alive look. Something eager there. Like he was expecting something to happen. What else could it be . . . excepting maybe a wedding back in Virginia. Ama would go to it and come back and tell us what the bride wore and what the food was like and where they went on their trip after the ceremony.

On his last day with us, I found myself out in the back acreage at twilight, looking for Old Red, who'd been bawling her head off for over an hour. Sure enough, I'd no more than got to the top of the hill when she stopped bawling, leaving me alone in the half light with the wind blowing in the grass and the trees, and the rustlings of animals and birds all 'round me and above me. Yes, and the first crickets of the night, for the sky had turned to darkest purple, me standing there ankle-deep in mud, wondering where Old Red had hid that new calf of hers.

"I think she's down the hill by that little creek," said a voice behind me, and I jumped, then turned to see Cole leaning against a tree, smoking a cigar in his shirtsleeves, his hat pushed back on his dark hair, his collar open. When I stood there gaping at him, not able to think of a word to say, he smiled and said, "Weren't you looking for your cow?"

I nodded and said, "Well, then I guess I'll . . ." But something kept me standing there, something about the expectant way he looked at me as if waiting for me to answer some question he'd asked me. But he hadn't asked it, just stood there taking another long draw on his cigar, the smoke white in the air. "So you're going on to Georgia then," I murmured, without nothing else to say.

He nodded. "That time has come. It's been the best six

63

days I ever spent at Symphony Oaks. You've all been extremely kind to me. I'll miss—well, everything, when I go."

His voice sounded kind of moody somehow, but I couldn't see his eyes, see if the emptiness was back. The deep purple air was like a velvet cloak shrouding us from each other, lifting only in sudden shiftings of light as day fought the night. All at once I wished I knew how to talk to someone like him, but that was impossible 'cause everyone he knew was so different from me. They could of almost been from another world. Fact is, they *were* from a different world.

"I'm sorry," I breathed, not expecting I was going to say it, "that I don't know how to talk better. Like the belles and the matrons from Richmond, I mean. You must forgive me, but see, ladies like them been taught what to say to gentlemen and nobody ever taught me."

A dead pause and then all at once Cole was laughing, peal after peal of laughter bouncing off the breeze into the night. I felt my face get red, standing there feeling like the biggest fool God ever made. Then he got control of hisself and started apologizing, saying sorry about four times before he finally said I'd caught him off balance, and how that was the first time he ever understood why the belles were so blamed dull.

"All that time," he said, sounding like he'd like to laugh again but was fighting it, "I wondered why they were so silly and it never occurred to me they sounded like that because they'd been *taught!* Can you imagine," he went on, *"teaching* someone to sound like that? Poor girls."

"Maybe so," I said kind of stiff-like, not forgiving him yet for laughing at me, "but at least they're trained to proper society. They know . . . well, graces, all that sort of thing. And I heard they're the most beautiful girls in the world. You said so yourself."

"Did I," he said. "Well, I shouldn't have, not having had anything to compare them with."

"Except—well, some of your clients." Meaning the girl who'd killed herself. She'd changed shape in my head so many times I couldn't even picture her no more. Black, brown, or yellow hair. Blue, green, or brown eyes. Thin, or a little plump. A face like a white oval. A face like a heart.

"So you heard that story," Cole said, sending another white puff into the purple sky. "Just incidentally, the effects of my clients' charms may have been exaggerated, along with the belles', I regret to say."

"Oh," I said, not wanting to say I'd already heard he hadn't loved the girl. I could feel his eyes on me, boring into me, as though he could see through the misty night as perfect as in sunlight. My nerves were all a-jangle from his silence. But maybe he was used to having the belles doing the talking. Maybe it was up to the woman to entertain the man. But no, that were belles and eligible bachelors. It was a confusion in my head, and still he stood there, smoking and leaning against the tree, watching me. "Well," I said after a few minutes of neither of us saying a word, "I guess you must be glad to be going back to city life. Probably a man like you must get bored in a place like this."

"Definitely," he said, his teeth flashing as he smiled. "That's the kind of man I am. Society every night, dancing, dining, flirting. I have to be occupied every minute. Out here, my blood would die in my veins."

"Are you teasing me?" I said, feeling sure he was.

"Well, partly," he said, and sounded thoughtful-like, not full of fun anymore. "Actually though, a man might be scared to live out here. That is, if there were darkness in any part of his being. Nights are especially eerie. You can actually hear your conscience talking to you."

"A man like you don't have to worry about that," I said. "You lead a good life. Ama told us about your causes. The work you do for all those people who can't afford to pay you much—"

I broke off, seeing the way he stared at me, the sky behind him growing deeper and blacker by the minute.

"I'll tell you something," he said. "Something that I don't expect a woman like you to know. There are . . . some people who have difficulty feeling much of anything. In a way, it's like they're blocked off from their feelings. They think, but they don't feel. I believe it's something like a curse. Or maybe it's bred into one who's born into a closed society. Who's trained into artificial responses. One knows every conversation before it's opened. Every action becomes so practiced, it inspires no emotional response. Hence, boredom. Insulation. An intense disinterest in the world around you.

"Still, one might be crazy enough to think something might break through after all. And one might yet be whole." Cigar in hand, he pushed hisself away from the tree and came toward me, so close that his body cast a black shadow over me, his eyes gleaming white in the dark.

"Well," I stammered, "when—when you help those people. You must feel something then. Don't you, Cole?"

In the silence before he answered, I could feel my heart beating inside my chest, so hard it hurt, and I couldn't move under his eyes that held mine. Oh, God, what's happening? I thought. But Cole only stood there, his teeth moving to tear into his bottom lip.

"The last case I had before—well, before there were no more cases, only war," he said finally, his voice just above a whisper like he was telling me a deep secret, "I lost. It was rather unusual for me to lose a case like that one. My client was an elderly man and was so clearly deserving and had so obviously been cheated by this unsavory speculator that when the judgment came down against him, the thought occurred to me that perhaps someone had slipped a bribe to the judge. Especially since he was a new man in the district, someone I didn't personally know.

"Well, as the judge was handing down the judgment, I was going over the whole thing in my mind, analyzing whether the idea of the bribe could possibly be correct or whether I had bungled some key element in the trial, even making a few notes, when all of a sudden I felt a movement at my elbow and I realized it was the old man, my client, and that he had started to cry. Do you see what I'm telling you? I had a client who had lost every penny! Everything that was supposed to see him through the rest of his life with dignity. And I was only sitting there thinking about the mechanics of the case I had just lost. I hadn't even remembered I had a client, much less that he was sitting there beside me in the flesh and weeping so hard that the tears were coursing like twin rivers from his eyes to both sides of his chin and rolling down to meet in the middle . . . oh, God."

I don't know when Cole's hands first gripped hold my shoulders, or when he started to shake me, or when his eyes welled up and he flung his cigar aside, crushing it under his heel. Just that all at once he grabbed hold of me like a drowning man grabs hold of a tree branch or a piece of root as he's being swept along by the current. Held tight against him, I could feel his chest heaving up and down, his heart hammering fast as mine and my whole body shivering same as his.

"It's all right, Cole. It's all right," I kept whispering, my hands against his neck, my fingers in his hair. Stroking. Soothing him like a child, him clinging to me, then all at once taking a sharp breath and letting go, the two of us standing there inches away from each other, trying to get our breath. I could see the pulse racing in his throat. My own pulse was just as fast.

"Dammit," Cole said half under his breath. "Goddammit."

"Cole . . ." Something was dizzy in my head. Something racing through me that made me feel like the sky had split in two by a streak of lightning and I'd seen something up there I'd never seen before. Or seen something inside myself I'd never seen before.

"I'm a fool," Cole said. "I deserve this. God, why did I ever come here to begin with. I just . . ."

He looked half crazy, standing there shaking his head from side to side, talking to himself. Seemed like he understood what he was saying. But to me none of it made sense. Deserve what? Why shouldn't he of come here?

"It's all right," I said, trying to make him see me. "You didn't mean nothing."

"Didn't I," he said.

"Cole," I pleaded. "Surely you can see that . . . well, that nothing happened. You was troubled. We all have our troubles. I comforted you just like you would of comforted me. That's all."

He raised his head and looked at me. Seemed like something died in his eyes. "How silly of me," he said, standing there looking at me with that vacant look. He could of moved over the boundary of Tennessee into Virginia, that's how far off he looked. I heard myself talking, the words rushing out of my mouth without me even hearing what I was saying. I could see that Cole wasn't listening, much less understanding my nonsense.

"Let's go home," he said after a while.

"Is everything all right now?" I asked him, feeling like I'd failed him in some terrible way. Seeing that dead look of him, that same look that Beulah had talked about, was like having a fist 'round my heart, squeezing.

"Everything's fine," he said, his voice dead as his face.

We walked home without talking to each other. Ate dinner without looking at each other. Then when us women took our sewing to the fire as usual, Cole excused hisself. He had a long trip in front of him tomorrow, he said, and must go to bed.

Sitting there sewing, I felt Ama's eyes on me but I concentrated on making tight perfect little stitches. What really happened out there? I wondered, snapping off a thread with my teeth. Nothing more than a man cried who said he didn't know how to cry. And I comforted him. Nothing more than that.

But in the end it was a sleepless night, me staring into my candle, the house sleeping 'round me. I knew Cole had probably forgot the whole thing already, and it was only me sitting there on the edge of my bed with a terrible confused feeling that wouldn't even let me lay down.

I haven't been unfaithful to you, I told Joe, wherever he might be. I didn't do nothing at all. It just feels like it, that's all.

Cole left with Ama early the next morning, wearing the same gray suit he'd come in, the same black cravat at his throat, and

68

looking down at us women gathered 'round the carriage. No one had asked me to go to the station and Ama said she'd be back soon as possible and could we get breakfast started for the field hands.

"You all take care now," Cole said from his seat beside Ama. His nod, something like a short bow, was for all of us. His eyes were on all and none. If this had been yesterday, I wouldn't of thought nothing of it. I wouldn't of expected it to be no different. Today though, I kept watching him, hoping he'd look at me. That would make it easier. But he didn't.

Then Old Docker was moving down the drive, pulling the carriage as easy as a young horse, and Melissa yanked at my skirt as they reached the final turn, where we wouldn't be able to see them no more.

I bent down to pick her up and she made a game out of it, lifting her legs and swinging on me, so that when I finally stood up again holding her, her arms tight 'round my neck, her cheek against mine, the carriage was out of sight, but the women were still waving.

"What are you waving at?" I said, kind of short-like, to Jinny.

"Well," she said, still staring off down the drive, "just there at the end, the man look back, honey."

"Seem like he halfway climb right out the carriage," Beulah added with a heavy shrug, then started for the kitchen door.

Jinny and Delilah hurried after her, for it was past time to start breakfast.

But I stood for a while holding Melissa and looking down the empty driveway, hearing the carriage get farther and farther away. It's like he never come, I thought.

Then feeling the world lay still and cool 'round me, I turned my back on the drive and carried Melissa into the house.

Six

With Cole gone, our lives at Symphony Oaks seemed quieter than ever, and more cut off from the world. We worked out-doors; the men finished the planting and left, and us women kept to ourselves and had our talks and our jokes. Though from time to time we mentioned Cole, where he might be, what he might be doing, in time he seemed to me like somebody I'd read about. Those few moments that had happened between us seemed so impossible that maybe I'd made them up.

In early May, Tom and Lucie Higgins come home to Free-land Farm. Old Man Higgins had been living in the big white house alone ever since his own slaves run off, almost as one, and Tom had left for the war, leaving Lucie and their boy, Benjamin, in Macon with Lucie's mother.

Freeland Farm was our closest neighbor and Ama used to send food to Old Man Higgins sometimes back before he'd turned in Moses to Mr. Jackson, but I'd never been inside the white fence that ran across acres of its land, though I'd looked across the long green lawn, peeked at the arbors with the twin swings and the bird basins and the gardens that had long since run to weeds. Freeland Farm were built like the slave planta-tions I'd heard about down South in cotton country, and Ama knew it well. She'd even known the Clark Williamsons, who'd built it and lived there for almost ten years. Without Ama actually saying so, I knew she'd never approved of old man Williamson, who'd tried to build an empire on the labor of slaves. Ama said slave economy was never a just enterprise, and here in our narrow Tennessee valley, it wasn't even good business. The closest thing to plantations we had were a few big farms with lots of field hands, but nothing like the hundreds of slaves some of the biggest Southern planters used. After Clark Williamson lost his money, he and Mrs. Williamson, who Jinny said were a yard wide in the hips and a inch wide in the brain, had moved to Washington to live with their daughter.

Five years ago Old Man Higgins bought the place, and moved here from Savannah with still more slaves and begun trying to rebuild Freeland Farm with its huge verandas and its row of slave cabins out back. Even from the road, it was something to see. Every time we drove past, either Delilah or me asked Ama to slow down so we could stare. You could feel the elegance of the place, even with the dirt and weeds and all that had cropped up in the last year since the slaves and Tom had gone.

The day after Tom brought Lucie and Benjamin home, Ama and Beulah and Delilah and I come to the farm with a wagon full of mops and rags and cleaning things and a basket of fried chicken and biscuits.

"We've come to work," Ama told the pale, freckle-faced young woman who opened the front door wearing a bandana over her head and an apron over her dress.

A little boy crawled right between her legs from under her skirt and she grinned at us and said, "I'm Lucie and that's my son, Ben. He's charming, but he's a devil."

At closer look, Ben was probably five rather than the three-year-old I'd took him for, and Lucie was full of more breeding than I'd first noticed with her bandana and all. In fact, nothing were exactly as I'd thought. The inside of that once elegant house were full of cobwebs, the roof had leaks, and the floors were caked over with dried mud. The kitchen had bugs and the cellar had snakes and rats.

"You're sure you really want to bother with this place?" Lucie sighed, showing us the dirt on her apron, the broken nails and scuff marks on her hands.

"Best way to make friends and neighbors I know of," Ama said. "Where's the water bucket?"

That first day, we worked without many breaks excepting for food and rest. The next day, we come back again and worked some more, and then Tom, Lucie and Ben, and even Old Man Higgins came to Symphony Oaks for supper, though he stood up and almost left us when he saw Delilah take her place at the table, for it were Jinny's and my turn to serve.

Ama said nothing. Lucie smiled polite-like. But it was Tom, who I'd hardly seen except as the tall busy man either in the fields or top of his house, always working, who settled things down. He put a hand on his father's arm and pulled a little and said, "Father, you've been craving a good pork roast and here's a capital one. And roasted potatoes, just the way you like them."

Old Man Higgins cut his eyes at the roast and the potatoes, then slid back down in his chair. I saw Ama's smile that was just a polite inch left of a laugh and heard Lucie's giggle that wasn't.

Delilah looked up from her plate then and gave a solemn nod of thanks to Tom, who nodded back as solemn, and I set the roast in front of Ama and went back for the gravy boat. When the eating started, if anybody looked solemn, it was Old Man Higgins, shoveling in pork and potatoes till his mouth was full and refusing to look at Ama's side of the table, where Delilah sat eating her pork with perfect table manners.

With the dessert course, Old Man Higgins started complaining. His legs hurt. His eyesight was going. The Yankees were lawless cusses, and his farm had gone to ruin since the niggers left. "How come slaves think they can ruin a man," he said, "when all I ever done was feed them, put clothes on their backs, and give them a roof over their miserable heads?"

Finally, Tom hauled him into the carriage and headed back to Freeland Farm, with a look of apology to us and a shrug to

Lucie. "I'll be back in a little while," he said, heading out. Beside him, Old Man Higgins kept talking nonstop, about the no-account slaves and the nigger-loving Yankees.

Ama and Jinny and Beulah cleared things up, and Delilah and me kept Lucie company on the porch, for Ama wouldn't hear of nothing else. Delilah and Lucie sat in the swing and I sat on the top step, my back against a pillar, my legs stretched out in front of me.

"Pleasant night," Lucie sighed, her eyes fixed on the full moon hung over the cornfield.

"Right quiet, too," Delilah added.

For a moment nobody said anything. Then, for no clear reason I could tell, Lucie slid forward cautious-like in the swing and started telling Delilah and me about Tom. How he'd been injured in the war, left for dead on the bloody battlefield of Bull Run, and how he was still carrying a piece of metal deep inside his shoulder. For all that, he had gone back to active duty until his year was up. Maybe except for the wound, he would have enlisted for another term, but maybe not, with his father walking 'round an empty house, dropping lit cigars on the floors and cussing people who weren't there to clean them up.

"It's a wonder," Lucie said, "that the house didn't burn down."

"Lucie," I said, and stopped. It took a minute to get my courage and then I said, "Did you know . . . I mean, there's something I want to tell you. Otherwise, we can't be real friends and I want that. I haven't never made friends with an educated young lady like you. To tell you truth, I never met a belle from Macon before."

"Tell you the *real* truth," Delilah said from beside Lucie, "I never even want to meet no belle. I seen 'nough on the plantation to do me for a life. Nothin' make me feel more like a slave than belle. Runnin' and fetchin', runnin' and fetchin'. And look from their eye could cut you in two. But you nothin' like that, Miz Lucie."

"Thank God," Lucie said, fingering her thin paisley shawl.

73

Then she touched the net that covered her smooth hair, and pushed at an escaped lock, and asked me what I wanted to tell her. Was it how much I hated belles too?

I took a deep breath and told her about Joe. How everybody thought of me as a Yankee. And how, truth to tell, I was starting to think of me as a Yankee, too. "You make a friend out of me," I warned her, "and right there, you've made enemies in this town."

"Good riddance," Lucie said. "I never met them anyway."

And we three giggled as the world lay beyond us in shadows. The war never seemed so far away. Maybe because we three were so young, with our lives in front of us. Without any older woman or man sharing our porch, we'd shed years and grown a little giddy. Something sweet wafted in the air and lightning bugs sparkled and dimmed, sparkled and dimmed across Ama's yard. Six or seven years ago, we might have chased after them with jars in our hands—men the furthest thing from our minds. Tonight though, two of us were married and the other one was waiting for a beau to come home from the war.

"Are you scared of the war?" I said in a low voice, my fingers locked over my knees.

"I been scared a long time," Delilah said.

"Nothing scares me," Lucie said, "except losing Tom or Benjamin. I can live through anything else without a bit of worry."

"Are we going to be close friends?" I said.

The moonlight played across Lucie's plain face, and she smiled. For the first time, she was almost pretty.

"Friends," she said.

"Friends," Delilah and I said together.

And we lost ourselves for a while like young girls who tell each other how they like to comb their hair, what their favorite colors are, what makes them laugh and what makes them cry. All half whispered, me creeping closer to the swing until I was sitting cross-legged in front of it, them leaning down to straighten my hair, put my necklace right, the way girls do for each other. And then under the bright moonlight, our faces grew

74

more solemn as in the distance we heard Tom's carriage. Heard a door shut inside the house and saw Ama pass the window, lighting a lamp. Before our own eyes, we started turning back into women, but friends.

The next week Lucie invited us to supper, but Ama said no, not until her house was ready. Lucie only had one servant, Narcissa Harwell, a poor white woman who were middle-aged and widowed and glad to move in with the Higgins family, though Old Man Higgins raged to anybody who would listen that it went against his grain to hire a white servant, when he'd paid good money for slaves. Tom had trouble finding a carpenter, too, but he finally found a carpenter's son, who was only fourteen but already experienced with his hands. How long Tom would keep him, though, he couldn't say, for the boy was already thinking of leaving for the war.

Tom worked from morning till night, with never a word about the impossible job of setting up such a big household at a time when help was hard to find and he was low on money. In spite of everthing, he seemed happy, striding across his property in great long steps, always with clear purpose, for he were a natural planter and a good carpenter. If he was almost buried under the care of his farm, it was easy to understand.

"That metal in his shoulder," Lucie said, watching him from the window. "It's going to kill him someday, you know."

I looked up startled from where I sat sipping tea. By now, it was part of my day to stop by for a half hour and either help Lucy with her work or sit with a cup of tea. "Kill him!" I said. "Why, I never saw a man in better health."

Lucie dropped the crochet she'd been working on, her eyes sick with sudden fear. "I guess I didn't tell you how badly injured he was at Manassas, Elizabeth. The surgeon sent for me but he—Tom—didn't know me." Her eyes seemed to search the walls, going from one elegant dark-framed painting to the next, but something told me she wasn't really seeing nothing but a strange hospital ward, Tom in a white bed, his

75

eyes closed. "He thought he was still on the battlefield," she said after a few more minutes of staring at nothing, her hand over her mouth. "He was screaming to some friend, somebody I didn't even know. His fever jumped up and down and . . . they told me he'd die. I screamed at them, Elizabeth. I swore at them. I even screamed at Tom. I told him to open his eyes and see me! Then I started crying and I got down on my knees beside his bed and I begged him to see me. I kept cold towels on his face and I rubbed his body and for nine days I never left his room for more than fifteen minutes at a time. And every day of that time, there was the doctor and one nurse after the other saying he'd die. That they didn't know what was keeping him alive from one day to the next."

Lucie's eyes started to water and she wiped the tears away with her fingers, smiling even while she was crying. "Then one day," she said, the relief spilling out of her as she must of felt it that day, "he opened his eyes and I was so scared I couldn't breathe. I thought he was seeing the battlefield again. I expected to hear him call out for his friend. But he said 'Lucie' and I just sat there with this idiotic smile all over my mouth and the tears running down my face. The next day he ate a little soup. He got better but . . . well, the metal's still in there. The doctors said watch for colds. Watch for infection, any kind of infection. Watch him . . ." Her voice broke. "Oh, God, I love him," she said.

Then she sat there beside me and told me about being born rich and not many of the eligible bachelors down in Macon being interested in her for she wasn't thought to be one of the prettier belles.

"You are so pretty," I said.

Her eyes met mine and she smiled. There was a bitter kind of accepting in her face. "No, I'm not," she said. "And you don't think so, either. Friends don't lie to each other, Elizabeth."

But by now, I wasn't lying. Her face looked altogether different to me now, after our talks together. Our cups of tea, our work. "I love your face, Lucie," I said. "I like your eyes and your nose. Even your freckles. And I never liked freckles before. Still, somehow I've come to like yours. You wouldn't be *you* without them!"

But the bachelors hadn't liked them, Lucie said, still smiling at me. And so she'd spent her time reading books and sort of believing that if she ever married, it would be to somebody who hadn't been able to find anybody else. Then Tom had come to Macon to look at some fine blooded horses and went to a party, where they fell in love at first sight.

"At least for me it was love at first sight," Lucie said, straightening her thin back, raising her small chin. In that moment, you could see her breeding, and her whole body fair breathed the elegance of the South. Her neck was beautiful; her wrists and hands all of a sudden took on a daintiness I'd missed. "He noticed me," she said, her face all aglow. "Me, out of all those pretty belles! Maybe it was the way I hung back away from people," she went on, her face falling some. "I wonder if he pitied me. He's too kind to say. Anyhow, we talked that night. I mean, we really talked. We'd read the same books, we were both students of world history, geography. We both planned to travel. And, well, he grew into loving me, I guess. It was never really the romantic way other men looked at the belles." She stood up all of a sudden and went to the window. I looked past her head and saw Tom heading toward the house carrying a bucket of whitewash.

"He's a wonderful man," I said. "You're so lucky, Lucie."

"Yes, I am. And I'm sure . . . I'm sure he loves me in his own way." Her voice was kind of sad, as if she doubted her own words.

"Loves you! Lord, of course, he loves you," I told her. "Why, the love just pours out of him. And the way he treats you! I never seen a man treat a woman like his best friend before. What more could a woman want?"

Lucie spun 'round and laughed, as if she thought I'd made some kind of joke. Then she laid her hand on my shoulder. "Is that what you want from your husband?" she asked, still with that teasing look.

I thought about Joe. Or tried thinking about him, 'cause every day he got further away, until I could hardly remember what he looked like. Sitting there in the elegant house, that was clean now and glowing from polish and elbow grease, I couldn't get a picture of Joe in my mind.

"Yes, I—" I started to answer, then out of nowhere, I thought of Cole. Of being short of breath, of seeing the pulse throbbing in his neck, both our hearts hammering so hard it shook our bodies. I saw Lucie staring at me and had to make myself speak. "I think," I said, "that it would be wonderful to have a best friend for a husband."

Her look changed from teasing to puzzled, then she said, "Oh, you're probably right, and much more sensible than me, when all's said and done. I suppose maybe I'm looking for something that isn't . . . well, that isn't in him. I wanted an intelligent man, and that's what I got, as well as being hand-some. And it's not that Thomas isn't a caring man. He is. For me and—and, of course, he just adores Ben. It's just that most of his *passion* is for the land, that's all."

"Ain't that like a man!" Narcissa Harwell said, coming through the door with a mop over her shoulder. Narcissa was a red-cheeked woman, tall as a man and with an appetite to match. Lucie said she looked for places to hide food, for once Narcissa caught sight of it, it was gone. No explanations, noth-ing. Just a clean plate and Narcissa humming in the kitchen.

"Narcissa, did you help Ben with his vegetable patch today? I was out there yesterday, and the weeds were so high they scared me," Lucie said.

"We did the patch this morning." Narcissa grinned.

"Did you bring in those ripe tomatoes? Some of them looked like they'd be perfect today."

"I didn't see a tomato on the vine," Narcissa declared. She licked her lips. "Not a one."

"But Narcissa, there must have been at least eight. . . ."

"Not a one!" Narcissa repeated in a firm voice, and passed on out the door, us hardly able to keep from laughing as she went.

Anyhow, Lucie looked happier. Maybe between Narcissa and me, we'd convinced her that all men were like Tom, that their deeper passions rested in the land. But deep inside me, I wasn't sure that this was the way of things. There were men, I whispered inside myself, who cared more for their women than for their fields and animals. There was . . . there was Cole. But why did I think that when Cole hisself had told me he couldn't feel nothing at all? Why couldn't I believe that when I could believe it real easy of Tom? Tom, I thought, is the man who can't feel deep passion. Not Cole.

"I guess part of being a wife," Lucie said, "is taking your man like God made him."

I looked at her. "Do you think men ever talk about their women like we talk about them?"

"No," she said. "Not their wives anyhow."

"What other kind of woman except wives could a man have?" I said.

"Kept women," Lucie said, her eyes wicked. "The kind they lust after and don't marry. Let me give you a hint, Elizabeth. These women . . . they aren't the pure sort. Just between the two of us, I wish Tom would treat me like one of those women. Not in front of people. Just in the bedroom. You know what I mean? I wish just once he'd almost lose control. But he won't. Still, you know what? I'll take what I can get!"

"I guess," I said.

But laying in bed that night, I couldn't push Cole out of my mind. I could see his eyes, see the crazy look in them before he'd grabbed hold of me. Like . . . like he'd lost control.

Trembling, I covered my eyes and told myself to quit thinking such things. I must never think about Cole like that again. Not ever. Whatever happened between us had to do with some hurt inside him and nothing to do with me. I'd just happened to be there. Anyhow, I was married and he knew it. Out of his class and he knew it. Let him go. That's all I could do, anyhow.

I laid still, my hands fists against my closed eyes, and after a while, Cole's tan face fell apart in my mind, as gentle as snow melting under the sun.

*   *   *

Before I knew it, we'd reached the end of June. The sun was hotter every day, the grass greener and the crops taller in the fields. And every night, Ama, Jinny, Beulah, Delilah, and me talked the hours away, our sewing in our hands, the teapot close by. It was one of the last June nights and the hottest, that we found ourselves on the subject of heaven and Ama near shocked everybody by saying she didn't believe in it.

"At least not Gabriel blowing a horn and everyone wearing gold crowns and the like."

"Ama, don't say that," I said. "God won't forgive you."

"Well, if He's going to be that much of a tyrant," Ama said, taking a biscuit, "I'd rather go to hell."

"I don't right know what I be sayin' 'bout that." Jinny frowned, rolling her eyes at Ama, then toward the ceiling, as if checking to see if God be listening.

Funny thing, I thought. It was only on the subject of God that anybody got so tense. Probably, because soon as you mentioned God, everybody got the same idea, that God was up there listening. You could talk and talk and feel like you was alone, but mention God, and all of a sudden you had an audience up there, leaning over with His hand cupped 'round His ear. Saying, "Shh, shut up, Gabriel, I got to listen. Somebody's talking about me."

Ama looked at Jinny for a moment out of her light-green, almost clear-colored eyes. There weren't no expression on her face. She just looked at Jinny for a time, then said, "You must be careful, Jinny, not to confuse religion with myth."

"What that, myth?" Delilah asked.

"Huh!" Ama snorted. "Myth is the brother of superstition. Next, you'll have me throwing a pinch of salt over my shoulder after I've spilt the shaker."

"Oh, I saw Jinny do that the other day," I said.

"Bet I did," Jinny said. "No tellin' what happen if I don't. That take the spell off."

80

"How about evil spirits?" Ama asked. "Does anybody believe in them?"

Jinny gave her a startled look, like a trapped calf. Then she looked down at the floor. The room was quiet. The only sound was Beulah shifting her weight in her chair.

Finally, Delilah cleared her throat. "I once seen a ghost," she said, not quite looking Ama in the eyes.

"You never!" Jinny said.

Still we all gasped and leaned in close together, like we knew Delilah was wanting us to.

"What that there ghost look like?" Beulah asked, getting to her feet.

"Well, it wearin' a sheet, course, that it were . . . a bloooooody sheet," Delilah added, her eyes glistening in the lamplight. "Yeah, now that I thinkin' 'bout it, that there ghost wearin' a sheet pourin' out bloooood!"

"Wait just here," Beulah said. "You mean you seen that there ghost down Georgia?"

"Yes, ma'am." Delilah nodded.

"You ain't talkin' 'bout the Morgan Hill ghost?"

"That the one," Delilah said. "You hear 'bout that ghost? Know why it cryin' and carryin' on?"

Beulah said, "It cryin' 'cause it got murder. It murder by Massah Morgan own young bride."

"That right?" Jinny asked. "I never heard that down Georgia."

"Oh, it a terrible thing," Beulah said, turning down the lamp. Her shadow fell large across the wall, and it looked like the spirits had come to visit. "See here," she said in a low voice, as she sat next to Delilah, "that Massah Morgan a rich man. Oh, he 'bout the richest man anywheres, but he a eeeevil man," she moaned, rocking back and forth with her eyes rolling 'round in her head. "He done fall in love," she went on, "with the most loveliest white gal in town, but she didn't want nothin' to do with him. So, he done catched her soul!"

"No!" Delilah cried.

"Yeah, he did now. And he done put that soul in a chicken! One of his own chicken in his own chicken house."

"And then," Ama said, "I suppose the poor girl married him to be close to her soul. . . ."

"Yes'm, that just the way it was, and y'all know Beulah wouldn't tell y'all no lie now. Pore young gal went up to that old Cyrus Morgan hill to be close to her soul. But ooooonnne day," she moaned, "that ole man . . . take that chicken . . . and he take a ax . . ."

"Oh, no!" I cried.

"Yes'm, now he did. He done take that ax and he kill that chicken!"

"He killed her soul?" Even Ama's face was kind of white.

"Yes'm, chop the head right off. And that poor gal had to go 'round and serve up that chicken for his supper. But! Later that night . . . close 'round midnight . . . she done take up that ax . . . the same ax what kill the chicken, the blood were still on it . . . and she done walk up the stair . . . up . . . up the stair . . . and right in his bedroom . . . and then . . . and then . . . she done raise that ax just high she could raise it . . . and with a *terrible* laugh, she done bring it down . . . *and hack his head right off!* There were blood everwhere. That prob'ly why that there sheet all bloody.

"Now," Beulah said, throwing her head back, her eyes getting bigger and bigger like growing flowers, "when old Massah Morgan seen what she done, he hoppin' mad, yes he were. So up he jump without a head and grab that ax right out of her hand. She take off runnin' and him chasin' after her with the ax a-swingin'. Now nobody know whether he done catch her or not. But to this very night, his ghost still haunt the hill. And evertime some pore person pass close by . . . he sneak out the bushes . . . raise up that ax high he can . . . then, oh mercy, he swing that ax down hard . . . and he chop off her head!!"

The words were barely out of her mouth, with us hanging on our chairs and not a ounce of air left in our lungs, when a heavy pounding broke on the front door like all of hell was just outside.

82

"Oh, mercy!" Delilah screamed, hiding her face against Beulah's shoulder. "It the ghost! The ghost sure's I sittin' here!"

Jinny dropped to her knees and commenced moaning and praying, a funny sound like the kind you hear at a funeral.

"You'll have to answer it, Ama," I said. "I'm just shaking."

"Oh, don't answer it, Miz Ama," Jinny moaned. "It Cyrus Morgan ghost with the ax!"

"Don't have to worry about me answering it," Ama said. "I'm scared to death. My blood's curdled in my veins."

The pounding came again, filling up the whole house.

"That there ghost sound mad, Miz Ama," Delilah whispered.

"Yes'm, it do now," Beulah agreed. "Best thing to do when a ghost mad, go see what it want."

"Not likely," Ama said. "Unless you're volunteering to go talk to it?"

"Me!" Beulah gasped. "Lord, no. My heart would stop."

The pounding went on, like a giant's heart that wouldn't stop beating for nothing.

Finally Ama declared herself recovered. "I don't know how I could be so silly. Of course that's not a ghost. I'll just go see who it is." She looked at us. "You'll all have to come with me."

"Oh, Ama, I can't!" I cried, and the others said it too.

"Well, you will," she told us. "If it's the ghost, you'll have to help me fight it off." Then she whisked off down the hall, me following her and praying every step, with the others hanging way back. She marched to that door, unlatched it, swung it wide, and stood staring, face to face with the ghost.

For it was a ghost. The ghost of Joe Crocker. With a face drawed up and changed, dirty and looking ten years older. But the brown eyes were Joe's. And the little scar on his chin. His mama said he'd got that scar when he was a baby learning to walk.

"I come for my wife," said the ghost. "Liz Ann . . ." and his voice broke and he looked ready to fall. For the first time, I noticed he was on crutches and then I saw the empty pants leg,

83

pinned up, and all of a sudden, I knew it was really Joe, living and breathing, and that he'd lost his leg.

"Joe, I'm here," I said and we were looking at each other then like we hadn't never looked at each other before. And right there in front of everybody, I put my arms 'round him and he broke down and began to cry. It was like having Melissa Sue in my arms but more. Inside me were relief and tears and heat and love and it all dissolved into hot liquid and poured through my body.

Ama, her face set fire with joy, took him inside and settled him in a chair with the others hurrying in with root coffee and food and brandy and him telling how he found Ama's note she left in the cabin when her and Jinny went to get Melissa's crib.

"How did you get here?" Ama asked.

"I've got a horse, 'most dead it's so tired. Neither of us rested for a day, just kept coming." As Beulah and Delilah went to see to Joe's horse, he leaned his head against the back of his chair and the lamp shone fuller on his face, showing the dark circles under his eyes, the lines across his forehead. "I ain't a handsome man no more, Liz Ann," he whispered, feeling how close I was watching him.

"Yes, you are," I lied. "You just need to rest your eyes, Joe. Anyhow, haven't you never heard it's the women supposed to be pretty? Not the men. Now I've got something to show you, Joe. Something that'll make you real happy." I left him sitting there, just starting on a plate of chicken and potatoes with biscuits and honey on another plate, and cake waiting. Won't you be surprised, Joe Crocker, I thought.

When I got to Melissa's bed, I stood looking at her for a minute, seeing her for the first time all over again like I was looking through Joe's eyes. I never felt so proud in my life. Then I waked her up and dressed her in the pink dress trimmed in lace that Jinny made for her. Then I brought her to Joe, and Delilah took away his plate so's I could lift her up to his lap. For a minute, there was silence in the room and Beulah was wiping tears out of her eyes as Joe looked at his little girl then with a cry held her to his breast, so tight I was afraid he would hurt her. "My baby," he kept saying over and over, and though Melissa squirmed 'round, trying to see me, upset to be held so tight by a stranger, she didn't cry but let herself be held.

I was so full of feeling I hurt inside. I don't know if it would of hit me so hard back at the cabin or if Joe had both legs and was all right. But seeing him in the dirty old clothes he was wearing with Ama standing next to him, pouring more brandy in his glass, somehow that filled me up till I could hardly say a word. I just looked at him and listened to the others talk. News of the war. How Joe had been hit by a Minié ball in the thigh in March, battle of Pea Ridge, Arkansas, this last said in such a short tense way that a silence fell and none of us dared to ask more.

"The Union's got all of Kentucky and most of Tennessee now," he said, letting Melissa squirm to the floor. He said "Union" like he was talking about an army full of enemies, not the very side he'd been fighting for. Melissa edged 'round the side of his chair and made straight for me, and Joe watched her, frowning. "I hear the rebels are ready to lynch Sidney Johnston just for losses in Tennessee alone," he went on without any more love in the word "rebels" than for the Union. He was still watching Melissa as she pulled herself up on my lap.

"Are there Union bases all over Tennessee?" Ama asked, leaning forward, her eyes keen and interested, not afraid.

Joe nodded. "Like flies on honey. . . . Liz Ann, give me back the baby."

I got up and put Melissa on his lap again, acting like I didn't notice her trying to hang onto me.

He looked at her real close, then tried to hug her again. But she squirmed away and began to cry. Nobody moved, and I could tell everyone were getting nervous.

"She don't know me," he said, his eyes as bitter as his voice.

And I wondered if he blamed the Union for that, or for cutting off his leg. I couldn't help staring at his stump. I hoped

I'd be woman enough where it wouldn't matter to me. It was just that first time when I'd be seeing it . . . that's what scared me.

All at once I felt Joe's eyes on me and my face turned red. As if he could read my mind. Well, maybe he *can* read my mind, I thought. Because sudden-like he held Melissa up to Jinny.

"I guess it's time we was leaving, Liz Ann," he said.

The next minute he was up out of his chair, holding onto my shoulder till Delilah got his crutches from the corner, and the feel of his body made me want to go to our home and live together with him, and learn how to love him all over again.

I looked straight into his eyes and hardly heard Ama's voice telling us we had to stay all night and go home the next day in a wagon with her horse. She wouldn't have it no other way.

When Joe and I went upstairs together, I was shy, especially when I saw Delilah giggle and give Beulah a punch. But there wasn't no reason to be shy. Joe was done wore out. He laid down on the bed in his clothes and before he could get up to get undressed, he'd passed out. I wouldn't wake him. I sat watching him by the moonlight and trying to understand why I was so glad to see this man, my husband.

Who are you, Joe Crocker, with pain lines 'round your mouth that I don't know nothing about? Without your leg—my God, Joe, your leg. He cried out in his sleep and I took hold of his hand.

"Hush now, Joe. Everything's going to be all right. I'll make it right. You'll see." And I sat there waiting for the night to turn into dawn.

Seven

*N*ext morning were still and hot, and Joe Crocker and me didn't have nothing to say to each other on the way home. His eyes never looked at me that I could tell. They were empty and tired and I was afraid he'd gone away from me like he'd never come home. Last night didn't really mean nothing, I told myself. I felt so low I could hardly lift my head. The worst thing about hope is when it goes away.

First Symphony Oaks, then Freeland Farm disappeared over the hill behind us. The white fences got brown and the long fields got shorter. Instead of mansions, there were farmhouses, most of them smaller than the barns that lorded over the property. Instead of Lucie running out the door and waving, there was Wade Long watching us pass his farm, his arms folded over a post, his mouth as grim as if he was watching a pack of wolves loping toward his henhouse. Then Milt Steedman halfway raising his arm from behind his plow and then putting it down as he got a better look at us.

I tried to keep my eyes on the road. A rolling road, not a flat stretch of land. Like life, I thought. Full of bends and hills and dales. Some land greener, some land rockier and browner. It had to do with irrigation. It had to do with bad breaks, maybe.

"You must be glad to be finished with the army," I said to Joe, looking to find words.

"You could say that," he grunted, his face sallow, his beard a shaggy growth, and it was hard to believe he were the same high-spirited boy that once caught girls' eyes. Brown eyes, brown hair. The kind of smile that let you know he knew he was looking good.

Joe was educated, too. He'd finished the Frisbin school and he even talked some about going to college, but even back then, I think I knew that was talk. It was the kind of talk that lets a person be more than he is without paying the price for it. I *could* go to college, Joe would say. That's the kind of man I am. If I don't go to college, that's my decision, but I could do it. And he let you know he had money. His father put up the money for Joe's land, backed him for the cabin. His father's slaves helped Joe put in his first tobacco crop. His only tobacco crop. He had an eye for a pretty face. Everyone in town knew that. He'd called on Gillian Brian, back when she was Gillian Kidwell. He'd looked a time or two at my sister Nellie. He'd even looked at women when we were together. In church and at socials. "You see me lookin', Liz Ann, don't you worry about a thing. That's just me bein' a man. I already got the prettiest woman for myself, but I can't keep my eyes in my pocket, can I? You just be glad you got a man who's a man, you know what I mean? The kind of man that loves a good-lookin' woman."

Joe approved of me not having much schooling. His family believed like my family. Women study cooking and learn to manage a house. Of course, they got to know how to read and write, he wouldn't have a woman that couldn't do that. But beyond that, it was more important that a woman knew how to sew a pretty seam. I never told him that sometimes I used to read my brothers' schoolbooks. Riding beside him now, I knew he'd be surprised to know how much I used to read at Ama's. Books I didn't even understand. Especially, since Cole had left. But to Joe, my six grades of schooling were plenty. Any more might of made him uneasy. Don't ask me how I knew this, but I did. Just like I somehow knew he was uneasy about the time I'd spent with Ama. As though I'd got hold of some dangerous information and might use it to make him less.

Of course, Joe was a Christian man. Lord, you can't get no more Christian than a Southern Baptist, he used to say, and laugh. But you never heard Joe talk religion; it was more like a suit of clothes he put on every Sunday. He didn't talk about the Reverend's message, he talked about how long-winded he was. He didn't talk about God, he talked about how much money his family had put up toward the new church. He prayed with his eyes open and winked at me over the hymnbook. He used to be an upstanding man of the church, but maybe not of God. I never heard him talk about heaven or hell. I never heard him pity his fellow creatures. But, if he didn't have a loud conscience, he had a lot of charm back when he was a young man.

It was only now, sitting beside him up front of the wagon, that I realized how little Joe ever talked about who he was. He talked more about *what* he was. A farmer. A good provider. A manly sort of man who was a good catch. He reminded you he was good-looking. He let you know he was from a good family. What I didn't know was whether he ever got afraid of life. Or whether he'd ever really loved me, or at least thought he loved me. Or if he'd been hurt by being raised by a mother like Mary Crocker who stared right through her children like they were the worst nuisances God ever sent her.

His father was always working, always planning, always making money. Hardly ever home. A farmer, a man of property. He'd invested money in the mill and that money had made even more money, a mint of money. Ethan Crocker, his grandfather, had been a farmer too, and a drunk. But then, none of the Crockers had much of a head for liquor, though they all had a liking for the bottle. You forgave them for it because, when they were sober, weren't no more charming a bunch of men and boys than the Crockers. And the Crockers were still popular in town. Joe was the black sheep that everybody except Mama forgave the family for. But they weren't about to forgive Joe.

"While you was gone," I told him, "after a while, I guess I started thinking of myself as being a Yankee. Isn't that something?"

He turned to me with a short bark of laughter. "This war

ain't over you and me being anything, Liz Ann," he said, dust flying up and insects buzzing and feeding on his sweat. "You think this war would ever been fought for anything *you* thought about being? This war is between giants. Them with the mills and them with the slaves and a bunch of fools in the middle, like Abe Lincoln, who think it's about niggers' rights."

"But you are a Yankee, though, Joe?"

"I was nothing but a body piled up with ten other bodies in a ditch. Happened I was wearing blue," he snapped, then wiped his forehead with his sleeve. "Whew, it's hot enough, ain't it?" he said. "Ask me, it's too hot to talk."

"I reckon so," I said, seeing he was staring straight ahead again.

A bird perched on a tree branch and cocked its head at me. A dog barked in a field. The trees were so still you'd think somebody painted them. There wasn't enough air to catch your breath.

While we rode, the wagon jostled up and down and we could hear Melissa's high voice, her shrieks that were the sounds a baby makes when it's in its own world and enjoying rolling 'round in a bouncing wagon. Twice she stopped shrieking and started crying in the sudden way that children do when they need something all at once. Both times, I slipped her pieces of dried apple, one of her favorites.

"Does she always cry like that?" Joe said.

"She hardly cries at all," I said. "You can't get a baby who cries any less. She's just not used to being away from Daisy, I guess."

Joe's eyebrows climbed toward his hairline. "You mean the nigger baby?"

I swallowed hard. "Yes. The Nigro baby, Joe. Daisy and Melissa weren't hardly apart since I been at Ama's."

"You got to watch that sort of thing," Joe said. "She'll forget who she is."

"Who she is?" I said, feeling myself fill up with anger.

"Yes, who she is!" Joe said. "You got something to say about that?"

After a minute I shook my head. No, I thought. And if I do, now isn't the right time to say it.

When we were right near the Alden Crocker farm, that belonged to Joe's pa, I almost asked Joe if he'd had news of his family. But then, it wasn't no use. Joe's pa had disowned him when he joined with the Yankees, and one of his brothers had threatened to shoot him. So there wasn't no wondering about Joe's family. He didn't have a family anymore, excepting for Melissa and me, and we'd probably spend the rest of our lives in our cabin, or one like it up North, and when we were dead, nobody'd notice. And the earth wouldn't have changed much for us having lived on it.

In silence Joe and I went up the side road to our place. It was so growed up with weeds, it was hard to get to. The cabin looked dull, almost rust-colored, and the flowers that once lined the path and grew in beds by the house had long since died. The garden were weeds and dirt. The fields were dry and empty. Everything that was run-down was evidence of no care being given to it, care I was supposed to give maybe.

"I was hoping you'd put in a few crops," Joe said.

"Weren't no use, Joe. I would have if there was, but there weren't. See, they dug everything up. Mostly, the Prewitts. The one I recognized was Ned, but he wasn't alone. I heard them all out there stripping the beans. They even took what they didn't need."

"Lord, it's a ruin," he said, pulling the horse up and giving the wasted field a disgusted look. "Somehow I thought you'd keep trying, at least. There's nothing. Nothing!" His voice shook in anger and then got moody and distant. "I guess there ain't none of the poultry left? The cow?"

"No. A fox or something got to the rooster and—and I had to eat the hens, Joe. One by one, just to stay alive. And the cow died of milk fever first of the winter."

"You didn't do very good, did you, Liz Ann?" He leaned over and spit off the wagon.

"Don't say that, Joe!" I said. "Don't say I didn't do it right! It was you went away to fight for the North. I never said nothing to you, 'cause I figured a man has to make up his own mind what side he's fighting for. But when things got hard, my own mama wouldn't take me in. Nobody in town would say nothing to me, lessen it were words of scorn. Then Melissa . . . she almost died, Joe. We were starving. I had to do what I could just to keep us both alive."

I turned on him, but there he was with his closed-up face, his vigor gone. A man lost to his own self, grieving. "Oh, God, I'm sorry, Joe," I said. "Please, forgive me. You couldn't know. I never wrote you how bad it were. I ought to not said nothing to you, getting home and seeing how bad they hurt you, your poor leg—" I felt him stiffen up and hurried on nervous-like, twisting my hands. "I—I'll help you, Joe. Help you forget."

He turned so quick and his eyes were so crazy that for a minute I thought he was going to hit me, but when I covered my face with my hands, he jerked them down and looked me eye-to-eye without touching me again.

"Forget?" he said in a hoarse voice. "Do you know what it's like having a glass of whiskey and they to be sawing your leg off? Your *leg*, Liz Ann." He grabbed me in a sudden close embrace and I felt his tears on my face. "I'm sorry. I don't know why I'm—this way, I just—"

For a minute his head dropped to my shoulder and I heard him sigh, like he was dying. But when I put my hand to his head, he drew away and sat there drying his eyes with his fist like an overgrown baby. Then he climbed down from the wagon, dragged his crutches from behind the seat, and went up on the front porch. The roof sagged from the two wood posts that held it, almost closing the space between his head and the rafters.

It's a tight cabin. That's how Joe had first described it to me. I remembered him taking me there before we were married and us walking through the door hand in hand, him walking through first and almost pulling me through. "See, you got to look at it like this, Liz Ann. We got a kitchen and a front room and a bedroom. It's got pine walls. Wood floors. Got real glass in the windows and a first-class chimney. The roof will hold us for fifteen years, maybe twenty. Let me tell you, it's tight as it can be. It's a beginning, that's the way I look at it. Every few years, when the children start coming, we'll add on a room or two until we have us something that'll make the whole town look at us."

That was the Frisbin way to look at a house. Houses weren't put there to stand forever the way you built them. They were like your children. They grew, they developed into something. When you were starting out, you lived in one or two rooms. But if you prospered, your house flowered out over the property. Took on porches, stairs, upstairs. Right now the outside of our cabin was weathered, still holding reds and yellows amongst the grays. The timber clear in its grain. Someday, maybe the cabin would be nothing more than two rooms of a sprawling white house on a hill, with children running over a green lawn, instead of a stony, mostly bare yard. The fields would be lush and full, not dry and empty.

And the inside would be light instead of a curious-like darkness that sent shadows over the walls and floors. That was the way I remembered it looking, anyhow. Dark and shadowy and the walls and the property growing shabbier every day, every week.

Joe put his hand on the doorknob; then his glance went once more to the barren fields and a wide pit of rocks and rotted planks that were our well. Whether he knew I was watching him, I couldn't be sure, but he came down off the porch, picked up a handful of dry dirt, and disappeared 'round the side of the house.

"He don't mean to be cross or nothing," I explained to Melissa, who was clamoring to get out of the back of the wagon. "It's just that life's kind of hard right now. But you don't understand none of that, do you, angel?" I lifted her down and she went running before me over the stony ground that was her yard toward the ugly filthy cabin that was her home.

For a few minutes I stood on the flat rock that served as front doorstep and didn't have the courage to open the door. I was actually trembling, my hands fastened together so tight my knuckles were white. If I go inside this cabin, I'll die here and nobody will ever know it, I thought. Elizabeth Ann Crocker, wife of Joe Crocker, soon to die of . . . of what?

You think in a different way in a place like this. Without people 'round you. No one to help you work. No one to help you with your child. You got to get through your days alone and you can't laugh away what comes into your mind. Like . . . what if Ama's wrong and life is really just one big coincidence? What if it's all an accident? You have children, but they just grow up and die. You die, everything dies. The grass dies, the animals die, the earth dies. The mountains fall down. The sun burns everything up. There is no God. There is no *anything*. Living is a terrible tragedy. You're born, you live, you lose everything, and then you die.

In a place like this, when you have thoughts like those, there's nobody like Ama to talk you out of them. You might get lost in those kind of thoughts. It's like looking up at the sky and feeling like you might fall into it.

And all of a sudden I remembered the look on Cole's face. "A man might be scared to live out here. If there was . . . darkness in any part of his being. At night, you can actually hear your conscience talk to you in this place."

I'm afraid too, Cole. But I'm not good enough to worry about my conscience. If I could just be sure there's a God, then maybe I'd worry about my conscience.

Like a blur, I saw Melissa fall over a rock, heard her scream, the kind of crying when a child gets hurt that won't go away until she gets your attention. Until she understands she hasn't broken her body for good, hasn't killed herself.

I scooped her up in one arm and felt a grin, sort of reluctant-like, lift the corners of my mouth. Your child makes you believe in God. Your child makes you strong. Your child makes you believe in the sense of life. I don't know how Ama does it without children of her own. Maybe that's why she adopts half the world.

"Ain't nothing going to kill us, Melissa Sue!" I said, something exploding inside me, and I threw open the door. " 'Cause we're strong!"

Inside, everything were just as I'd left it. The china cups and plates on the shelves, the doilies on the sofa, the mirror behind the glass girls in their painted skirts that stood beside glass men and glass animals. But a year's dirt was over all. And a strange smell of rot and stagnant water and yesterdays.

Lord, I'd never seen nothing that bad. Even Lucie's house weren't that bad. Filth and spiders and goodness knew what. Something ran across the floor at my feet and I jumped. It could be anything from a rat to a rattlesnake. Melissa were screaming and holding onto my leg with both little arms. "Nothing to worry about, I reckon," I said, soothing her. "We got to have some light here. Well. I'll start carrying in things from the wagon. No, I guess I'll clean up first. Can't bring nothing in here yet. I'll get oil for the lamp."

When I headed back to the wagon, I saw Joe standing out in the field hunched over his crutches, staring out across the empty acres. He looked like he belonged here with the lonesomeness and the shabbiness all 'round.

I got the oil and started to work, jerking back the bedspread so's Melissa could sit on clean sheets, but she wasn't to be contained and ran outside and inside, back and forth, like a wild creature that don't recognize its surroundings. No matter, no matter, she'll learn, I thought as I began washing the walls. I ended on my hands and knees, scrubbing the floors. I never gave much thought to my throat aching and my eyes stinging, because I wasn't crying. Lord, no. My eyes was dry as dust.

That same day Joe went and emptied out the wagon, leaving supplies laying everywhere over the ground, and took off driving without telling me where he was going. But I knew he was taking back Ama's horse and Ama's wagon just as soon as he could. Sure enough, later he come back riding his poor old horse that was so bony it was a sin, and a flour sack filled with a few boxes of crackers and what looked to be bottles.

"Joe," I said, "I'm sure Ama never meant you to bring back

her horse so soon. You could of kept him a week or two and gave your own horse a rest."

"Liz Ann," he said in a patient voice, reaching into the sack and taking out one of the bottles that was full of whiskey. "The Crockers ain't never been charity cases. You know we have our pride."

I thought, Yes, I know about your damned pride. But I never said nothing, because he looked like he was trying his best to be civil, even carried some of the things from the wagon up to the cabin and stacked them 'round the front door.

"You got to learn," he said, taking up the bottle of whiskey and the flour sack, "how I do things. Once you learn, then you and me won't have no more trouble between us." The smile he gave me was polite, but distant as a winter sun, and before I knew it he'd disappeared 'round the side of the house again. He was gone before I remembered to ask him where he got money to buy things.

That night I smelled liquor on him but he wasn't drunk, just slurred in voice. We ate dinner from the basket of things Beulah'd cooked for us, and I was too tired to ask him if Ama'd sent me any message or if he'd thanked her and said how owing we were to her. My back ached and Melissa was cross and the only thing I wanted was to go to bed. By the time I got Melissa down, Joe was already asleep in our bed with his back turned to me. Such a hot, still night. Such a little bed.

As tired as I was, it took me a while to sleep. It was odd to be laying next to a man more stranger than husband. Just like the cabin was too strange to be home.

Just sleep, I told myself, shutting my eyes against the shadows that flickered on the ceiling. Sleep and pretend that when you open your eyes, you and Melissa will be back at Symphony Oaks. And Joe will be . . . Joe will be back at the war.

It were three days after we moved to the cabin that Ama come to see me, her and Jinny and Delilah carrying boxes full of vegetables and preserve jars. Then I saw Beulah coming last, lugging a big ham, with Daisy flying along behind her with a loaf of fresh bread in both arms.

"Melissa! Look!" I said, jumping up from the kitchen table, where I sat sewing up the left leg on Joe's old pants. "We got company!"

But Melissa was ahead of me, blundering out through the door like a great clumsy moth heading for the light quick as she could get there, and went running up to Daisy, the two of them hugging with their arms so tight 'round each other that the bread got squashed in the middle. With a catch in my heart, I realized that Melissa and Daisy been together since Melissa was just a baby in my arms and that she and Daisy'd never been separated since. Until now.

"It's all right, honey," Ama said and it took me a minute to realize she was talking to me, not Melissa, and that tears were streaming down my face.

With water whistling in the teapot, fresh cakes from one of Ama's baskets laid out, the babies laughing outside the open door, and us women gathered 'round the kitchen table, nothing seemed so terrible anymore. Delilah sat beside me, smiling and hemming up the leg on a pair of Joe's pants, just like I was doing, and Jinny bustled 'round the kitchen getting the tea while Ama and Beulah sat knitting socks that Joe was sore in need of.

Finally Ama said, "Well, Delilah, whatever are you waitin' for? Give it to her."

Delilah looked up from her sewing, shy-like. "I be waiting for a special moment, Miz Ama."

"Oh, lord." Ama laughed. "Then I'll give it to her."

Ama started to reach into the basket, but Delilah got there first. She put her hand over her mouth and giggled. Then she brought out a small flat box and handed it to me.

"This here from me and Lucie," she said. "So you never forget who the three of us be. You and me and her."

"Lucie wanted to be here," Ama said as I opened the box. "But Ben's got a summer cold and Tom's just plain worn out."

All eyes were fixed on me as I took out the daguerrotype. Two girls in a swing. Ama's swing. And the two girls were Delilah and Lucie, wearing the same clothes they'd wore that night on the porch. Hair combed the same. Both smiling and leaning forward.

"We leanin' toward you," Delilah explained. "You can't see you, but you there, sittin' right there on the porch in front of us. It were my idea, but Lucie got the man to come and take it."

"Oh, lord," I said, half laughing, half crying, the others smiling, and Jinny coming over to give me a hug.

Beulah said, "Ole Man Higgins tell us give you his regard too!"

All of us women laughed full-out then, Delilah going back to her sewing and Jinny pouring the tea, when a shadow fell over the table and Joe come stumbling inside, one of his crutches slipping to one side and falling on the floor with a bang, to be picked up by Ama and dropped again by Joe. And when he was finally balanced on it saying his regards to the women, he sounded like whiskey and smelled like whiskey. His eyes on the pair of pants in Delilah's hands were boiling, and though he smiled at me, the smile was like a slap in the face.

"Liz Ann," he said, still smiling that way and speaking in a tone that scared me for its very politeness, "could I see you in the bedroom, please?"

Once we were inside our room, with the door closed, he told me to get out there and tell the women to go.

"Oh, Joe, I can't," I said. "They just got here. They haven't had their tea yet. And they brought us all sorts of things. We can't—"

"Sure 'nough, we can," he said, wobbling some. "They ought to knowed we weren't set up for company yet. Just tell them to leave the food and say how grateful we are for it, then tell them we can't entertain today, we have our work."

"But they're helping me with the work, Joe."

"Yeah," he said. "I saw how they was helping you. I saw the nigger sewing up my empty pants leg, probably laughing at it, every stitch she sewed."

"She wasn't!" I gasped.

"I say she was," he snorted, tight-mouthed, swallowing.

I took a deep breath and looked him in the eye. I was afraid, but said it anyways. "No, I can't do it, Joe. I can't throw them out of my house after everything they done."

He laughed sudden-like. Then he stared down at his stump, his face growing even tighter. "I'm afraid you'll have to, Liz Ann. Or I will."

"Joe, I'm begging you. Please don't make me. You don't know, you can't imagine what they—"

"Get out there and tell them!" he yelled, eyes on fire, hand pushing damp, sweaty hair off his forehead. "And if it's going to be like this between us when they come 'round here, you can tell them not to never come back!"

I leaned toward him, breathing in the whiskey smell of him, and whispered, "You don't want them to see you 'cause you're a mess! You're a drunken mess, and you're ashamed of yourself, Joe Crocker!"

He wheeled round, struck the heel of his hand against the door frame. "Damn you!" he cried. Then he came forward and almost fell, straightened up, and slapped me twice full-face, and when I put up my hands, he pulled them down and hit me again. "Get out there! You hear me? You git!"

I don't remember moving after that, only seeing all the women on their feet, their faces long and haggard. I probably didn't need to say nothing, because before I'd got a word out, Ama grabbed me and hugged me tight against her, but it was like I was somewheres else. The only thing I could feel was the shock of Joe's open hand against my face.

"You better go," I said with no feeling, and I heard my voice like it was a stranger's, all broke and flat.

Ama still held onto me and I heard her whisper against my ear: "You don't have to stay here, Elizabeth. You don't have to let him do this to you."

What was she talking about? I wondered in that dead calm head of mine. You had a husband, you were stuck. That was the way it was. It never had been no different in my family. The Allen women had always prided theirselves on keeping peace in the family, even if the men yelled. All of a sudden I remembered something Mama told me the night before I married Joe. "Always remember, Liz Ann," she said, "it takes two to make a fight. A man has to vent his temper. If you let him, and you don't say nothing back, then you'll have a good marriage."

Then I heard Beulah saying something. "Miz Ama, you don't understand. Being a woman sometime same as bein' a slave. My first man this way. I know. We stay here, Miz Ama, it go worse for her. It go a lot worse."

I felt Ama let go of me, heard somebody, maybe Delilah, crying, felt the cabin empty out. A few minutes later, I heard the wagon start up, the horses' hooves trot down the path.

It was past dark, with Joe Crocker passed out and snoring in his chair, when the feeling come to me. I tiptoed over and picked up Melissa where she was playing on the floor with a bowl and two spoons and carried her to the rocker.

"Was it good to see Daisy again, honey?" I whispered in a choked voice.

But there be no answer from Melissa. No answer I could tell, but she laid her head against me, her tired eyes closing as I stroked her hair away from her face.

"Mama's sorry, Melissa," I said.

There was a lighted candle on the table, and the flame died and came to life again as a breeze blew through the loose boards 'round the window. As the night drew on, my own head nodded, my own eyes drooped shut. I slept. Yet some part of me stood guard against the man laying asleep in the next room.

And would always stand guard, from that day forth.

Eight

At first, there were strained grins on Joe's face, and him telling me in the most reasonable voice that he hadn't meant to hit me, that he'd make sure he never did that again. On the other hand, he'd appreciate a word of apology from me for driving him to such a thing. I apologized, and it was true that he did better. He fixed the latch on the door. He raked over the lawn, and seeded. He even tried to put a few crops into the ground. And for a time, he never touched me, he just yelled when I drove him to it. When he hit me again after two weeks, it was the liquor and his not being able to do the work he'd been trying to do.

Nothing could look as pitiful as Joe in the field after that, hobbling along after his horse, dropping seeds in the dry ground. Knowing as I watched him that the seeds would die practically as soon as they hit the earth. What could grow here? The irrigation ditches were as dry as dust. The ground was stony. Cracked and hard.

There won't be any corn this year, I thought, watching him drag hisself along. Why don't you put in a few tomatoes, Joe? Just a few beans and maybe some okra. Some lettuce and a melon patch. Why aren't you growing a garden instead of acres of corn that won't never grow? We might be able to water a few feet of land, but all that acreage, never. Never.

He seemed to of forgot how to work. How to pound a nail.

101

To hammer a loose board in place took him two hours, and the next day you was likely to see the same board hanging there loose as ever, the nails still in the wood. He spent a week working on a new walk, but the new stones weren't no better than the flat stones he took out. In fact, you were like to turn your ankle on them. They set too high. The bucket of white-wash was mixed too thin. It run off the barn as soon as he brushed it on.

I heard him cussing to hisself as he worked.

Yet sometimes he came home with groceries from the store. The kind of things you buy, not the kind of things you dig out of the ground. Crackers, cornmeal, dried beans and peas. Lye for soap. And finally, he admitted to me that the army sent him some money every month. How much, he wouldn't say, even when I told him it was my right to know. Wasn't I his wife? Wasn't I hungry same as him? Wasn't I worried same as him? But if I knew, then maybe he wouldn't have as much money for whiskey.

One night, I saw him put a wad of money into his pants. He went out without saying nothing and come home drunk, but no bottles of whiskey or nothing. Yet the money was all gone. I tried to think who could be giving him whiskey. There weren't no saloon in town, the church wouldn't allow it. Was there a farmer in our town who'd drink with a Yankee? Was there a farmer in our town who'd even let Joe onto his property? I might of thought of Nat Hawkins because they used to be friends in the old days, but Nat stopped by one day and before he left, he and Joe had come to blows in the front yard. Nat said before he left that he'd just come out of old friendship, but that was all for him, the friendship done wore out and he hated Joe as much as the next man now. So it couldn't be Nat. It couldn't be any of the Crockers, because as much as anybody hated Joe, the Crockers hated him more. Anyhow, that's what Joe said.

And what could be taking him out after dark?—him going at a faster clip than I ever saw him go at any other time, his body rocking back and forth between his crutches, the moon glinting down on a man in a hurry.

One night I followed him. For two weeks, I'd been thinking of doing it. Itching to do it. But there was Melissa Sue alone in the cabin. You don't leave a baby alone in the middle of nowhere. What if she cried and there weren't nobody there? What if she got up and wandered outside? But she was sound asleep and full of my milk. She *wouldn't* wake up, I told myself. She never had before.

And before I knew what I was doing, I was slipping out the kitchen door, following Joe at a safe distance. As full of curiosity as I ever was. Were we heading to town? To the Tyler farm? Maybe Elvin Tyler was giving Joe liquor. If it was some still in the mountains, Joe would of taken the horse. And yet, hurrying along over the hard, dry ground, the caked mud crunching under my heels, something was starting to sink into my head. Wasn't this the way toward Gwen Coleman's house? She lived off by herself, as isolated from folks as if she was a leper or as if she was a Yankee, like us. It had always been that way with Gwen, but there were reasons. I'd heard whispers about her way before her husband killed hisself by shooting hisself in the head. I heard Mama tell Bertha Long that no wife in town was safe from Gwen, though when you'd see her in town, Gwen spoke so nice to everybody you'd of thought her tongue was made out of molasses. That didn't fool nobody. *Every town has a woman like Gwen Coleman,* Bertha told Mama. *She's got a red-hot you-know-what. I guess it itches her and she has to get it scratched, if you know what I mean.*

Hush, Mama said, looking at me.

It's just as well Liz Ann knows. Bertha shrugged. *She'll probably grow up to have a husband that calls on Gwen.*

By that time, Mama said, *Gwen will be an old woman.*

She'll still be itchin', if she lives to be a hundred, Bertha said. *And where there's an itch, there'll be a man to scratch it. I bet you there ain't a man in this town hasn't scratched it.*

Mama drew her back up. *Not my husband,* she said.

Your husband been scratchin' it for years, Bertha said. *Now don't look at me like that. My Wade's been scratchin', too.*

103

Only thing I know, he don't get nothin' more from me. Not comin' from a woman like that.

I remembered once when I was in the hayloft, crawling 'round looking for eggs. Papa was down milking cows. Maybe he didn't know I was there. Maybe he forgot I was there.

Only thing is, all of a sudden I heard a soft knock on the barn door and I looked down to see Papa open it and Gwen standing there. Her body kind of heaving up and down. Her fingers doing something to her blouse. And then Papa sort of yanking her through the door and pulling up her skirt. I closed my eyes and hid in a corner of the loft, but you could hear the way they went on. Gwen moaning and Papa moaning louder.

Oh, God, I thought now, not Gwen. Gwen must be over forty now. Joe couldn't be going there. He couldn't.

But I recognized the old barn that marked the beginning of her property. Saw her house in the distance with smoke puffing out over the dark field. Saw the light in the front room.

No, I thought, seeing Joe open her gate. Seeing him swing up the walk, his crutches moving slower now. In the next minute, he'd lifted his fist to the door and Gwen was there. I couldn't see her face, but her red hair spilled over her shoulders like a schoolgirl's as she took money from Joe with one hand and put her other arm 'round him to draw him through the door, closing it behind them.

Leaving me standing out there, with my arms wrapped over each other, hugging myself, and hearing my teeth knocking together as I shivered. I knew what they were doing. I even saw a shadow of them against the window, a man with his arms wrapped 'round a woman with long hair swinging against her back. Two heads together. A skirt being lifted.

Then I was running away from them. Back toward Melissa. Some kind of wild thought in my head to pack us both up and take off before Joe come back. Leave a note and tell him what I saw. Or not leave any note, just leave. He didn't deserve any explanation.

But when I finally got home, I found Melissa screaming. She was running from room to room, falling, scrambling in the dark. She'd looked for me and I wasn't there. I grabbed her up in my arms and tried to soothe her, but she wouldn't quit crying. Her arms were locked 'round my neck so tight I could hardly breathe.

"Maa-maaa!"

"I'm here, Melissa. Everything's all right."

It's just your father. Don't you worry. He's not worth worrying about. But these were things I couldn't tell even her. These were things worse than no light, no mother in the house. Oh, baby, I need to get you out of here. I need to get us both out. But she wouldn't let go my neck and in the end, when Joe opened the door, we were both still in the rocking chair with her arms still 'round my neck, the tears still wet on her face.

I opened my mouth to tell him what I knew, but he swung past us without a word. And like a slap in the face, I seemed to hear Bertha Long. *As long as there's an itch, there'll be a man to scratch it.*

Mostly, we lived in silence after that, without nothing to tell one day from another. Excepting some nights, we'd hear Ama's wagon pull up and stop. I'd feel Joe tensing every muscle, probably wondering if she was going to knock on the door or if I'd jump up, but I'd just lay there and we'd hear things being left by the door and the wagon leaving. And the next morning, there'd be bread and eggs and a few bottles of milk and maybe a package of bacon and sometimes a few dollars. And one morning, there was a letter from Ama. I slipped it inside my dress before Joe followed me out on the porch, and waited till he disappeared with the money before I opened it.

"Dear Elizabeth," Ama wrote.

> The major has been taken prisoner up north. Please pray for him that he'll be all right as he's at Elmira, New York, not noted as an easy place for a Confederate officer. I only

hope they'll be able to see he's far more decent than one might expect, given he's a rebel. I've heard from Cole that he's been able to establish some sort of correspondence with the senior officer there, and that my husband is well, although Cole says he's lost a lot of weight, or so this officer reports.

We at Symphony Oaks go on as well as we can, which is, as you know, my one main philosophy. Never a day goes by that we don't talk about you and Melissa. We know that you are busy and that it must be hard for you to write, so don't trouble yourself if it's impossible or even difficult. Nevertheless, if it should be possible and *easy* for you to do so, just a line from you saying that both you and Melissa are doing well would make us all draw an easier breath.

Oh, if only you were with us! There now, I'd promised myself I wouldn't say that to you, but now that I've written it, I leave it as is. After all, *I want you to know how much you are missed in this house!* God bless.

Love,
Ama

After that, there were more letters and I read each one with my heart pounding, almost afraid to breathe. At night, I lay still either beside Joe's sleeping body or alone in bed. Listening to a silence so deep it rang in my ears. Wondering what on earth I could write Ama. No, better that I sneak away and see her. But what would Joe do if he knew I'd gone? The twice I'd mentioned visiting Symphony Oaks, he got furious and drunk. So in the end, I finally wrote and hid the letter in one of Ama's empty baskets that I left on the porch for her to take when she brought new supplies.

It wasn't much of a letter. I said how big Melissa was getting. I talked about the weather and asked about the major. I didn't lie, but the truth were buried in the awkward way I avoided saying anything about Joe. What was I to say? That when you're in a bad marriage, nothing else matters, even the

war? Ama was smart enough to know that already, so I talked
about the leaves falling off the trees. The water freezing in the
pump. And Ama wrote back that their water had frozen too.

I never did tell her how Joe's army money wasn't coming
to the cabin no more. How he'd sometimes go out at night and
come back a few hours later with vegetables and fruit he'd taken
from other people's fields and orchards. He never said so, but I
knew where it all come from. He'd line everything up on the
kitchen table and I'd start putting things away. Neither of us
talking or looking at each other.

Without Ama and without Joe's stealing, I don't know
what we would have done, and we had yet to face the winter.
Sometimes, I'd look at Melissa, growed so thin and so white,
and I'd think, Oh, God, what is it going to be like when the
winter comes?

I didn't know if Joe was still seeing Gwen Coleman or not.
Somehow, I didn't think so. If I was to guess, I'd say that Gwen
and winter and life had all fell away from him like the leaves
that fell from the trees. And he was just left staring down at his
stump and feeling it. As time passed, it seemed more important,
not less, and after a while it seemed to me that Joe's missing leg
must of had most of him in it. Sometimes, he broke down and
cried, like crying was the one worthwhile thing left to him.
Melissa would sit watching him with tears in her eyes, too, and
one day she lifted her little arms to him to be picked up.

"No, Melissa, come here!" I said quick as I could. Something about the way he turned to look at her worried me, the
nervous working of his mouth, the way his eyes almost closed
into slits.

"What's the matter, Liz Ann?" he asked half lazy-like,
picking up Melissa by her arms.

"Be careful, Joe, they say don't pick a child up by the arms.
You could pull them . . ."

"I guess I know how to pick up my own daughter, Liz
Ann." He never took his eyes off Melissa as she put her hands
to his face and began stroking his face, wiping away his tears
with her fingertips.

107

"Why, course you do, Joe. I didn't mean nothing by it." I tried to smile, forcing down the sick feeling inside me.

"I think your mama's 'feared of me, Melissa Sue," he said to the little face. "She don't think I'm a very decent fellow, you know. Always lookin' at me, watchin' me to see what evil thing I'm gonna do next. She don't like it when I go steal food for us to eat. No, she thinks that's not right. That's a sin. Ain't that what you think, Liz Ann?"

"Oh, why . . . why, no, Joe. 'Course not. We got to eat and how else . . . I mean . . ."

"She means how else a mutilated man gonna feed his family, a man who don't have a leg. How else a poor pitiful man gonna git somethin' lessen he sneaks out and steals it? Ain't that it? Look here, Melissa, don't you stare at me like that too." Melissa Sue was afraid and tried to crawl down. "Trying to get away from your pa? From your poor disgustin' pa?" His voice were so loud and fierce, she started to cry and struggle to get away.

"Shut up!" he yelled at her, covering her mouth till her screams were muffled.

"Oh, God, Joe, get hold of yourself! She's a baby, she didn't do nothing to you." My heart was going double speed inside me. "Come here, Melissa." I tried to take her, but he knocked me away against the table.

"Just leave me alone!" he shouted. "Why don't everbody just leave me alone? Everbody at me all the time. Yellin', squallin' brat! I told you to shut up!!" His big hand was on Melissa's throat and I couldn't stand it. I just couldn't stand it.

"Jesus, Joe. Jesus. Please stop it. You're killing her. You're killing her!" God, I couldn't get his hand off her throat. Seemed to me the harder I pulled, the tighter he squeezed. She was gagging now, oh, God, she was going to die. I was hitting him just as hard as I could, hitting and clawing him and hitting him and it was all no use because he had a man's strength. Then I saw the ax leaning against the wood box in the corner and it come into my mind that I'd kill him. I would. Just that quick, I stepped back from him, ready to run for the ax and to come back swinging. I only hoped I'd be in time. That's all I hoped. But when I was turning to go, he screamed. Screamed like a man in mortal pain and shoved Melissa into my arms hard.

My legs wouldn't hold me and I fell into a chair thanking God and feeling Melissa's arms 'round my neck and her whole body shaking. Then Joe got down on the floor like a low creature and come crawling on his elbows and grabbed hold of my legs and held on crying and begging us to forgive him. "Please, please, say she's all right," he begged. "Say I didn't hurt her. Oh, no, oh, God. Did I hurt my little girl? Oh, God, my little girl."

How could I forgive and how could I not forgive? Do I love you, Joe Crocker? No, it's just pity now. You used up all the love. My hand was trembling as I laid it on his poor head and somehow we found there in that dark sad room a moment of peace together.

Nine

$\mathcal{S}$ometimes now, there was the sound of gunfire from the mountains and I knew soldiers had really moved into the Cumberlands and were snaking through the forests, camping along Lula Lake, looking down on our valley from boulders and jutting cliffs. For a while Joe would take to riding his horse miles and miles, coming back to tell me that the bridges on all sides of us had been burned out. That railroad wreckers from both sides were tearing up trestles along twenty miles of the Louisville and Nashville main line. That the armies were contending for the Tennessee River.

But something must of happened then—maybe Joe had been gossiping with some men, even soldiers, who'd found him out to be Federal—because he stopped going out one day, as sudden as a bird in the sky stops flying and falls with a hunter's bullet in him. Just one day he wouldn't go out, wouldn't hardly get up. After that, he'd scarce leave the cabin at all, only to go for liquor with the money Ama sent. And it was only when he was drunk he'd take his pleasure with me, me gritting my teeth and counting till he was through. He was rough and hurting, and after, he'd push me away and say to leave him be.

Before I thought about it, winter was there and it wasn't no worse than the dull plainness of just everyday living. Though our skin was raw and we sat shaking for hours by the fire, there was the wood I chopped for fuel and for cooking. We had a roof over our heads, and so far the rains and the snows hadn't soaked through. We survived. That's how I'd come to see life. How much emptiness you could stand and how long you could stay alive.

And there come one of those nights that seemed to go on forever with us laying in the same bed and worlds apart and, maybe just to hear a human voice, I said to the dark shape of his back, "Joe?"

He took so long to answer, I didn't know if he was sleeping. Or pretending to sleep. But finally he said, "What you want now?"

"Joe, why did you go fight for the Yankees? Don't get mad, but if I could only know, maybe it would be easier."

You never knew with Joe, but tonight was lucky because he sounded too tired, too drained, to get mad. "Oh, I tried to sign for the South," he said, "but they put theirselves up to be a gentlemen's army. Too proud for poor white farmers or peckerwoods, that's the way the word come down. So, to hell with them. I signed on for the North."

"*What?* You mean . . . you didn't have no other reasons? No loyalties for the Yankees? Nothing? It was just that the South turned you down?"

"To hell with them," he said again, and it were his last words of the night. They left me trembling. Needing to get up and walk and afraid to move. Needing to scream at him and afraid to whisper. *You mean you did all this out of pride? You mean it didn't mean anything? Nothing?*

I put my fingers in my mouth and bit down hard. No use to cry, I told myself. If he hears you, there may be trouble. Just keep quiet. This night can't really last forever. You can make it. One second, one minute, one hour at a time. He did it for nothing. He didn't even want to be a Yankee. The night wrapped itself 'round my head like a long black scarf. The only thing that moved was wind against the windows. The only sound inside our room was a gurgling sound. Either Joe's stomach or mine. Somehow, it didn't much matter which.

I watched the sun come up without a hour of sleep between

111

the night and the morning and went to see if I could put together breakfast for Melissa. I found Ama's basket on the front porch, but no eggs no more, no bacon, no flour, no packages of chicken, so I knew the war was getting to Ama's pantry too.

I sat down weary-like on the front step and lifted Ama's letter to the dim light. My eyelids were so heavy I could hardly see what I were reading, my face and hands so numb I could scarce concentrate. But I liked reading Ama's letters outside in the open, where thoughts and feelings had a chance of being free.

"Dear Elizabeth," she wrote.

For some time now, there has been no word of the major. Cole had been trying to work on an exchange—the major for a captured Union officer who was being kept in a converted tobacco warehouse along the James River. Unfortunately, the Union officer either died or escaped (it's not clear which) and Cole found no enthusiasm on the Federals' part to effect another trade, so for the time being, we must leave the matter in God's hands. No, not that man in the sky we talked about. I have come to realize more clearly in these hard times what God is to me. He's the air that I breathe, the whisper in my ear when I'm lying in bed at night that sounds like the major is talking quietly to me across the miles.

God is the conviction in my soul that there is a reason for this war and that the reason is huge enough and noble enough to deserve the rivers of blood that flow through its veins. God is the predetermined victory for the United States government. He is Mr. Lincoln's Emancipation Proclamation that frees all black men and women from bondage and frees the consciences of the white men and women. Elizabeth, without seeing the major or communicating with him in any way, I feel absolutely certain that his views on the rebellion have changed. *I know* that if he had to do it over again, he would be a supporter of the Union and an abolitionist.

Perhaps, if I hadn't forced him so hard in the direction of abolition, he would have come to it on his own. In fact, I'm certain he would have as it's such a good cause and he's such a good man! This is another of my concepts of what God is—He's *movement*. The something that lets us keep mulling things over and feeling free to change our minds. Whenever you meet a stubborn man, a man set in his opinions and his ways, that stubborn part of him is . . . I won't say the devil, but definitely not God!

I suppose you've heard of the huge Northern victory at Sharpsburg, Maryland. Or, as it's called in town, "the soulless slaughter of *our boys* by the *damned Yanks.*" I wonder what they'd have said if the rebels won! And the Fredericksburg battle. What a tragic loss of life that was. I begrudge every single battle that does not further the cause of the Union, and thus the end of the war.

But I am distracted. How are *you,* my dear?

Is the winter very hard for you? The last snow was so deep that we were concerned you were cut off. But at least, I doubt you've been raided as have we and most of the town. There are so many soldiers in the hills now—and I'm afraid they simply come down and take what they want. So far, all Confederates.

Do you need anything I haven't thought of? With the steamboats blockaded, supplies of certain foods are terribly short. Sometimes, I actually dream of coffee. And what I wouldn't give for just half a sack of flour! Or even a *jar* of flour!

Well, I must close and go drive in the cattle. I want to take a head count as I have a sneaking suspicion we've been rustled again. Daisy wants to send Melissa a kiss. Make sure you give it to her and tell her it's from her best friend who is like a sister, Daisy.

We miss you both more every day, not less! Write when you can. All send love,

Ama

Putting the letter aside, I breathed in and out once, conscious-like, and my body felt warm and alive. Even on paper I could feel Ama's goodness. Feel her reaching out to me—to the whole world, in fact—and that gave me courage and strength and a smile.

I wrote her back that day that everything were fine, that Melissa sent Daisy a kiss too, and that it was kind of them to leave firewood stacked by the porch, but we didn't need to bother them for wood. That was something Joe could do. Actually though, it was me that cut the wood and split logs into kindling, bringing the ax down so hard that it felt like I was chopping the heads off demons. Winter, I thought, was nothing much to bother about. Just colder than the other seasons, that's all.

For the next few weeks there were no more letters from Ama. Those weeks stretched to a month and I began to worry. Only two baskets come to the cabin, and they were near empty.

Cold was everywhere. Frosting the windows. Freezing the water and the creek and keeping the land hard and still. Most mornings Melissa woke at dawn, hungry, and I'd feel her anxious fingers on my face. Her touch sent off an alarm in me that sent my feet to the ground, my arms reaching for her, while I was still half asleep. *Don't let Joe hear her* was what jumped through my head. Shh, Melissa. Quiet, angel. The two of us creeping across the floor, the cold air at my ankles, my throat. Then lifting Melissa and feeling amazed that she could feel so warm.

It was one of those cold mornings, the two of us in the rocking chair, her nursing as hard as she'd nursed as a small baby, when my eyes drifted out the window and caught a glimpse of a thin body standing near a tree in the early gray light. A woman, for her skirts rose in the wind, and she seemed

114

to be staring hard at our cabin. Maybe trying to decide if anybody was up.

With a cry, I was out of the rocker and running for the door. Something's happened, I thought. I knew it in the tense way Delilah stood there, one hand clutching at her shawl, the other at her head as if she needed to help hold it up. The second I opened the door she saw me, took a scared peek as if checking over my shoulder expecting to see Joe standing there, then come running across the yard, the wind whipping at her hair, her clothes.

A few seconds later, she was in my arms, Melissa between us, and I heard the ragged sound coming from her throat. The sound of somebody crying and trying to choke it back.

"Is it Ama?" I said, pulling her inside the cabin. My knees shook so hard, I had to sit down or fall, and so I staggered to my chair without even offering her a seat. She stood there leaning against the door, then she was beside me, kneeling by my chair, her fingers in Melissa's soft hair as if seeking the same comfort I always looked for in my baby.

"Oh, Lizbeth . . ."

"*Is it Ama?*" I cried out, grabbing her by the shoulder, my fingers pinching her flesh.

"No," she gasped, and then the tears came pouring down her face. "It . . . it Lucie," she said after a minute of that kind of hard crying, and I stared at her, not able to understand what she could mean.

Lucie? Was she in some kind of trouble? Sick? Had she done something . . . had some kind of trouble with Old Man Higgins? What?

"What?" I said, sounding so blank that Delilah stopped crying and dried her eyes.

"She been expectin', only nobody know. Only me, that all. I only one she tell. She 'fraid Tom be all upset. See, she had a hard time deliverin' little Ben and the doctor say she too thin 'round the hips and she shouldn't have no more children. Thing is, Lucie say she die to have more babies. And . . ." Delilah's scared eyes met mine. "And she . . ."

"What?" I whispered, and all of a sudden I was afraid to hear any more. "Delilah, she didn't . . . ?"

Delilah saw what I was thinking and she nodded. "Yeah, she did. God, Lizbeth, Lucie really did die last night. I can't believe it, but she did! Oh, God. And . . . and Ama say I shouldn't come here, she say you have 'nough trouble of your own, but—but I prowlin' 'round and prowlin' 'round and all of a sudden, I don't know, I just here."

She stopped talking and the two of us stared at each other. We could of been hearing of each other's death. If Lucie was dead, anything was possible. If a young woman, a mother of a child, a wife, a freckle-faced girl just twenty-two years old could be dead, anybody could be dead. I could be dead.

Delilah's head was in my lap. I heard her say, "It only me and you now, Lizbeth, we ain't three girls no more, only two."

"It's all right, it's all right," I said.

But it wasn't all right. I sat there with a heart as cold as the room and heard how Tom come banging on their door at midnight, saying that Lucie was in trouble. Then them going over to Freeland Farm and Tom showing up with Mattie Simpson.

"But there weren't nothin' Mattie could do," Delilah wept. "Weren't nothin' nobody could do. Just listen to her scream. Beg her to keep calm as possible. Tell her we'd do anythin' she told us. Take care of Ben. Take care of Tom. Lie to her—tell her she be fine. 'Course she don't believe that. She know she dyin', same as anybody would of knowed. Sweet Jesus, you never see nobody in so much pain. I 'bout died to see her. And Ben . . . Ben broke my heart," she finished, sobbing harder than ever.

Somehow, I found myself on my feet. Making Delilah a cup of tea in the kitchen. I couldn't feel the floor under me, it was like I was floating 'round the room. It was so early in the morning, that half of me still felt like I must be dreaming. Some terrible dream that makes you desperate to wake up and you can't. You just keep dreaming.

By the time we got our tea, sitting there at the table with the teapot between us and our cups in our hands, neither of us were crying anymore. We were so exhausted we almost couldn't speak—our words fell out of our mouths like stones.

"You mean she was pregnant and Tom couldn't tell?"

"By that time, he knowed. Her belly out by then. She just so sure everthin' be fine, how could you worry? Even me. I so dumb, I think the doctor wrong. But he weren't wrong. . . ."

'Course, even while we sat there, both of us knew any minute Joe might wake up and come in raising the roof. Let him, I thought. Let him scream his head off. Maybe we should all scream. It might feel wonderful to open up my mouth and scream. Scream for Lucie. Scream at God for taking a twenty-two-year-old girl, when there must be a bushel of old women for the taking.

"You never mentioned the baby," I said finally. "Was it another boy?"

"Yeah, and it look just like Ben. Only thing is, it never take the first breath. Now that be a moment for you." Delilah nodded solemn-like. Her eyes sparked some. "Can you picture this, Lizbeth? It pitch black in Lucie room. All us bent over the bed—"

"And Mattie?"

"Yeah, Mattie there. Her and Ama, they keep theirself calm somehow. They know all the time, everthin' doom. They know this, and they work. Smile at Lucie. Put they hand up inside her, her screamin'. Try to turn the baby, pull on the baby. He prob'ly dead already. I seen Mattie get real still. Her arm up inside Lucie, way up there, her touchin' somethin'. Right then, she know that babe be dead. I knowed from her face, just wouldn't let myself believe. Ama smile at Lucie. Say, What a brave wonderful girl you are. You should be proud of yourself. The sweat pour off Lucie, but she try to smile back. Say thank you. The baby all right? And Ama say, Let God take care of the

117

baby. Let God take care of everythin'. And Lucie say All right, she do that. Then die. Just like that. Act like she can't get her breath. Fight for a few minutes, then she gone. Mattie . . ." Delilah swallowed. "Mattie reach up inside her and she . . . somehow she yank that babe out but he dark blue as the sky. He so dead, you can see he never live. Never have a chance. That were when Ben . . . he run in screamin' for his mama and grab hold of Lucie with Tom right behind him tryin' to pull him away. . . . If God let me forget just that one moment, Lizbeth, it more than plenty."

I looked her in the eye. I reached out and took her hands in mine. "We got us," I said. "And though Lucie's gone, we still got our friendship with her. Friendship don't have to die with the friend, does it? Isn't she still a part of us? Isn't she still sittin' in that swing, Delilah?"

We thought about that so hard, we could hear each other think. I could see Lucie in Delilah's eyes; maybe she could see her in mine.

"Don't worry," I whispered after a long while. "We'll keep her alive, Delilah, you and me."

And she nodded. Then she got up and helped me clear away the tea, hugged me and left as silent as she'd appeared. She had so much in common with me and she had this one other thing . . . she didn't want to see Joe Crocker that morning no more than I did.

Lucie was buried behind the house on Freeland Farm. Someday, other Higginses would lay beside her. Joe wouldn't go to the funeral and wouldn't let me go neither, 'cause he said they'd be calling us names, those that be there, maybe even raise their fists at us. Strike blows.

Ama wrote that Mrs. Reverend Harper was there in her husband's absence and offered the prayer, holding one of the Reverend's own personal Bibles. Mattie was there too, and had dressed the poor little baby, who was buried in Lucie's arms. Besides Mattie and the Mrs. Reverend and the folks at Symphony Oaks, there were the Higginses and Narcissa Harwell and some people of the church. All kind people, she said, who had wept when the pine coffin had sunk into the new-dug grave.

Ama said she could hardly bear to see the men shovel the heavy clumps of earth on the coffin, and that the wind blew fierce and she'd said her own private prayer then for Lucie. I don't know about the gates of Heaven, she said. But the Lord will surely be welcoming Lucie in His own way, never fear.

Me, I worked on God, too. Mainly begging Him to bring Lucie back to life, though I knew He didn't do things like that. Or just crying, taking long walks with Melissa in the frozen glimmering mornings. Looking at icy blades of grass, the twisted bare limbs of winter trees and thinking that all of nature looked like it was praying for Lucie. Every day was quieter than the next. Every morning hungrier. Joe less alive every hour he lived. And after a while, I wasn't just talking to God about Lucie. But about me and Melissa, too.

I know I got to do something, Lord. Life can't just keep going on like this. But what do I do? You know these things better than me. Lord, do you leave a man for being half evil? What about the half of Joe that's just pitiful? Help me to understand, Lord. Lead the way. Tell me what to do. Are you listening to me, Lord?

When spring finally come, I hardly noticed, and on April seventeenth, in the dark of the night, I was laying in bed with my hands clenched to the sheet waiting for my husband to have done with me, him breathing his whiskey breath in my face, groaning as he worked his way up to his satisfaction, when I heard the door open.

At first, I thought I be imagining things, the bed squeaking and all, Joe making his noises. But I heard sounds in the front room sure enough. "Joe!" I hissed, trying to push him off me.

"Stay still, woman!" he said, gripping my shoulders.

"Joe, listen. Somebody's here."

"Ain't nobody here," he said in his slurred voice, and kept on. He was long at it tonight, and it was making him angry.

I pushed myself up on my arms and my ears were strained to hear. "Joe, listen. There's somebody here. Right here in the cabin."

He stopped still and I couldn't see his face, but I could feel the fear in his body all of a sudden. We laid there hearing the soft steps come closer and closer and then the door to the bedroom opened, but nobody said nothing.

I couldn't move I was so scared, and I could feel Joe's heart beating fast right next to mine. Then from the door, a match was struck and held up to a lamp and several men's voices all yelled, "Surprise!" then broke into loud laughing.

"Did we come in at a embarrassin' time?" asked one. He was the tallest and his face were bearded and gleamed in the light like a pumpkin all lit up.

Joe rolled off me. "What you want?" he said, his voice shaking.

"Well, looky here," said one of the smaller men, coming over to the bed and staring down at me in my thin wore-through gown. I pulled the sheet up and tried to cover myself, but he ripped the bed covering clear off the bed and laughed again.

Joe wet his lips nervous-like as the men crowded round us on both sides. In that first minute they all looked like the same man to me. Dirty faces, dirty hair. The ugly look of men who had their minds set on evil.

"Can I do somethin' for you?" Joe said, trying to sound friendly, but it came out like a scared whine.

"Can he do somethin' for us?" said the bearded man to the other three and they all laughed again. Then his face got serious and mean. "Well, maybe you can help us kill a few Yankees—if they's any 'round, that is. Would you help us do that?"

For a moment Joe said nothing. I could see the godawful fear in his eyes, feel the way his body started to tremble. "Well," he said, "I'll help any ways I can . . ."

"Like I said, we want to kill us a few Yankees. Do you know where's any 'round?"

"No . . . no, I don't," Joe said.

"Hank, do you see any Yankees anyplace?"

"Well, Lord, yessir, I b'leeve I do now, Ferris. I surely b'leeve I do," said the one called Hank, taking his gun out. He was almost as tall as the other, with longer darker hair. More hair on his face too—a full, almost black beard.

"Well, where on earth do you see one?" Ferris said, looking round innocent-like.

"Well, Lord, I b'leeve I see one . . . right . . . h'are." And Hank raised up his gun till it was even with Joe's head. At that the four of them about fell down laughing. It was strange how they all looked alike. Two tall, two shorter, but they could of been from the same family.

"Please," Joe said, like he couldn't think what to do. He tried sitting up straighter, then slouched back, his leg moving under the sheet.

The heaviest and shortest man grinned. "Please, what?"

"Well, looky h'are," Hank said. "It shore 'nough is a Yankee. And a beggin', snifflin', whinin' Yankee at that. You say, you'll do just about anythin' for us, boy, that it?"

"Anythin', anythin' you say," Joe said in a rush.

"Well then, suppose you just open up your mouth and put it right 'round the head of my gun." And the gun inched forward.

Joe tried to push me in front of him, but one of the other men jerked me back and pulled Joe out of the bed by his hair. He fell against the floor hard, and I could see him there and his missing leg never looked so pitiful as then, him squirming 'round in a circle, pushing hisself with his one leg.

"Now don't be scared, boy," Hank said. "You just do as we ask you and nobody gonna get hurt. Just open your mouth . . ."

"You promise . . . promise you won't shoot?" Joe begged. His shadow fell on the wall, twisted there. His eyes twisted too, away from the barrel of the gun.

"Well now," Hank said. "I can't go promisin' no Yankee nothin'. But you do as you're told, and I b'leeve it'll work out all right. Now open your mouth or I'll shoot you through the head." And his finger moved a little on the trigger.

"No!" Joe screamed. "I'll do it! Just don't shoot . . . don't shoot. All right? All right?" His lips opened and then closed, and then as the gun moved again, they opened in a hurry and closed 'round the barrel. A bead of sweat rolled down between his eyes.

"Now, you just shake your head yes or no if you agree with what we want. All right? Would it be . . . all right . . . if us four was to bang your slut wife? Just shake your head yes or no, 'cause of course we wouldn't think of doin' nothin' you didn't approve of. . . ."

Joe, his mouth 'round the gun, nodded yes over and over again.

"Look how anxious he is to share his woman with us," Ferris said, undoing his pants. "And I bet you're real eager to have us too, ain't you, whore?"

Just be quiet, I told myself, and shut my eyes tight. Let them do whatever they want, it don't make no difference. Nothing matters but that gun in Joe's mouth. Then I felt the front of my gown tore open and cold hands settling on my breasts. I could hear breath coming in short rasps. His hands got rougher as he pushed open my legs, and all I could do was groan inside as his beefy, overweight body came on top of me.

I couldn't keep my eyes closed no longer, and when I opened them I saw what I couldn't help but see—a filthy, half-naked creature above me, his skin against mine, and with all his strength, he forced hisself inside me and I tried to stiffen, but it was no use. He was in me then, and when I made a last effort to tear away, his hand slammed down on my chest, keeping me flat on the bed.

"How I doin', Yankee?" Ferris yelled. "Am I doin' it right?" and I could hear Joe's groaning sound that meant yes.

When Ferris was done, he and Hank tried to get the heavy man they called Charlie and the older man who they called Junior to have a turn, but they wouldn't. Charlie said he was afraid of catching a nasty Yankee disease and Junior just wasn't

122

interested. So that only left Hank who was holding the gun. "Now how am I gonna bang the slut whiles I'm holdin' a gun? You do want me to bang her?" he asked Joe.

Joe nodded, groaning, and I shut my eyes again.

"Well then . . . lessee, we got a problem. . . . Well, hell, I'll just have to shoot you, I guess," he said, and pulled the trigger. The room felt like it exploded inside my head. Then a terrible silence, then men breathing heavy. Then boots walking over the floor. The sound of fabric rubbing against the gun and I knew Hank was cleaning it. Getting rid of the blood.

"Shit," somebody said, sounding almost awed, and I could imagine them standing there looking at pieces of Joe's head splattered all over the walls, the floor.

Thank God I didn't see it happen 'cause I had my eyes closed. Dear Lord, Jesus, I prayed, forgive Joe for his sins and take him into heaven.

"Stupid son of a bitch," someone said. "Now you done it. Jesus!"

"Shut up." That came from Hank.

"Ain't shuttin' up. No reason to kill the poor son of a bitch, was there?"

"Not in front of her. You got somethin' to say to me, say it in private."

Eyes half open, half shut, I heard footsteps leave the room, saw the door slammed shut. I just laid there listening, afraid to move. Afraid to turn my head, knowing already what I would see. After a while I heard them clinking bottles 'round, and knew they'd found Joe's whiskey. For a time their voices were low, then got louder with argument, and sudden-like I thought about Melissa.

Oh, dear God, through some miracle she hadn't made a sound, somehow sleeping through everything, even the gunshot, and they'd never seen her in the crib in the corner of the room.

I got out of bed and steered clear of Joe, trying not to look at his poor corpse, still seeing it though I looked the other way, arms out, staring, and went to Melissa. I didn't want to move her 'cause I was afraid she'd cry, so I piled up a stack of clothes, leaving her some breathing room. Dear Lord, what would they do to Melissa if they found her?

Outside, I heard them start arguing again, then footsteps coming toward the door. I got back into the bed, and when they come into the room and Ferris threatened to have another turn, I pressed my lips together and never said a word, for I wouldn't have Melissa cry. If he was going to do it again, it wouldn't be no worse than the first time.

"Let's git the hell out of here," said Junior and Charlie and then even Ferris seemed nervous and wanted to leave, but not Hank.

"Aw, shit, Hank, we've been all over this. Ain't you caused enough trouble?" Charlie said.

"Not yet," he said, grinning. "That's good meat, boys."

Junior sniffed. "You stay then, I'm gettin' out." Ferris and Charlie grunted in agreement, and Ferris started strapping something 'round his waist.

"Hell, Hank, you're too drunk to even enjoy yourself," he said, swaying himself. "Maybe you should do her some other time."

"I'm gonna do her now," Hank said, glancing at Joe's body and looking away again as if he'd seen a ghost. *"Now*, goddammit! And nobody, not even you, gonna stop me." He unstrapped his holster and flung it on the chair. The handle of the gun struck the wood and made a loud sound.

"Suit yourself," Ferris said, shoving the others from the room and slamming the door behind them.

"But watch out she don't do you!" somebody yelled, and I could hear them laughing as they got their horses. Sudden-like the horses' hooves died away, the laughter too, and Hank was starting to the bed unfastening hisself when Melissa Sue started whimpering.

"What's that?" he said, stumbling a little.

"Nothing." Be still, baby. Be still.

But Melissa was crouched in her crib, staring straight at Joe's body, and what had been a whimper turned into a scream.

"What the bloody hell," Hank said, and started toward her.

I don't remember getting up from the bed, pulling Hank's own gun from the holster on the chair. All I remember is cocking it and pulling the trigger. Even when he fell sprawling on the floor, I couldn't believe I shot him. But I did. I really did shoot him. I knew I did when I saw the blood pouring out of his body. He was still alive and he started to crawl toward me, his eyes staring at me, bulging out of his head, but I took the handle of the gun and beat his head and his face till he fell and then I watched him and he didn't get up again.

When he quit moving, he wasn't no more than a foot from Joe's body, that silent huddled-up thing with the stretched out arms that used to be my husband. Whose head I could only bear to look at out the side of my eye, never seeing it direct, but still shuddering at a distant impression of a face with a hole in it, a body laying in red, covered in red and red stuff sprayed all over.

Melissa, still screaming, come running and threw herself at me.

"Honey, honey, stay real still. Just a minute, honey, just a minute," I crooned to her. But it was several minutes before I could get her arms from 'round my neck, get her to stay in the crib, while I stretched out my hand and took Hank's wrist in my hand and felt for a pulse. My own blood was shooting through my veins so fast, that for a minute I couldn't judge him alive or dead and it was only when I took hold of him with both hands and looked into his sightless staring eyes that I were sure he really was dead.

Then I tore my gown off and threw it over his body and a blanket over Joe's head. Seemed like there was a ringing inside my ears. I never remembered putting the gun away, but there it was, back inside the holster on the chair. Once I thought I heard myself say something, but I wasn't sure if I did. I got dressed in the first clothes I grabbed and took up Melissa in my arms, her legs wrapped tight 'round me, her arms too, and went to get the horse. I didn't have to ask myself where we were going, 'cause the only friends, the only family we had, were at Symphony Oaks.

125

Ten

The sky was misty with just a piece of the moon showing when I rode up to Symphony Oaks on horseback with Melissa Sue screaming and us strapped together. Then I went running through the yard holding Melissa, crying for Ama to come, and when I got to the door, I beat on it like I'd lost my mind.

I was thinking they would never answer, that nobody would ever come, when the door swung open and Ama, her hair in a braid, set her candle on the table and caught me in her arms just as I fell, still clutching onto Melissa with both hands.

The others came running behind her, Delilah shivering in her nightgown, Beulah in her wrapper and Jinny with a shawl over her gown, probably the first thing she could put her hands on. She took Melissa from me and wrapped her snug in the shawl against her body, Melissa staring out at me with eyes wide and scared as Delilah's.

"Ama, Joe's dead," I said, and I felt the scream raising up inside me. Then it was outside, getting loud in my ears, till I felt a hand shaking me.

"Elizabeth! Stop it! Delilah, get the brandy. Be quick. It's all right, Elizabeth. You're here now. Hurry, Delilah. Yes, that's it. Get that down, just a sip, it'll help you relax."

I felt the glass pressed up to my lips and raised. When I swallowed, it felt like it was burning a hole inside me. "Ama, I'm going to be sick."

"No, you're not," she said. "Take a deep breath. That's right. Now hold it. Again."

I put my hand over my mouth gagging, but the brandy stayed down and after a while, I took some more. Somebody put a cold towel on my forehead.

"Where's Melissa? She all right?" I asked.

"Yes'm, she doin' fine," Jinny said. "She done quit that cryin' and carryin' on, yes she have now. She know her old Jinny ain't gon' let nothin' happen, no sir." Jinny was sitting in the rocker now, with Melissa in her lap, Melissa's face against her neck and not making a sound. The rocker was creak-creaking against the floorboards and for a few minutes that was all I heard, the sound comforting to me as the motion was to Melissa. It meant we were home, that we'd really made it back to Symphony Oaks.

"Can you tell us now, Elizabeth, what happened?" Ama said, brushing my hair out of my eyes.

My voice was so low I could hardly hear it myself when I told them. I felt their eyes watching me, but I didn't look up. I just kept saying those words, simple everyday words, but when you put them together, they said how two men were dead and how things had been done to me that never ought to been done. When I was finished telling my story, it was quiet, excepting for the sound of us breathing and the rocker rocking and the clock in the corner beating, telling us that time was passing.

Then I heard weeping and saw that Delilah's face was wet, and Ama's too. Jinny's face was buried in Melissa's hair and Beulah had her chin down, shaking her head, both eyes closed.

"Why?" Delilah said, sounding fierce. She was squatting on the floor in front of my chair, her hands on my arms.

Ama wiped her eyes. "Elizabeth, you say they mentioned that Joe was a Yankee . . . ?"

"More than once," I said. "Kept teasing him with the word."

Delilah said, "Could they be soldiers?"

"Wait. Let me think," Ama said. After a few minutes of us watching her while she thought, her chin in her hand, her elbow propped up by her other hand, pacing, she asked, "Are you quite sure that Joe and this Hank are . . . ?"

"They're dead. If you'd seen Joe, you wouldn't have to ask. Oh, God, his head was most blowed off."

"And you're sure about this Hank, too?"

"He's dead," I said, and put my head in my hands.

"We must go back and get rid of the body," Ama said sudden-like to Jinny, who moaned and grabbed hold of her as if to keep her there. "Yes, I know, I don't have the stomach for it myself. But we have to go back."

I looked at Ama like she was talking gibberish. One thing I knew for sure. I was never going back to that place. Never. When I told Ama so, she put both hands on my shoulders and said, "Elizabeth, you don't have to go back. In fact, I insist that you lie down. But some of us will have to go. We have to bury the body. And from this night on, as far as you are concerned, there never *was* any body. Do you understand? You didn't kill anyone. Hank left about an hour after the others."

The whole time she was talking, I could hear Jinny moaning, but nobody said nothing. We watched Ama turn away from us and go to the window. She stared out like she could see through the dark, one hand up to her throat like it was hurting. Somehow I knew her mind was made up, that she would be the one burying the man that laid dead on my cabin floor. When she turned back 'round, she told Delilah to find something warm for me to sleep in and said I should lie down and rest. She'd decided on Beulah to go with her.

Beulah made some sort of noise, more like a grunt than a yes or no. Her eyes roved the room and she kept her own thoughts.

It was Jinny who finally spoke up. She wanted to go with Ama. If anybody should go, it was her, she said. Wasn't she always there to look after Ama, and wasn't that the way it should be tonight too? But Ama held up her hand, and in a stern voice, a voice almost demanding, insisted Jinny tend to Melissa while Delilah looked after me. Then Delilah was to bring Melissa and me to her in three hours. Not to the cabin. We were to meet Ama beside the oak grove just this side of the Anson Taylor homestead. She wanted Delilah to bring the carriage and tie my horse behind. Jinny was to stay at Symphony Oaks and look after Daisy.

When she was finished, we stared at her for a few seconds, then one by one, we nodded that we understood. Only Beulah didn't nod, didn't look direct at Ama. But when Ama said "Beulah?" in a certain way, Beulah muttered, "I get dress. Delilah, me and you hitch the horse to the wagon. We take Omaha and one o' the mares. You use Docker."

"I'll help you with the horses," Ama said, turning her back on the room. "It won't take me more than a few minutes to get dressed. Delilah, you take care of Elizabeth." This last over her shoulder.

Then Delilah had me by the arm, dragging me toward her room, and all I could think about was how folks in Frisbin would be calling me a murderer now. It wouldn't matter to Frisbin people if Joe's head were blowed clean off his neck, he was still a dirty Yankee. And it wouldn't matter if I got raped by a dozen men, I was a Yankee slut who must of deserved what I got. I wondered if they'd hang a woman for murdering . . . if she be a Yankee woman. And if so, what must it be like to be hanged?

A half hour later, I was laying in bed in Delilah's nightgown listening to the last sounds of the wagon rattling down the driveway. I crawled from between the sheets and crept over to the window and saw Delilah standing there staring after Ama and Beulah. Both her hands were up to her face. Then she turned toward the door. It seemed like she was shivering.

I was back in bed when I heard my door open and then close and I knew Delilah had peeked in at me and left the room. A few seconds later I was out of bed again, reaching for my clothes.

Dressing seemed to take forever. My fingers were numb. I couldn't find my shoes. But finally, I were dressed and sneaking down the stairs and out to find Joe's horse. He was tied to the side hitching post, still saddled but covered with a light blanket.

It were quick work to uncover him and check the saddle girth, then I was on his back galloping away. A voice yelled behind me and I looked back to see Delilah at the front door, then running down the driveway after me, her nightgown billowing under her half-open wrapper, her hair blowing 'round her head like a cloud of black ink. Both her hands were in front of her, fingers stretched out like she was trying to reach through the air and pull me back.

"You got to understand," I whispered, feeling somehow that she could hear, that she could understand. "This is something I have to do."

I only wished she could have seen my thoughts while I was tossing around on my bed, listening to the wagon leaving. Remembering Beulah's face. Picturing her and Ama out there in that cabin, lifting Hank between them, and all the time me back at Symphony Oaks, safe, warm in bed.

Better this way. Cold and afraid and running toward the last place in the world I wanted to be.

Eleven

*T*he cabin was there waiting for me in the gray mist of a clouded night, full of its dead. That narrow sweep was the front porch. . . . It seemed to know me. . . . *Come, Liz Ann, you no-good trash, I'm waiting for you, Liz Ann.* The trees were gray-misted too and blowing hard in the cold wind, and I could hear the old barn door banging open and shut and I almost jumped out of my skin thinking it were the men coming for me. All 'round me was the land. I couldn't see much of it, just dim stripes of empty bare acres. Any minute it ought to be raining. The sky was filling up with it, but it weren't falling.

Hurry, Liz Ann. Hurry.

The whole place, even the sky, seemed like it was talking to me. The cabin seemed like it was laughing about how scared I was. In front of me the wagon had stopped and Ama was climbing down from the driver's seat, her hurricane lantern in her hand. She had seen me coming a ways back, but I had stayed behind the wagon and she hadn't slowed or gave me any kind of signal. Now she turned 'round, holding the lantern high with one hand, and her other hand stretched out to me.

"You shouldn't have come here, Elizabeth," she said, but her eyes gleamed odd-like, almost like pride come shooting out of them, even as the first lightning bolt shot across the sky.

"None us ought be here," Beulah grumbled from the wagon. "We lookin' for trouble here. We beggin' for it."

131

I was off my horse when something moved out of the shadows behind me, something coming quick, looming up over me. "Ama! It's them!" I screamed.

I fell against the wagon, my insides hammering at me till I was almost vomiting. It took me a minute to realize that it was Hank's horse, running crazy from the lightning.

The horse reared and Ama managed to get one hand on the reins. He almost come down on top of her, but she stepped back, still holding on. "Easy, boy," she crooned, as if reminding him it wasn't his fault he was owned by a man of the devil. She had a way with horses, even this one, and somehow she managed to quiet him, though his eyes still jerked from side to side and his feet never stopped moving. She handed the reins to Beulah, who'd finally come down off the wagon. She were in a dark mood, but she took hold of the reins and started for the barn when Ama said to put Hank's horse and Joe's in the barn, then to hide the wagon in there too. Beulah's head was down and she was mumbling to herself.

I was wishing Jinny would of come instead, when Ama took my arm and started guiding me toward the porch, holding the lantern so's we would see where we was walking. Somehow I knew she was listening, just as hard as I was listening, for the sound of running horses or men's voices.

"They're coming, Ama," I whispered. "I can feel them coming."

"Hurry," she whispered back.

We almost tiptoed over the porch. Then Ama let go of my arm and reached for the door handle. The latch was broke, where one of the men had put a foot to the door, and the door swung open the minute she touched it.

We waited a minute, still listening for the sound of voices, then we went across the floor and into the bedroom. Ama turned her lantern up full and held it up and we saw the place was full of blood, just like I'd left it. There was Joe with his pants half down and a blanket over his head, oozing blood. Hank was on the floor beside him and he was bloody too. There was the trail of his blood where he'd come crawling after me. And the blood on his head where I'd bashed him with the butt of his gun, and the blood that had gushed out his back.

"Oh, lord," Ama breathed, and I could feel her body sag against mine. But she drew herself up just as quick. "Rags, Elizabeth. We'll need water and rags."

There wasn't time to think. To do nothing but what had to be done. I brought out old sheets and tore them up. Ama brought the water bucket from the kitchen.

"Now lie down on the bed," she said. "You shouldn't even be on your feet."

I dipped a piece of sheet in water. "I'm not going to stop," I said. "Not until it's over. Until it's *all* over," I added, seeing her ready to protest.

"Still," she said.

"I have to do this, Ama. I'll rest when it's finished."

She watched me squeeze my rag in the water, then wadded a piece of sheet and dipped it in the bucket. We were down on our hands and knees scrubbing, rinsing our rags in bloody water, when Beulah came back and found us there. She got down on her hands and knees too, but she kept looking at Hank's body, asking how come I shot him in the back.

"You shoot somebody protect yourself, you shoot him in the front," she told me, then said it again, almost to herself.

I started all over again telling her about what Hank had done to Joe, that she should just look at Joe's body with her own eyes, and how I *knew*, I just *knew* he was going to do something just as bad to Melissa, and I was saying all this whiles we swabbed up blood and dipped our hands in the bloody bucket to rinse our rags. Blood be hard to clean. Even the clots burst open and more blood comes out of them.

Then all of a sudden we heard it. A horse coming. We looked at each other and I wondered if my face could be any worse than theirs. None of us moved, just stopped right where we were, our rags still in our hands. Waiting.

"Hank? You in there?" a slurred voice shouted after a

minute. The horse was out front now. We'd heard him neigh when he was pulled to a stop. "Hey, Hank, ya son of a bitch. You in there?"

"Drunk," Ama mouthed to Beulah and me, then leaned over and put out the lantern. Now we were in the dark and couldn't see each other, only vague shadows that crouched near the floorboards. Heavy breathing that belonged to all and no one in particular. A sharp thud as somebody knocked against the bucket and a flood of water that drenched my legs and my dress. I heard Beulah moan "God almighty," and the rattle of the bucket as she set it up.

Then we heard the man grunt as he got off his horse, heard the sounds of him moving across the porch, then into the front room, the door creaking closed behind him.

"Hank?" came his voice.

I felt Ama's fingers squeeze my arm. "Answer him," she whispered, her breath warm on my face.

Trembling, I made myself call out, "He's gone. He—he left 'bout ten minutes ago."

Boots sounded on the floor. He's coming in, I thought. Then he stopped. "You musta been havin' a big old time together." He laughed. "Maybe . . . hell, maybe I should take another turn. Bet you'd like that."

Ama's fingers tightened on my wrist, but I couldn't think of anything to say. I felt the tears coming out my eyes, felt myself choking on fear and hate, and all of a sudden I wanted to go out there and kill him, too. Maybe I moved or maybe I didn't, but Ama's fingers pulled at me, telling me to wait.

Then he laughed. "Hell, ain't probably nothin' left of ya, seein' how long Hank took. Maybe later, though. After you bury that Yankee bastard of your'n. I may be back one of these nights. Who knows."

He walked away then, his boots stomping as he left the cabin, slamming the door behind him. A few seconds later we heard him call to his horse and gallop off.

Beulah's voice rose up in the dark, cold and wavering. "No,

sir," she said. "This here ain't our business, Miz Ama. Out here, moppin' blood. Get ourself kill maybe."

"Quiet," Ama said, still listening.

There were nothing to be heard now. Only the sound of wind coming through the window, and Beulah's quick breathing. A tree branch started tapping on the window. It was a sudden thing, like fingers on the glass, and when Ama finally managed to get the lantern lit, we halfway expected to see a grinning face looking in on us. Instead, only darkness.

Beulah got to her feet, standing up tall in her long dark coat, her breast heaving, her face hid in shadows. "What Daisy gon' do if'n I get kill? What then? Daisy need thinkin' 'bout, too, Miss Ama. Not just *her* baby"—jerking her chin at me without looking at me—"but *mine!*"

Deep down, something stirred in my mind: Beulah staring at Melissa Sue. That look on her face. Hate struggling to rise up.

Ama turned up the wick and the light shined brighter as she stared at Beulah. "Go then, Beulah. Just start walking," she said in a colder voice than I ever heard her use. "If you go," she added, more gentle, "I won't hold it against you. But I tell you this: Elizabeth and I need your help."

There was a minute of Ama and Beulah looking at each other, then Beulah swallowed hard and dropped her eyes. She said, "I sorry, Miz Ama. I stay with you. Do the best I can do for you."

"Good," Ama said, and the three of us began working even faster than we worked before, this time without nobody saying a word.

When we finished the floor, Ama said to leave Joe's body as it was, Joe's blood where it was. But water had been spilt and who was to know what blood was whose. We rinsed out the bucket and put it out back. Then we rolled up Hank in a blanket and started dragging him out the door. His head banged against the floor, and Beulah cried out like it was a living person we had hold of. Hank was a heavy man, hard to pull along, even for three women.

135

Ama fell once, and Hank's body slid clear out of the blanket. When his boot flipped up and kicked at my leg, I slapped it back down hard. Then we rolled him up again and got his blood all over us and no way to clean it off.

Ama was upset and told me to stay back, that she didn't want any blood on me, but it was too late for that, it was smeared clear down Delilah's dress I were wearing.

Somehow we got to the barn, half wore out from dragging Hank, and we'd just started pulling him up into the wagon when we heard horses. They were coming fast, and we just got the barn door shut when two men come galloping up.

We looked through a crack in the door and saw they were going inside the cabin, just busting in like it were the natural thing to do. Then a few minutes later they come out and started hollering for Hank again. Angry drunk voices that carried on the wind. That howled.

"They see he shot in the back, us same thing as dead," Beulah said in a dark voice, looking hard at me.

"They don't know anything's happened to him," Ama said, trying to calm her.

"They *gon'* know. They here lookin', ain't they?" she mumbled, still with that look on her face.

"Looking for what?" I asked her. "Why should they think he's here?"

"Maybe they not lookin' for him," Beulah said. "Maybe they lookin' for you."

She turned toward Ama, who was listening to the men outside. We couldn't see them now, but knew they were close. What we could see was the lightning that lit up the whole barn in flashes. It crackled through the air until the walls trembled 'round us and thunder shook the earth under our feet.

"Miz Ama," Beulah said, pointing to a busted board in the side of the barn. "We can get out that there crack. They never know we with her. They be thinkin' she 'lone."

"Listen!" Ama hissed, eyes staring. It was quiet now, but the night sounds were there, animals scurrying for shelter, a coyote howling from far off. Then the thunder again, even

136

louder, and the wind whipping the trees. And all of a sudden we could hear the men's voices again, close to the barn this time.

I pressed my eye to a knothole and watched them run toward us. Then behind them one of the horses screamed and rose up on its hind legs. It came crashing down, then up it went again, crashing down even harder, and I heard one of the men scream, "Oh, hell!"

"Here comes the rain!" the other one called, looking from the barn to the horses and back again. The first man had run to the horse that was acting up.

Then the storm finally started, and all at once it seemed like I was back at Ama's place when Moses went hiding, rain and all, only now I was the one hiding. What would they do if they found me? Beat me? Brand me? Kill me like they ought to done, maybe, when they killed Joe? Maybe they were sorry they hadn't killed me too.

What I should do is walk out there and let them see me, I thought. Then maybe Ama and Beulah'd be safe. But I knew I couldn't turn myself over to them, and it didn't help to remember how Moses couldn't hand hisself over neither.

"Get the horses!" the second man yelled. "We'll wait it out in the barn!"

He come rushing toward us. He nearly missed seeing the old well hole, stumbled 'round it and kept coming, through the mud and past the old shade tree, water splashing, rain slanting down, and I shuddered.

I knew if I didn't move now I never would. I took a last look through the knothole, saw him still coming. Saw the first man over his shoulder having trouble with his horse. It plunged down toward him, its mane flying in the wind. In the next instant it broke free and went whirling from the man, who went chasing after it on foot, losing his balance and falling face forward, then up and running again. The other man went for his horse, vaulted into the saddle, and, when he reached the man on foot, stopped until he could climb on behind. Then the two of them rode together after the loose horse, whistling and yelling as they went.

"Hurry," Ama said, "they may be back."

We finished lifting Hank into the wagon and got the wagon out of the barn. Then Joe's horse kicked up when we tried leading him out into the rain. Finally we had him tied on behind the wagon and the barn door shut and were hurrying off with Hank's body in back. Ama'd decided to bury him along Anson Taylor's creekbed, those low swampy acres where just about the whole town had hung their fishing lines from time to time. The creek would of overflowed with all the rain we'd been having in the past few weeks and the digging would be easy. Anyhow, we didn't dare bury him close to the cabin. If his body was ever found, it should be way off somewhere.

Later, I remembered dragging Hank down the wet hill, sliding in the mud, then wading in the mud at the bottom. Rain or no, digging was hard, and in the end, we had to bury him shallow 'cause our backs were breaking. He laid there in his grave with a slit of moonlight on his face, eyes open, staring up at me like he was seeing what I was doing.

I took a shovelful of dirt and threw it over his face, and then Ama shoveled dirt over him, too, and then Beulah, then all of us until he was finally under the ground.

"Come on," Ama said, already headed for the slippery hill.

Delilah was waiting for us at the oak grove, Melissa asleep in the carriage, her head in Delilah's lap, Delilah's arm 'round her. When she saw us, all covered with dirt and blood, she said, "Lord God," but we were all too done in to explain.

Ama untied Joe's horse from the carriage and helped me in the saddle. Then her and Delilah lifted Melissa up and handed her to me backwards, facing me, still asleep, but with her arms clutching 'round my waist as if part of her was awake and knew she had to hang on.

"The blood on your clothes is Joe's," Ama said. "You know what to say, Elizabeth. Stick to the truth until you get to Hank. He left after his friends left. That's all you know. Once the sheriff is done with you, come straight back to us. I won't sleep till I see you."

The past is done, I thought, hugging Melissa to me. She

slept on, like she was in her bed 'stead of on a galloping horse. Pure and childlike she was, while I practiced up the lies I'd be telling for the rest of my life.

The wind blew hard, the trees bent down to touch us as we went riding for the sheriff's office. The very first lie I'd be telling was about the blood all over me. The blood, yes. I had to remember how . . . it belonged to my husband.

Twelve

The strangest thing was when I was telling it, the truth didn't seem no more true than the lies and the lies no falser than the truth. I could of been dreaming it all. The sheriff and his deputy, both up cleaning guns and talking war though the night was 'most over. The prisoner in one of the two cells, up talking war too, sitting on his bed in his sock feet saying how General Braxton Bragg was the biggest fool of a commander in the whole Confederate army, though it grieved him to say it. And me sitting there at the sheriff's desk with a cold messy sweat streaming down my face and my neck. Dirt on me like a second skin. Blood on my skirt, both my sleeves ripped from grave-digging. Melissa hanging over my arm like a dead weight. My shawl lost somewhere on the road.

And Mama's voice, part of the same dream. "Now, Lizbeth Ann, don't you go near that place. Don't look at me like that, you know what place I mean. A lot of men always sitting in there talking about goodness knows what. Go on now. If you and Nellie want to walk to the courthouse, walk on the other side of the street." When we could, we'd sneak a few peeks inside the jail, and sure enough we'd always see men sitting 'round with their legs crossed, talking to each other. Probably about murder, Nellie and I used to whisper to each other. Or terrible things we couldn't even imagine.

In those days, Sheriff Ben Oates had been almost young.

140

Handsome, too, enough to make girls and women look at him, though he never seemed to look back. He'd never been married, never been a churchgoing man, and didn't go to parties or the like. He spent his time at the jail or hunting or having a meal at an eating spot. Now he was at least forty and his hair had gone gray and his teeth near black. Instead of being handsome, now he had the gritty, puffy-eyed look of a man who'd spent most of his life awake. Yet, in this place, he was right strange compelling. Powerful. You knew just to look at him he was the sheriff. A person who gave the orders. There was a lack of fear in him, a calm sort of sizing up the situation that made me understand in the blink of my own eye why all these years, whenever there was trouble, whether it was from the law or just a drowning or a bad accident, folks came straight to Ben Oates, sometimes even before fetching the doc.

When I stopped talking to take a long breath, Ben Oates said, "Go on," sliding his eyes 'round on me. Up to then he hadn't seemed to be listening much. He was standing by his desk, his foot on the chair, his rifle open over his knee. He'd been swabbing out the barrel and throwing in a word every now and again to the men's conversation behind him, that was all about the war and our hills filling up with soldiers, their voices louder than what I was saying. He was looking at his rifle, not me. Even when I said I'd been outraged, he never looked away from his gun. But now all of a sudden, his attention was all on me and I couldn't even remember just what I'd been saying.

When I just sat there looking up at him, my mouth open, he said, "Who came back? Which one?"

"I—I'm not sure I—"

"After Hank left," he said. "You said one of the men come back. Which one of them? Don't you know?"

"Well, sir," I said, "I'm just not sure which it was. He never came in, you see, just called out."

"You never looked out the window or nothin'?" he asked, his chin lifted and looking at me curious-like.

"No, sir, but even if I had, I couldn't of seen nothing. I didn't have no lights on. Not even a lantern lit. Nothing."

141

"That right?" He put his rifle on his desk with a clatter and leaned over to make a note in an open book, his tongue curled up under his bottom lip. Then he sat down and squinted at me through the dim light of the lamp that sat between us on his desk, pouring black smoke out the top, smelling to high heaven of bacon grease.

Lord, what did I say? I thought, watching those eyes of his get even narrower. He could of been peeking at me through a keyhole. Through the eye of a needle.

Be careful, Liz Ann, I told myself. Say everything just the way Ama said to say it. Nothing more. Nothing less. Of course, I was already keeping my deepest wounds in my heart where he couldn't see them. That my family weren't my family no more. That the people of Frisbin weren't my people. That everything was starting to scare me, even black nights. Even the mountains I'd looked at all my life. The mountains that were like long fingers around our part of the world. Now there were soldiers up there, and who knew how close to us they were, ready to kill. Yet, after tonight, what was there to fear? Could war be any worse than tonight?

"You know, Frank," Ben Oates said, interrupting his deputy, Frank Wright, who was describing the Spencer repeating rifle to the prisoner with the same joy as if he'd designed it. "I recognized the names straightaway. Damned if she ain't been talkin' about the Greenwoods. I've shot birds with them boys over at McMinnville. You've heard me talk about Cecil Greenwood. Well, Cecil's got four boys. Oldest named after him, Cecil Junior, then there's Ferris and the big heavy one, the one they call Fat Charlie. And Hank's the Morgan Raider. They're raging Confederates. Raiders took Hank first. I don't know what units the others went with."

"That so?" the deputy said, turning full 'round. Even the prisoner got up from his bed and came to the bars. Now that the talk had turned army, they both acted more interested. Before, I'd just been a woman interrupting their talk.

And I was thinking, Brothers. It was brothers that killed Joe! No wonder they all looked alike. Though now, I couldn't picture any of them. Even Hank was gone from my brain. Sitting there in the near-dark jail, all I could see was Joe's face. His mouth 'round the gun, moaning. Begging. Then I heard the gun go off. I covered my face with my hands and smelled blood on them. I jerked them away, feeling like I might throw up any minute.

"So that's all?" Ben Oates said real soft-like. He looked dangerous as a snake trying to decide what part of me to have for dinner. If I didn't know better, I'd of sworn he knew everything that had happened. His eyes were so almighty knowing, he could of been hiding under the bed or something.

"I guess that's about all," I said, staring at my hands and seeing blood under my fingernails. I started picking them out, using one bloody nail on the next. If I didn't watch myself, I'd be screaming out *I killed a man tonight! Is that what you want to know? He's covered with dirt right this minute!*

He said, "Well, time of war and all. Everything's different. You know how it is. Raiding, that sort of thing. Hell, soldiers do things. A bunch of damned Yanks hung a whole town not more than forty miles from here. Children and women, everything. Some farmer complained when they shot his pigs. Like I said, everything's different, soldiers and all. I doubt I do anything."

"But . . ." I started to say, then stopped.

"What?"

"I just don't see how, well, something like this could be *military.*"

"Hank Greenwood's a Raider. You know the high jinks of them Raiders." The prisoner laughed, going back to his bed.

The deputy said, "Hell, yes! They're liable to be up to anything."

The sheriff was keeping his eyes on me. "Like I said . . ."

I almost laughed. So he wasn't going to do anything. Why did I ever expect you to? I felt like saying. Instead I said, "Can I go, then?"

"Just a minute," he said, motioning me down in my chair. "About this other thing. . . . You know, you being outraged and all," he went on. "You actually want me to write somethin' like that down in my report? It's just that I'm curious. I'd have to say in all my years of sheriffin', I never heard a woman admit to somethin' like that. Friend of mine was on a wagon train got attacked by savages," he said, tilting his chin toward Frank Wright to include him in on what he was saying. "Well, the redskins took some of the women prisoners, and two of them got rescued about three months later. All tattooed. Couldn't hardly recognize them, or so they said. You don't mind my saying this, ma'am, one of them had a red baby some months after they released her. Now here's the thing. Neither one of them, even the baby's mother, ever said a word about being outraged. That's being a strong woman, wouldn't you say?"

Frank Wright nodded, his finger in his ear, his belly stuck out like he was the one having the baby.

"Mind, I'm not tellin' you what to say," Ben Oates said. "I'm just sayin' maybe take a while to think it over. I don't have to write that part down. The bein' outraged part. Women just don't say that kind of thing. I could forget I ever heard that."

"I don't want you to forget nothing," I said, and watched a slow grin creep over Frank Wright's face. He'd started to watch me as close as the sheriff. He had a less sly mind than the sheriff, but dirtier.

"Course, that's entirely up to you, ma'am," Ben Oates said, exchanging a look with Frank.

"Can I go home now?" I found the strength to hoist Melissa to my shoulder and push myself out of my chair.

The sheriff's eyebrows raised. "Home?" he said. "You say you're goin' *home*?" Joe's body back in the cabin laid in the thick silence between us.

"I guess I'll go to Ama Hadley's place," I said, trying to seem like I just thought of it. "She's always been real kind to me. I guess she'll take us."

"Woman's a fool," Frank Wright said. "Damned highfalutin ways."

I looked at the floor.

"One more thing," the sheriff said. "Since I'm writin' this

144

down, this part where you claim to be outraged. You want to go on record sayin' how that made you feel? You feel guilty? Angry? What? Anythin' you want to say about that?"

"Right now," I said, Melissa hanging in my arms till I was about to fall, "it feels like it never even happened. Like it was a bad dream or somethin'."

I saw him dip his pen in the ink, heard the scratch-scratch as he wrote on his paper, Melissa getting heavier in my arms every second. Finally, he pushed the paper toward me and told me to sign. I blinked down at it, and the scribbled words swam before my eyes. I shrugged and wrote my name.

I was half out the door when I heard Ben Oates mutter, "I'll have to take a trip out to your place tomorrow. Don't move nothin' till day after. You hear me?"

By "nothing," I guessed he meant Joe's corpse. "All right," I said, wishing I'd never have to move Joe or touch him or see him again. I remembered his body as something froze. Arms stuck out. Fingers reaching for something invisible. Funny thing. Every time I thought of Joe, he was deader.

Thirteen

*I*f I dreamt of death in that next day of sleep, if I dreamt of Joe, of Hank, of Mama turning her back on me, it wasn't no more than ripples on a cow pond. Seemed like I cried out. If I did, it was like the croak of frogs hopping beside the water. And if my fingers grabbed hold my pillow and squeezed like they were squeezing the life out of somebody, that was like grabbing hold of a tree branch and pulling your head above the water, so you could breathe.

Once I opened my eyes. The curtains were drawn shut and the room were dim and quiet. Delilah was sitting on the foot of my bed with tears on both cheeks, her eyes looking straight into mine.

"You did better than me," I told her, remembering all her stories of how she'd fought the men on her plantation. Ready to die, before she'd let any of them touch her. But then she hadn't had Joe kneeling before her, a gun in his mouth. Maybe then, even Delilah would have done what they said.

But her head was shaking and more tears come to her eyes. "No," she whispered. "No, I didn't do nothin' better than you."

"What do you mean?" I whispered back, seeing from the look of her she had something she needed to say.

"It happen to me, too," she said like the words been locked up in her a long time and come busting out.

"You mean . . ."

146

"What he done to you. That man," she said. "It happen to me, too. On the plantation. Marse Klein boy. He done it to me."

"But you—"

"Hush," she said, drying her face. "It all be all right. Everthin' be all right. I just wantin' you to know."

She slipped her hand under my neck, lifted a cup to my lips. I sipped tea and looked into her eyes. Water swimming in them.

"I'm sorry, Delilah," I said when she took the cup away. "I'm sorry it happened to you."

"I sorry it happen to you, too," she whispered back, and sat there holding my hands while I let my eyes close. I heard her take a long breath, felt a breeze on my face from the open window. It was warmer today, and I drifted backward into sleep.

It was later, I don't know just when. A child screamed and I forced my eyes open. Melissa was there, holding out her arms to me. "Mama-Mama!" she was screaming.

"Shh, baby," Ama's voice said behind her. "Let Mama sleep. Everything's all right."

But sooner or later, widows had to wake up. Else, how their husbands get buried? So after a while I sat up and drank soup and let Delilah brush my hair. Both little girls were wrestling on my bed, and Beulah came in, frowning, and picked up one under each arm as easy as if they were still babies, and left with them hanging half upside down, shrieking and laughing. She never said nothing, never really looked at me.

Jinny pulled the curtains, and long fingers of light streamed over my bed. I flinched and closed my eyes. When I opened them, Ama was standing there with a dark gray dress over her arm.

"It's light for afternoon," I said, staring toward the window.

"Not afternoon," Ama said, smiling, laying the dress over the foot of my bed. "It's the morning of a new day. You slept almost thirty hours, off and on."

Half an hour later, standing at my window dressed in the dark gray dress that Ama told me would serve me just as well as black, I looked out on little green buds on the trees, leaves shooting out. Tender new grass in thin patches over the ground, like hair on a baby's head. Windy, but sunny. It's really spring, I thought. And I'm burying Joe today.

It was a poor sort of funeral. Ama had sent word to Joe's family, but nobody came. Besides us women and the babies, there was just Tom Higgins and little Benjamin, inches taller than when I'd last seen him. It was strange to see Tom and Ben without Lucie, strange to be back at the cabin looking down on an open grave with a plain wood box at the bottom, knowing that Joe was inside with the lid nailed shut over him. Tom had dug the hole and made the box. There wasn't any casket to be had in town as Davis Garrett, the man who usually made them, had died at Fredericksburg last winter. There wasn't no preacher, either, with Reverend Harper up in the hills being a chaplain. Even if he was home, I doubt he'd of prayed over a Yankee grave.

We stood around the hole in a small circle, with Ama next to the grave, holding an open Bible; Daisy was running everywhere with Melissa following right after her and copying everything she done. They even had to be jerked away from the grave.

Ben was as quiet as a little man, though. He kept looking down at the grave, eyes sad as a dove's. He was almost seven now. Old enough to be remembering his mama's funeral.

Pray, Ama'd told us. Pray as best you can. But I was blank inside. I thought of the other funerals I'd been to in Frisbin. Folks and a preacher and flowers and people crying. I felt like everybody must be studying my face to see what I felt. When the truth was I couldn't feel anything. When you were the widow, you were supposed to feel something. I remembered those other funerals and women crying, even screaming, when they started throwing dirt over their husbands' coffins.

It should be somebody else standing here, I thought. Not me. It should be somebody who knew Joe as a boy, maybe. His mama, Mary Crocker. His sister, Pauline. Somebody else. Not me who hardly knew him.

I saw Delilah's face turned sideways, watching me, and her hand reached out and squeezed mine and held on. Then I felt Jinny's hand on the other side grab hold. Beulah came in beside Jinny then, and stood real close, shoulder to shoulder, and Tom Higgins put down his shovel and picked up Benjamin.

With us standing there together, Ama read from the scripture. Voice like music. Wind blowing her dress, ruffling the pages under her fingers. Sunlight on her face. Grasshoppers jumping 'round in the grass at our feet. The season's first butterflies floating over Joe's fields.

Ama'd chose the prayer of the afflicted and when she read of eating "ashes like bread" and "the sparrow alone upon the housetop," she looked at me. Ama was right to read such sad words, I thought. It was right and fitting to speak of enemies that reproached and days "like a shadow that declineth." If only I could find a prayer for Joe, I entreated God. But I couldn't. My heart laid as silent and dark as that grave box.

Finally Ama stopped talking and nodded to Tom. He put his hand on Ben's head for a minute and the two of them looked at each other. Then he set Ben down and picked up his shovel.

It wasn't until that first spadeful of dirt hit Joe's box that all of a sudden, without no effort at all, I started to mourn the waste of Joe's life. Poor Joe, he hadn't done much. He wasn't much of a husband or father. Even back in the old days, I remembered he'd had a reputation for being stubborn. He hadn't ever been close to his brothers. Since he come home from the war, he'd never mentioned his own ma and pa. In all of Frisbin, he was the only one to fight for the Federals, and the only reason he done it was 'cause of pride when the rebels wouldn't take him.

You're dead now, Joe. It's too late to do anything different.

Tom Higgins looked up from where he was standing near the grave, and his eyes looked at me as if he knew what I was thinking. Knew I wasn't grieving. That I was standing up there judging Joe like I was God. When maybe none of it was even Joe's fault. Maybe it was me failed Joe instead of the other way 'round. Maybe the whole world failed him. The army that wouldn't take him. His family that disowned him.

"Good-bye, Joe," I whispered as Tom started shoveling on dirt again and Joe's box disappeared from sight forever. Right then and there, I felt my eyes burning, something wet sliding down my cheeks and I knew I was crying. Crying for what never was and never could be. Crying for Melissa who wouldn't have nothing to remember about her pa and me with nothing much to tell her if she asked. Crying for pity of Joe who wouldn't be here to watch her grow. Crying because I really didn't care that Joe was dead and I wished I could care.

It was done finally. The hole was filled in and the dirt pounded down and packed in. Ama planted wildflowers all 'round the grave. Then she put a little wood marker in the ground. It said Joe's name and the years he'd lived.

Nothing more.

Fourteen

As we made our way back to Symphony Oaks under low clouds the color of soft cool smoke, me up front next to Ama, and the other women and the girls in the back of the wagon, we heard the horses coming. Everybody stopped talking and we heard breaking bushes, hoofbeats galloping down the hill behind us, and then a man's voice called "Yee-haaa!"

"Good lordy, who that?" Jinny asked.

But just hearing that voice, the strain of it, the way it rose ugly on the air, made me know who it belonged to and I almost stood up, almost jumped down from the wagon right while it was moving.

"It's the Greenwoods," I cried. "Ama, it's the Greenwoods!"

Ama's hand pulled me down from where I was half standing, half kneeling over the seat. "Don't be absurd." Ama frowned. "It could be anybody. You're just worn out and imagining things."

But she called to her horses to giddap, and we come up fast on Tom Higgins who was ahead of us in his buckboard. I caught a glimpse of Tom's face as he glanced back, his eyebrows pulled in together, and then he touched his horse with his riding crop and the horse leapt ahead.

Ferris, I thought, my teeth gritted together as we hurried on behind Tom and Ben, all of us bouncing and hanging on best we

151

could as we hit ruts and roots and dead tree stumps beside the path we skittered from. For the first time since I left Ben Oates's office, I could see the Greenwoods clear in my mind, could put a face to every name the sheriff had gave me. Cecil Junior, the oldest face, with the nose that sniffed and the eyes like ice-blue chips. Fat Charlie with the big lips and the puffy eyes. Ferris with no mercy in his face who took what he wanted. I knew it was the Greenwoods, coming on faster every minute. Demons on horseback. I stared up over the hill that was without a real road excepting for the cleared stumpy path through the thicket of trees, and I could see them now, charging at us over the rim of the hill. The horses' heads pushing forward, the men on their backs, good horsemen all of them, stuck tight to their saddles, plunging down at us.

I felt Ama draw a sharp breath. "Elizabeth? Is it?"

"Yes," I said. "It's them."

The horses sounded like thunder now. Seemed like there was fifty of them. A hundred. Like they were coming at us from all directions. But, no, it were just the three of them and the closer they got, the uglier they got, until they were right on top of us, so unshaven you couldn't see a mouth among them. Hair oily. Their shirts so filthy and so full of sweat, they were clinging to the men's bodies. Before you could look them in the eye, you could smell them. The kind of smell that gets up inside your nose and lays in there like a salve you can't get rid of.

The horse that Ferris rode come at one of Ama's horses with his teeth bared, but Ferris jerked his head to one side. I heard Ama cry out and her horse whinnied and shied. Something black as bat wings moved inside my head.

"Even your horses are devils," I snapped at Ferris, without even knowing I was going to say it, then felt Ama's elbow under my ribs telling me I didn't need no more trouble with the likes of the Greenwoods.

But Ferris only grinned at me and raised his hat to Ama. It was a gray hat of wool felt, round in the brim. A Confederate hat. So Ferris really was in the army. He turned to me and said,

"You lookin' good as supper on the plate, Missus Crocker. Ain't you goin' to introduce us to your lady friend?"

But his brothers, neither Fat Charlie nor Cecil Junior, weren't looking at us. Cecil Junior said, "Ferris, that buckboard up there ain't going nowhere." He jerked his thumb to where Tom Higgins had pulled to a stop ahead of us.

Ferris said, "Who gives a goddam," not even bothering to look at Tom, who was already walking toward us, a rifle under his right arm. Ferris was looking at me in such a personal and evil way that he seemed to have beds in both eyes. Me and him in those beds doing what he wanted.

"What do you want now?" I said, and then all the Greenwoods looked at me, laughing a little, as though I'd been trying to make a joke.

"More feisty today, ain't she?" said Fat Charlie, and Ferris added, "Now me, I find that right appealin' in a woman. Shows she has some life."

Then Cecil Junior rode up closer, pointing toward Tom again and shaking his head, and Fat Charlie rode closer too, scratching at something matted up inside his beard.

While they were talking among theirselves, Ama whispered, "Careful, Elizabeth, you're sounding angry. God knows it's normal, but this is the wrong time. And don't look at them any more than you have to. You look like you'd like to kill them."

"How else should I look? Like I'd like to kiss them?" I said, turning my head to look her in the eye.

"The babies," Ama whispered, taking my hand in hers. "If you set them off, they might hurt the babies."

My heart stopped at what she was suggesting, but I whispered back, "You're just saying that to get me sensible."

She smiled a little at that, but still she said "Hush," her hand over mine tightening and relaxing, tightening and relaxing. Maybe, I thought, Ama was caught same as me. Somewhere between what she wanted to do and what she thought she should do.

By that time Tom was there, standing between me and Ferris, the barrel of his rifle pointed toward the ground but his finger on the trigger. I looked up to where his buckboard sat parked, trying to catch a glimpse of Benjamin, but he was out of sight. Tom must of told him to stay down. I felt myself calm some. It was going to be all right, I told myself. Being between Tom and Ama was like being a valley, wedged between two mountains. Both so strong. So still.

"Why don't you fellows move along?" Tom said. "We've just come from a funeral. Lady's lost her husband. I suppose you couldn't know that."

Ferris and Tom were staring at each other. The one clean and tall and clear-eyed. The other with slits for eyes, stringy hair wilted flat against his skull and sagging in his saddle.

"Hell, she told you, did she? Told everybody everthin'? A decent woman wouldn't said nothin'—that should tell you somethin' 'bout her character. Damn you, man, don't look at me like that. She weren't no pure little thing or nothin'. Fact is"—he grinned—"only thing bothered me was whether or not she had the nasty Yankee woman disease."

"If you don't move on," Tom said, "I'm going to put a bullet in you."

"That right?" Ferris said. A bleat of sound that might of been a laugh burst from his lips. His fingers inched toward his gun.

Cecil Junior said, "Hell, Ferris, I'm too done in for brawlin'. I ain't goin' to shoot nothin' out over a Yankee woman. Ain't worth it. Besides, we're after Hank." His ice-cold eyes slid over me like I wasn't there, and found Ama. "See, ma'am, we've been lookin' for our brother since night 'fore last. Problem is, we can't find him nowhere."

Ama said something, I couldn't tell what. All at once Daisy called out, "Horsies! Big, *big* horsies!" and somebody said, "Shh, baby, shh." Maybe Beulah, maybe Jinny. There was a creaking in the wagon and, without looking over my shoulder, I knew the women were picking up the children, trying to keep them quiet.

154

Ama's horses were moving 'round, pawing at rocks on the path. Seemed like the world had stopped, like we'd been standing there for hours. Ama'd quit talking now. I found myself staring 'round like desperation. Seeing that every brother wore or held that same gray rebel hat. Ferris's saber at his waist, a long evil-looking thing that glinted in the sun. Ferris's uniform pants; the other brothers in plain pants, but homespun. Pistols strapped to every waist, Ferris's over top of his saber. A shotgun between Ferris's saddle and his rolled-up coat.

What I stared at hardest was Fat Charlie's chins, flabby sacks of evil, lines between them like creekbeds collecting oily water, dirt. Looked like fat dripping down his neck. God, this one was ugly, I thought, and I couldn't quit staring even though he was glaring back at me. Look at that hair, not as long as my thumbnail, and greasy as the rest of him.

Cecil Junior said, "Still, we can't figure out what happened to Hank." Then he glanced at me. "Lessen you know somethin' we don't. He did leave pretty near after us, didn't he?"

"Hank was all right last I seen of him," I said as quiet and blank as possible.

All of a sudden I could hear Ama breathing. Her shoulders rose and fell, like it was an effort to get the air into her lungs, and I knew she'd picked up what I already knew soon's I said it. I shouldn't of been so blank. I should of asked, "What do you mean? What about Hank?" Something like that.

Ferris was saying slow-like, a frown between his eyes, "Hell, he didn't ask you if Hank was all right. He asked you—" when Cecil Junior interrupted him, said, "Wait a minute, wait just a damned minute, somethin's wrong here."

"You bet your sweet ass there is," said Fat Charlie. "This slut's done somethin' to Hank. Somethin' awful!" he wailed, and I saw tears come to his eyes. Real tears. And of everything that had happened, that struck me the strangest. That Fat Charlie could cry over what might of happened to Hank. Grief could live, mystery of God, even in the lowest form of the human heart. For here were three men of the worst sort still looking for Hank. Crying over his miserable hide. How could one brute love another brute so much, even if they were brothers?

"Dammit, woman, you better start explaining," Ferris said, mean-like, never taking his eyes off my face. "What the hell time did Hank leave your bed, anyhow?"

I felt Tom on one side, Ama on the other, tensing against me. I shook my head, trying to ward them off. No need to shoot or be shot, I thought. These men don't know a thing. They're just guessing. They don't even know for sure that Hank's dead.

"Hank left about an hour after you left," I said, seeing Tom's finger playing with the trigger of the rifle. If Ferris makes a move, I thought, Lord only knows what will happen.

But Ferris kept both hands on his saddle horn, even though his eyes were crafty. Murky, too. Snakes could be swimming in there. He said, "You're lyin', woman. Lyin' sure as that snivelin' husband of your'n were a Yankee." He spit, and a gob of it landed near Tom's shoe. "So we're goin' to the sheriff, how'd that be? 'Cause we Greenwoods are keen on justice. We got to get justice or die tryin'."

"If you don't move on," Tom said in an even voice, "you'll be trying and dying any minute."

Ferris sat there staring at me for a few seconds more; then he touched two fingers to his hat. "I'm goin'," he said. "But this ain't over. Not till we find Hank. And I surely hope we do find him. . . . For your sake," he said to me, "well's our'n." Then he dug his heels into his horse's sides and took off riding without looking back, his brothers behind him. Fat Charlie's hollering and cussing could be heard even after they disappeared over the hill.

"Thank the Lord, they gone," Jinny said, and Delilah broke down and started crying on Beulah's shoulder.

Beulah said, "No need of that now," in a kind of absent way, petting Delilah's head like she was a pet dog while she was thinking something private inside.

Tom Higgins just stood there looking at me. Until this very day, I'd hardly had a thought in my head about Tom except to know he was a good man, a hard-working man, and, most of all, Lucie's husband. But Lucie was gone now and Benjamin didn't have a mother and Tom didn't have a wife. And the longer Tom looked at me, the more I started staring back.

Fifteen

The rest of April passed without word from the sheriff or from the Greenwoods, and by the first of May, we heard thunder in the hills again. We stopped working, one at a time, put down our hoes, wiped the sweat off our brows, and listened.

"That must be Bragg's soldiers," I said to Delilah.

"Solid shot and shell, if you ask me." Tom nodded, on his way to the hilly backfield with the mule he called Bessie. By this time, he was working both farms as one. Delilah and I watched him for a moment, his strong tall frame disappearing over the rise, the mule plodding beside him.

When he was gone, Delilah looked at me funny-like, then went back to work. Beulah looked at me too, just staring hard in that way she had. Words had got scarce between us since the night Joe got killed, and yet I could tell she had something deep on her mind.

With a sudden quick swipe of her hand, she cleared away more sweat from her brow, then hunched over and went back to her hoeing.

A half hour later, Ama found me by the well where I was pumping water into jugs to take to the fields. She sighed and dropped to the wooden block, pulling me down beside her. "Let's take a few minutes," she said.

There was something in her voice that made me turn to her. She looked wore out, hair a bit grayer, eyes without some of their glow. In the outdoor light, I saw lines in her face I hadn't noticed before, and her hand that reached up to take off her sunbonnet was rough from work, and trembling.

"What's happened?" I said, expecting the worst, and she said in her usual abrupt way that she'd heard from Cole and that the major had caught pneumonia.

"Oh, Ama, I'm sorry," I breathed, struck by a grim knowledge in her face.

"Pneumonia," she repeated in a short way that fought to have no emotional nonsense. "He was never any good in damp cold places. God only knows if he'll even get medical care." There were tears in her eyes, but she blinked them away. "Only fool thing he ever did was fight for the rebels and he had to end up in a hellhole like Elmira. You'd think God would have allowed him one mistake, wouldn't you?" But her eyes stayed dry as she went on talking to me about the war and how it was going to bring about a new world. We all had to be willing to make sacrifices, she said. Whatever was needed—nothing was too much to ask. She made herself comfortable against the pump and I had the feeling she might sit there all day. It was like she could see through her own pain and all the destruction that the war was bringing to our people. She said she had a theory that both sides, not just the North, were really working to abolish slavery. That the South knew deep in their consciences that slavery were bad and wrong, but couldn't bring themselves to give up their plantations and rich way of life. So, they'd more or less forced themselves into the whole thing by having this war that even the worst fools knew the South couldn't win. Part of their penance, Ama said, was bringing the war into their own part of the country.

"When it's all over," she said, running her fingers through her hair, "the plantations are going to be level to the ground and the slaves will be free men and women as they were intended to be."

"Is our part of the world going to be leveled, Ama?" I asked.

"Let's put it this way," Ama said, her voice a little grim

now. "We're the floodgates to the South. We're on top of the most important railroads—the Nashville and Chattanooga and the Memphis and Charleston and the Western and Atlantic—and all of them are vital to both armies. They depend on the rails for all their supplies. Their guns and ammunition. Their food. Their textiles. President Lincoln says that if the North can hold Chattanooga and eastern Tennessee, a quick victory is certain. General Rosecrans is likely to attack Chattanooga any day now."

"Chattanooga," I said. "What are we going to do?" Wary as any animal, I raised my eyes to check my surroundings. But the world was as silent as before and there wasn't a soldier on the horizon.

For a while, Ama thought over my question of what we were to do, pressing her palm against the wet grass beside the pump block. "I thought," she said finally, "that we'd put corn into that back field. You know the one I mean? Downhill? It's never been planted but it'll likely irrigate just fine."

"I meant what are we going to do about Chattanooga."

"Chattanooga," she said, "will have to take care of itself. Corn, however, cannot plant itself."

Out there under the sun, we made our plans. She saw my eyes on her face and smiled at me, knowing I was thinking about the major. "We go on, Elizabeth," she said, her voice quiet, and I knew she'd released any demons, that she'd made peace with fate. "We plant our corn. Beans. We bury our dead, and more babies come. Our job is to go on. Just go on, that's all, like the earth. There's sense in that. You can *feel* the sense in that, can't you?"

From where I sat with my back against the pump, shoulder to shoulder with Ama, I could see Delilah and Beulah in the garden, bending over rows of what would soon be beans and lettuces and squash. And just by turning my head away from the sun, I could see Jinny standing in the back porch of the house, watching us, her face long as a slat. The children were inside the house having their naps. And the earth was still, lapping up the thin sunlight that shone over everything the oaks didn't shade.

160

Green was pushing out everywhere. Everything smelled sweet. And I thought that perhaps Ama was right.

The last week of May, Tom brought Ben over to live at Symphony Oaks because Ama agreed with him when he said a small boy needed the care of women. And then there was Old Man Higgins acting a mite strange, shooting off his pistol in the middle of the night, walking 'round stark naked in the moonlight hollering for his niggers to come back, and if they didn't, he was going to kill them.

And Narcissa Harwell quitting her job 'cause the food at Freeland Farm had grown scarce, and she wasn't about to take care of a mansion and a boy and a crazy old man on no empty stomach. No, sir, she wasn't so off she went to live with her sister in Texas, whose cupboard was full, whose husband was dead.

And last, Tom had told Ama, there was the war. It was so close to us now that Tom felt the boy'd be comforted in a house full of women.

Like Tom, most of the white men were alone now and worked their own fields or the fields belonging to their fathers. The few Nigroes left in Frisbin had jobs at the sawmill. Only Mr. Sam Cook kept most of his slaves by holing them up in his barn and shooting anybody that tried to escape, Emancipation Proclamation or no, but hardly anybody else in our town owned enough slaves to bother trying to hold onto them. The few that was left, like Henry Gallagher's old cook, Mary, was too old or sick to run.

With the war *coming*, which is what they said all over town, Jinny wanted the children with her everywhere she went. She wanted to be able to see them or hear them and if she didn't, she went running to check. "Got to know where they is all the time," she said, her head shaking, her eyes on the hills.

Ama's copy of *DeBow's Review* said that General Rosecrans had spent the winter at Murfreesboro and was to attack Chattanooga at any time. On the other hand Bragg was dug in solid along the Duck River between Rosecrans and Chattanooga. So Bragg was between us and the Yankees yet. That thunder we heard up in the hills must have been cavalry raiding parties, or so Tom told us.

"I'm not going to lie to you," Ama told us, her ears as alert to the shooting as ours, "we're in the thick of it. Being square in the middle of Chattanooga and Chickamauga right now is like being in the middle of a dogfight."

One night in the second week of June, us sleeping in our beds, something that sounded like an extra heartbeat waked us up. Made us sit up in our beds, wondering if we'd dreamed something or if our own hearts had picked up a beat.

We met in the hallway, carrying our children who were still half asleep. Tom came from Benjamin's room, where he was in the habit of dozing off on Ben's bed, sleeping there so often, you might say he half lived at our house. Ben was on his shoulder, his small face yellow in the candlelight. The rest of us swarmed out of our rooms in our nightclothes and Tom smiled sudden-like when he saw me standing there half naked in my shimmy. Delilah was in her shimmy too, with tears running down her cheeks, and Beulah had a blanket draped 'round her and Daisy. Only Ama and Jinny had taken time to put wrappers over their nightgowns, and as Jinny hurried over to take Melissa from me, I ducked back in my room for my own wrapper and a blanket for Melissa. By the time I come out, Ama had a burning lamp in her hand and Delilah was sharing Beulah's blanket.

"Drums, I think," Tom was saying, nodding to Ama. "Troops on the march."

Ama's face was grim, but in a second or two she said in a calm voice, "No use in not seeing the spectacle, is there? Everyone who wants to go, hurry and get dressed. Tom, can you hitch up the wagon for us?"

Tom said yes, and stuffed his shirt in the pants he'd fallen asleep wearing. Right away, he headed for his coat and the horses and the rest of us went to dress as fast as we could pull on our clothes. We were just climbing into the wagon when Old Man Higgins come screaming out of the dark, cussing Tom for leaving him alone and wondering what in blazes all the noise was about.

Finally, Tom got him into the wagon and it wasn't long till we were all bouncing along under a heavy sky, the sun just breaking over the hills, and the sounds of an army on the move growing louder and louder in our ears. When we reached it, we found that the main road was overflowing with what seemed like thousands of men. Soldiers riding fine horses or marching along at a good clip. Driving ox carts. Pushing cannons with shouts and loud grunts as their machinery slid off the road and wheels got caught in ruts or behind big rocks.

Yankees! Flying the red, white, and blue. And Old Man Higgins, head rolling ever which way as he looked out on the swarm of grand blue uniforms, said, "Look at them! Our boys out there in butternut, barefoot and starving, and these here scum decked out fit to kill! Look at the boots! Look at the bellies on them! No starvation here. I'd just as soon be home than seeing this here. Makes you sick. Godamighty, look at the grins of them lookin' at us."

Of course, they knew that Frisbin was a Confederate town. Half the wagons of the other folks from Frisbin that were gathered by the road with us, come to watch the soldiers go marching by, were flying little Stars and Bars and the people yelled at the Federals and sang "The Bonnie Blue Flag," or tried to, because the Yankee drums and marching drowned out all else. The Yankees looked at us. Grinning. Laughing.

Tom had driven, but had come in back of the wagon to try to quiet his father and when at last the old man sat muttering to himself, his chin buried in his coat, Tom sat back, his shoulder against mine on the wagon gate, the back of his hand resting against mine. My mind seemed like it spun in a hundred different ways at once. Joe asking me to marry up with him. Cole staring at me and then reaching out. Lucie saying how much she loved Tom, though there wasn't no passion in him. I could feel my hand shaking and Tom slipped his hand around it in the dark. It was a comforting touch, calming. I took a deep breath and felt myself stop trembling.

"I guess we're watching a part of history," Tom said. "And I have a hunch which army is going to win before I even read about it in the history books."

"The North, you mean," I said because that's what Ama had said so many times I thought it had to be true.

He nodded. "The army with the shoes." And together we sat there looking at the United States flags flying, the cannons and wagons of lead balls. Rifles and pistols and sabers.

Within the hour, most of Frisbin was lined up along the road on foot, horseback and in wagons, like us. "You going to Tullahoma?" folks cried to the soldiers. "You going to Stones River? Chattanooga? Where you going? Where?"

Mr. Ed Drew, a man I'd knew since I was a baby—he was a distant relation of Papa—was on his horse not a yard from us and he yelled at a foot soldier. The soldier raised his hand to his ear like he couldn't hear, and come closer, then before Mr. Drew or anybody else realized what was happening, the soldier drew his gun and ordered Mr. Drew off his horse right there with dozens of Frisbin people all 'round. He said he was *commandeering* his horse for the army. A minute later, he was riding off on Mr. Drew's horse and Mr. Drew was on foot, staring after his horse too shocked to even cuss or shout.

I heard a laugh from the ranks of marching soldiers and saw several of the Yankee men looking at each other, then out at the town people.

"Oh, no!" Tom said, jumping to his feet all at once, then lunging up front to the wagon seat.

"What's the matter?" I cried, but he didn't answer, just scooped up the reins and started pulling the horses 'round quick.

"God, I was a fool to bring the horses here," Ama muttered, and I looked over my shoulder where she was looking and saw a soldier aiming a pistol in our direction.

"Oh, please, Ama! Stay down! Everybody down!" I screamed and for a terrible minute I couldn't see Melissa. Dear Jesus, she hadn't climbed out of our wagon, had she? Then right after my heart stopped beating, I saw her head sticking out of the crook of Jinny's elbow.

164

We all rolled in a heap together at the bottom of the wagon, Old Man Higgins moaning and Ama murmuring to him to be quiet, that everything was going to be all right, and all the time us rolling this way and that. The wagon rocked and almost turned over and our heads banged against wood. My hands were full of splinters from trying to catch hold of something to get my balance and every second I expected to hear a bullet crashing into our wagon. Jinny was praying out loud, the others were just hanging on best they could, Daisy and Melissa in little balls with Jinny's arms 'round them and Beulah holding onto Delilah. I ended up with my arm 'round Ben, who was the calmest of us all somehow, him with his round serious eyes.

Tom never slowed the horses, and somehow the soldier never shot. We were halfway to Symphony Oaks before he said to go ahead and sit up, that nobody was following us. And we threw off the quilt we'd been shivering under and crawled up and looked at each other, feeling like history had rode too close tonight.

"I wonderin' what happen 'bout the soldier," Delilah said, staring behind us. "You reckon he—"

"Probably stole somebody else's horse," Old Man Higgins snarled, but Ama said thank goodness they hadn't got Docker, he was too old to go to war. For the rest of the trip back, Ama was in deep thought, her finger stroking her chin like she was studying what to do.

The next day, I knew what she'd been deciding about. She said we had to make preparations, that now it was only a matter of time before the war came to us. Tom stood nodding beside her and I felt the last little bit of hope drain out of me. In some kind of faraway place in my mind, someplace that was distant from my own fear, I was thinking that war times are like no other. Almost every day amazing things could be getting ready to happen, terrible things, and yet after a while, they didn't seem so amazing. In any other lifetime just one of those things would be the biggest thing that ever happened to you. Now life was one thing after another. You expected things to happen and when they didn't, you were almost surprised.

*   *   *

For the next four days, we didn't work in the fields. Instead we made up trunks of silver and china and whatever else we could think of that we didn't want to lose, even Ama's good rugs, and we buried it all on back acreage. All of us helped Tom dig the seven holes, all in different places, and everyone put in what they cherished most. Tom buried some things of his own, things that had belonged to Lucie and that he was saving for Ben's wife when Ben would grow up and marry. Ben himself slipped in the locket that had belonged to Lucie, holding it for a few seconds in his fist, pressed against his cheek, then dropping it into the chest and running from the room like something was chasing after him.

When everything was in the ground, we filled the holes and beat the earth with shovels, then ran the horses over top. We would have run over top with the wagon, too, but we dug in the lowest ground, where the ground would be wetter and softer and Tom was afraid we'd have trouble getting the wagon back up the hill. But in a month or two, when the grass grew in, wouldn't nobody know nothing was buried there.

"We're safe now," we told each other a hundred times a day. I think we hoped we were safe from everything, even the Greenwoods. For as the days went by and nobody, not the Greenwoods or the sheriff, came to our house, even Beulah relaxed some and there were times she even hummed to herself like the way she used to when I first come to Symphony Oaks.

The long slow days suited us and we worked side by side weeding and irrigating the crops and doing our cooking and cleaning without worrying about who was doing which job. The children were happy and Ben started laughing again. And Tom seemed ten years younger than that day at Joe's funeral when we were first seeing each other again.

More than once he caught me alone and we'd stand there talking about farming and everything else that was safe to talk about and all the time I felt him watching me. I started imagining myself married to him, secret imaginings not even shared with Ama, and I could see myself walking through the front door of Freeland Farm. Tending to Ben and Melissa and a new baby. Cooking in the huge kitchen. Dusting rooms full of elegant furniture. But there would have to be servants in such a big house. I couldn't imagine that part. Me ordering people around.

The other part I couldn't imagine was Tom taking his man pleasure with me. He had to do it with Lucie or there couldn't of been Benjamin. When Lucie said he didn't have passion . . . did she mean in their bed? Would he be like Joe, hurrying through what he had to do? Would he still be the same Tom or would he turn into another person up there on top of me? When I thought about that part of marriage, I thought I'd rather stay a widow and never have to be bothered or disgusted again.

Yet right in the middle of me thinking about that part of being a wife, I'd always get the same thought. That when it was Cole who had his arms 'round me, it hadn't been disgusting at all. He was trembling and I was trembling and in my heart I knew it was the first time I ever really wanted a man to do to me what Joe done. Everything in my body had burned and in those few seconds with my arms 'round his neck, my fingers in his hair, I couldn't get close enough. This with a man who was so far out of reach, he could be living on the moon.

As the summer went on, I took my wedding ring and laid it away in my bureau, wondering how long before somebody noticed I wasn't wearing it. Sure enough, Delilah stared at my hand before breakfast was over and said, "Somethin' missin', huh" and I looked up to see everybody looking.

"No secrets here," I said, smiling. But blushing a little, too. I wasn't altogether sure why I put the ring away. Whether I just didn't want to wear it anymore or because of kind of an understanding that was growing between Tom and me. Really, I think I put it away because it seemed like it weighed a ton. Without it, my finger seemed light as a butterfly wing.

Almost without knowing it, I found myself petting Benjamin more, almost like I was his mama, and he come to me for help with the same things all children go to their mothers for help with. Tying bows and getting Melissa and Daisy out of his private play area. And sometimes he come to me for no reason he would say, but I'd know from the look on his face that he was thinking about Lucie.

God, I love this child, I would think, holding him with his head on my shoulder. And I care about his father in a way that I never cared about any man. I respect him, I trust him not to yell, not to turn ugly, to respect me and to accept Melissa as his daughter. This is the way I talked to God with my eyes on the hills, hoping the soldiers wouldn't never come. That the Greenwoods or the sheriff wouldn't come neither. That we would just be left to live out our lives in peace, with the rest of the world forgetting we ever lived.

A hundred times a day I told myself, There isn't nothing going to happen to you, not now, Liz Ann. You're finally home safe and free. But then I'd turn sudden-like, thinking I heard horses. I'd find myself staring down the empty driveway toward the road. Expecting *them* to come, whoever *they* were.

Ama found me at the window once, my face in my hands. She said, "It's natural to keep thinking you're going to lose everything, Elizabeth. You always have. But you're not going to this time. You have me now. All of us."

Even so, there were nights when I'd feel myself being shaken and I'd sit up covered with sweat and fall into Ama's arms crying that I'd been having the dream again. Did I cry out again in my sleep? She'd say yes, but not to worry, she was there. That's what she was for, to hold onto and cry whenever I needed her.

"Exactly what is this dream?" Ama asked.

"Oh, Ama, I'm dreaming about lynching parties," I confessed, shuddering to think of it because at least half the time I believed it might come true. "People showing up to lynch me. Recognizing their faces. Folks that used to come to my mama and papa's home for supper. They come for me and take me away in the back of a wagon and—and they smile while they tie a rope 'round my neck. Am I crazy as a loon?"

"Yes, you are," Ama nodded, throwing back her head to laugh. The patch of moonlight on her head was something like

168

a halo, but she looked too eerie to be an angel. Too full of mischief with her teeth bared and full of some kind of raw humor that was not exactly the kind preached in the pulpit. She looked like she knew all humanity inside and out and was laughing at it all.

"Ama," I said, "sometimes you remind me of a witch."

"I know it," she said. "I've always been something of a supernatural."

"Can you tell the future?"

"I can tell that you *have* a future. Is that what you wanted to know?"

"No," I said, stubborn as a child. "I want you to tell me what it's going to be like. Do you see me . . . do you see a husband for me? More children? Will I live here in Frisbin or somewhere else where I won't have you?" Fresh tears welled up, but Ama only smiled.

"If you want to know your future, maybe you only have to look at today," she murmured. "It seems to me there's a man looking at you. What I don't know, and you haven't given me one clue, is how you feel about him." She tipped up my chin and gave me one of her looks that searched deep. "Are you in love with Tom Higgins, honey?"

I felt my face get hot, but I didn't pull away. "I care about him, Ama. And I care about Ben."

"And do you want that for your future?"

"I think so," I whispered. "And I want the rest of the world . . . all of *them* . . . to go away."

But in the middle of June, when I'd started to let myself believe that maybe everyone had forgot about me, Sheriff Ben Oates showed up. I stared at him, my jaw dropped open, as he tramped mud inside Ama's parlor and sat on her brocade sofa wearing dirty pants, an old stained pouch strapped 'round his waist. He acted like no time had passed and seemed surprised that I was surprised to see him.

"I told you I was going back to your cabin," he said, as

Ama left the room to check on the tea tray. "Well, I did just that. Day after you come to my office. I looked 'round and all. Examined everything."

"Well, wha—" Before I could get the words out of my mouth, I caught a glimpse of Ama's face at the open parlor door. She had her eyebrows pulled down close over her eyes and she was mouthing something to me and shaking her head from side to side. Probably she was trying to tell me not to talk too much. A second later, she laid her finger over her lips and disappeared.

When I was sure she wasn't going to come back for a few minutes, I said, "Did the Greenwood brothers go to see you? They did, didn't they?"

"Why would they?" Sheriff Oates said, crossing his arms over his chest.

"Well, they—they said they would."

"You seen the Greenwoods?" he said, looking surprised.

"Right after Joe's funeral. They said they'd be goin' to your office."

The sheriff nodded. "They come in just about that time. That was right before my trip to Richmond. I'd made up my mind to enlist in the army. I knew a man there and he said there'd be no problem about my commission. I wasn't asking for nothing big. A second lieutenant, something like that. But I wasn't going to be no common foot soldier, not at my age and a lawman all these years."

Ama came in the room with the tray. Delilah was behind her carrying a pitcher of sorghum, our only sweetener. When the tray was settled and the sheriff served with tea and a small plate of food, Ama said, "How is Richmond these days?" and the look she shot at me told me she'd been listening to every word we'd said while she was out of the room. Delilah glided out, giving me a rather scared smile before she closed the door behind her.

Ben Oates took a noisy sip of tea and said, "Richmond is in the worst mess you ever saw." Wiping his lips with his thumb, he went on: "Soldiers. Congressmen. Every hospital full, or so I heard tell. And course, every woman a nurse. And the prisoners! Maybe four thousand of them holed up in the warehouses! Livin' like animals. Folks can't feed theirselves, can't feed their soldiers, how they goin' to feed four thousand Yankees? Other hand, there were hotels with plenty of good food, if you wanted to pay fancy prices. One night I ate at a place called the Oriental Saloon, paid three dollars for a plate of roast beef. Believe that? Then had to pay another dollar for potatoes—"

"Excuse me," I said, startled at the sound of my own voice. I hadn't known I was going to say a word. In fact, I'd been determined to sit there and hear everything he had to say about Cole's city, even without mentioning the only person living there who was of any interest to me. "I just—I mean, I was wondering why you're here."

Ama stirred in the chair beside me, and I dug my nails into my palms so hard it wouldn't of surprised me to see blood. It was too late, though, to keep my mouth shut. "Why," I said, kind of stammering over the words, "you aren't off bein' a soldier."

Ben Oates's face darkened and he set down his teacup so hard it rattled in the saucer. "That's what I told them in Richmond!" He glowered at first me, then Ama. "They said they don't need no *silk-glove* volunteers. You imagine that? What an insult that is to a man who's lived for the law? You ask me, a lawman's the next of kin to a soldier. Anyhow, they turned up their noses, said they wanted men to volunteer their blood and guts with no strings attached. They wasn't lookin' for officers nohow."

"What a shame," Ama said from her straight-backed chair. She'd been working in the field all morning; her hair was dirty, her face was red, and she had a summer cold. Yet, her eyes were clear. Calm. Just looking at her, I felt calmer myself. Breathed better. She went on listening while Sheriff Oates rambled on about Richmond. Half the citizens masquerading as officers, and the blacks acting so uppity with the whites, you could hardly get your boots shined anymore. As he went on talking, I let my thoughts slide toward Cole, wondering what he was

171

doing, if he was getting any cases through court. If there were any pretty belles catching his eye these days. If he ever by accident thought anything of us here at Symphony Oaks. Not of Ama—I knew he thought of her, even wrote her often about what he was trying to do for the major. But the rest of us. Beulah, Jinny, Delilah. Me.

On his second cup of tea, Ben Oates told Ama he'd made formal application for a commission and still had hopes it would come through. Meantime, there was his sheriffing. And business to take care of. Then his eyes shifted sideways, toward me.

"Anyways," he said, "the Greenwoods are raving something awful. Wanting to know what happened to Hank, you know. They seem stuck on the idea that Hank is . . ." He cleared his throat. "Well, they're suggestin' some pretty extreme things. Filled out a statement and all." He drew out some papers from the pouch strapped 'round his waist and studied them, frowning over what he read. "To be right honest with you, ladies, there's some things here I don't understand myself," he said finally.

"What are those things?" Ama asked in a crisp let's-get-down-to-it voice.

"Well," he said, "to begin with, there's the door."

"Really," Ama said with a shrug. "The door." As if to say what can a door amount to.

"Of her place," Ben Oates said, tilting his head at me. "There was a trail of dirt startin' right at her door."

A trail of dirt, I thought, seeing it in my mind. Where the Greenwoods had come busting in. And where Ama and Beulah and I had walked through the mud and in and out carrying water from the rainwater barrel out beside the cabin.

"Yet inside the bedroom," Sheriff Oates said, "there weren't no trace of dirt. Nothing. 'Ceptin' a floor scrubbed clean as a whistle. There was your husband's body on the floor, ma'am. Just like you said. Not as much blood as you'd expect, somehow."

He mused about that to hisself for a while, and I thought with my eyes on my lap, Oh, God, we cleaned up too much

172

blood and he noticed. It was spilling that bucket of water. But I couldn't say that, of course. I didn't dare look at Ama. Just forced myself to glance up now, not exactly into his eyes but at his jaw, at the brown stain on his leather pouch that looked like it might be a tobacco stain. I tried to look puzzled as if I was as much in the dark as he was.

"What I keep asking myself," he murmured, scratching his cheek, "is how a woman mops out one room neat as you please and leaves dirt and mud and such all over the rest of her house. You think of any reason, ma'am, you did that?"

My eyes flickered up at Ama and her head shook a little from side to side. Her lips said no.

"To tell you the truth," I said, "I can't think of no reason why I done such a thing. If I done such a thing."

He caught on the *if* right away. "You mean you ain't sure you left it like that? Well, let me ask you this," he said. "Do you remember scrubbin' the room? Or not?"

Ama's shoulders raised and lowered, such a movement as you make if you're tensing a tired muscle, nothing more.

"I can't remember exactly," I said. "After everything that happened, you know. Maybe I did. Maybe I got busy or something and never finished. But like I said, I don't exactly remember."

A minute passed without nobody saying a word. We were all still as Ama's china figures on her shelves. The clock ticked and a dog barked in the distance. Sunlight streamed through the wide windows.

"Somethin' else," the sheriff said. "When I got there, the floor was still wet. Water all down in the cracks 'tween the boards. You could see it there, just settin' there. Streams of it. That the way you wash a wood floor? Flood the room with water? Don't dry it or nothin'?"

"Well, you know, I have a little girl," I said without looking at Ama. "Melissa had an accident there that night. She still wears diapers, she's just now being trained. And, well, I had to mop up the floor. And while I was mopping, Melissa turned the bucket over."

173

"Aha," he said, writing it down. "You see, that helps. It helps to talk, see. Now was that close to your bed where your little girl had the accident?"

"Yes, it was," I said, feeling Ama looking at me and knowing that by inventing stories I was going against what she'd told me to do.

"Closer to your bed, that is, than the baby's crib?"

In my mind I could see Hank standing just in front of my bed with his back to Melissa. Then when she'd cried out, he'd turned and took a step or two toward her. Right then, I'd thought I was living out the last minutes of my daughter's life.

I said, "I guess it was about halfway between our bed and Melissa's crib. Where the accident happened."

"Not right next to her crib?"

"No," I said, worried about what he was getting at. "Not right next to it."

"And, of course, you already said it was on the floor. Not in her crib, nor nothin'."

Ama was right, I thought. Once you start lying, it leads to a trap. Lying is confusing. You don't know which thread is starting to unwind on you.

"It was on the floor," I said, trying to sound firm. Like I knew what I was saying. "Maybe just a little closer to her bed than ours, if I'm remembering right."

"Well"—he sighed—"looks like I'm still in the shade. You want to know somethin'?" His eyes went from my face to Ama's and back to mine again. "That little gal's crib was as wet as the floor. I felt the legs, the sides, underneath. You must of scrubbed it same as the floor."

"I just went ahead and scrubbed everything," I blundered. "That much water spilt and all."

"That so," he said, looking at his notes. "You brought in a whole bucket of water to clean up one little spot?"

"Yes."

"Ha," he said absent-like, his finger moving down the page. It stopped toward the bottom and he read for a while to himself, his mouth moving 'round the words.

Ama's face was thoughtful, but she didn't look angry at my lying, at my raising questions without really answering anything.

"This here part," the sheriff said after several minutes of reading. "When Ferris and Charlie and Cecil left but Hank stayed on. Just how long was it you say he stayed?"

This time I did look at Ama, but she made no sign. Probably, she didn't know any longer what to do, no more than me. "Maybe an hour," I said. "Or less, maybe. It's hard to say. I wasn't thinking about time."

He cleared his throat. "Yes. All right, let's look at it a different way. After Hank finally did leave you, you say one of the Greenwood brothers come back and, I should say, the Greenwoods agree with you on that. Ferris Greenwood did tell me he come back lookin' for Hank that same night. Now my question to you is, How long was it after Hank left you before Ferris showed up?"

Not knowing if there was a right or a wrong answer, I said, "Maybe another hour. Maybe a little longer."

"All right," Ben Oates said. "Now Ferris Greenwood said in his statement that when he got to your place, he found the whole place dark. Would that be right?"

"Yes, that was right," I murmured, seeing that Ama was frowning into her cup like there was a bug in there. But even if she was seeing something I didn't, I couldn't ask for her advice or nothing. She wasn't supposed to of been there that night.

Ben Oates leaned forward on the sofa, his breath heavy on the air. "You mean," he said, holding my eyes prisoner, "you stayed there in that dark house with your husband dead on the floor all that time before you come to town to tell me about it? You didn't even put no light on nor nothin'? Just sat there in the dark with the body?"

"Well," I began, seeing the spark in his eyes, "I—I don't believe I had the fuel to burn the lamp." But before I'd even finished saying it, I knew by his face that I'd made a mistake.

"There was a lamp on the chest of drawers," he said. "That thing was half full of kerosene."

175

"I forgot about it!" I snapped, wishing I could wipe that look off his face. "Everything that happened to me that night, I didn't remember I had the kerosene."

"Though all three Greenwoods said the lamp was burnin' the whole time they were there."

I felt the blood drain out of my face and knew I must be sheet white.

"It's just powerful strange," the sheriff said in a soft way, almost smiling to himself, "the way it all happened. For instance, the way you waited all that time in your house 'fore you came to town to see me. No matter how hard I try, I just can't understand it."

Through the swirling mist in my brain, I heard Ama's voice, saw her get to her feet and the sheriff stand, too. "Do you understand four men killing one man in cold blood?" she was saying. "Do you understand three men *watching* while their brother outrages the widow of the man they shot? Do you understand the one man who stays because he wants to heap more outrage on the poor woman whose husband lies dead on the floor?" One of her hands were a fist and she was clenching it with the other, as if to keep herself from attacking the sheriff, while he mumbled something about acts of war.

"Acts of war," Ama repeated, her voice shaking from the rage she was holding inside.

"You'll never be able to understand any of this," Ben Oates said, "unless you understand that the war's a part of what happened."

"Then I'll never understand it," Ama said, her finger pointing him toward the door. "I want you out of my house," she said in the low, just bare controlled voice she'd been using. "And I don't want you to come back here for any reason. Not for *any* reason!"

Ben Oates looked down to where I still sat on my chair, my hands locked together over my knee, my knuckles white.

"I'm goin'," he said. "But I can't swear I won't be back."

It was Ama's hand under my elbow that lifted me, that give me the strength to see the sheriff out the door, to stand beside her watching him ride off on his horse without once looking back at us. Instead, his eyes were looking everywhere over the ground.

"Is he looking for something?" Ama hissed.

"Oh, yes," I nodded. I felt a grim smile curve my lips as Ama turned to look at me.

"What the hell is it?" she demanded.

I laughed and the sound was as hollow as if my voice were in the bottom of a barrel.

"Don't you know?" I said, watching him look left and right. "He's looking for Hank's grave."

Sixteen

Here are some of the things I wondered after the sheriff left Symphony Oaks that day. If what the Greenwoods done to Joe and me was just part of the war, then why wasn't what I done to them part of the war? How could people seem so sure of what were right and wrong, when I never could be certain of it myself? After the war, how could North and South ever be one nation again, with all the hate that divided us?

I kept asking myself these questions over and over again, but I knew there were no true answers, not for me anyway. Not at night, when I was doing most of my wondering. Not in the mornings, either, when a thick wet fog rolled in on us, hiding the mountains and carrying the sound of fighting. It was really as if the shooting was right on top of us. We'd get up, one by one, and find each other standing at the windows and sometimes at an open door. Just standing there in all that white fog, straining to hear, wondering if soon we'd be able to hear the famous bloodcurdling rebel yell, that half-human scream that would mean the war had sneaked down out of the mountains at last and come into our own hometown. And when the wind was just right some kind of echo blew over the whole valley, where one shot sounded like fifty and fifty sounded like ten thousand.

Standing side by side with Delilah at the kitchen door, the two of us listening to that evil echo, I said, "I doubt with all that's happening that I'll ever live to be lynched."

"That a big comfort," Delilah said, never batting an eye.

On June twenty-fourth, the rains began to fall. Not the gentle steady rains that would of helped our crops grow in the fields, but a fierce pelting downpour that poked holes in the ground and washed everything away, all the corn, all the squash, the lettuces, the radishes, everything we'd worked so hard to put in. Everything was mud, and the back field that Tom had worked from dawn till dusk, plowing it, planting it with corn, was nothing but a muddy river. He waded down there to check on it and came back to say he'd found a slew of new cornstalks floating there, and as many snakes as corn.

Day after day, the rain kept up and we sat inside the house and talked about how we'd have to ration our food even more than we were already doing. Soon we'd be living like the soldiers. Old Man Higgins, who was used to busting into the house now, looking for Tom, and who was getting crazier by the hour, complained as much about Yankees and niggers as about the rain, until we all felt we'd go crazy ourselves just listening to him. But for Tom's sake and also out of politeness for his father's age, we kept our patience and told ourselves at least we had a roof over our heads—and, thanks to Tom's hard work and good sense, enough firewood in the cellar to keep a roaring fire burning in the parlor and in several other rooms as well, so that the damp was at least part ways burnt out of our house.

"Anyhow, how long can it rain?" Jinny said. "Y'all don't think we got no Noah flood goin'? Mayhap, though. I ain't never see nothin' like this here. Rain never stop for nothin'. Look, there go the clothesline."

The smell of cedar and pine drifted through the house and the fires kept our home dry and warm. But the rain kept on coming and coming and the thunder rolled and the lightning cracked until the children screamed and even Ben took to hanging 'round Delilah and me, putting his head in our laps when the sky was screaming the loudest.

And still the sound of fighting, cannon now, carried on the wet air, like muffled thunder, so much of it that Delilah said she felt like killing somebody, she so restless to find out what was going on.

On the fourth day of the rains, it slacked some, and Tom braved the road to town to bring back papers and news from the new telegraph office that had been built because of the war. He said that his horse had to wade through water and mud up to his chest, that the roads had turned to streams, and that he'd found two farmers stuck in a wagon, trying to get to town too.

Though he come home soaked and cold and muddy, he rubbed his horse down and bedded him before he come back from his barn, his father close on his coattails, to say he'd heard some news in town. "The man at the telegraph office said he'd got word the Federal Army of the Cumberlands is on the march. Already left Murfreesboro. Probably headed toward Shelbyville."

Several of us had met Tom at the door. Almost pulling him into the parlor, him trying to dry himself, us pelting him with questions. Water seemed to spring from him like a fine spray as Delilah run to hang up his coat and Jinny come rushing out with several thick towels. I got the kettle going for tea, and flew back from the kitchen, desperate for every scrap of news.

Ama said, "Let me see the *Review,* Tom. Jinny, get my spectacles." The fire jumped up, sparks popped, flew and landed on the floor. Old Man Higgins stumped them out like he was killing snakes.

"All hell's broken loose now," Ama said, staring through her thick lenses at the front page of *DeBow's Review.*

"What is it?" I said. "Ama, read it!" And a hush settled over the room, with the only sounds being the rain drumming down and Ama's voice, raised some to carry over the storm.

The papers Tom brought were new ones and gave enough details to make us even more anxious than we already were. Fierce fighting at Liberty Gap with Major General Cleburne mixed up in it, the man the *Review* called the best leader in the Southern army. The Yanks had finally got Cleburne's men out of Liberty Gap by just clawing their way up the mountain and flanking him on both sides of the pass. Even more devastating, the article said, was Wilder's brigade's attack down the main road toward Hoover's Gap.

"Cavalry?" Beulah asked, her lips clamped together so tight they were white round the edges. She alone had never talked war, or for that matter, much else during these last days of rain, but we knew she was worried for Henry. She hadn't heard from him in months. Either he hadn't been able to find a soldier to write a letter for him or he was injured or dead.

Tom nodded, frowning toward the hallway where Ben and Daisy and Melissa were hanging onto the open door, trying to understand what we were saying.

"Go get my tobacco pouch, Ben, honey," he said in a gentle voice. "I left it on the table in the kitchen. It's all right. Go on now." When all three of our children had left to find the pouch, he closed the door behind them and said, "They said that Wilder's men galloped through the pass. Rain and all. Never slowed down. Raged through the pass. Spearheaded by the Seventy-second Indiana," he muttered, this last part for hisself, as regiments didn't mean nothing to us women. Still, we could imagine Wilder's men charging through the pass, could almost hear their horses' hooves as the Lightning Brigade, as they'd come to be called, ran through bullets and rebel war cries and mountain mud slides to claim Hoover's Gap as their own.

"Them goddamned Yankees," Old Man Higgins groaned, jumping to his feet again and walking wild-like up and down, up and down, pounding his fist against his other hand.

"Here it is, Papa," Ben said, coming through the door with Daisy and Melissa trailing him and Tom's tobacco pouch in his hand. Looking at the three of them, we were struck dumb and couldn't say another word about war until later, when they were in their beds.

Only Old Man Higgins kept walking and muttering, saying things like "Damned Yanks" and "Goddamn the rain" and how he'd like to go out there and take on the murdering cusses with his bare hands.

Like in a dream, I saw Jinny with Daisy and Melissa crowded together in her lap. Delilah with her head down and Tom's hand on her shoulder. Beulah sitting off to one side.

Later, after Jinny tiptoed back from the children to say they were all three sound asleep, Ama and Tom took turns reading aloud. Fighting in Manchester. The Confederates had left Shelbyville and fallen back to Elk River. Closer. Much closer than we'd believed. And the *Southern Illustrated News* actually wrote "The southern army has been driven out of Middle Tennessee. Bragg is surely heading toward Chattanooga."

We sat there wringing our hands and saying "Chattanooga" to each other. Chattanooga was home. All of a sudden Beulah put her face in her hands. Ama went and knelt down in front of her and murmured something so quiet none of us could hear, but we could hear Beulah's choked voice rambling on as she let Ama stroke her arm, put her fingers through her hair.

"Maybe he cookin' for one them regiment up there in them hill. Maybe he dead. Sick. Maybe he just feel like he dead. Fightin' all 'round him, maybe. Bein' treat like a dog." For we'd heard that the blacks was treated scandalous up in the Northern army camps, much worse than in the Southern camps.

Beulah raised her head sudden-like from her hands, looked at all of us and said like she was choking on hate, strangling on it, "I wonder why my Henry serve any side. They won't let him fight like a man, he got to go cook for the white. Even this here war that suppose to be 'bout slave. It all 'bout one white man fightin' another white man. One man try to say what he gon' do. Other man say no. First man say he use a whip if he want. Second man say a whip no good. Only allow to yell the black man in line, spit on him. Nothin' else ain't moral."

After a while, she got up and went to her room. She'd never been more separated from us, more withdrawed into herself, even from Delilah who adored her like a mama.

We sat there staring at each other. Delilah said after a while, "She say I like the white too much. Say me and Jinny both. Say Jinny just fawn all over 'em. Make her sick."

Jinny said, "She don't like nobody no more. That her trouble. Hate black and white. Everybody make her sick."

"I like that," Old Man Higgins growled from his corner by the fire. "White people making the black sick. Hah!"

"Be quiet, Father," Tom said.

"Maybe," Ama said in a slow thoughtful way, "maybe Beulah's right to be sick. Henry's up north, isn't he? Why *isn't* he fighting for the Federals, instead of cooking for them? Why aren't there more black soldiers, if the North is fighting for the rights of black people? Why are the few black soldiers confined to black regiments? No, this isn't right. Maybe we all have to look at ourselves."

"Not you, Ama," I said.

"Oh, yes," she said. "Maybe someplace deep inside me, hidden away so fiercely that I can't even see it myself, I have tolerated slavery. Not the whip. But perhaps I have tolerated the *benevolent* slaveholder. I have actually called them that! Benevolent. They walk around smiling. Treat the blacks like their children. Throw a blanket on the floor of a woman's slave cabin so she won't freeze, but no bed. No pillow. The kind that scolds with a frown rather than a lashing. Will never permit starvation on *his* plantation. So he hands out an extra sack of meal, the guts of the hogs and the cows, rather than throw them to the dogs. No fruit. No sweet cakes. Yes, I'm afraid I have a terrible something hidden away somewhere in me. Me in my big house, wearing my pretty dresses and my swishy petticoats and calling myself benefactress. Me, with my husband on the wrong side of this damned war!"

Old Man Higgins couldn't listen to such words—he'd tried to interrupt, then stomped out when Ama kept talking. But Tom was shaking his head.

"What about me?" he was saying, casting his eyes over to where Jinny and Delilah sat together, their hands clasped in their laps, heads bowed. "I wore a Confederate uniform—do you know why? Because my father couldn't have stood it if I were with the Federals. I told myself there was morality in that.

Honoring the beliefs of your parents, no matter how wrong you might believe them to be in your own heart. Thank God I took the bullet that day at Manassas, not the boy who shot me. And thank God, the infection took me out of action." He looked at Delilah. At Jinny. "If I hadn't been due to get out, I believe I'd have deserted," he said earnest-like, begging to be believed, and when he finished talking there was a dead weight of silence in the room.

Ama was the quietest of us all, sitting very still in her chair, her knitting balled up in her lap, twisting her rings on her fingers, her eyes looking into space as if she could see Major Hadley riding his horse toward the house. Then all of a sudden she stopped twisting and started really seeing her rings, then took them off.

"Darn it, I should have buried my rings with the rest," she said. "Sentiment or no. And God knows what else I should have put under the ground. Well, we'll just have to go through the house again. Tom, go through your place, too. Will Ben let you have the daguerrotype of Lucie? I know he keeps it beside his bed, but the frame is valuable. Oh, hell, maybe you can take it out of the frame, even if it is a sentiment. Lucie's hair inside and all. We've got to find some good hiding places for our jewelry and our money. What do you think? The well?"

"Everbody gon' stick everthin' they got down the well," Jinny said. "Me, I go straight for the pump if I a thievin' soldier."

Delilah said, "What 'bout we sew things in the hem of our dress or underneath our clothe?"

Both Ama and Jinny said that wouldn't work, because if we was to walk 'round too much, the dresses were sure to bounce funny, even if they didn't already hang crooked, which they likely would. And nobody was in the mood to dig holes in the swamp our land had turned into—half river, half mud that sucked like quicksand.

It was Tom who finally came up with the idea of tying everything up in the trees. Not necessarily the ones closest to the house, more like the trees 'round the creek. The pines on the thickest tree-grown acres where the land had never been farmed and where the trees were left untended for years to grow tall as they wanted.

After seventeen days, the rain finally quit falling. At dawn the next day, Delilah and Beulah and I followed Tom over the fields, dragging ourselves through acre after acre of water and mud, legs wore out from pulling our feet out of the soft sticky earth, and weighted down with silverware and jewelry and money and the like. I lost a shoe; Delilah lost both shoes. Only Beulah had the sense to walk barefooted through the cold wet mud, silent as she always was now, head down as she followed Tom's deep footsteps that he made in his long boots.

But when Delilah fell down, Beulah threw her a glance, like she was ready to go over and jerk her up by the hair, and said, "I don't know how old I be. Never had no chance to know my own age. Nor you all age neither. But I sure as hell 'bout ten year older than you, gal. And if'n I can drag myself 'round, I guess you can drag yourself 'round, too."

Though Beulah hadn't even bothered looking at me, I threw away the one shoe I had on and used both hands to haul Delilah out of the mud, and we waded on together behind Beulah, holding onto each other and shivering until we reached the muddiest acreage of all, a dark brown river of a place almost a mile from the house. Then us three women had to stand there in water up to our knees while Tom climbed trees and sent down a basket on a rope for us to fill with what we'd brought. While he was up there, hiding things, I tried best as I could to write down where every tree was that we hid things in, and everything we'd put in each place. When we was finished, Tom had put things in eight trees and in twenty-six places in those eight trees, including birds' nests and squirrel holes and just tying bunches of valuables onto tree branches with the twine he'd brought along.

When we got back home, we were all drenched to the skin

and freezing with a kind of chill that I couldn't get out of me all night, no matter how close to the fire I sat. My hands shook and I jabbed a needle into my thumb when I tried to sew. I thought, *The soldiers are coming any time. They're really coming.*

Seventeen

The waiting went on day after day, week after week, even though we kept getting word of battle up in our hills, heard them fighting up there, shell enough to kill God knew how many. Fighting in Gettysburg and Port Hudson, too, closing off the Mississippi and cutting off another Southern supply route. But though our vegetables were all washed out of the ground and the firewood had gave out a week before, and though our house had finally got the damp moldy smell of water, our town was left to itself, while we strained our ears for the sound of guns or cannons in our own streets.

Ama explored the sorry state of our fields and came back to say, "This is it. Our supplies are almost gone and our crops are destroyed. We're finally going to feel the hunger of war poverty." She went 'round making lists of what we had and what we could eat and making charts of how long it would take us to get to the point of true hunger if we had to use only what we had and couldn't get more supplies. Day followed day in an aimless vague sort of way, like time was drifting in a still river.

In mid-August I found myself alone in the yard, out taking clothes off the line on a late, hot afternoon. It was the kind of heavy day that seems to sink into layers 'round you, pulling you down same as if you was walking in mud up to your ankles, bringing the sweat to your brow and making you do everything in slow motion. I was pulling a sheet off the line and looking down to see how many other sheets there were, for sheets was the thing I hated most to fold, when all of a sudden a man's hands reached up and took the sheet beside the one I was pulling on, and when I looked 'round, Tom Higgins was standing beside me. Not looking at me, just helping with the work.

Something about him being there, something about the way he wasn't looking at me, something about the serious look on his face told me this was it. Tom was really going to ask me to marry him. In something like a panic, I realized I still didn't know what I was going to say. I should of knowed. It had been plain in his eyes that someday he might ask me. Lord, I should of had an answer ready. But shouldn't I just *know* what to say? Without trying to figure it out? But I didn't. I hadn't never been so sure of anything as I was sure I didn't know at all what I wanted to do.

Marry Tom? I thought, working on my sheet. Be a mother to Ben? That part I knew I'd like. But get married again? Even with waiting for the Greenwoods to come, waiting for the sheriff and the soldiers, there was a kind of freedom in not having a husband. Not having to answer to anybody, not having a man use your body whenever he wanted his man pleasure.

"Elizabeth," Tom said, facing me, and all at once he was smiling. His eyes shone like glass, the sun lighting them up, and everything in his face was gentle. Caring.

"Oh, Tom," I said, wishing I could make him stop. Because I still didn't know what to do, what to say, and if he asked me and I said the wrong thing, everything would change between us and I didn't want nothing to change.

But Tom shook his head at me a little, his lips smiling some as if to say, Relax. I don't mean you no harm. And as I took a deep breath and let it out, I knew that I was going to say yes. That I really was going to live at Freeland Farm and be wife to Tom and mother to Ben and that my life would unfold in a way that would make beautiful sense.

"You're like family to me, Elizabeth," Tom said, and reached out to put his hand on my shoulder. "I like everything I know about you. I know that you'd make a wonderful mother to my son and a life companion to me. We'd get along, we'd be there to get each other through the hard times, and I promise you, I'll do everything in my power to see that you're happy. I'm not a man who loses his temper much, as I hope you've noticed by now. I'm not a drinking man. And my family means everything to me. If you marry me, your daughter will be my daughter just as much as my son will be your son. If I die early, as enough doctors have told me I may, you'll have enough money to take care of you and the children. If I surprise them and live to a ripe old age, as I believe I may, I'll see that you never want for anything." He never took his eyes off me. He was like a man taking an oath or something, that's how solemn he were. And so calm that I felt all my fears grow quiet and slide away. And when he finished by saying, "I believe that we see life the same way, Elizabeth, and I know that we love the same people," it seemed to me that he had chose the exact right words to make me realize how destined for each other we really were, and when he finally said the words "Will you?" it wasn't no effort at all to say I'd be glad and proud to.

After that he said how very happy I'd made him, and it was that simple. We went on folding clothes; he never mentioned it again except to say that he'd make some quiet arrangements in the fall if that was all right.

Maybe there was something triumphant in the way I walked back to the house with Tom carrying the two full baskets of clothes as if they were nothing. I felt like shouting, *Look at me. I've got myself the best man in the whole world. I'm going to live in a big house, people in Frisbin are going to have to respect me, after all, even if it sticks in their gullets. I'm going to be somebody. I'm going to be Tom's wife!* But I didn't say nothing, just took a basket from Tom at the door and went to the kitchen table and started to stack clothes. Tom laid the other basket beside the first and went out without a word, but Delilah turned to face me, a mixing spoon in her hand, her face curious blank.

"He ask you, didn't he?" she said.

"Well, he . . . Oh, Delilah, he . . ."

"So he did ask you," she said. "That nice for you, Lizbeth. That real nice." She smiled then, a glad smile, and opened her arms to hug me. I felt the mixing spoon at my back. "I real happy for you, you got yourself a man like Tom," she said. "I real happy for you." And when she pulled away, she had tears in her eyes and she was smiling. "You be a real lady now, live in a house like that there," she said, dabbing the tears away. "You ain't forgettin' me now?"

"Forget you?" I said. "Oh, don't you understand? That's what the whole marriage is all about. It's so I'll never have to go away from any of you. We can go on just as we are, only I'll be in another house just up the way. And Melissa will have a father and I'll have a husband who respects me and won't yell at me."

She was staring hard at me, her eyes puzzled. "And you love him somethin' fierce, too?"

"I love him like my own family," I said, firm-like.

"Like *family*?" she said.

"Don't look like that," I told her, wishing she could see inside me and realize just how sure I was I was doing the right thing. "That's the best way to love your husband. Believe me. I know what I'm doing, Delilah."

"I not so sure you do." She frowned at me. "Here I think you desperate in love with the man . . ."

"Everybody's not like you and Sinclair, Delilah."

She sighed. "Sinclair."

All at once I wondered how long it had been, anyhow, since I heard Delilah mention Sinclair. I couldn't even remember the last time.

"You may be right 'bout this lovin' thing," she said. "It may be that love better when it ain't so desperate. Anyhow, Sinclair gone. Never hear nothin'. He ain't never comin' for me. It like that part of me dead. Never think 'bout him no more. He a healthy young man. By this time, he got a woman. Don't make no difference to me now. Only thing is," she said, her face clouded, "who gon' love me? I young, too. Who gon' love me?"

I studied on her face for a minute, then I said, "You remem-

190

ber when I first come back to Symphony Oaks, Delilah? What you said? When I was sleepin' that first day and I woke up and you was sittin' on my bed . . . what you told me?"

"Oh, yeah," she said in a minute.

"Did you mean it?" I near whispered. I'd been thinking about it ever since, but this was the first time I'd ever mentioned it. I'd thought she'd bring it up, thought we'd talk about the man who'd had her, same as the man who'd raped me, but she'd never said a word about it.

"Yeah," she said. "It happen to me. I use to say it didn't. Pretend it never did. Act like I were pure. Yeah, I even told Sinclair that. Told him I fight all them white men off. He so proud of me."

"You never had to pretend with us," I said. "Not with me and Ama and Jinny. Not Beulah either. Beulah loves you, Delilah."

She was quiet and her eyes were wet. "I were lyin' to everbody, Lizbeth. To me, too. Try so hard to make like all that stuff were a dream, all that bad stuff. I guess that it. And all my talk and jabber 'bout how pure I were and how it all happen to everybody else but me—I guess I just try to make *that* the real stuff. Like by sayin' it, I make it so. Change the past and all. Just bein' a fool."

We were nothing but girls, Delilah and me. Right now, looking into her eyes that were like planets I never been on, I felt like we both could be old women. Her without a man. Me lucky enough to find a husband who wasn't going to be no problem to me. I took hold of Delilah's hands and pulled her down into a kitchen chair, then sat beside her, pulling my chair until it touched hers.

"Delilah?" I whispered, since I'd gone this far and had a feeling she was waiting to say the rest, *wanting* to say it, like she was casting a weight out of her heart, a weight that had laid there a very long time. "You know those babies you said some of the black girls had? Some half white, half black?"

She looked at me with those eyes. "I had a little pale-like babe. Boy. Then a baby gal. Kept them 'bout twenty minutes

191

each maybe. Boy were first. I never know they take him from me. I think they take him to show him off, that how dumb I were. Laid there, expectin' they bring him back any second. I—I just couldn't believe they do somethin' like take a new babe from his mama. Gal come, I knew what would happen. Couldn't do nothin', just cry, try to hold onto her. They come, friends of the missus. Weren't there for the birthin'. Just come after for the babe. Claw open my arms. I told them, Why don't you take my heart out? Take my guts out? They just take my babe, though."

"They must of took good care of them, though," I said. "They wouldn't . . ."

"No," she said. "They wouldn't kill 'em. They property. Worth money. Don't matter their pa livin' at the big house. They just property."

I said, "No, wherever they are, they aren't property. They're flesh and blood. They breathe in the air. They breathe in God, just like me and you."

She nodded. "That help some to think that. Help when it warm. When it warm, I know they ain't layin' on some dirt floor freezin'. I hate winter. Hate cold rain and all. Hate to think they hungry," she said, her voice breaking.

For a while, we held each other and cried. But we went on. No choice but live or die.

Later that day, staring out over the pitiful rain-soaked fields, Ama gathered us together and insisted we try draining the soil best we could and replant what seed we had, though it was the middle of the summer. So for a week, we reploved the earth and the next week we put in every seed we had left in our cellar. One cup of seed corn was all we had left, this shook out of used bags that were stored in a barrel. A few grains in one, a few more in another. As I sowed the row, being careful as I could, I never noticed that one of Ama's three hens, all bought off a woman who'd broke up housekeeping and moved to Mississippi, were following along behind me, eating every kernel, till Jinny looked up from where she was trying to tie wilted beans to a line and screamed, "Stop, you nasty ole bird!" And before I knew what she was up to, Jinny got to her feet, flew after that hen, and wrung her neck without another word. Then, calm as you please, she fished every kernel from the hen's craw and sowed them right back in the earth. The hen was our first meat for weeks. She was scrawny but delicious and not a pick was left on her bones.

But with all the draining and replanting, hardly a thing come up in the fields. All of us were hungry, Old Man Higgins—I supposed I'd be calling him Father Higgins soon—being hungriest of all, to listen to him. He was a thin old thing, sort of like the hen, and his stomach did growl something awful when he'd show up mealtimes and Beulah would set his plate on the table with a little dab of this and a little dab of something else.

By now, it was like Beulah was gone. She never sang 'round the house no more. She cooked in big pots with lids on them, peeking in like it was a secret what she be cooking. Counted out peas, one, two, three when she served them, us all looking at her. To me, it seemed like her plate had more peas on it, more potatoes, than the rest of ours. And we'd all seen her tasting while she cooked. In the old days when there was plenty, no one minded, but every spoonful meant something now. Even Ama studied Beulah's plate some, and Delilah did too, both frowning a little, but nobody said nothing.

Tom, as the one who did the hardest work, had more on his plate too, Ama saw to that, and when he tried to share, nobody would take so much as a taste. His father would of, but every time that came up, Ama would quick put a little extra on Old Man Higgins's plate, saying that Tom needed his food, every spoonful of it that could be spared, else how could he do the work that had to be done if we were all to survive? The one of us women who grumbled most were Jinny. She said a woman her size had to have more food or die, and when she'd say that, Beulah would give her a spoon more peas, a dab more potatoes. Something else. When Beulah gave the children cornpone spread

193

with sorghum, Daisy's piece of pone was bigger even than Ben's, though he were years older, and Daisy's had a gob of syrup, while Melissa's and Ben's pone were spare on syrup.

"Syrup!" Melissa said, holding up her pone, expecting Beulah to spread some on, like she'd done before.

"Ain't no more," Beulah said, without even looking at her. "Everbody get the same. Anyhow, I the cook, wait on everbody like always. My chile get a treat sometime same as the white."

This last to all of us, and my heart seemed to fall inside me. Beulah was so mad all the time, it was like she hated everybody, even Delilah who she used to dote on so, comb her hair and all. She didn't comb her hair now. Didn't even glance at her most of the time, nor at nobody else but Daisy. It was like she was trying to keep her and Daisy in a separate world from the rest of us, a private world for just them two. But Daisy didn't want no part of that world, and when Beulah would pick her up and try to carry her away from Melissa and Ben, try to shut her up in the bedroom with her, Daisy cried and screamed until she had to give in.

Nothing's the same, I'd think in the evenings, watching Ama work at her desk and Delilah sit staring out the window like any minute she'd jump up and start down the driveway toward the main road. She told me she was thinking about moving up north, where she had an uncle, but his family were poor, eating less than when they were all slaves down in Georgia. She didn't want to take food out of no one's mouth for no reason—but still, what to do? Time was come she ought to be moving on, maybe. On account there weren't no black men 'round for her to get interested in or to get interested in her and she had to get somebody whiles she was still young, it was either that or live the rest of her life alone. Without a husband, without a child to raise, what was the use of going on living? She said if she still had her babies, then maybe she wouldn't care so much about it, but since she didn't, she couldn't quit thinking about leaving.

Tom spent half the day working our fields, repairing our house, our leaks, our clogged-up rain gutter, and the other half of the day working over at Freeland Farm, so I hardly saw him except at supper. He was too tired now to sit in the chair that Cole had once sat in, too tired to read the books about places I'd never heard of. Too tired even to play much when Benjamin pulled on him and tried to start a game.

And the talk was *Anytime now, the soldiers will be coming.* And with everybody in Frisbin saying that Chattanooga would be the next battle, the ladies started having sewing and knitting benefits for the soldiers over at Mrs. Reverend Harper's house. The soldiers were running out of everything. No gloves. No socks. Shirts and pants like rags. They needed Ama's wool and her thread, so Mrs. Reverend Harper stopped by in person with an invitation. After she left, heaving her stout self up into her buckboard and flicking her switch over her mare's neck, Ama found me raking over the ruins of our garden, and said she'd been thinking about the sewing benefit and we ought to go.

"Go sew for the rebels?" I said, raising my eyebrows at her.

"I've already told the reverend's wife that everything we make is to go to the Hess family. Mrs. Hess has seven children, all of them in rags and barefoot, and her husband killed at Vicksburg."

"Oh, no, not me," I said. "I can't go to any kind of a town social."

"Why not?" Ama asked. "Are you afraid you'd be unpopular?" She threw her head back and laughed.

I frowned at her. "Is there any doubt?"

"None at all," she agreed, still chuckling a little. "But then do you think the popular people are the only ones that go places? It wouldn't be a society if it weren't made up of everybody."

So I ended up at the sewing benefit sitting on a hard wood chair, without a cushion, wedged between Jinny and Delilah in their wood chairs who looked as uneasy as me. I thought, I'll sit, but I won't talk! Jinny and Delilah just sat, too, their needles flying, their eyes fixed on their work.

For the first half hour I looked up every time the door opened, expecting to see Mama and the girls walk in. Half of me wanted to see them and half of me was afraid. Maybe they'd see me and just turn 'round and walk back out the door. But maybe, just maybe, Mama might walk over to me with tears in her eyes and say, "People make mistakes, Liz Ann. I was wrong." I was ready to forgive her. I was even ready to forgive Jessie Lee.

Bertha Long caught me looking and said, "If you're looking for your ma, don't. Her and your sisters never see the light of day, much less go out at night. I never thought I'd live to see Carolyn Allen living like that. That dark cold house. They're living like hermits."

"I'm sorry to hear that," I said. After that, I quit looking and paid attention to my sewing. And after a while, I even got interested in the news of the war. Naturally, most of the talk was about Vicksburg, on account nobody had expected it to fall after the way the Confederates had held through the terrible Vicksburg siege of '62. But this time, after forty-seven days of new Yankee attacks, being low on food and outnumbered and the city half gone under enemy shell, General Pemberton had surrendered the city to Grant.

"My boy said Pemberton had no reason to surrender," Bertha Long said with some pepper in her voice. "He said all the troops were mad enough to lynch him."

"Oh, to a man." Gillian Brian nodded. "And they all said they'd never serve under him again, that miserable man, though they was to be lined up against a wall and shot for their refusal. My husband included."

"Let's hope it doesn't come to that," Ama said in a dry voice that sliced through all the little murmurings in the room and silenced everybody for a few minutes.

In the quiet, little Jessica Long's high, childlike voice rose to ask, "Is it true, Cousin Gillian, that the Vicksburg soldiers all ate mule meat?" Gillian blushed at the question, but Jessica was only thirteen and more interested in knowing the truth of that shocking rumor than in standing on propriety.

"Of course, they did, everybody knows they did, those gallant men," Mrs. Reverend Harper said real calm-like, sounding like it was a Christian honor to exist on mule meat, if for the Cause, and Gillian relaxed some.

"Talk about disgrace," Martha Lewis said, "what about all of Vicksburg taking the oath of allegiance to the Union?"

A murmur of "Terrible" and "Oh, the shame of it" went across the room, heads wagging, needles busy.

"Although," Gillian said, "there were one of the city merchants that my Walter personally knew that *wouldn't* take the oath. Walter said it cost him his whole store of goods, but it was a glorious moment anyhow. A German man. *Jewish*," she added, her lips mouthing the last word.

"How much did the poor man lose?" Mrs. Reverend Harper asked, her eyes sparkling with interest.

"Walter said he guessed twenty thousand dollars, can you imagine?"

There was a sigh that went over the whole room just hearing about twenty thousand dollars, more money than any of us would ever see. But I noticed a few smiles, too. Seemed a heap easier for poor folks to hear that somebody had lost twenty thousand, rather than earned it.

Truth to tell, the ladies at the sewing didn't seem all that friendly to each other. In fact, all the time they'd been knitting and sewing together, they were having little flare-ups. Most of them were about conscription and desertion and it all went on between those women whose husbands and sons were serving in the Confederate army and those women whose men either hadn't showed up to honor their conscription summons, or who had got fed up and deserted the army before their time was up.

"Now just a minute!" Esther Wells snapped out, throwing her knitting needles on the table in front of her. Her stomach was full of her newest child and the rest of her body looked as large as her stomach, down to her chins, all wobbling with snake venom. "My Ed ain't been well!" she howled. "And his pa is dyin', as everybody in this room knows full well, and there just ain't no way he can serve now, though he has every intention of servin' at some future date."

" 'Some future date,' " stout little Josephine Steedman sniggered, and other ladies in the room laughed, too.

"That sounds like something out of some highfalutin lawyer letter." Gillian sniffed. "Is that what your Ed wrote back to General Robert E. Lee? 'Maybe, if you're still fightin' in 1870 or so—' "

"I'm not going to stand for this insultin'!" Esther screamed. By now she was so mad, looked like she was going to pop her bodice. Maybe start having her baby right there on the spot.

In something like a second, half the room was screaming at each other. Good Lord, I thought, were these the people I'd been afraid to face? Look at the silly hens. Just look at them!

"Just a minute!" A voice rose up, cutting through the hubbub like a thin sharp knife. It took me a minute to realize it was Ama, who hadn't stirred from her seat next to the quilting group.

"If you've been reading the papers, and I assume you have," she said when everyone calmed down, "or if you've been talking to your neighbors, and I assume you have, you must know that conscription is a very unpopular law and it's practically the exception to honor it. Especially in an area like ours that hasn't much to win from the war. We're a poor area, we don't own many slaves, we keep to ourselves and always have. Most of you don't hate the Yankees as soldiers. You and your mothers and fathers and *their* mothers and fathers have *always* more or less disliked Northerners in general. As *people,* not soldiers. New Englanders, in particular."

"Soldiers, people, they're all the same," snapped Mary Brian, Gillian's sister-in-law.

All over the room, women agreed with her.

"Yes, I know," Ama said, her voice once again raising above the babble. "But do you really love the big planter who's ordering you into war while he sits at home on his plantation, fully protected by the twenty-slave law? And how do you feel about the rich hiring the poor to take their place in the service? I imagine there are those in this room who have husbands earning salaries by serving in the ranks for rich men who can afford to stay home with their families."

At this last, Esther Wells turned to her left and said, while staring accusing-like at Camilla Johnson, "We all know those kinds of soldiers for hire, don't we?"

Before Camilla could fire anything back, Ama said, "Why, this war isn't even popular in the deep South, let alone here in Tennessee, which is at best a border state. Half of our people didn't even want to secede. North Tennessee is hardcore Federal. Just what the devil is there about this almighty Cause that makes everyone in this room so patriotic?"

"But the war *is* about states' rights," Mary Brian said, with her square jaw set. "We've the right to govern ourselves if we want."

"Do you like the way Jefferson Davis is governing you now?" somebody asked in such a confident way that I was shocked to realize it was me that said it. Then I was horrified, because almost as a room they turned on me. I was at least someone they knew they hated. I was the Yankee they were fighting, and they could understand what they felt for me better than why they went to war in the first place.

Ama stood up and faced the room with her arms folded across her breast. "What about slavery?" she said.

"The war ain't about slavery, not *just* about slavery, anyhow, though the Yankees are screaming to the world it is," Mrs. Reverend Harper said, trying to tidy her long white hair, which had come loose from her hairpins and were straggling down both sides of her face. "It's about states' rights, like Mary said," she went on, her face flush, fist to her chest hard enough to make you remember that a year ago she'd had months of indigestion and bad pains right where she was pressing.

"Everything I read is slavery," Ama said, but in a gentler voice. "What right do you suppose the Southern states cherish the most but the right of human bondage? Without it, the cotton yield certainly wouldn't be doubling every year. Why else does the Southerner feel so adamant about being allowed to bring his slaves to California? Oh, believe me, this war is most certainly about slavery, no matter what other words are being bandied about."

"If I can take my horse to New Mexico or California, why can't I take my slave?" Josephine Steedman demanded.

"*What* slave?" Ama blasted back. "In the name of God, this poor town doesn't own forty slaves put together. That is, of course, if you eliminate the ones Sam Cook closed up like chickens in a coop, poor souls, and the ones Adrian Higgins owned before they ran off. But most of you in this room never owned more than a couple of slaves in your life, some of you not even one! In a town like this, why would you even care about the right to own slaves? You *don't* care about it in the feeling parts of yourselves. You've just been fed a pack of lies so that you *think* you're for slavery, just as you've been told you're better than black people because of the color of your skin. So help me, patriotism is beginning to sound imbecilic! If you ask me, the big planter has got you all buffaloed!"

All this with the women cutting their eyes at Delilah and Jinny. Probably hating that Delilah was the prettiest woman in the room. Probably forgetting that Jinny was next thing to a saint.

In the end we marched out of there with our heads held high, Ama and Jinny armed with baskets of wool and thread and behind us a slew of women screaming as much at each other as at us.

"So much for society," Ama said back in the carriage, with all four of us collapsed against each other and laughing until we cried.

When she could talk, Jinny wiped her cheeks with her fist and said, "Miz Ama, you could make a cat laugh."

"I wonder how they're going to feel when the war comes to Frisbin," Ama said, wiping her eyes, then finally picking up the reins. "Then we'll see who's willing to pay the price of being a patriot."

We didn't have long to wait.

Eighteen

*B*efore dawn on the seventeenth of September, young Billy Meeker come riding hard. He said he and a handful of friends were delivering news all over town and the news was that "something might be happening." Bertha Long had got word from her son, who was stationed with Bragg and camping close to Lee and Gordon's Mill. He had paid a mill worker to bring a letter saying that all sorts of armies were on the move, that there were already skirmishes around the mill area and there was no telling what might happen next.

Not half an hour after Billy rode off, we heard the thundering sound of troops on the march. I stayed in my room, kneeling at my window, and heard knuckles brush against my door. Before I could answer, the door opened an inch and I saw Tom's face. Without me asking, he come in and strode right over to me, kneeling down beside me and putting his arm 'round my shoulder for a minute.

"Are you afraid?" he said in his slow, quiet voice, and when I turned to look at him, I saw that his eyes were empty of fear.

"I never been to war," I said, but already felt more peaceable just looking at him.

"Sure you have," he said with a little smile.

"Not this kind of war."

"I'll take care of you," he said. "That's what I'm here for."

201

I didn't want to hurt his feelings by asking how he thought he could protect me from a whole army, and besides, he looked like maybe he really could, so I just smiled at him and said, "Where will they come from?"

"Everywhere," he said, following my gaze toward the mountains. "The hills and the roads and wading across the creeks and swarming across the railroad trestles . . . Ama's hung a United States flag on the gate. I wonder if I should rip it down."

"Why?" I asked.

"Because if we go hanging up flags, we may incense someone," he said. "As we stand now, we're just civilians, and both armies are supposed to leave us strictly alone, especially during fighting."

I reached over and squeezed his hand. "Go tear it down," I whispered, and it was the first time I ever felt that Tom and I was a little unit complete in ourselves. Even conspiring in secret to tear down something that Ama had hung over her own fence.

Before I knew he was going to do it, even maybe before *he* knew he was going to do it, he leaned over and kissed me on the mouth. It was a nice kiss. I could feel his self-confidence, and nothing at all pushed in too close or made me feel afraid. And I knew I'd be all right being married to Tom and that he'd done right in asking me and I'd done right in saying yes.

I closed my eyes and put my hand against his neck and felt his finger stroke my cheek. Gentle. Peaceful, even with the war really coming at us now. This is the way love is supposed to feel, I told myself.

"I'll see you later," I heard Tom whisper. "I have a flag to tear down." A second later he was on his feet, moving across the room.

Who needs passion? I thought, smiling, touching the place on my cheek that he had stroked.

By midmorning, there was cannon fire and not long after that come rifle shot. We stared at each other and knew it wasn't so far away. It wasn't up in the mountains, not all of it. The rifle shot was from somebody's field, not close by, but still . . . Frisbin. Yes, Frisbin for sure.

"Maybe some of the farmers are getting carried away," Ama said, without much conviction in her voice for once.

"Where's my rifle, son?" Old Man Higgins asked, so nervous he couldn't stay put. He had a flush that burned into his cheekbones and the energy of a child, going up and down, up and down in front of the house, shading his eyes from the sun and staring one way and then the other over and over again.

Tom had put the guns away and wouldn't be persuaded to hand over his father's rifle, no matter how loud Mr. Higgins demanded it. Instead, he saddled his horse and rode to a high spot with his field glasses. After hours of being away, he come home to say he'd been keeping his eyes on most of the valley and so far it was mainly bushwhacking fire. He said this like it were good news and when we stared at him, he went on to say that at least all-out war wasn't raging through the town. Still, miles of army snaked through our town, even more troops than we'd been imagining from the noise. There was army everywhere, Tom said. Not just the main road, which were clogged with wagons and cannons and hundreds of head of oxen and horses pulling army equipment. The firing, he thought, had probably started when two regiments, both heading south, maybe toward Lee and Gordon's Mill or maybe toward a railroad bridge or some battle site, had chanced to intersect each other. Tom said most of the fighting looked to be square in the middle of Sam Cook's long fields. Probably, his slaves had been caught in the fire because the big barn they'd been cooped up in had been burned.

"By now," Tom said, "the Cook slaves are probably free men or dead men."

"Either way, they better off," Delilah said, and Tom nodded.

By late afternoon, all of Frisbin rang with the volley of bullets, and smoke followed by dust clouds blew over our town, so thick that when Tom rode back to his lookout spot, he could only see the blur of battle and a few riderless horses running here and there, bridled and saddled. The fighting grew worse later in the day and by five-thirty we were wearing wool in our ears and choking on the dust and smoke of battle.

I was praying. Making beds, praying. Eating, praying. Cleaning and sweeping, praying. Not only me. Delilah was down on her knees, her elbows on Ama's footstool, her hands clasped under her chin and her lips moving. I saw Tom go to her, kneel down beside her and put his arm 'round her shoulder just like he'd done to me earlier and, just like me, Delilah seemed to quiet. I saw her hands come down, saw her take a deep breath and smile at him. Listen to whatever he was telling her. Old Man Higgins was still pacing, still cursing the Yankees. Jinny worried over the children and Ama stood at the window, her hand on her throat like she always stood when she was deep in her own thoughts.

Jinny said, "Sound like they right about on top us, don't you think, Miz Ama? Miz Ama? Everthin' all right, Miz Ama? What you think 'bout everthin'?"

Ama didn't say nothing, didn't seem to hear what Jinny said, and we all looked at each other, not able to do nothing about the vacant look of her. Finally, Tom went to her and took her by the shoulders and turned her 'round to face him. For a minute she seemed to sigh. She leaned on him and patted his cheek, then let him go and turned to the rest of us, the vacant look gone from her face. Her eyes went from one of us to the next, smiling, reassuring, and my eyes clung to the sight of her.

"Where's Beulah?" she said after a while, and it was only then we saw Beulah wasn't in the room with us, though Daisy was with the other children over by the bookshelves with children's books spread 'round them and Benjamin reading some and pretending to read the rest while Melissa and Daisy clung to every word. It wasn't strange how we'd missed Beulah's being with us. She was so seldom with us that we never looked for her, never expected her to be with us, unless it was for meals or common work.

"Elizabeth," Ama said, "would you please get her? Tell her I asked her to come."

"Yes'm," I said, but when I stood up, my knees buckled. Then I stumbled when I tried to walk, sort of jerked, with my body going two ways every step I took. I finally found Beulah not in her room or at the hall alcove, staring out the windows as I'd expected, but in the kitchen, standing over by the stove, eating something out of a long-handled spoon.

Any other day, maybe I would of thought something. Like she was sneaking food, or tasting food when nobody much cared whether it needed more salt or seasoning, just how much of it there was. But today I just thought, *Thank God, there she is!* As if somehow I'd expected her to vanish into thin air, or maybe run from us now that the fighting had really started.

"Ama wants you," I gasped out, hardly able to get the words out.

Beulah gave me one of her looks that told me she knew how scared I was and was scornful about it. It were like her eyes were saying, "You yellow-livered white trash, look at you snivelin' 'round, don't you have no guts?"

"Please," I whispered through dry lips, wanting to get away from her eyes, and she shrugged and looked at the floor.

"Come on then," she said, and started off without waiting for me, me stumbling along behind her, trying to keep up.

Ama smiled at us as we come through the door and said she'd like for all of us to stay together and listen just as close as we'd ever listened to anything in our lives.

"You hear that sound?" she said, and stopped talking so we could listen closer to the whistling, cracking, screaming of shell. Awful explosions in the air. All mingled together with human yelling, maybe the rebel yell we'd heard so much about. Or maybe the sound of rebels and Federals all together, so much yelling or screaming, so many voices, that this human crying-out rung over the land and made a wilder, more frightening sound than the savage piercing and whirring of weapon fire.

"We've all got to get used to living with that sound," Ama said. "If we get used to it, we won't be so afraid. It won't make us so crazy."

"You call me here for that?" Beulah sniffed. "I weren't

scare then, I ain't scare now. Ain't got no cause to 'sociate with the war, one way or other."

Ama looked into Beulah's eyes, a patient pleading look, and finally Beulah dropped her eyes and said, "All right, Miz Ama. You a rich white woman, still you been good to me. You want me to listen at the war, I listen."

We all stayed together until night, and all of us listened, taking our children onto our laps when they got frightened, letting them back to each other when they wanted to run and play so they could pretend there wasn't no war. More smoke come, pouring over the land in billowing clouds, and the winds seemed to spring up from nowhere, those same winds that had been so absent from the skies all September, and carried the smoke down the chimneys and into our home in great gusts, choking us, making us cough. Making us wonder if our whole town was burning 'round us.

Out of all this, there suddenly come a screaming, a desperate squeal like a wild animal was trapped inside our walls and screaming for freedom. It took a minute to realize that it was Benjamin, who had left his picture books and come racing to Tom's arms, flinging hisself against Tom and screaming.

"Mama!" he cried, over and over again until the sound of it could of wrung tears from a stone. "Papa, please! I want my mama! I *need* my mama! I *need* her! Oh, please! Pleeese!"

"It's all right, baby," Tom said, both arms 'round his boy. And little at a time, Ben collapsed against Tom, his cries muffled against Tom's neck, his thin little body only trembling now and not heaving so hard. And me all of a sudden realizing what it was going to mean trying to take Lucie's place, when there wasn't any possible way to take her place. The thought froze me and I couldn't move.

In the end, it was Delilah who crept over to Tom's chair and leaned 'round back and stared whispering to Ben, whose head now hung over Tom's shoulder, as limp as a doll's. I saw her smile, saw her touch the tip of Ben's nose with her finger, and in a minute I saw him reach out with one hand and play with a strand of Delilah's long black hair.

206

More shells exploded in the air, followed by screams. The whole world seemed filled up with loud cries of agony. "Whoever expected to go through something like this?" I said after a while, too ashamed to look at Tom, too frightened to look at Ama. "Do you know all my sisters and I ever talked about as little girls were what kind of man we'd be marrying, what kind of farm we'd be living on, how many children we'd have. Things like that. And all the man had to be was handsome and all the farm had to be was big. We never thought about something like this."

Beulah laughed. Actually laughed out loud. "Is that what the white talk 'bout? *Worry* 'bout men and they property?"

Old Man Higgins snorted, "No slave ever had to worry about nothin'. They were taken care of same as children."

Beulah looked at him. "Sorta like we take care you," she said.

Mr. Higgins flew 'round to Ama, his head wagging at her, his eyes about to pop out his head. "Are you goin' to let that— that nigger cook of yourn insult me? Insult me right in your presence?"

"I'm sorry," Ama said absent-like, still staring out the window. "I wasn't listening. I missed the insult."

"You miss an awful lot 'round here," Mr. Higgins said, but caught a dark look from Tom and lapsed back into his gloomy silence.

"I wonder how many folk dead over there," Delilah said after a while. She was sitting on the floor beside Tom's chair and somehow Benjamin was on her lap, still playing with her hair, looking comfortable and content, the desperation gone. "With all that shootin', must be a passel of dead."

"Don't rightly know," Jinny said, blowing her nose. "Anyhow, it late. I hungry as a horse."

"It eatin' time, sure 'nough," Beulah said, sounding cheerful, even friendly. She heaved herself up. "I get right to cookin'."

"No, now you stay put," Jinny said. "You listenin' at the war."

"War," Beulah said, sitting again, "ain't all that much to listen at."

"It right annoyin' though," Jinny said. "Crack, crack, crack, never stop."

"Must be even worse bein' out there," Delilah said.

"It *is* worse," Tom said. Something about his eyes made you know he was seeing Manassas again. "You see the man next to you fall," he went on. "You throw him in a common ditch. Or you duck down beside his body, if it's between you and the shooting. You think to yourself you'll do anything. Anything at all. Just to make it stop."

"Stop talking like a damned coward!" Old Man Higgins snarled. "You was on the right side."

"Was I?" Tom said, sounding a little sad.

Then it was very quiet, the room filled with down-to-the-floor glances and heavy sighs. I wanted so much to go to Tom and take him in my arms and hold him, but I could see he were miles away, thinking hard. All of us thinking. In and out. I were stone dead and also, for a while, standing there listening, not knowing what I was listening for no more. It might of been a human voice with fire in it, a rebel yell. It might of been Old Man Higgins screaming into the night that he were wanting his slaves back.

Then there was nothing. I turned and saw Ama running her hand absent-like along the windowsill.

I could hear the wind outside, could imagine the woods dense and dark, and there was nothing in them that knew me. There were creatures with one forepaw lifted, not wanting yet to put it down, for fear of sound. There were eyes made for seeing in the dark, but none that saw me. Not outside. Not inside, either.

Not really.

"Night's here," Ama said from the window, and we all looked at her. "That means the fighting will soon be over for the day. And I have a feeling that the troops will be leaving before the sun comes up. Yes, I'm sure I'm right."

I ran over to stand beside her, to see what she was seeing,

hear what she was hearing. But standing beside her, I never saw nor heard any change. But I could hear Ama's easy breathing, see how calm she was, staring up at the sky, watching the smoke move like blown clouds over the land, not casting shadows no more like they done when the sun was high.

"It's going to be all right," she told me, then turned to the others. "Tom, you can go check on the animals. Beulah, you and Jinny can go start the food and I'll set the table. I think the children need to eat. In fact, we'll all be better off for a meal. There, I thought that would get a smile. Delilah, go wash your face, honey. No more crying today. It's over for a while."

That we believed her shows the kind of unquestioning blind faith we had in her.

Nineteen

$\mathscr{B}$ut the next morning, the eighteenth of September, we heard more than the loud gunfire we'd growed used to. We heard a mountain storm of it, the explosions bouncing off Missionary Ridge, off Lookout Mountain, caught in that terrible echo that bounced from hill to hill, and Tom, back early from the telegraph, said they were fighting at Reed's Bridge and all 'round the Chickamauga. Then on the nineteenth of September, about eight o'clock in the morning, the hills seemed to go up in one giant explosion and the sky filled with fire and smoke.

In our house, all three children were screaming. The rest of us went 'round on legs so weak they barely held us, trying to comfort the children, trying to cook and eat and keep a cheerful face for the others, but always with the feeling that peace, as we knew it, was over forever. Maybe even life was over forever, for it sounded like the world was exploding. Could this be Judgment Day? Could it? The crashing of cannon was so close, seemed like it could kill us all in one terrible roar.

Carrying Melissa everywhere, her arms 'round my neck, her legs 'round my waist, I stared out the windows and saw the clouds of smoke rolling toward the house and wondered, Where are the soldiers? Oh, God, how close are they?

Delilah followed me like my own ghost, hand in hand with Benjamin, stooping to hug him every time he started to cry, for

210

Tom was out trying to calm the horses, which were screaming in the barn.

"Maybe we should hitch 'em up," I said in a low voice to Delilah. "Try to get away."

Her wide eyes met mine. "Try to get where? Chattanooga? God only know what happen in Chattanooga."

"Just keep going, maybe. Till there isn't no fighting," I said.

Beulah passed by and said, "Ain't no way to go. They everwhere. Too late now. Way too late"—her head wagging and her voice sounding like she wished she'd gone away a long time ago. But she was trapped now, like us.

By noon a line of bloody Confederate soldiers come straggling up our drive from the main road, asking for water. They cried like babies. Said men were running everywhere, that all organization was lost and men were retreating in all directions. From the hills, from the banks of the Chickamauga. They told us ambulances of wounded were making their way along the main road toward town, where they were setting up a military hospital. That the wounded on foot was falling thick by the wayside.

Ama looked 'round at us standing on the porch. "We'll have to fill the wagon with water, and linen for bandages and scissors and . . . oh, anything else you can think of. Just hurry! Hurry! We're needed!"

I had to tear Melissa from me, her screaming "No, Mama, no, no!" when I pulled her arms from my neck and gave her to Beulah for comfort.

"Melissa! Listen to me, honey! Mama's coming back! I promise, honey, I promise you. You got to be a big girl now. Got to help Beulah." All this with her screaming and the world exploding 'round her and strange bloody men on her doorstep, some of them with tears streaming down their cheeks.

With Tom already running for the horses, Delilah was on her knees in front of Benjamin, who'd been clinging to her all day, saying, "Ben! Benny, boy. Delilah got to go down yonder

211

and help the soldier men. Now what you gonna do, you gon' help Beulah here, strong little man like you. Oh, my, you plenty strong 'nough to be the man of the house while you daddy take us down yonder. You hear me now? 'Cause I don't want to come back from no ride and hear you ain't been doing you duty! Don't let me hear that, now!"

When we left in the wagon with Tom driving and Delilah, Jinny, Ama, and me trying to organize supplies in the back, Melissa's and Daisy's screams followed us, for Beulah'd had to set Daisy on the porch, where she clung to her mother's one leg and Melissa clung to the other. But Benjamin, with tears still draining down his red, swole-up face, ladled out water alongside Beulah to a line of men that thickened even as the front of the line moved on or collapsed under the trees in the front lawn. Some of them, sitting there with their hats in their laps, their eyes vague and puzzled, looked almost as young as Ben. And some looked as old as Mr. Higgins, who stalked among them in his nightshirt, crazy-like, demanding that somebody give him a gun.

Down by the main road, 'mongst a mob of soldiers, a man on a stretcher waved his hat at us, grinning so cheerful-like it took me a minute to realize his whole stomach were ripped open.

"The boys was holding their own last I seen!" he called out, raising his head some while the two men who'd been resting beside him dragged theirselves up and lifted the stretcher.

"Wait!" I called, struggling down from the wagon with a jug of water and a ladle. The water was all I could do for him, but he thanked me like I'd saved his life, though his death warrant was in his stomach, in the blood that dripped from the stretcher, in the flies that buzzed over him and covered his wounds.

I stared after him, trembling, until I felt Ama's hand on my wrist. "There's so much to be done," she whispered, and I turned 'round sharp, thinking *So much to do and I haven't no idea how to do any of it!*

But likely none of the others did either, so I did the best I

212

could, bathing wounds and faces, tying on tourniquets, ladling water, comforting the men who cried, even as I closed the eyes of a man next to them who'd passed away right where he laid. Some of the men was soaking wet. They said they'd waded in the creek up to their armpits, this in weather so cool that I shivered all the time, half with nerves and half with chill. The wet-soaked men shook so hard their top teeth rattled against their bottom teeth.

Jinny and I ended up on the north side of the road and Tom, Ama, and Delilah on the south, with ambulances rattling between us and soldiers staggering toward town and soldiers trudging across fields and stopping to ask for water or for help with their wounds or just stopping to die.

"Oh, God, Jinny, there's no end to this!" I cried, and she looked up from the man whose head laid in her lap with her eyes full of nightmares.

"Still," she said, swallowing hard, "we got to do what God give us to do."

As we worked our way up and down the uneven lines, even the most dreadful wounded soldiers turned their heads to each other and talked of the war. All morning we heard of the most ghastly kind of battle, the likes of which the men said they'd never seen, and some of them career military men who'd fought in the Indian wars.

"That Chickamauga, you know the one the damned Indians named River of Blood?" a man said whose face was burnt black, the flesh shriveling on both sides.

"Know it? I near drowned in the damned thing, didn't I?" the second man said as I wrung out my cloth and pressed it to his bloody head.

"River of Blood!" the first man whooped. "Lived up to its name today, sure 'nough." He grinned a little. "Damned thing's running redder than a tomato patch."

Then both men saw the look on my face and hushed up, and I glanced across the road to find Ama and saw that she was calm as usual, bending over a man's face with a cloth in her hand like she was holding onto his tongue, maybe to keep him from swallowing it. Ama, with her ideas about the war being the South's penance for slavery. Probably, all this didn't seem so terrible to her, I thought. More like what she'd expected all along. Not far from her, Delilah was trying to drag the body of a soldier from the road. Tom saw her and went over to help. As he lifted the man, he looked at her and said something, and she drew a long breath, then wiped her tears, maybe smiled, maybe not, but looked like she'd found the strength to go on.

Jinny and I scarce said a word to each other as we worked, only things like *Could you tear up that sheet and make me a long bandage?* or *More water over here.* For we didn't want to scare the soldiers by saying how terrible their wounds looked, how close to death so many of them seemed.

"It the Lord will, you just 'member that," Jinny said once. "Nothin' ever happen ain't the Lord will."

I looked at the man I were tending to, collapsed in the dirt, his face young, oh God, so young! And so hopeful as I turned him over, only to see the front of his uniform so red with blood you could of wrung it out.

What I thought, what I wanted to say was *The Lord never shot this man!* even as I tried to straighten his body into a more comfortable position and gave him water and bathed the blood from his hair and face.

I lost track of the time, but it must of been midafternoon when a man in a Confederate uniform passed, carrying a young Yankee soldier over his shoulder, and said in an anxious way, "Ma'am, could you please tell me how far it is to the hospital?"

"Hospital?" I gasped out, forgetting about the tent in town they were supposed to be setting up for the wounded. Then when I saw the look on his face, the way he put his hand over the young soldier in blue, I added, "Oh, I think they've set up something in town. Yes, I'm sure they did. Oh, please, take some water before you go."

He drank a ladle of water, but he wouldn't sit down. He said, "Thank you, ma'am, but I must be going on now. He's pretty bad, I think. I have to find a doctor."

"Is he your friend?" I murmured, dabbing a damp cloth

over the young cheek that hung in air over the man's back, eyes closed.

"He's my son," the Confederate soldier said with such a look on his face that I fell silent. He moved on, leaving me to wonder where they'd come across each other and whether it was the man that shot his own boy and if so, how long had it taken him to realize who he'd shot.

I watched him carry his son over the small rise, his body holding up straight under the weight he carried. Somewhere off in the distance a dog barked. Then barked again before it begun howling, a horrible yapping that spread across the valley until the sound was thin and distant as an echo.

When I turned I saw Ama come rushing toward me. "Elizabeth," she said, motioning off down the road toward the man and his son. "There's folks that need a doctor quick! Who might pull through with the help of a good medic."

I nodded, and in no time we'd loaded a whole wagonful of the most desperate wounded, men who needed help we couldn't give, and Delilah and Ama in the back tending them best they could. As Tom drove off, Ama raised her hand to me and I ran after the wagon waving back and sending up a prayer that they'd be all right.

I was saying another prayer for the father and his son, hoping Ama would find them on the road, would get them to the doctor in time, when I heard a low-spoke "Hello there" and turned to see a soldier sitting against a tree, separated from the others. He was drinking out of a canteen and didn't seem to be in any pain, though his arm had a rag tied round it and his sleeve was blood-soaked.

"Oh, what—" I started to say, but he answered my question even before I could finish it.

"Saber," he said without any more details. His eyes stared at the rolling countryside all 'round him, rather than at the misery and death at his elbow. I found myself looking too, drawing a deep breath of something like relief to see the peaceful old trees whose leaves were just turning crisp, the mountains on all sides, too big to be touched by war.

"Is it always this quiet?" he asked.

For a minute I almost laughed. Quiet? With the sounds of battle exploding not so far away. With men moaning. With another ambulance clattering 'round the bend even as he spoke. Quiet!

He held up his hand for silence as I started to talk, and it was in that second, when I stood there kind of hesitating, in the pause between the beats of my own heart, with him watching me, that I heard it. The beautiful silence all 'round us. A silence that hadn't nothing to do with all the screams and pain of mankind, or the rattling of our wagons, or the firing of our weapons. Just a silence that come rolling off the hills, as clear as the sounds of battle. Something of nature, deep and pure, untouched by all the noise man could make.

"It is quiet, isn't it," I said to the calm-eyed soldier, who had put his hand flat against the tree he was sitting under.

"It's even quiet up there," he said, tilting his head toward the very hill that the men were retreating from. "If you listen close enough."

I felt a tug at my skirt, and turned to find an injured soldier at my feet who needed a drink of water, needed his face washed and needed a calm word, for his eyes were frantic. He hadn't heard the silence of the hills. He was like the rest who'd talked of the awful roar that was part of the battle. Noise so terrible that men could not hear each other's shouts from a distance of ten feet. It was like being swallowed alive in the terrible explosions, with the men in front of you screaming as they were hit by canister, with neighing horses scared wild by the whirring shrapnel, with the crack of bullets and the roar of cannon fire, and the savage yells of enemy to enemy.

And yet, I knew the soldier was right. Somewhere under all that terrible noise, there was the silence of the hills, the peace of old trees whose leaves fanned soldiers' faces even while the thick forest made it almost impossible for them to know who to shoot at. Made them accidental shoot each other. And when the soldiers spoke of the thick smoke of the battle, the smoke that blinded them, disguised enemy from enemy worse than the thick growth of trees, maybe in that smoky hell there could be clear vision as well as peace. A way to see through the trees, the smoke. Wondering if the soldier had found a way to see the crisp leaves over his head and light filtering down through the smoke, I turned, expecting to see him there with his hand still resting flat against the tree with that calm look in his eyes, but he was gone.

Voices called to me on all sides and there wasn't time to wonder where he'd gone. There were too many men to see to, most of them bloody. And the men told me as I worked over them that if I thought they looked bad, I should only see the ditches full of dead and wounded on the battlefields. That the dead was actually stacked, one on top of the other, like cord-wood.

After a while, I found myself shaking, had trouble tying a simple knot, and scraped my nails more than once against the foreheads that I was kneeling over, trying to soothe. I heard myself muttering "Oh, God, oh, God" over and over, though I wasn't sure if it was or wasn't a prayer. But I had to say it somehow, just to pull myself from one minute to the next, from one bloody soldier to the next.

It seemed to me like that day wouldn't never be over, that the gray-like sun would stay in the sky forever, but finally, it dropped lower and twilight come in like a darker gray cloak. I could of cried from relief when little by little the terrible sound of battle started to grow less.

"That's about it," said a soldier whose hand I was holding like I was his mother, though he looked older than me. "Fighting should be about over for the day."

Even this was not to be, though, for all at once we heard a sound like the very earth had blowed up under us, sending up a scream of human voices, the sound of which could almost kill you to hear it. It was the longest unbroke blast of artillery of the entire day, and I looked for Jinny and she come running into my arms. We stood there hugging each other with tears streaming down our faces, and the soldiers who had been smiling just a minute before were crying, too, and saying, "Oh, Lord, they'll be killing theirselves in this light!" Meaning, I guess, even worse than before. Nothing made sense. Nothing could make sense when it sounded like the world was coming to an end.

Not until dark did the terrible sound finally die, and then we all collapsed to the ground thinking about the loss of life, everybody crying, and more wounded pouring out of the hills. No jokes now, no smiles. Just crying.

Ama finally come back about nine o'clock and she was alone in the wagon. Tom and Delilah had stayed to work all night at the army tent, but Ama had come for us. She said she'd decided to take us back to Symphony Oaks, both for the rest and for food and wine supplies.

Come midnight we were still sitting in front of the fireplace talking over the day, Beulah with us, trying not to look too interested in what we had to say. She'd worked all day herself, ladling water along with all three children, who'd proved a godsend and a joy to the wounded, handing out crackers and whatever food they could lay hands on.

Ama had already took inventory of the food and gathered the canned goods we had left, as well as preserves, apples, and two dozen potatoes. There weren't no more crackers, not a single cornpone, not an egg, not even a jar of our homemade coffee brew. We had so little now, when there used to be so much. Still, what there was, we loaded into the wagon with a fresh supply of water and a stack of sheets and towels. And our last bottle of brandy, along with a half-dozen bottles of wine.

"Three tents have been set up on the courthouse lawn," Ama said. "Half the town's there working. The men are building shants for the overflow of military, and the women are trying their hand at nursing."

"I can just see Gillian Brian nursing!" I said. "Even for *her* Walter. She'd get one whiff of blood and have to be carried to a bed."

"Actually, she vomited." Ama grinned with some satisfaction.

218

"She really did?" I said, and surprised myself by going into a fit of laughing. Imagine laughing, when men were in town right this minute getting their arms and legs sawed off. Dying. And me laughing.

"And she wasn't alone," Ama said. "Our women weren't ready for the worst cases. The only two women who could be found to help in surgery were Mattie Simpson, who's been a wonder, and . . ." Ama stopped talking and bit her lip.

"Who?" I said.

"Delilah," Ama murmured. "But it hasn't been easy for her. She doesn't say a word, just works. Does very well helping the surgeon, but I can tell it's . . . it's very hard for her. And despite all she does, half the women still don't have a kind word for her."

"What happened to the Confederate father?" I asked. "The one who was carrying his son. Did you catch up to them on the road?"

Ama nodded, smiling. "Actually, that's a piece of good news for you. The father was so worried, he had us all convinced his son was at death's door. The boy woke up on the way to town and do you know, there wasn't a mark on him. The blood on him was from another soldier he'd been fighting beside. The boy shot his rifle and saw his father a second later and thought he'd shot him! Between the shock and having been sleepless for close to three days, he fainted dead away. He was one hundred percent unharmed."

"They ain't gone back to the war, have they?" Jinny exclaimed. "Oh, Lord, don' tell me they gone back to kill each other all over 'gain."

"Wouldn't doubt it, they white." Beulah sniffed.

"I don't know that they went back to the war," Ama said in a rather cross voice. "And I must say, Beulah, that as a white woman, I'm getting tired of hearing you put down the whites all the time."

There was a kind of gasping from the hearts of all of us. The kind of awe that comes from hearing the hard truth spoke at last. I held my breath for a moment. Then I saw Beulah's face.

219

Saw her eyes and knew she were deciding, going back and forth for a minute.

Finally, she sat up straighter in her chair, met Ama's eyes direct, and said, "Miz Ama, you ain't never done nothin' to me. You been real decent, even more than decent. But the white done claw the soul outa me. I ain't got 'nough love for one to make up for the hate I got for all. That just the way of it. Can't do nothin' 'bout it, me or you."

Ama nodded. Just like that, she accepted what Beulah had to say. Didn't try to hold out no olive branch or pretend what were said hadn't been. "I'm tired," she said, pushing herself out of her chair, and she hadn't never sounded so tired since I knew her. "We'd all best get some sleep. Tomorrow's going to be as hard as today."

We all walked back to our rooms like spirits from different worlds, all prisoners locked in different boxes. I could hear Jinny sniffling, but Beulah's face was worse than grief . . . it was like she'd started changing into a different person right there on the spot. Somebody I'd met in quick glances, in things said just under the breath or right out loud but fast-said, like a mouse that jumps out of the mousehole for a second daring the cat to come after him. Now it looked like the mouse was out for good and the cat be damned. Beulah's face, more than anything else, looked glad.

Laying in my bed that night, I tried to order myself to sleep. For every bone, every nerve in my body ached. But sleep was as far away tonight when I needed it as it was close on nights when I hadn't needed it at all. Men dead. All that blood. Beulah with that face. Beulah with those eyes that rejoiced on being left free to finally hate as much as she wanted to. Oh, God, hate was everywhere. Hate was camping along the banks of the Chickamauga this very night. Hate getting ready to kill or be killed at first light.

"Oh, God," I moaned, muffling my own voice in my pillow so's not to wake Melissa. I'd been saying "Oh, God" all day. But this time, I knew I was really talking to God, finally getting around to begging him for mercy. Make this war be over. Make

220

Beulah stop hating us so. Let me be married to Tom soon as possible, God, and let us find peace together and have time to watch our children grow. All this while weeping so hard into my pillow that the linen was soaked.

Then my door opened and Ama slipped in, a tall, thin shadow with a white candle in her hand. She sunk to her knees beside my bed, setting the candle on the nightstand and comforting me with little pats.

"The only way to get Beulah back," she whispered, "is to go ahead and let her feel what's been boiling in her heart for a long time now. Probably for her whole life."

"Oh, you can tolerate anything!" I said, weeping. "You even talk about leveling the whole South without getting riled up about it."

Ama looked at me keen-like and drew closer. "Just keep remembering what it's all about, Elizabeth. Horrible as it is, perhaps the war serves a greater purpose. Beulah has come to a final realization. Otherwise, she might never have come to it. She's got a cause now, a grand cause, and she knows that now. She'll probably dedicate the rest of her life to the fight against bigotry. If I know her, she'll soon take her argument into the streets. She has a strong voice, I've always known that. She'll be heard. And sooner or later, we have to believe she'll come to hear us. Come to realize that all white people aren't like Mr. Higgins. When she does, she'll come back to us. Understand?"

I thought for a while, then I dried my tears and nodded. Ama smiled at me, but she didn't say no more.

Twenty

We left for town the next morning after breakfasting on apples and mush, washed down with weak tea. There was very little talking 'mongst the four of us, but Beulah wrapped a meal for Delilah and Tom while Jinny finished checking the wagon and I went in for one last check on Melissa. I wanted to wake her, wanted to hold her and feel her warm little face against mine, but standing there, looking down at her as she laid there in the kind of heavy sleep that comes after a hard, exhausting day like yesterday, I knew I wouldn't. If I did, she'd only cling to me and beg me not to leave and start crying all over again. So, bending over her, so close that several strands of her silky hair touched my lips, I whispered, " 'Bye, baby. I'll be back soon" and almost ran out of the room before I changed my mind and shook her awake.

"Everything all right, Lizbeth?" asked a small voice from the stairwell as I put my hand on the banister.

I looked down to see Benjamin, near invisible in the curve of the landing. His white face twisted 'round to stare up at me and he gave me one of his smiles. Serious. Thoughtful-like.

I swung past him, giving him a light tap on the head as I went. "Why, sure, Ben, everything's just fine! Don't you worry about a thing!"

He didn't say nothing back, just let me run past him without another word to stop me. It was the empty pattering of my

222

own words that made me turn back, wiped the smile off my lips. "Oh, Ben," I said, and after a moment of neither of us saying a word, I sunk to the step below him. "Nothing's fine, is it? It's all . . . scary and terrible." I met his childlike eyes and thought I saw the man he would be someday, looking back at me. How long am I going to keep running away from you? I wondered. Am I going to be your mother, or don't I have the guts for the job?

I reached out my arm and put it 'round his shoulders and he beamed at me, bouncing down the step on his bottom to be close to me, to snuggle up next to me.

"Nothing could be any scarier," he confided, still peering at me, "not even falling down the well. Still, what I thought . . . Well, we don't have a choice, do we? I figure I'll just act brave. That's what Pa told me to do when I'm the worst scared." He held his hand out straight in front of him. "See?" he said. "Not shaking or nothing. If you want me to, I'll look after Melissa for you while you're gone."

I grinned at him and hugged him tighter. "I want you to, all right. But who's going to look after *you* for me?"

"I'll do that, too," he offered, and threw both arms 'round my neck.

When I come down, Ama was already behind the horses, reins in her hands, and Jinny reached out a hand and dragged me in back with her where we huddled together, cold though we wrapped ourselves in quilts. Beulah stood on the steps watching us go without moving or waving, and the last we saw of her was a dark stout figure, arms crossed under her breasts, shoulders hunched down and head turned up to the dark morning sky. She looked like a statue, too still to be alive.

"Shouldn't the fighting been started?" I asked Jinny, clutching the heavy coat we were bringing to Delilah. She had spent yesterday in a long-sleeved dress covered only by a black shawl that was looped 'round her shoulders in a knot, more awkward than warm. Last I seen of her, she had taken it off and done without any overgarment at all.

Ama heard me and looked back over her shoulder. "It's almost seven. I expect we'll hear something any minute now. . . ."

But it were still quiet by the time we reached the road. Even the soldiers who had slept all night at the roadside were quiet, barely glancing up as we rode by. And the whole town, the shady streets, the two-story shops and the fields beyond, even the cold air that we gulped into our lungs as we drove were almost frightening still.

"Maybe," I said after a while, "there isn't going to be no more fighting. Maybe—maybe the soldiers have moved somewheres else. Maybe Chattanooga." I could hear my own voice falter, like it got caught in my throat, and I swallowed hard and added, "Or maybe farther south. What do you think, Ama?"

She looked doubtful. "I don't know anything about war, but—" She broke off, clicking thoughtful-like to the horses.

"Only thing is," I said when she'd let a minute go by without saying nothing, "there was so *much* fighting yesterday. From all directions. You'd think it would—"

Ama nodded. "Exactly. What could have happened?"

"Surrender?" I asked.

"I hopin' that it!" Jinny said with some relief. "Yeah, I think that prob'ly it."

Ama flung her hands out toward the mountains that rose 'round us from all directions. "Who surrendered *what* to *whom*, then?" she said. "Could all of those battles we heard yesterday have reached some conclusion they hadn't reached at twilight last night? It doesn't make sense." She shook her head.

Still no fighting when we pulled in front of the courthouse yard, which was filled with three huge tents, and people hurrying in and out of them, and wounded in the yard being tended by women and both local and army men. There was a rushed feeling 'mongst the wounded, ambulance bearers moving stretchers, murmurs of "Water, please" as me and Jinny followed Ama into the middle tent. But even here it was much quieter than I'd expected, and the least wounded kept looking here and there, their faces set with strain, and I knew they couldn't understand the quiet no more than us. Inside the tent there were rows of narrow beds filled with men, and a terrible odor of dirty bodies and festering wounds. Women were at work, moving up and down the rows with wet towels, trying to soothe men who vomited into basins held by Mrs. Reverend Harper and Martha Lewis and Bertha Long and a dozen more of the tough-minded women who had not vomited themselves or passed out like Gillian Brian.

Even here men were listening, sitting on the edges of their beds, ears strained to hear what they expected to hear and didn't—the sound of fighting.

Screams come from the back. Ama said "Surgery" with a white, set face and I could imagine from looking at her the horrible operations that were going on back there. Legs, hands, arms coming off, and the men conscious the whole time, without no drugs for the pain.

"Wait here," Ama said, disappearing behind the surgery curtain with a box of wine and the one bottle of brandy. She come out a few minutes later and said that Delilah had been sent on a break by the surgeon, her first in hours.

"Lord have mercy," Jinny breathed as Ama led us down another row, this one of men so bad that it was sometimes hard to tell who was living and who was dead.

We found Delilah sitting out back of one of the tents, her back against a pegged rope, her head in her hands, and Tom standing facing her, gulping something from a cup. When she heard Ama's voice, she jumped up with a strangled cry and took the three of us in her arms, all at one time, kissing one, then the next, her cheeks wet against ours.

Her eyes were frantic, all trace of calm gone. "When the fightin' start again?" she begged to know, rubbing under her eyes with the towel Ama handed her, and shaking so hard that there wasn't no calming her. Ama put her hand on her shoulder and this slight touch was enough to send Delilah to the ground like she'd been struck from above. She sat there crying in a weak shudder of sobs that seemed to come from her very heart.

"It's been terrible," Tom said, coming to me and speaking in a low voice. "After a while, I lost track of time. I would never have left you, if I'd known I'd end up staying here." His eyes searched my face. "Did you get any rest at all? Did you see the children?"

I smiled at him, put my hand on his arm. "They're fine, Tom. Benjamin is as strong as . . . you," I finished in some surprise, for the words had come to me out of nowhere. It was true. The boy was like the father. No matter how hard life came at either of them, they came back just as hard. Only way to defeat them was to beat them to death, for as long as there was a spark of life left in them, they'd struggle up to their feet and keep fighting.

Tom stood there, one hand locked 'round my wrist, looking ready to collapse, yet worried for me. Asking me whether or not I'd be all right here, this place where women held basins as men vomited over everything. Or held towels and handed instruments to the surgeons and tried not to listen to the men scream. "What I don't want," he said, still holding onto me, "is anything else to happen to you. You've gone through enough already."

I shrugged and remembered Ben's words. "Aren't there times when there aren't no choices?" I said, trying to look strong, but Tom stared harder at me and shook his head.

"It shouldn't be," he muttered, and he seemed trapped by the idea, wrapped in his idea of saving me from seeing the misery of the tents, and knowing he couldn't. "I care about you," he said after a long minute of standing there with his empty cup dangling from his fingers, and he bent down to give me a swift kiss and was gone before I could think what to say. I watched him head between the tents, his long legs stumbling as he stepped on ropes and tools on his way back to surgery, and I knew that for Tom those few words were the same as another man howling his love out under the moon.

A minute later, Delilah's head fell to one side and we knew she'd passed out asleep right where she sat. Jinny sat beside her, taking her head in her lap, and Ama sunk down beside her and smoothed Delilah's hair with gentle fingers. Such beautiful hair, and such a lot of it that, even tangled and standing as though she'd been running her hands through it time after time, it were

226

a riot of curls and more becoming to her than when she wore it up.

"Go on," Ama mouthed to me. "They'll be needing you inside. Jinny, let me have her, I want to stay with her until she wakes up. I want to talk to her." She gathered Delilah's head and shoulders onto her own lap and sat glancing down at Delilah's face, where the feathery black lashes fluttered restless, like demons chased through Delilah's dreams.

I nodded and took one last look at Tom, who was out beyond the tents, pacing in long strides, his own demons pacing behind him.

Jinny and I headed for the sick wards and there was so much to do that nobody had to tell us nothing. There were bodies to wash, bedpans to carry, eyes to close, water to give, shovels to dig filth from the dirt floors, rakes to smooth out the soil. Modesty was gone.

At ten o'clock that same morning, the fighting started again. At first, there were just scattered gunshots, then musketry, heavier and heavier, and the soldiers who had been sitting up listening, with strained frowns over their faces, seemed to relax. They fell back on their pillows and said, "There now, there now" to each other like some terrible suspense had ended at last and they could breathe again.

We still didn't have no idea of why the fighting had started so late. It took hours for us to hear what had happened, or at least the new wounded soldiers' version of what happened.

"It would seem," drawled a Texan who'd took a Minié ball in his left arm and had it amputated right behind the line before being sent out of action, "that the Army of the Cumberlands decided to hold where they were and just wait for us to come and get 'em. Guess we musta been tryin' to throw 'em off. Kept 'em waitin' till all our boys got breakfast, a shave, and a haircut."

"Breakfast part true 'nough," another soldier said, laughing. He said he'd been serving under D. H. Hill. "Word come down bright and early this morning that nobody was to fight on a empty stomach! You 'magine that?"

227

"Put the blame on Polk," objected a soldier from the next bed over, fitter than most. Only his arm was in a sling, not like the poor Texan, whose head felt raging hot under my hand. His eyes were glassy and bright, but he was still talking and still listening to every word said. "He was reading a damned *newspaper* this morning," the fit soldier went on. "And waiting for his own breakfast when Bragg found him sitting there in front of his tent. Raised holy H, the general did."

None of the news mattered to me. I don't know if it mattered to any of us women who walked up and down the rows of mangled soldiers, some of them too far gone to even listen to war news, some of them in such pain they were moaning and screaming and nothing any of us could do for them. We washed them and gave them water and tried to explain to them there wasn't no morphine, wasn't nothing for the pain, that they must try to take deep breaths, try to think of something else, try to stand it best they could. There wasn't nothing else to do. Nothing.

By the afternoon, Mattie Simpson come out of surgery spent, her gray and brown hair out of its tight bun and hanging down to her waist like a young girl's. Yet calm. Her eyes looked at the women, one at a time, as if deciding something. I saw her look from Mrs. Reverend Harper to me, back to Mrs. Reverend, then settle on me.

"Liz Ann," she said, coming and taking the wet towel out of my hand. "I got to lay down outside. I got to take at least two hours. The surgeon needs a good pair of hands."

"Oh, God, Mattie," I started to say. "I never—"

But Bertha Long, behind me, finished the sentence for me. "You never done it," she said in a grim exhausted voice, "and you ain't never goin' to do it. Not here. Not with our boys."

I turned 'round and saw them. Mrs. Reverend beside Bertha. Josephine Steedman with a towel over her arm and her hair ever which way. Martha Lewis stooping over a cot, but with her eyes on me, dark and unfriendly. Other women looking at me from all over the tent.

"Why ain't she?" Mattie said, her hands on her hips, facing them.

"Because," Bertha said, taking another step closer until she and Mattie were no more than a foot apart, both glaring at each other, "because we ain't havin' Yankee eyes look at our boys screamin'. We ain't havin' her carryin' their precious arms and legs away on her tray. Not when it's her kind that done it to them!"

"Don't be no fool," Mattie muttered, but her chin come down and she stared at the floor.

"Don't you be no fool!" snapped Mrs. Reverend. She slapped down the instrument tray she was carrying and started past Mattie. "You rest," she said. "I can help the surgeon." She half raised the curtain and I saw Tom over her shoulder, pressing a man back onto a high bed as the surgeon pushed a thin knife into the man's arm. The man screamed, a hard pulsing scream that cut the air same as the knife cut his flesh. I heard Tom's steady murmur, "Hang on now. He's got to find that bullet. . . ."

And for a moment we all froze. Mrs. Reverend let the curtain fall. Her old hand trembled and she wound it in her apron. She glanced toward the curtain but she didn't take another step toward it.

Mattie's chin was back up and she was looking at the women again. "I tell you, Liz Ann can do it," she said. "I seen her give birth. She got a whole heap o' courage."

"You tryin' to say the rest of us don't?" Bertha Long asked, her eyes puffy from lack of sleep.

"No," Mattie said, not backing down, "but some women can do this sort of thing and some can't. It ain't no disgrace not to be able to. But she can do it." Mattie's hand closed on mine. She nodded to me. "It'll all be fine, Liz Ann. Come on, you come with me."

Martha Lewis drew a long breath and looked from Mattie to the curtain and back. "It ain't right," she muttered, but she didn't make no move to stop me as I started to follow Mattie.

What stopped us instead was a long whistle, a rude sound that sent me whirling 'round, looking for somebody that I couldn't see at first.

"Shame on you! Shame on all a ya!" I knew the voice before I saw the man. A rough voice, mocking. Loud enough to be heard over the man in surgery, who'd started screaming again, after stopping for a moment or two.

"You let a Yankee do your work," the voice went on, "and that don't make you no better than the Yankee, that's the way I look at it!"

I stared across the dim-lit tent to where a sliver of daylight cut through the lifted flap.

Ferris Greenwood stood there, dirtier than ever if that was possible. Crafty-eyed.

Delilah pushed into the tent behind him, her face worried, but there wasn't no sign of Ama, who'd been outside working with the men on stretchers. Delilah's eyes burned in her face and I saw her reach for Ferris's shirt with outstretched hands.

"Stop!" I said before she could touch him, and saw her hesitate as Ferris swaggered toward me, his hand on the gun he wore at his hip. "What are you going to do now?" I said in the dead silence with everybody watching Ferris, probably wondering who he was. "You want to shoot me? Call me names? Spit on me? What?" Seeing him smile, I went on, impatient with tiredness, looking to get rid of him, "Well, whatever you're going to do," I said, "go ahead and do it!"

"I like all them ideas," Ferris said, his eyebrows raised at me. He shot a glance at the women, who were watching him without making a move, hardly breathing, it seemed. "What you ladies think? That sound good for a Yankee? Come on, what you think?" His voice was raised now, almost yelling at them, and Mrs. Reverend cleared her throat.

"Calm yourself now, we can't just—"

"*Why can't we just!*" Ferris screamed. "Have you forgot who you are? Have you forgot who she is? The woman's a damned Yankee. She shot my brother! You know that? She ever tell you she shot a Morgan Raider? Didn't know that, did you?

230

But you damned sure know what side the war she's on, and that don't stop you from lettin' her go all over, puttin' her hands on your wounded. Sweet-talkin' 'em. Flirtin'. 'Let me wash your head, honey!' You'll have her on her hands and knees kissing their you-know-whats before it's over! By God, it's a disgrace! A damned disgrace!"

Josephine Steedman had been biting her fist. Now she looked up, took a deep breath, and said, "The man's right!" Nothing more than that. She was known for her blunt ways. But her eyes raged.

"God knows he's right," Bertha Long said. Her fingers were digging into my arm as she yanked me away from the surgery curtain. "I told you all she didn't belong here. Just like she didn't belong sewin' with us! Did you see what happened with her there? Did you see us yellin' at each other? Fightin'? You see what she done?" She gave me a hard push toward the tent flap, so hard I would of fallen, but Delilah was there, grabbing me with both hands and whispering, "Let's us get outa this place. Let's us run fast as we can. Just go!"

"That's right, go!" screamed first one woman, then another as they started coming from all directions, too many of them to count, and Ferris laughing in the middle of them, his eyes never leaving my face.

"Wait," I managed to say to Delilah, me holding onto her as hard as she was holding onto me. Even with them all coming at me, there was something I had to know. Ferris's eyes. Why were they so self-satisfied? What did Ferris Greenwood know all of a sudden that he hadn't known the last time I saw him?

He saw me looking at him, saw my mouth open, and before I could say a word, he spit hard at the floor, aiming for my ankles. I felt the spit hit my leg, but stood my ground.

"Why are you here?" I said to that grinning face and saw the grin get wider, till every crooked tooth in his head showed itself.

"The body, Mrs. Crocker," he said, the words teasing me. Whistling 'round inside his huge wet mouth, then shooting out at me like they were whirled from the round opening of a cave.

"They found the body! Yeah, they did. You know the one I mean, 'course . . . my brother Hank Greenwood's body? His poor body? The Morgan Raider?" He lowered his eyes then, so nobody couldn't see the dancing light in them, and said in a mournful voice, "Ladies, your sweet nurse there murdered a soldier, same's the kind you're letting her tend. No telling how many of your men she's let die today . . . just holding a towel over a face quiet-like, him too weak to struggle. Letting a man bleed to death rather than tie on a tourniquet. Who knows what she's done to your boys, ladies!"

As a roar come not just from the women but from some of the men on the cots and the floor, the same men I'd helped tend all the morning, I also heard for the first time, mingled in with the roar, the terrible sound of the rebel yell. First the men, then the women, too. Such a sound I never could of imagined. Something of human that made the sound worse than animal. All of them screaming, as for a kill. A letting-go of pity, as maybe a mountain lion lets go of pity to down its prey. And I knew I was the prey. I heard Delilah scream, felt her fingers cutting into my arm, and we drew back together as a swarm of yelling people come forward.

I told myself, *Be calm, be still. Don't be a fool. Take it. Take it. Beat them that way. God, help me. Help me beat them that way.*

But it was no use. My body had a deeper mind, a mind that knew its own fear, so that sudden-like, in spite of the reasoning, this other strong spirit come over me, come flooding over my insides. From my belly, into my arms and legs, and I ran for the tent flap with a scream of my own, pushing, shoving, then diving toward the speck of daylight that turned into gray sunlight that left me blinking, stumbling over a pegged rope. Then I was running down the open path between the first two tents, Delilah right after me, hanging onto the tail of my skirt, the only part of me she'd managed to grab after I'd broke free.

"Wait!" she gasped, trying to pull me to a stop. But I tore my skirt from her hands and took off even faster. All I knew was

232

I had to run. Hank's body was found and there wasn't nothing to stand between me and the noose. Not no more.

Behind the third tent was a hitching post with a half-dozen horses tied to it, nags mostly, for the good horses had been given or stolen in the name of war. Ama's two horses were there with the wagon still hitched to their backs.

Before Delilah could stop me, I half jumped, half climbed to the driver's seat and was already turning the horses when she grabbed Omaha's muzzle. "You got to tell me where you goin'," she begged as I brought the switch down on first one horse's back, then the other.

"Let me go," I cried, struggling to be free. Any minute they'd be after me, I thought, my heart pounding in my throat. "Don't tell Tom. . . . Don't tell Ama. . . ." The words come in a confused jumble and I weren't even sure what I was begging her not to tell them. Just let me go, that was the only important thing.

A noise behind Delilah made her turn. Then she glanced back at me, such a frightened look in her eyes that I knew somebody was coming and who that somebody must be. In that second, she made up her mind.

"Hurry!" she whispered, eyes huge in her head. "Just go! Go, Lizbeth, and don't look back!"

That fast I was gone. I beat old Docker and Omaha harder than they'd ever been beat, and still the miles felt like they were crawling away. Hank's body found. But could they prove it was me that done it? They don't need to prove much! You saw them back there, Liz Ann! You saw that mob. They would of strung you up on the spot, if you stayed 'round to let them do it.

The cold wind whipped the horses' manes into a flurry, brought my hair into my eyes. Hurry. Faster. Where's Ferris? Is that horses' hooves behind me now?

I passed an ambulance going the other way, swerving so close I almost run the driver off the road, him raising his crop at me, yelling. Saw men beside the road raise their eyes to see me go, but without much curiosity. One man lifted his hat. Another tried to wave me down. But I kept going until I reached the side road leading to Symphony Oaks, then finally the drive. I was so out of breath I could of been doing the running myself.

Only when I reached the top of the circle drive did I slow the horses to a stop, throwing myself from the seat to the graveled drive in one leap, then running toward the house. A second later, the front door flew open.

"Mama!" Melissa come screaming. Behind her, I saw the round eyes, the pale scared face of Ben.

I packed without thought, throwing things into a cloth bag, anything that could serve as clothes for me and Melissa. A sweep of my hand cleared out a dresser drawer. Little-girl things went into the bag. I ripped two dresses off their hangers and stuffed them in, too.

"What happen? You got to tell me what happen!" Beulah was screaming at me, both her fists grabbing at her apron. I saw *Run* in her eyes too, but she weren't thinking me, she was thinking her. Her and Daisy. "It the war?" she yelled, the veins standing out on her throat. "They comin' out here? You got to tell me!" she kept saying, first with her voice, then with her hands on my shoulders. Shaking me so hard, my head went back and forth.

I could hear Melissa screaming again, Daisy too, and caught sight of Ben's face as he tried to pull Melissa toward the bed. Daisy clung to Beulah's dress. "Mama!" she screamed, and Beulah bent and scooped her into her arms. Then through the distance, like horses racing across the sky, come the hoofbeats. I stopped packing and felt the last bit of air leave my lungs. Beulah's eyes sharpened on me, but some of the desperate light went out of them. A thought seemed to of come, something that brought her to the window. She stood there holding Daisy, chewing on her lip, watching, as both Ben and Melissa went to me, both of them reaching to save me from something they

234

couldn't understand. Only knowing in the way that children know things that I was in some sort of terrible trouble.

"It's all right," I whispered, trying to keep my face blank, my voice without no fear. With my arms 'round both of them, I made my way to where Beulah was standing by the window. Looking down, we saw the sheriff and Ferris get off their horses. Heard the sheriff's heavy knuckles rap on the door. And I thought: Every bad dream seems to come true.

Twenty-one

"Them rains," Ben Oates said, "washed up the body."

He stood near the steps of the porch trying to act dignified, his gray eyes like iron and so steady. But I saw nervousness pop out all over him like hives. Ferris was beside him turning the world into brown slime, but he wasn't batting an eyelash. Just smiling.

For some reason, I stood there nodding. Yes, I see. The rains. But after all this time? I tried not to look at Ferris. But I could still see him in the corner of my eye, like a speck that was jammed in my eye, that wouldn't go away. Something in him flickered a moment, made me think of the instant when a snake shows its tongue.

"Anyways," the sheriff went on, "he was found by two boys rowing a boat down by the fishin' hole. Foolin' 'round, you know boys. First thing you know, they see a man's body half floatin', half buried in a bog. Course I went down there and had a look. 'Pears to me from his clothes he was shot in the back."

" 'Pears, nothin'," Ferris snapped. "She shot him in the back, sure and certain."

"Not so much left of his body, you understand," the sheriff said, me still nodding. "Fact is, he was identified by his clothes and his lower right tooth."

"Broke it on a sparerib bone." Ferris grinned at me. "No

236

mistakin' that tooth. I'd stake my life on it. Or make that *your* life!" He laughed out loud.

The sheriff sighed. "Not that I want a woman in my jail," he said. "I never had one in my career and I don't want one now. But Ferris here and his brothers are pressin' the point. I'm afraid I'll have to ask you to get some clothes together and come on with me."

I heard guns in the distance, thought of a world half tore apart. And only now he'd come for me. All those silent months and now, when the earth had turned the maddest, here he was.

"She tried to make a run for it," Ferris said, hopping round the sheriff's boot heels. "I want that in the record."

Ben Oates turned a sour face on Ferris, probably because he was making him arrest a woman, but he didn't say nothing to him, just to me. "Get your things—" he started to say, but he never got finished because there was Beulah coming down the stairs behind me. My bag in her hand.

"Look there! You see that?" Ferris yelled. "She already packed! I want that in the record too!"

The sheriff took the bag out of Beulah's hands. Before I could say I'd seen them coming and that's why I'd packed, he was rummaging through the bag, pulling out handfuls of little-girl things. He held up a little dress. He said, "She was runnin', all right." Then he threw Melissa's clothes toward Beulah and said, "Come on, ma'am, we'll be headin' in."

But Ben and Melissa were standing together on the porch, crying, so I turned and made a last try. "You got nothing," I said, my voice shaking. "Nothing to say I was the one that done it. For God sakes, Sheriff. We're at war! Anyone could of shot him."

Ferris opened his mouth and gave out with the worst scream of laughter I'd heard from him yet. When he could talk, he shrieked, "Only Hank's gun, that's all!"

Ben Oates nodded and his eyes, fastened on my face, were nothing but serious. "It was left on a chair beside your bed, ma'am. In your cabin."

"Hank's gun, no mistake!" This from Ferris. "Three notches carved in there for the three wildcats he killed."

I stood there staring at them, thinking, *The gun.* We'd got down on our hands and knees and scrubbed out a whole bedroom from top to bottom. And we'd left Hank's gun on the chair!

"I took it away with me the day I checked your cabin, ma'am. Didn't think much about it at the time. When Hank's body turned up, I right away showed it to Ferris. He identified it right off, and well, ain't no way Hank would of left your cabin without his gun. Unless . . . unless, of course he was drug out feet first."

"That's right!" Ferris yapped, stuffing a plug of tobacco in his jaw, chewing and spitting like he was raring to go. "Let's take her in, Sheriff. Get her arrested, 'cause she guilty as sin!"

"Just a minute, Ferris," the sheriff said. "I'll do this my way. It's my job."

"He was my brother, yeah. Now I'm gonna get justice!" Ferris said, his face flushed dark red. For all the yelp of laughter that broke out of him, and under the slick shine of his eyes, a strange fear lurked, something hard as bone, something that rattled 'round in that terrible mind of his. For all his braying clamor, it was there.

The sheriff stood silent a while, waiting for Ferris to calm down. "There were two bullets missin' from the gun," he said then. "One was where Hank shot your husband—"

"In self-defense," Ferris interrupted.

"And one was where . . ."

The sheriff hesitated, and I run my hand across my forehead to clear off the sweat that had popped up on my brow. "Where I shot Hank," I finished. For some reason, I was still nodding.

If there wasn't a thimbleful of mercy to be found in Frisbin, there were quarts of curiosity, and folks come from everywhere to crowd 'round the doorway of the jail and get a look at me

238

sitting on my cot behind bars. The news spread within the hour. Ama, Jinny, and Delilah all come flying from the hospital and crowded into the jail, almost wading in men, old and young, who were sitting 'round Sheriff Oates's desk and over at the fire and just about anyplace there was to sit, even the railing that curved 'round the cell space, separating it from the sheriff's office. The other women wouldn't go past the door, just stood there peeking in and whispering to each other.

The sheriff opened my cell door and let Ama and Jinny and Delilah inside. We all four sat on my little bed and stared at each other. With everybody looking at us, we couldn't even talk. It was like we were on display or something, like a cake at a church social. I could hear Ferris snorting out there in the crowd of men.

I thought, If they wanted to lynch me right now, they could. There's too many of them to fight. Too few of us. I heard them laughing, saw hands slapping pants, heard breath wheezing out of mouths, like they were leaking air—heee, heee, heee. Tobacco juice squirting between teeth into cans. A musty smell floated over the room. Smelled like dirty, sweaty clothes.

"Tom wanted to be here," Ama said real low, leaning so close to me we could of been one person. "It's too dangerous, Elizabeth. There was a fight at the hospital after you left. Tom did his share of the damage and now the men hate him. There was talk that if he showed his face here . . ."

"I understand," I said.

"What us gon' do?" Delilah whispered.

"There's nothing to do," I whispered back. "It's over. Only way they'll let me out of here is in a box."

Ama cut me with her eyes for saying such a thing. She looked toward the sheriff, who weren't far outside the cell, sort of hovering 'round, looking miserable at having all these people inside his office and a woman in one of his two cells.

"We need privacy!" she said in a very loud, very clear voice. And the laughing and the murmuring stopped cold, everybody listening to her. Wanting to get the inside story on what we was all going through.

Ben Oates stared back at Ama. He looked so helpless, I could almost of liked him if the situation was any different. "How I'm goin' to do that?" he said. "The way the danged cells are made is so's you can look through them."

And the room rocked for a minute, everybody laughing like he'd made a wonderful joke. Then quiet again, everybody trying to hear what Ama would say.

"I want something to hang up," she said. "Get me something. A sheet or a blanket. Something so I can have a private conversation with the entire damned town eavesdropping."

"*Ohhh!*" at that, whether because Ama swore or because she'd insulted the whole town. But Ben Oates went upstairs to his rooms and come back with a horsehair blanket. He pushed it between the bars and Ama and Jinny took it and tied the corners top and bottom to the bars. It was a big blanket and a little cell, so pretty soon, we were away from their eyes. I could of fainted from the relief of not being stared at. What I did was finally cry, trying to cry soft so's not to be heard, Delilah holding my hands so tight it felt like she was fair wringing them off. They let me cry, looking at each other, their faces solemn as death.

"I'll get you a lawyer," Ama said, kneeling in front of me.

"No sense to do that," I said, drying my eyes with the back of my hand. "We don't have trials in our town. We have justice, remember?"

For as long as I could remember, folks had said that. That in our town, we didn't have trials, only justice. We had a courthouse, but we'd never had even one trial there, not a real trial with a jury nohow. A prisoner got hauled into court and faced the only judge in town, Judge Early, a thin wiry kind of man. He was an old man, been judge since before I was born, and had the energy to keep going forever, or so it seemed. A prisoner would tell his side of the story to the judge and either he'd promise to pay a fine or give part of his crops to another farmer for a debt owed. Or he'd have to promise to stay sober. Maybe he'd have to stay in jail for a while.

And sometimes, a higher justice was needed. That's what

the town said when it was a case of rustling cattle. Or something uglier even, like the mountain man who come down to settle a score with a man who'd bothered his wife, so the story went, and ended up killing Billy Waycock, who never had been right in the head. Then this higher justice was needed, and it took place in the dark of night, and when it was over, the prisoner was gone, just disappeared without no questions.

Delilah was looking round the tiny cell. It was maybe ten feet by twelve feet. "How you goin' to the bathroom?" she said. " 'Less you ask the sheriff right in front everbody. Tell him you got to pee, and everbody laugh till they sides split while he walk you out the door."

Ama looked at a pail standing in the corner. It was a rusty old thing, looked like it was an old milking pail.

"You can't mean it," I said, feeling myself get white. "I have to go in that *bucket*? Who's going to empty it? How am I gonna use it with everybody outside? And what about a bath . . . ? I can't take a bath here. Oh, Ama, I'm afraid to be *human* in a place like this. Anything I need is just one more thing they can hold over my head."

Just then we heard a scratching at the blanket and a work-worn finger pushed up the bottom and a face like a friendly monkey peered up at us.

"Thank God," Ama said. "It's Miss Margaret. Sheriff? Are you there? Would you let Miss Margaret in, please?"

A minute later little Miss Margaret Caldwell was inside with us, looking at us with a lively air, her tongue twisted up inside her upper lip. "Well, now, I been cookin' for the sheriff for over twenty years, but I never had a woman to look after," she said, not smiling, but with a smile somehow in her voice and in her being. "You won't have to worry about clean sheets and pillowcases, and I can cook out of anythin'. One of my regular gentlemen—he has a drinking problem that brings him through the door ever so often—claims I could make up a wonderful soup out of a bucket of dirt if that was all that was available, and I believe he's right."

Ama sat back down on the bed and put her arm 'round me.

"With Miss Margaret and all of us besides, you'll make it through," she said.

As it happened, the sheriff threw everybody out of the jailhouse at six o'clock. Even Ama couldn't persuade him to let her and the others stay the night. "Everybody goes," he said, rubbing his chin with his fingers. He looked weary and fed up with having his jail overrun. "Besides, a prisoner don't get to have no servants. I've never had it before and I ain't havin' it now." He glanced over at me with kinder eyes than I'd ever seen from him. "It'll go better for her without that mob 'round," he said. "I suspect she'll collapse from the relief of it."

"Go ahead and leave," I told Ama and the others, looking from one worried face to the next. "Really. Miss Margaret will look after me. Besides, they'll be needing you at home and at the hospital, too."

"I wait outside all night," Jinny said. "See that little hole of a window you got? That little runt of a thing? I be right outside. You need to talk, I be there. You worry 'bout somethin', I be there."

"I want you to go home to Melissa, Jinny."

"No. No, I can't do that, Miz Lizbeth."

"You've got to," I said.

"No. I be here. They have to blow me out here with a rifle, they want me goin' someplace."

I stood up and hugged her hard. She felt good and tough. She'd been through so much, it was near impossible to kill her. I looked into her eyes and saw something stubborn looking back at me. "Please," I said, picturing her squatting outside the jail all night with God knew who saying God knew what to her while she waited for the sun to come up.

Ama had put her hand on Jinny's shoulder, but she shrugged it off and leant closer to me and spoke in the kind of voice you'd expect to use if somebody had both hands 'round your throat. "Night my family burnt," she said in that strangled voice. "My little boy sick. He need me but Miz Jane need me at the big house. Won't take no. So I go and some fool start a fire.

242

Burn my angel up. Burn everthin' I love up. I ain't much on leavin' folk."

"But think of me knowing you're out there," I said, trying not to flinch from what I saw in her face. "I'll be more worried about you being out there than me being in here. Anyhow, I'll have Miss Margaret."

Miss Margaret looked up at Jinny. She was so short, she would of had to look up to almost everybody, even tall children. She couldn't of topped four foot nine. She had a square body, full of energy. A thick head of gray hair. Hazel eyes that snapped and a mouth that was most usual pursed out while she thought. Seldom smiling, but something about her face made you think she was smiling, even now when she was most solemn, peering from Jinny to Ama to Delilah.

"I'll take care of her," she said, and there was something in her voice that made Jinny sag down against Ama, both of them letting out their breath like they'd relaxed all of a sudden. Delilah nodded.

From that minute on, I was under the care of Miss Margaret. When the others were gone, I watched Miss Margaret bustle 'round my tiny cell, dusting and cleaning, even getting down on her hands and knees getting the corners clean. Me too weak to even offer to help. Just sitting on my bed with my feet drawed under me, watching her work. Then she went out into the office and opened a closet and found a nicer sheet and pillowcase for my little bed, and when everything was just so, she handed me a cowbell.

"My place is right out the back door," she said, pointing through the back door of the jail. "If you need me for anythin', you just ask the sheriff to fetch me. Or if he ain't here, you take that bell and ring it for all it's worth. I'll be sure to hear you. Course, I ain't leavin' yet, don't worry."

She took me outside to the outhouse, not even checking with the sheriff, who watched us out of the corner of his eye while pretending to read over some papers at his desk. She

243

unlocked and locked my cell door herself, even taking the key right out of Ben Oates's top drawer without asking leave.

"You may not like being here," Miss Margaret said, shaking her gray head at my cell. "But you're not goin' to lack for anythin' I can bring you, I can promise you *that* at least! A woman don't belong in no jail cell. Not even a hussy, which you ain't."

She waited for the sheriff to go upstairs before she left me for the night, sitting up sewing in a small rocker that she dragged up in front of the bars outside my cell, and somehow I knew that this was Miss Margaret's own chair. That she had brought it here, probably without even asking the sheriff's permission. But when the sheriff had finally gone up to his rooms, she got up right away.

"I suspect," she said in a kind voice, "that you'll be needin' some time for yourself. Now if there's nothin' else tonight, I'll see you bright and early tomorrow mornin'."

I'd untied the blanket after Ama and the women had gone, feeling like I was in a tomb and wanting to visit with Miss Margaret. But now that I was alone, I tied it back in place and laid on my bed, letting my muscles go limp. Aching from where I'd held myself tense for so long. Laying there on the bed in my everyday clothes, I felt my eyes stinging from tears I'd been holding back, but the tears come now, flooding through my fingers as I tried to stop the flow. Probably, I thought, Miss Margaret had known that I needed this, needed to be alone, needed to cry, just like she'd known that I needed the nice pillowcase and a trip to the outhouse so I wouldn't have to use the rusty bucket during the night.

I cried for a long time, then dried my eyes and stared 'round me. It's really true, I thought. You're really in a jail cell, girl. Thin moonlight shone through the small square window high over my bed and streaked the bars with light. I looked up. Such a small square of a window. My head would hardly fit through . . . that is, if I was to try to fit it through. Outside that window was a free world and friends and Melissa. Inside were me and disgrace.

Melissa! I thought, calling to her in my head, trying to make my thoughts sail through the window and through the space that divided us. To find a way into her dreams or something. If the worst happens and I never make it out of here, baby, don't you fret. You got people to look after you. You got Ama and Jinny and Delilah. You got Benjamin and Tom who love you, too. And maybe, somehow, I'll get home to you. I never heard of a woman shut up for life, or lynched. . . .

"Elizabeth? Can you hear me?"

I sat up sudden-like, and the voice was as close as my own mind. I could be thinking the words, not hearing them.

"Tom!" I said, imagining him standing beyond my window. As quiet as the moon. Steady. And I felt my heart quicken.

"Elizabeth, listen. There are a few who might cause trouble," he said in his quiet way. "If they knew . . . well, about us. Me being local. You being Joe's widow . . . I wasn't sure you understood why I stayed away."

"Ama told me," I said. "But even if she hadn't, I'd of known. I know who you are, Tom. What you are."

"That's good," he said. "We all miss you. The house is empty. I stayed with Melissa until she went to sleep. She wasn't crying. Nothing like that, just worried. But I gave her my word you'd be coming back and she said she'd believe anything I'd ever tell her. Then she went to sleep, peaceful as an angel. Isn't that amazing?"

"No," I said. "I'd believe anything you told me, too."

"Then," he said, "you can believe this. Elizabeth, no matter what happens, I'll always be here for you. And I'll always . . ."

But there was a murmur of voices, and then a jumble of voices, and a moment later I felt him go. Just disappear into the night. Then even the other voices faded away.

It was so quiet I wondered if he was ever there. Or whether I'd imagined him.

* * *

The next day the sheriff and his deputy led me down to the courthouse, me between them, Ama following behind. Jinny and Delilah watched from the door of the jail. "No niggers in the courthouse," Frank Wright had said in no uncertain terms, and the sheriff had growled, "Watch your mouth, Frank. No need to sound like a overseer." Anyhow, the women stayed behind to help Miss Margaret scrub the whole place, probably as some kind of personal thank-you for her looking after me. Although, knowing Jinny, it might also be an excuse to make sure the jail was as clean as she wanted it to be, now that I was living there.

"I smell smoke," Ama called just as I'd caught whiff of it. "Is there a fire?"

Ben sniffed. "Somethin's gone up somewhere. Smells like a big one."

Even as he said it, the big gong sounded, and we knew the fire brigade was being called to alert, and that the war was still raging. Someone had said earlier that Bragg had taken Lookout Mountain, that his sharpshooters were camping all along the Tennessee River Valley below the ridge. Even so, the Federals were digging in again, and wounded and sick were still coming over the mountain, enough so Frisbin looked to have a permanent hospital in the middle of the town square.

Chattanooga was under siege, too. It had used to be a pretty town. Most of the grown-up people of Frisbin had visited Chattanooga and said how beautiful a city it was. A delightful place and prosperous, with lovely homes and tree-lined streets. Now it was a poor city, with army everywhere and people's homes tore down as fuel for army campfires. Ragged men, women, and children from Chattanooga were on our streets now, calling themselves refugees and saying how they'd left filthy cold shacks and certain starvation in favor of picking their way along the road, hoping for something better.

"Wonder where the blazes are?" Frank Wright said, and I saw him frown and lay his head to one side. "We ought to be on our way out there, Ben."

"We will. Let's hurry up and see Abner Wilcox. Then we'll get goin'!"

Ben jerked open the right door of a pair of double doors leading into the white courthouse and I stepped into an open area full of round columns and pictures hanging on long white walls. I breathed in polish, not smoke, and saw shining windows and gleaming wood doors and a double staircase leading up on both sides to a white railing. The railing was topped with an oak hand rest that curved out to a big upper landing and led back to other doors facing me, and in the middle was a hallway that led back to still more doors. I must of walked through the courthouse yard a hundred times, but I'd never walked inside.

"This way," Ben Oates said, hurrying me along, and a minute later we were inside a huge room with at least fifty seats inside and a platform bigger than a pulpit. A chair for the judge was built into the middle of the platform, and the Stars and Bars were to one side, not far from a big empty picture frame.

Ama come up beside me. "I'll bet that used to be a picture of George Washington," she said, jerking her thumb at the picture frame.

Next thing I knew Abner Wilcox come out wearing a suit and a rather yellowed shirtfront. He laid a few papers on a stand at one side of the platform and leaned toward me. "All right," he said, "let's hurry before our whole town goes up in smoke. How do you want to plead? Guilty or not guilty?"

I stared up at him, remembering how Abner used to try to see how much money people dropped in the church collection. And if he didn't think you put in enough, he'd tell you about it.

"She's not guilty, Abner," Ama said, and gave my arm a warning squeeze that said *Pay attention!*

Abner frowned. "I want to hear her say it."

"Not guilty," I said, and heard him sigh.

"Have you thought about this plea?" he asked. "You should think about it."

"Where's the judge?" Ama asked.

"He's gone to be with his son," Abner said. "You heard

that Wayne took a shell at Port Hudson, didn't you? That was back in July and the boy's still critical."

"Judge or not," the sheriff said, "I want to know from somebody whether or not I have to go on keepin' the woman inside my jail! I can't take a man prisoner while she's there. I can't do my work or nothin' with people crowdin' 'round to get a look at her."

"Not to be unfeeling," Abner said, "but all that has nothing to do with me. Christ, Ben, we're in a war!"

"But why should I have to get caught in the middle of this whole mess?" Ben Oates demanded. "You know as well as me that jail's no place for a woman. I got people laughin' at me, makin' jokes all over town. It borders on the downright ridiculous, Abner."

"Listen, Ben"—Abner frowned again—"it's a mess for all of us. Still, we've got to arrange things."

He finally said he'd get off a telegram to the judge. In the meantime, since the Greenwoods were so set on charges being pressed, there wasn't nothing to be done but to keep me in jail. A bail hearing was out of the question, unlikely even if the judge was in town. Ferris Greenwood said there was ample reason to believe I'd head north at a second's notice, what with my political loyalty to the Yankees. "And God knows," Abner added, "he's probably right. All right, I've entered the plea, Ben. You take her back to the jailhouse and—"

"Let's get to that fire!" finished Frank Wright.

"Wait just a minute," Ben snapped, and headed up front. He started a long conversation with Abner, out of our earshot, the two of them leaning toward each other, the tops of their foreheads almost touching. Ama and I sat waiting, hearing the shuffle of feet behind us as Frank Wright went back and forth between two windows.

"Ben, the sky's blacker than tar," he said. "More soldiers are pourin' in. We got to get out of here!"

I saw Ben stop talking, saw him and Abner turn toward the window. "Sweet Jesus," somebody said. Next thing I knew, I was in the courtyard, half running toward the jail, squeezed

248

between the deputy and the sheriff, them dragging me by the arms and Ama trotting in front of us, her face lifted to the black smoky sky.

"It's coming from all directions!" she said. "It must be . . . Oh, Elizabeth, it must be . . ."

Sheridan! I thought before she even said the word. I heard Ben Oates gasp as we all realized in the same instant what was happening. Sheridan's order from Grant: Make a wasteland of the enemy, Grant had said. Steal what can be stolen and burn the rest. And all of a sudden, we knew it wasn't a bluff. Our valley had fallen under those orders. Our town was burning.

"Oh, Ama!" I cried, grabbing hold of her sleeve. "Do you think Symphony Oaks . . . ?"

Her face turned to me, white but controlled. "As soon as we get you back to the jail," she said, "I'm going straight home and see about things."

"Ama, Melissa's back there! And Daisy and Benjamin! Go right now! Hurry! Hurry!" My voice come out in a frightened wheeze. I'd never in my life seen such an eerie blackness spreading over the earth, not even in the darkest rainstorm. Already, I was choking on the smoke. Already, I knew the fires were too many to fight, that barns and fields and hay and wheat and whatever crops were left in storage were gone. Houses gone. Everything gone.

People poured out of the shops, out of the hospital tents and shants. I heard screams, saw people running toward houses that were miles away. Saw little Jessica Long with both hands wound up in Bertha's long skirts, trying to pull her back toward the cook tent, and Bertha trying to claw Jessica's hands free. Saw Josephine Steedman and Esther Wells crying with their arms 'round each other. Men run for their horses, while others stood and shouted at the sky.

"Sheridan's burnin' us!" somebody yelled at the top of his lungs.

And from everywhere there were screams. Shouts. Somebody beating his fists against the courthouse.

People wept into handkerchiefs or against their sleeves or

just let the tears run without trying to dab them away. "Oh, damn the Yankees for doing this! Damn them!"

"The Yankees!"

"The damned Yankees are doing this to us!"

"Oh, Lord, get home, Ama," I begged her, trying to push her away. "Get Docker and go! For God's sake, go as fast as you can!"

But the face she turned to me was full of trouble, and her huge eyes seemed to see something I didn't. In the split second before I knew what was happening, I saw Ama try to wrap her body right 'round me; then somebody grabbed her, tore her away from me, and I heard a woman screaming, felt fingers tangle theirselves in my hair and yank. Somebody else got their hands on my dress and I heard a loud rip as one of my sleeves were tore clean off my arm. A rumble of "Yankee!" Seconds later they come at me from everywhere.

"Help her!" Ama gasped to Ben Oates, but he had jerked me into his arms before she spoke, used his body to shield me as the first rock was thrown, followed by another and then another. Big rocks, and I heard the sheriff swear as him and the deputy pulled me between them, all of us running best we could toward the jail.

"Come on!" Ben Oates snapped at me, and struggled to push through the shabby folks that swarmed the street, a fair number stooping for rocks. Hands reaching for my clothes, my hair. Women's nails digging into my arms when I covered my face with my hands. Then Delilah was beside me, coming from nowhere and shielding me on one side with Ama on the other. Jinny was in front of me, wrestling with two women who had their arms straight out in front of them, their fingers made into claws.

Somehow we were at the jailhouse, little Miss Margaret holding the door wide and half dragging us inside. The sheriff and the deputy pushed their weight against the door, but they couldn't hold it. It opened and closed, opened and closed. I stood there trying to scream, my voice raising and falling like a young bird trying to fly, and saw Ama and Delilah and Jinny putting their weight against the door too, and it still wouldn't hold against the crowd.

"Get her in the cell!" the sheriff barked, and Miss Margaret come running to me, pulling on me, the key in her hand.

Trembling, we got into the cell, slammed the door shut, and locked it behind us. Miss Margaret dropped the key down the front of her dress and picked up the blanket. She had to climb on the chair to tie the top corner to the bars and, rooted to the floor, I saw her dragging the chair in one hand, the blanket in the other. She was standing tiptoe on the edge of the rickety old thing, almost going over, when I finally ran to get the other end. By the time we heard the mob inside the jail, heard the sheriff's voice shouting at them to get the hell out of his jail, Miss Margaret and I were huddled on the bed together, shivering, our arms wrapped 'round each other and the blanket shielding us from view.

I'd never seen a mob out of control, not like that, and never could imagine how a lynching must happen. But it was about to happen now and I knew it, and as something like a roar rose up on the other side of the blanket, Miss Margaret knew it too and pushed me against the wall with her whole strength as if she was trying to push me right outside the jail.

"It's no use," I kept telling her. "There's just too many of them!"

She was shaking her head, trying to tell me something, pointing out toward the mob, and I heard Ama's voice shouting, caught a glimpse of Delilah's scared face peeking in at us from one side of the blanket, then her back as she used her body to block off a space we hadn't covered.

Then like a crack of lightning in a thunderstorm, a sound so shocking and loud that it quiets even a screaming mountain lion, a gunshot rung out. And in a second, everything stopped.

"You know me!" the sheriff snapped in the sudden quiet. "And you know this ain't going to work! First man or woman sets one foot closer to that cell is a corpse. Now I never made a threat in my life I weren't ready to keep and you know it. That's why you made me sheriff."

I whispered to Miss Margaret, "Would he really shoot somebody?" and she shook her head, her face as gray as the cell walls.

But if it was a bluff, it held. For a while they argued. Then I heard the energy draining out of the crowd. I heard the anger droop into sadness. Little by little, the murmurs died as people started dragging theirselves out the door. I could imagine them hanging onto each other as they stared out over the land, maybe trying to tell theirselves they had a chance. Maybe their house hadn't burned with the rest. Maybe their fields, their barn of hay, their last cow hadn't been destroyed. I heard the long wails, the "Ohhh, God, ohhh, God" that rose to heaven outside the wall that separated us, the sound mingling with the smoke that drove them into coughing fits as, one by one, they started to go home. Finally, Ama and Jinny went too, hurrying home to Symphony Oaks and our children and Beulah and Tom. Wondering, like the others wondered, if anything was left.

Twenty-two

All day Delilah helped Miss Margaret wring wet sheets and hang them over the windows and by the door to battle the smell of black smoke, the terrible smell of loss that hung over the town. Then just before dark, we heard the horses. A regiment of horses, for that's what it were. The call of "Yankee!" rose as a blue army thundered through the streets, torches in their hands, come to finish what had started in far-off fields. From inside my cell, I heard shouts, a few guns firing, but not many. Ben Oates stood by the door watching, his rifle propped beside him, and said there were just too many of them to fight.

Instead, the Frisbin people fought the fire that raged through the heart of our town. Eating the two-story shops, the trees that lined the street, and the courthouse. Sheridan had said, "The people must be left nothing but their eyes to weep with over the war." That's what the blue army tried to leave us with. Nothing but our eyes.

"Oh, God," Delilah moaned, putting her face in her hands. "Somethin' awful happen back home. I just know it. To all them. Somethin' terrible!"

I put my hand through the bars and patted her shoulder. "Ama always knows what to do," I said. "Besides, she's got Tom to help her."

She gave a sort of strangled sigh and put her hand over

mine. Then in the next moment she pulled away. "No, I got to go to them!" she cried. "I got to see they all right!"

"There's fighting in the streets!" I screamed back at her, and grabbed hold of her arm before she could get away. She stared hard at me with the same look Beulah gave Ama that night. "I'm worried too, Delilah. I don't feel I can stand another minute of not knowing. But I won't let you go!"

Miss Margaret passed by then, sweeping the dry ash that blew in under the door and down through the chimney, settling on everything like dust and coming back in flaky clouds the second she swept it away. "There's worse things than not knowin'," she said, sending ashes flying with a shake of her white hair. "Believe you me, bad news is heaps worse than not knowin'. What's killin' you is not gettin' any *good* news."

I saw the flush on her face, saw the gleam in her eyes, and knew she was thinking of her own good luck. Today, while most houses had burned to the ground, Miss Margaret's neat little two-room cottage still stood behind the jailhouse, spared like the jail had been spared for reasons known only to the Yankees. Maybe they'd had more compassion for prisoners than for the common citizen.

Delilah looked at Miss Margaret with a cold stare. "We at war," she said. "Only good war news is when it all over. Nothin' till then."

But when Delilah left for the hospital late that night, Ama come twenty minutes behind her, crashing through the jailhouse door, eyes peering, hair stuck out where the wind had blown it, and bearing the good news that Miss Margaret had talked about.

"Symphony Oaks is still standing, Elizabeth!" she cried out. "The Yankees saw the flags. Saw them flying. They only stopped for food and water and left several sick and wounded in our spare bedrooms. Dear Lord! Symphony Oaks still stands!"

"Flags!" I said, staring at her. "But Tom took . . . I told him to . . ."

For a few seconds, Ama's jaw hung slack; then she grinned.

254

"I hung another flag on the gate last night," she said, coming toward me through the cell door as the sheriff swung it open. "Hung another in the back, and two more on both sides. Had flags everywhere. The children were scared, of course. They saw the smoke, smelled the town burning, but they're fine. Last I saw them, Beulah and Jinny were fussing over them, trying to get them to bed."

I felt my heart jump, and my arms went 'round Ama so tight she said, "Elizabeth, please, I've only got so much breath left."

When I stepped back, I saw for the first time that her face was tired under her smile and she wasn't holding herself as straight as usual. She looked chilled, and something like a shiver trembled through her body.

"There's bad news, too, Elizabeth," she said, and settled herself on my bed. "Freeland Farm is gone. There's nothing left. Only things standing are the chimneys."

"Oh, no, Ama, they couldn't burn something that beautiful. They couldn't!"

But she just stared at me, hands fumbling to undo her cloak, coughing some at the same time. Her breathing wasn't right, neither, 'cause she kept taking in short gasps of air. "I'm afraid they did," she said, clearing her throat. "You should have seen Mr. Higgins. Screaming and hollering and carrying on. He nearly got himself killed."

"And Tom? What about Tom?" I asked. The words fell from my lips without feeling, sounding numb as I was.

"He's like he always is," Ama said with a slight shake of her head, as if doubting her own words. "He just goes on, Elizabeth, not really saying much about anything. When you see him, it will be as if nothing happened. He just goes on."

I looked at the gray plank walls of my cell. The bleached cloth curtain that hid a makeshift clothes rack in the corner. The roof overhead that shook at any racket. "Maybe I won't be seeing Tom no more," I said, and could feel Ama sigh next to me.

"We'll all see each other again," she said. "It's like roads.

255

Where is the beginning and where is the end? A road is a road. It just goes on. And Tom is part of *your* road. Just as you're part of his."

Ben Oates was sitting on top of his desk, watching us and shaking his head. "So your house didn't burn, huh?" he said. "Something else for the town to hate you for."

"I didn't think of that," Ama said after a minute. "They *will* hate us for keeping our house."

The deputy turned from the open door to face us, smoke drifting up from his feet like fog rising. There weren't much to the frame buildings the Yankees had torched, and the fires close to the jail had 'most burnt out. The courthouse fire still burned, but not roaring, not raging, just finishing the supper of mahogany and oak and rosewood it had started.

"I lost my house, too," Frank Wright said, fingering his deputy badge. His stomach, so big just weeks ago, was almost flat now. "And to tell you the truth," he went on, his eyes hard and small, "I ain't got no fondness for Yankee-lovers that get their houses spared while the rest of us get burnt. My whole spread's black and flat."

"I don't love the Yankees neither," Ben Oates said, "but as long's I'm sheriff and you're deputy, you'll uphold the law, Frank. I want that clear between us. And shut that damned door. It's freezing and the air's worse outside than inside. I can't breathe and I'm gonna catch pneumonia."

Frank's eyes turned back to the street and he stood staring for a few seconds before he shut the door.

"Lock it," Ben Oates said with a look that made me wonder if he'd really been cold or had the door shut for a different reason.

"Listen, Elizabeth," Ama said in a soft voice, putting her arm 'round me and pulling me against her. "Help will be here soon. I sent a telegram."

"What kind of help?" I said, still thinking about how Frank Wright looked as he locked the door. "What do you mean?"

Ama laughed, the sound of it drifting through the cell.

256

"Why, I mean Cole MacPherson, of course," she said, her eyes gentle and teasing at the same time. "I've sent for him."

I studied on Ama in a black silence for a minute before she puckered her eyebrows together and said, "What's wrong? I thought you'd be glad."

"Cole MacPherson," I said, my voice coming out flat and desolate as the burned fields that must still be smoking under the moonlight, "is the last person alive I want to see me like this, Ama!"

Ama looked at me curious-like; then her mouth opened, but no words come out. Only a cough, born of too much smoke and too much night air. A second later, she was tying on her cloak and heading toward what she called the sheriff's "barricade."

"You can pump water out of a pump, but you can't never pump the real story out of somebody lessen they tell it to you on their own," Miss Margaret said, making herself comfortable in the one chair inside my cell. I'd had a basin bath (a cold business in jail), and I was shivering on my bed, a blanket 'round my shoulders and a hot cup of herb tea in my hand. "You *wantin'* to tell me who this MacPherson man is? Otherwise, pay me no nevermind."

"He's a gentleman," I shuddered out. "In a way, I barely know him."

"You're not drinkin' your tea," she said. "That'll warm you faster than anything except love." She gave an evil laugh, her eyes dancing at me. "And love gets you so warm, only way to cool down is to get hitched. *That* soon gives you a chill."

"I believe you," I said, shaking.

"You're not drinking your tea."

I strangled down a gulp of tea. "Were you ever in love, Miss Margaret?"

"Men"—she frowned—"are just babies. They ain't so bad.

257

They just don't hardly grow up. Just ever once in a while you find one that does."

"Maybe nobody grows up, even women," I said. "And men just complicate things. So you never did love a man, then?"

Miss Margaret crossed her arms tight under her breast and hugged herself for a few minutes without saying nothing. I'd known her as Miss Margaret my whole life. But now I knew her as a woman. I knew her hands, all twisted up with arthritis, must bother her something fierce sometimes, yet she worked on without complaint, and her needlework was better than the work of many a woman with straight fingers. I knew she hadn't no vanity at all, but she went 'round with a touch of red on her all the time, sometimes just a piece of ribbon pinned to her dress, because that was her favorite color, she said, since she was a girl. I'd heard the women of Frisbin call her a shy little woman, so shy that she never went to socials or church or even funerals, though she was often called to help dress a corpse or watch children so somebody else could go to a dance. And she marched through the jail, where no other woman would dare to go, as fearless and sassy as she was tiny.

She wasn't a smiling woman and yet I saw her laughing to herself sometimes when the sheriff or somebody else acted like a fool. And she knew how to bake and sweeten without milk or sugar, how to make the best hot-water cornbread I ever ate. How to make people feel she cared about them. Most of the time she was silent, yet she was one of the easiest people to talk to that I ever met. She had wicked cheerful eyes that looked young as a girl's though she was maybe seventy. And without her saying so, I knew that telling about her love life would be something like inviting somebody in to watch her take a bath. In that, I guessed she was like most women. Still, I wished she would tell me.

"Well," Miss Margaret said in that voice of hers that made you feel she couldn't ever tell you a lie even if she wanted to, "maybe there *was* a man I cared about. He didn't want to get married and neither did I. You might say we kept company for almost forty years."

I looked into her wide unblinking eyes and said, "I never heard you was seeing a man, Miss Margaret." I thought, You were able to keep company with a man for forty years without nobody in this town hearing about it? Then, like I was pulling the name out of magic, I all of a sudden remembered Raymond Hill, who had lived up the road over the top of a shop. He did some work at the jail, did some tending of property for folks. I could almost picture him driving Miss Margaret's father some-place—maybe I'd run across them some time or other, although if I had, I couldn't remember quite when. He was a quiet man with shy, sweet eyes, and you couldn't help liking him—when you noticed him at all. Raymond, I thought, enjoying the idea of him and Miss Margaret.

Miss Margaret gave me a look that let me know she knew how to do things without the whole town knowing her business. "He's dead now for eleven years and three months and five days," she said. "I trim the grass over his grave and dig out the weeds and make sure there's flowers growin' there. And when I die, there's a spot for me beside him with the headstone already made out. My name and the year I was born and just '18' with the last part left out. When you're alone, you want to do as much as possible for yourself ahead of time, because there ain't no guaranteein' what can happen once they bury you. I do kind of worry they won't put the year of my death on the stone. It won't look, well, *finished* somehow if they don't. I won't feel proper dead."

I looked into her eyes and said, "Miss Margaret, to tell you the truth . . . Well, I doubt with all this that I'll outlive you. . . ."

"A young woman like you, you hush," she said, working her jaw at me.

"Well, if I *do* outlive you," I said, "I promise you I'll make sure everything's done the way you want it. I'll see to your casket, plant flowers, and take care of your grave and Raymond's, too."

"You'd really do that?" she said.

"I swear to you."

259

Her eyes marveled at that. "That'll be a load off my mind," she said, almost to herself. Then, looking up: "It's that plot behind the Baptist church. You'll see my name on the stone."

After a minute with neither of us talking, I said, "Cole MacPherson's a lawyer. I just got a silly idea about him once, nothing more than that. But somehow, I don't want him to see me like this. Even though if he comes, I'll be just a client to him."

"You sure about that, you bein' just a client?"

"Outside of being a friend of Ama's," I said, trying not to think about that night in the back acre. "Except for Ama, he'd probably have a hard time remembering my name."

"Well," she said, after mulling on it for a minute, her tongue in her cheek. "If you are just a client, then it don't make no matter, does it? He won't be lookin' at you. Not as a woman, anyhow. And if you're wrong and he's kind of interested, if you know what I mean, then he won't be lookin' at *where* you are, he'll just be lookin' at you. Either way, it'll be all right, you see."

Later on, in the middle of the night, tossing and turning in bed and hearing the sounds of the people who more or less lived on the streets, refugees turned out of the overcrowded shants by the residents of Frisbin who'd been burned out of their houses, I found myself repeating her words. If I was just a client to Cole, then it *didn't* matter. He really wouldn't be looking at me. Then how come I was all of a sudden worried about how I looked? Wondering how to get a looking glass without somebody laughing at me for asking for one. How to ask Delilah for a fresh dress . . . when there was hospital work to be done? How to get some ribbon for my hair without anybody wondering what I was up to? All of a sudden, I thought of Tom and felt my face grow red. Tom was my future, not Cole. And if Tom was to see me, I wouldn't worry, because I'd *know* Tom would find me pretty. What does Cole have to do with anything, I thought. But . . .

The next morning when Miss Margaret fetched the key from under the sheriff's nose and poked it in the lock, she had a looking glass in her hand. "You want me to brush your hair for you?" she said after she'd brought me to the outhouse and after I'd washed up. She had me sit on the floor and she sat on the bed above me. I felt her twisted fingers in my hair, then the brush, and I felt myself start to relax. "You got nice pretty hair," she said. "And the prettiest face I ever did see. If you want a man, I reckon you'll get him all right. He won't have a chance."

Instead of telling her about Tom, telling her that I already had a man, I murmured, "Imagine that." Then, before she could follow that line of talk any further, I said, "Miss Margaret, what does it feel like to work 'round nothing but men all the time? And practically living in the jailhouse?"

"Well, you do kind of feel like your whole life is one little corner of the world," she said in a dreamy voice.

"Didn't you ever want to go anywhere else? Out west, or have adventures? Or maybe just take trips or something?"

"No," she said, "I never wanted to be anyplace I wasn't."

Delilah come later without Ama or Jinny, but with two clean dresses over her arm, and gathered up my dirty laundry to take home. My laundry was one thing the women at Symphony Oaks wouldn't let Miss Margaret do. It was their way of doing something for me and they wouldn't be denied.

Delilah said Ama and Jinny were at home, nursing the sick soldiers that had been left at Symphony Oaks.

"A Yankee die last night," Delilah said, making a bundle of my laundry. " 'Nother one 'bout dead. Miz Ama and Jinny up all night. I don't know how they keep on. Neither one get a wink if somebody need somethin'. Look here," she said, unpinning a folded-up handkerchief at her sleeve, "what Miz Ama send you."

There was something inside the lace handkerchief in Delilah's open hand. She held it out to me, and my hands trembled as I took it from her. It was Ama's cameo necklace, one I'd admired since I first come to live at Symphony Oaks. It was the most beautiful cameo I'd ever seen, small and delicate, and hung on a thin gold chain.

"Miz Ama say tell you it your'n now. It ain't no loan. It your'n." Delilah took it from me and fastened it 'round my neck. I felt the cool chain 'round my throat, the small solid weight of the cameo under my collarbone. Then she stepped back to get a look at me. "That look outstandin'. Just look beautiful."

"But . . . but she can't do this," I stammered out. "This cameo was Ama's since she was a girl. Her mother wore it."

Delilah snorted. "Nobody tell Miz Ama what she can or can't do. She say just wear it. Say you tell Lizbeth not to worry, Cole MacPherson be here soon. Say believe it."

Three days later, he was. The door opened and a chill blew across the room. Then Cole swept in, dark cape whipping 'round him, his hat in one hand, a bag in the other. He was thinner and his hair were long and blown. He needed a shave and his cravat had come loose.

And I thought, The moment never comes the way you imagine it. He was all business, serious. Almost at once we were sitting in chairs, him outside the bars in Miss Margaret's rocker, me on the hard-backed little chair inside my cell, facing each other. He was holding a polished board on his lap. It was something like a desk, with paper and an inkwell. His hand shook when he reached for his pen, and he frowned.

"I'm sorry, Cole," I blurted out. "I know you don't want to be here."

His head came up and his eyes met mine direct. "When you don't want to be somewhere," he said, smiling for the first time, "it takes a darned sight longer than four days to get there. I had to bribe my way onto a military train!" He laughed.

It was a full-bodied sound, from deep within, and after that he was the same as I remembered him. The same reckless glint in his hazel eyes, his jaw thrust out, his grin devilish, and I felt

262

my head spinning just looking at him. He was more alive than any man I'd ever met, and more vital, telling me about his train trip, how he'd shared the food in his hamper with a ragged Confederate soldier, how he'd gambled some and lost four dollars, and how it saddened him to see at last the blackened streets of our town. At this last, the smile fell from his lips, but he shrugged and lifted his hands as if to say, This damned war. I asked him if he'd been to Symphony Oaks yet, and when he said he hadn't, I told him about the Yankees there and how I hadn't seen Ama or Jinny in days; they were nursing the sick men who'd been left behind. That I hadn't seen Melissa once since they'd locked me up. I talked on, telling him everything except about the Greenwoods, and finally fell silent, my eyes on the floor. It was dark. Night had come early.

"You're going to have to talk to me about it, you know," Cole said in the most gentle voice I'd ever heard him use. I looked up then, not at Cole, but at the sheriff, who was over pretending to warm his backside against the stove. Really, he was looking over at me and Cole, nosing in on what we were up to.

"I'm guilty, Cole," I heard myself say in a low voice. "Ama said to say not guilty, but I did it. I shot the man."

Cole raised his finger to his lips. There was a warning spark in his eye. "I never met anybody who wasn't guilty of something," he said in a voice just above a whisper. "Smile for me. Turn your shoulder just a little more this way, and lean your cheek against your hand. There, he can't see you, and if you'll keep your voice low, he can't hear you either. Just aim your words for me, like you're whispering in my ear. And stop looking like it's the end of the world. The whole way here I kept trying to imagine what you'd look like and I just kept hoping you wouldn't look like it was the end of the world and now you are."

"Do we have to talk about it?" I said. "I'd rather talk about Richmond."

"Forget Richmond," he said.

We sat there staring at each other so hard, I forgot where

I was. It was like no time had passed since I last saw him. It was like I'd never lost a husband, never been engaged to another man after that. Life is strange. One minute you're in jail. The next, you're something close to flying. I put my head in my hands.

"Elizabeth? What's wrong?"

"Nothing," I said, with my eyes closed, seeing myself back in my cabin laying on that shabby bed. Joe on top of me with his trousers half down. I could smell the whiskey on his breath. Pretty soon, I could see Ferris on top of me, too. Feel him inside me. See Fat Charlie wiping his lips, watching us. Cecil Junior with that look of disgust on his face, his nose in the air like he was smelling something rotten, but no mistake, he was looking, too. And I knew out of everything that had happened to me, the worst thing in the world would be to tell Cole these things, and have him see me the way I was that night.

With my eyes still closed, I said, "I can't use you as my lawyer, Cole."

I heard him take a deep breath, but he didn't say nothing. Probably shocked. Relieved was more like it, no matter what he might try to say. Now he could bribe his way onto another train and be rid of his obligation to Ama. Maybe he could be gone in days—in hours, maybe. I felt seconds, then minutes, tick away and neither of us moved, me sitting there with my hands pressed against my eyes. Go on, I thought. Make some nice little regret speech, then pick up and go.

Then I felt a warm hand take my hand and draw it out through the bars of my cell, the metal just grazing my wrist. Lips against the spot on my flesh the bars had touched. And when I finally opened my eyes, Cole was sitting there holding my hand against his cheek.

"Elizabeth," he said. "Don't you understand yet? I've loved you ever since I laid eyes on you. And I've hated that bastard Tom Higgins ever since Ama wrote me you were planning to marry him."

I stared at him. "That's . . . that's impossible," I said.

"Don't you think I know it's impossible?" he said, sound-

264

ing halfway exasperated. "I must have told myself it's impossible every day since I left you at Symphony Oaks, and still I couldn't forget you. It's absolutely impossible, but it's true. I love you, Elizabeth."

There was no air for me to breathe now, no time or space to get away as he drew himself close to the bars. We were so close I could feel his breath on my lips.

"I fell in love with you through Ama's letters," he said. "I invented the trip to Georgia just to meet you. And I knew the second I saw you that I'd been right. There were no airs about you. You were so real that you stunned my senses. I didn't seem to have any defenses against what you were doing to me. I was happy I'd found you, and I hated myself for coming to Symphony Oaks and finding you and knowing I had to leave you again. Then when your husband died, I made myself wait before I came back. I knew I'd hardly be able to restrain myself when I saw you—knowing, of course, that you were in mourning. When Ama wrote me that you were more or less engaged to Higgins, I was ready to kill either him for taking you away from me, or myself for being stupid enough to have waited."

Listening to him, I thought it seemed that no one in my life, not even Ama, had ever talked to me with so much love in his voice, so much tenderness in his eyes, amazing shy for such a man of the world. No one had ever held my hand against his cheek and made chills shoot right through me. All this in a jail cell with the sheriff trying to pretend he didn't see nothing and giving us sidelong glances.

"I didn't mean to tell you any of this," Cole said after a while, and he took my hand down from his cheek now and held it kind of loose on his knee like he was giving me the chance to draw it away. His face was flushed high along the cheekbones and his dark hair was wet at the temples as if he was sweating in this cold place. "I know you're engaged, Elizabeth. You can forget what I said, or act like it never happened. But when you said you weren't going to let me represent you . . ." He broke off and leaned forward. "What are you thinking, letting me ramble on like this? What's on your mind?"

"I guess that it's dangerous," I said in a slow voice, "to let down my guard with a man like you."

"Why's that? You've got the best protection," he said with a little smile, eyeing the bars that caged him out and me in. "But then you always have. Bars, a husband, a fiancé. And still, here I am, a hopeless case. I've had no encouragement from you whatsoever. You've been out of my life, even out of my sight. Yet, no matter where I go, no matter what I do, I can't seem to get you out of my head. One three-sentence wire from Ama telling me you need a lawyer and I jump out of my skin and come racing to you like a lover. Either I'm in love or I'm a lunatic. I don't know which."

"Love," I said, "must be a lot easier when it's just two people in the dark someplace."

"We were alone in the dark once," he said. "It wasn't all that easy. Every time I'm around you, I make a fool out of myself. Now tell me. Tell me what happened to you, Elizabeth. Can you do that for me? Tell me about the Greenwoods."

I was silent for a moment, realizing again that we weren't alone. Behind us was the sheriff, prowling and curious. Cole and I were supposed to be client and lawyer, I reminded myself. Client and lawyer. In a sudden rush, the cold, damp night air pressed in on me, everything pressed in, and I straightened and with my heart hammering away in my chest, I said, "I'll try, Cole. I'll really try."

266

Twenty-three

 *S*omehow the truth I finally told Cole that night with my shoulder turned toward the sheriff, my cheek leaning on my hand so the sheriff couldn't read my lips, was a more complete truth than I would of told any other lawyer. Even how I'd come to marry Joe without much more thought than a moth takes when it flies into a lantern light and gets burned alive. You get married because that's what girls do. You wait until somebody picks you and if the person looks all right and has prospects and if both families approve, then you get married and you have a handful of babies. I told him how nice Joe looked when he married me and how pleased and proud Mama had been to have him in the family. And how shabby he got and how Mama had come to hate him, and hate me, too. About the leg he lost, and his whole soul that he seemed to lose along with it. How we lived with hardly a word between us except when he'd get mad and yell. How quiet the cabin would get at nights until you could hear the mountain creatures screaming on the cliffs. How loud the rain would fall on the roof until I wondered what we'd do if the roof just fell in.

I even told Cole, looking straight into his eyes and speaking without a falter, how it was when Joe would take his pleasure with me. How he wouldn't even take his clothes off, just pull down his trousers and tell me to hush. How I'd close my eyes and count just to get through it, and Cole's eyes, grim, angry,

locked so hard on mine that it seemed to me he was remembering it with me.

"I wish to God he weren't already dead," he said. "I'd like
the pleasure of killing him myself."

"He was actual dead a long time before Hank Greenwood
killed him," I said, slow-like. "Walking 'round, eating, drinking, but dead. It was almost like he was waiting for that night.
Like it was destined to come to him. Like it was some nightmare
he'd been having for a long time. At least, he had something
hopeless about him. More than what already happened to him,
I mean. Sort of like a tragic past leading to a tragic future. Like
he was just sort of hobbling along toward some terrible end that
only he knew about. If he didn't exact know it would be the
Greenwood brothers, he knew something horrible was going to
put an end to him. You could almost read it in his face."

It all come flooding out of me. Thoughts I couldn't remember even thinking. Fears, sadness. Sometimes I'd cry and Cole
would stop writing and wipe his own eyes. Into the night, I
talked and talked and Cole sat beside me listening with the
polished board on his lap, taking pages and pages of notes, and
Miss Margaret would bring us food and melt away like she
never come. Delilah's face appeared at the front door and then
she was gone, too, shutting the door behind her with a muffled
rattle. For a while Frank Wright hung 'round the stove, trying
to have a loud conversation with the sheriff about the destruction of the town and the looting that was going on with people
helping theirselves to goods from stores, and how the law ought
to take action. Finally, the sheriff said he was right and he was
officially sending him 'round to put an end to the looting, or as
much as possible, as he hisself had to protect the prisoner. Still,
he said, there must be dozens of men Frank could round up to
help. Frank strapped his gun to his waist and bustled away. I
had a feeling that the sheriff had sent him away on purpose,
leaving only hisself as a silent watchdog in the background of
our talk.

Sometimes, Cole would turn to ask the sheriff a question.
One of the first questions were about Hank's gun. Whatever

made him remove it from the cabin? Evidence, the sheriff said. After all, a man had been shot. Later on, Cole asked him about Hank's body. When exactly was it found?

To my surprise, the sheriff looked a little put out at the question. He said he wasn't exact sure. With all that had happened, who was about to remember the date? He looked almost hurt, like he'd befriended us, gave us our privacy, and now Cole was putting him on trial.

"Just a minute," Cole said, soothing him down. "I'm just trying to get something straight. This is September. Mrs. Crocker was arrested on the twentieth of this month. How long before that was the body discovered?"

"Well . . ." the sheriff said, shuffling 'round.

"A few days, a week, perhaps?"

"Second day of this month."

"September second!" Cole exclaimed.

"Now wait a minute. We had to contact the Greenwoods and they live up in Murfreesboro, which is a far piece, so . . ."

Cole's thick brows pulled together. "They live in *Murfreesboro*? What in blazes were they doing in Frisbin?"

"Turns out," the sheriff said, "they was on a raidin' party. Requisitionin' for the Confederate army. I thought it was only Hank who was in service, he was a Morgan Raider, but Ferris Greenwood done informed me the whole family is in the military. 'Ceptin' for the pa, who's home tryin' to take care of the farm. We contacted Cecil Greenwood, the pa, in Murfreesboro and he wasn't right sure of Ferris's unit. . . . That's why it took Ferris a spell to get here, I reckon."

"He's a soldier and he's hanging around this town during wartime?" Cole exclaimed. "Now that's an odd turn of events!"

The sheriff grunted. "Odd or not, that's what's happened. And you know as well as me, there's a heap of folks supposed to be in the army that's doin' pretty much as they like. Farmers go home for plantin' and again for harvestin'. They're not even botherin' to call them deserters in some regiments. They're too glad to get them back when they finally sign back in."

"I know very little about the military," Cole said, writing

everything down. "But you say the Greenwoods are all Morgan Raiders?"

"Hank was a Raider. The others are in different units. Let's see, Charlie and Ferris are Army of the Cumberlands and I believe he said Cecil Junior is in Virginia. . . ."

"And they were all in the same raiding party." Cole whistled. "I can see I really *don't* know anything about the military!"

"Anyways," the sheriff said, barely looking at Cole. "I got things to tend to upstairs. It's long after hours, so it's best you be quittin' now."

Cole waited until the sheriff had disappeared up the narrow wood staircase, then turned sudden-like to me and said, "There's two ways for us to go, Elizabeth. Self-defense or just a simple 'not guilty' plea. There are two main problems with self-defense. The first is we're leaving the door open for opinion. And, remember, once we opt for self-defense, we're coming right out and admitting you shot Greenwood. I don't like to do that when the circumstantial evidence is so very slim. Apparently no one saw you with a gun, no one saw you burying Hank's body, no witness has stepped forward to even say he heard a gun go off on that night. . . . What have they really got? I want to sleep on it, but I think just sticking to the story you told the sheriff may be the way to proceed. The Greenwoods came, shot Joe, raped you, and left. Keep it simple. Hank Greenwood took off on his own and you have no idea what happened to him, but he was very drunk; that's why he left his gun. Changing your story would open a door that I personally don't want to open. Not in this town." He chewed on his lip for a minute.

"Elizabeth?" he said. Then, in a very soft voice. "Is there really nothing other than the gun to link you with Hank's murder? Nothing at all?"

"Nothing that I know about," I said. "Our place was so far away from any other houses . . . Nobody would of been close enough to see or hear anything."

"Then we'll go with 'not guilty,' Elizabeth. Now I believe

270

I'm about to be thrown out of here. And you've had a long day. You need your rest."

But how was I to rest when Cole had noplace to go? I was surprised he had decided not to stay at Symphony Oaks, but he was determined to stay close to the jail. It wouldn't of been a problem if the hotel was still standing, but the sheriff said it was nothing but an ash skeleton, top to bottom. The few beds and the charred furniture that had survived the fire had been scavenged, whether for fuel or furniture, he wasn't sure. There were no other hotels or boardinghouses left standing. Even the shants were full, and some people were living in tents and some were sleeping right beside the streets, without any kind of roof over their heads. Cole said if he had to sleep under a tree, then he'd do it, but he had no intention of leaving me here alone after what I'd told him of lynchings and a higher justice.

Miss Margaret, who'd served us both dinner, come in to take the dishes away then. "Well, now," she said, gathering them onto a tray, "there's always my place. He could stay with me and that way, he'd be right out back."

"A man stay at your place?" the sheriff hooted, as he come back down the stairs. "Well, that would look just fine, wouldn't it?"

She put her head back and laughed. "You mean, you think folks would bother talkin' 'bout a seventy-year-old woman taking in a young man like this one? With everything else that's happened in this town, they'd have to be addled in the head to pick on that bone of a tidbit! Besides, lots of women in this town have took on boarders, and some of *them* didn't have a man in the house. Let me tell you, they'd be glad enough to take him now if their houses hadn't burnt down."

The sheriff put his chin out. "It wouldn't look right. You ain't never been married, Miss Margaret. A widow woman takin' in boarders is one thing. A old maid like you is somethin' else."

"The reason I ain't never been married," Miss Margaret said, sticking out her own chin in his direction, her wrinkled lips

271

pursed together, "is that I never would let a man boss me 'round. And I'm not plannin' to start now. I said I'd take him and I'll take him. I'll stay back in the bedroom and he can sleep in the front room and no one will be the wiser unless you open your damned mouth, Ben Oates!" She looked over at Cole and added in a real casual way, "You can move in tonight, young man. Put your money back in your pocket for right now. You can pay me whatever's fair later, and I'll feed you, too, well as I can. Though with food supplies what they are, we'll all be eatin' mud pies pretty soon!"

As I laid on my bed that night, listening to the fine spray of rain that blew against the outer cell wall, it seemed to me that Cole had done to me what the war had done to the town: taken away all the old landmarks that I used to recognize myself by. Shaken me down to the core of who I was. Brought fire to me, confusion to me. Made every other feeling I ever felt less. Because when he was in the room, there was no other world. I had no friends, no family. I couldn't even hold still to think of Melissa. All I wanted to do was watch Cole, think of him, feel what he made me feel.

And what of Tom? I had trouble even remembering his face. He was a tall shadow in my mind. Somebody I'd been teaching myself to feel something for. Somebody my mind cared about. Not like Cole, who my body still remembered after all this time. I never had to try to feel a thing for him—it all come over me like a firestorm.

The safe one was Tom, of course. He wouldn't bribe his way on trains . . . and don't forget, Liz Ann, trains run two ways. . . . Tom could tell you something and you could believe it forever. "I'll always be there for you," he'd told me, and I believed him like Melissa had believed him. He'd be there or die trying.

And yet this night was Cole's night. He washed over me like the rain washed over the town. There were no Tom or anybody else as I imagined the rain hitting the ash, sending black streams rushing toward the river.

Either I'm in love or I'm a lunatic, he'd said. You didn't know with Cole, like you knew with Tom, but I knew at least one thing about me.

I felt something. And that probably made me the lunatic.

Twenty-four

A week later, on the second of October, Judge Early come back home from Mississippi, and though he found his own house burnt level and his barn gone—wheat, hay, and corn with it—and every animal he'd owned requisitioned by the army, he was at the jail by eight o'clock the next morning. He stood warming hisself at the stove while he shook his gray head at the sheriff and said that the missus and him were living in a shack on the property now. In the few days since the fire, his two daughters had hurried to fix up a toolshed that had escaped burning, and that's what he was calling home now.

"Main thing, though," he said, brightening some. "My boy's much improved. He's amazed all the doctors. Not that I don't grieve over losing my house. It was my pa's and his pa's before him. But it isn't just me on the losing side. *Everybody's* lost everything, don't you know, and it's not right to complain over a house when you've still got your boy." Looking at Cole, he said to the sheriff, "Is this counsel for the lady?"

Cole had just come through the door after breakfasting at Miss Margaret's, and he stuck out his hand to the judge. They shook hands with force, like they were measuring each other's mettle and giving back proof of their own.

"I deeply appreciate, sir," Cole told the judge, "that with all your trouble, you came to us so promptly."

"You do, do you?" Judge Early barked right back at him.

"Where do *you* come from, where the judges lay in bed all morning and keep the law waiting?"

Cole laughed and glanced at me sitting in my cell, pretending to write a letter to Ama, which was what I'd been trying to do all morning. Ama had only been to see me once in the past week. She had her hands full looking after the Yankees who were still holed up in her spare bedrooms. They were gravely ill, she said, not looking well herself. There were deep hollows between her neck cords, smoke blue. As Delilah helped her on with her cloak, I'd looked into her eyes and saw that her eyelids were wrinkled like walnut hulls.

But not to worry, Ama said. Cole was there to look after me now.

And he was. He spent most of his time working beside me. Sometimes silent, sometimes asking me questions. And writing, always writing. So intent on his work I'd think he'd forgot I was there, when I'd look up and see his eyes fastened on me. Last night he'd read poetry to me from outside my window as a protest against the sheriff's early closing hours. It was the bawdy kind, full of steamy images, and when I told him to stop, he laughed rich and full. "Good night, Elizabeth," he'd said, and I heard him whistling clear into Miss Margaret's house. Exasperating, I thought. And I couldn't wait until the next morning to see him again.

Now when I heard him say "Why, sir, I'm from that great city of Richmond," I lifted my eyes from the letter again, and sneaked a peek at the three men, who had gathered by the stove.

"Ah," the judge said. "That makes sense, then. I hear Richmond's in the hands of a pack of fools, the biggest one being Davis, in my book. And how about that face on Douglas? With that body of his, he must do nothing but eat. I'd lie in bed, too, if I had to deal with those idiots. Are you really going to go ahead with this trial-by-jury nonsense, son?" All this was said in the same tone without stops or starts.

"I don't know how you came to hear such a thing," Cole said. "I shouldn't think there'd be any need for a trial at all. I'd simply like to appear before you in an official capacity and suggest that you dismiss the case and set Elizabeth Crocker free to go back to her daughter. Dismissing her case would be in the interest of the whole town. The hospital tents are full and the town's overrun, what with citizens being burnt out of their homes and refugees marching through the town on a daily basis. People are poor and hungry and there have been too many atrocities committed in the name of war to prosecute them all. Easier and more expedient to simply dismiss the matter, wouldn't you say? Especially in this case," he added, meeting the faded blue eyes of Milton Early, "with the lady wrongly accused."

"Hold on there, boy. Not so fast. So," the judge murmured, warming his hands over the stove, "you're going for a not-guilty plea."

"The case is laughable. There's not a particle of evidence that Mrs. Crocker shot anybody."

"The Greenwoods disagree with you. They say she shot Hank in cold blood while he was in the act of requisitioning supplies for the army. And they're on the popular side, being soldiers and all."

"Do they claim they saw her pull the trigger?"

"You know they didn't see it. They spent some time looking for Hank, hoping against hope he was still alive. But Ferris does claim her husband took a shot at him. That, in fact, is when Hank was forced to kill him. And there's a signed statement from all three of them that with her husband lying dead on the floor, the lady herself grabbed a small pistol from under her pillow and threatened to shoot them if they went after her stored goods. They finally took off, but Hank stayed to try and talk reason to the lady. He didn't know she was a Yankee. Being a Raider, Hank had a stubborn streak in him."

Cole put his foot on the front part of the stove beside the judge's. "Off the record," he said in a low voice, "how do you feel about these charges by the Greenwoods?"

The judge's eyes snapped. "As a secessionist state and town, we don't allow anti-Confederate citizens to shoot our army just for requisitioning supplies. These are not only my words, understand; they represent the feelings of Ferris Green-wood. He made a trip to see me last night the minute he heard I'd come home. I must agree, he has a point. Wouldn't you say?"

"You mean regarding the army's right to civilian sup-plies?"

"Exactly," the judge said. "There's a list of Tennessee farmers as long as my arm who got injured or killed while refusing to give up supplies to the Confederate army. I have compassion for them, but I support the reasonable needs of the army."

"Does rape fall under the category of reasonable needs?"

The room fell silent then, the sheriff and the judge trying hard not to look in my direction.

"Mr. Greenwood mentioned Mrs. Crocker's charge of rape," the judge said in a low voice. "But he says it's a lie. It's just her word against his and that of both his surviving broth-ers."

"Just as Mrs. Crocker says their allegation of murder is a lie. And that's not even their word against hers. They didn't see her shoot anyone. They didn't even know their brother was murdered. As you yourself pointed out, they looked for him for a good long time, hoping he was still alive! Mrs. Crocker had already buried her husband while the Greenwoods were still riding over the countryside looking for Hank. Probably he raped some other poor woman and her husband shot the bastard."

The judge gave a long sigh, hissing it out through his pursed lips. "Look . . . what was your name again, son?"

"MacPherson," Cole said, never taking his eyes from the judge's face. "Cole MacPherson."

"Listen to me, MacPherson," the judge said in a level voice, keeping his jaw square. "I've never had a public trial in this town. Never called a jury. I'm the law here. That's how it's always worked."

Cole looked deep into the judge's eyes and said, "Give me some idea of what that would mean to us. We'd come before you; you'd hear me speak; and then you'd come to some sort of a decision? Is that what you mean by 'I'm the law'?"

"Something like that," the judge said. "Look here, even if this trial goes through, it'll be on my own terms. We're not a part of the United States. I won't be held accountable to any part of the federal Constitution. If I decide to try the lady, it'll be to free up our jail and get rid of this whole mess. I don't want to hear any complaints about my methods being unconstitutional, and nobody in this town's going to hang around saying things about higher appeals and the like. Believe me, if she weren't a woman, you wouldn't be here. There wouldn't even be a prisoner over there to bother about."

"Are you referring to this higher justice I've heard so much about?" Cole snapped.

"It's the way we do things, that's all, and I've lived too long and been the only judge in this town for too long to give a goddam what you think about it, son. I've never been challenged, and if you feel like challenging me now, we won't bother about this trial at all. We'll figure something else out."

There was something so mild and yet so dangerous in the judge's face that the anger drained out of Cole. All of a sudden, he looked just plain scared.

"Judge," Cole said, sounding almost pleading now, "just for a minute, let's pretend Mrs. Crocker actually did the shooting. *If she did it,* she would have killed in self-defense against the act of rape. She would also have killed the man who shot her husband in the face. And Ferris Greenwood, the man who's bringing these charges, is as much of a murderer as his brother. Hank Greenwood pulled the trigger, but each and every man in that room is legally and morally responsible for Joe Crocker's murder. Hank Greenwood killed the lady's husband by shooting him through his mouth right in front of her. With Mrs. Crocker's small child right there in the room to see what was going on! In the name of God, sir, why don't you tell the sheriff to just walk over and unlock the poor woman's cell?"

The judge watched him for a while without saying anything. When he did talk, he looked down to search his breast pockets, finally pulling out a long cigar. "Is that so," he said. "Well, what if my opinion says the Greenwoods have got the

278

favored claim? They've got the body of their brother, they've got their brother's gun that was found in Mrs. Crocker's bedroom, and they reported their suspicions to the sheriff right after Hank came up missing. And don't forget the body was found right here in this town, shot in the back. The back, mind you, not the front! Not the usual sort of shot that's fired in self-defense."

Cole stared at the judge for a minute as though he could hardly believe what he was hearing. Cole knew law, and he'd said my case was as flimsy as they come, not even enough to bring me to court if this was Richmond. But he didn't know Frisbin. He didn't know that Milton Early took care of everything legal, just like Doc James used to take care of everything medical. If the judge said you were guilty, you were guilty, just as if the doc said you were going to die, you were same as dead.

"I think," Cole said, drawing a long breath, "that I'm going to ask you for that jury trial."

Pretty soon, the two men were in chairs pulled up close to the stove, with the sheriff sitting on top of his desk listening in. There was all sorts of things to be decided, the judge said. First of all, where to hold the trial, since there weren't no courthouse anymore. Biggest buildings left in the center of Frisbin were the long wood shants. Other than that, there were tents, or the jail, or a few half-burned stores, which were too small to be used as a makeshift court.

Cole said what about throwing up a building quick, something like a barn raised up by the community. In fact, it would be a shant, just bigger than the ones we already had. It could be built in a matter of a few days. Then after the trial, it could be used as housing for refugees and anyone who needed temporary housing while they rebuilt their homes. The judge nodded and said that was probably the best idea.

Next thing was to set a quick trial date. A woman in jail wasn't to the judge's taste and, "speaking frankly," he said that I wasn't necessarily all that safe in jail. In these times, tempers could flare; then who knew what the devil might happen. When Cole asked him point-blank if he was hinting about a lynching, the judge puffed on his cigar and said hell, no, he hadn't said a word about lynching, who was talking about lynching? Still, there were such things as a drunk wandering in with a loaded gun, things like that. Anyhow, a quick trial would help the sheriff out and free him from protecting one prisoner so's he could help the whole town, which was more or less still under siege.

With all that in mind, Judge Early said, how about one week from Monday? Nine days from now. That would be October twelfth.

Cole said if he agreed to that, would the judge agree to releasing me into Ama Hadley's custody? He'd personally put up a bond, if such a thing could be agreed upon. The judge said this town was too damned hot for any such idea. They'd have his hide if he freed me for any reason whatsoever.

"How about if the jury finds her not guilty?" Cole asked. "Are they going to have your hide if you let her go free then?"

Before the judge could say anything to that, Ben Oates coughed, and the judge turned 'round to exchange a long look with him.

"We'll worry about that when it happens," the judge said, his eyes still on the sheriff, a puff of cigar smoke curling 'round his ears. "Yes, sir, we'll worry about that when it happens!"

I looked up and it was sundown. I was alone in my cell, shivering, when I heard Deputy Wright call to the sheriff, heard the sheriff mutter something back from above. Then I heard him slam his door closed.

Frank Wright laughed and turned to the other two men I didn't know, and who he'd been talking to for almost an hour. One of the men, the taller, with deep-set eyes and shaggy beard, wore a blue overcoat he said he'd taken from a Yankee prisoner. The other man were small and stout and wore civilian clothes, but had on a pair of Yankee boots.

They passed a bottle of whiskey among theirselves, and I

could tell by their voices and by the way they come and went from the outhouse that they were all drunk. Stumbling some, holding onto the chair one time, the desk another.

At first, they talked war. How all of the Federal army had slipped through Bragg's clumsy fingers and had found a safe home in Chattanooga. How in our town all of the railroad bridges were burnt now, and all the roads east and west were lorded over by artillery. The only escape from Frisbin were the mountain passes—steep, rocky, twisting trails that were nothing more than footpaths. And as if to confound both armies, more rain.

It was heavy now, coming down on the roof of the jailhouse, pelting the window of my cell and rattling it some. Every time lightning cracked, or thunder roared, they'd all stop and look at each other and then go back to talking.

During one of the pauses, the small stout man started telling Nigro stories.

About the nigger that did his wife dog-fashion so much that she got to chasing horses, and that's why he kept her chained in the backyard—to keep her from getting trampled to death.

About the nigger whore who told the white man he could have some free, but just on one condition. "What's that?" And she said, "Raise my dress up high as taxes, pull down my britches low as wages, and give me the same screwing that Lincoln gave the South!"

After each story, Frank Wright's face flushed dark red. A yelp of laughter broke out of him like a cry of pain, but when he saw me putting the blanket up in front of my cell, he sobered up quick and said, being reasonable, "Well, goddam, didn't I tell you to shut up, Luke? Didn't I tell you twice? We got us a lady present, and wasn't you actin' vulgar? Sheriff runs a clean place here, you understand?"

The tall one drug another swig from the whiskey bottle and smiled across the room at me. "You need help, little lady?" he said, still smiling.

My hands were cold and I couldn't get the blanket up right.

One side kept falling down, and I was just pulling it up again, not paying attention to what I was doing, when the door to the office opened.

Delilah come rushing in first, and then Tom right behind her. Both were drenched through and through, coats soaked, boots caked with mud, wind pushing them through the door like helpless ghosts. After he closed the door, Tom's eyes found mine and he smiled some. Then his face got serious.

"We've come to talk to Mrs. Crocker," he said, turning to Frank Wright, who let him stand there for a moment dripping water on the sheriff's clean floor.

"That right?" Frank said. Beside him, the two men got to their feet, stirred up at the sight of Delilah.

"Hell!" the tall one said. "If it isn't Massa Higgins with one of his slave gals. You two been out neckin' in the rain?" He spoke from behind clenched teeth that held a stubby cigar. Frank Wright and the other man laughed at what he'd said, their eyes on Delilah.

"Wouldn't mind doin' her myself," the short man said.

"Hell," Frank said, "you peckerwoods are all alike. You can't stand niggers but you're taken with that ole soul snatch."

"Listen, Frank, no more of that," Tom said, looking at the deputy, then toward me. "We've got some news for Mrs. Crocker. We'll only be a minute, then we'll be on our way."

"You don't say boo-diddy-shit to Mrs. Crocker, you understand me, Tom? You up there with that Hadley woman nursin' Yankees. Turnin' nigger-lover on us. You got a goddamn nerve, waltzin' in here like this."

The two men beside Frank had turned quiet, their eyes slanted toward Tom, and I was certain there'd be trouble. Tom stood for a moment, his eyes locked on mine. Sadness was on his face, something like love. More than anything, though, he looked desperate.

"All right, Frank," he said. "I'll wait outside. But let Delilah have a few minutes with her. It's important. She really must be told."

It was then I felt my legs give way. My stomach, too. I said

"Tell me" in a hoarse whisper, watching Tom back out the door, Frank Wright get the keys from the desk drawer.

When Delilah got closer I looked to see whether she was crying, but who was to know where the rain stopped and tears began. Then she was inside the cell, and the two of us were hanging the blanket. And all the time this dread inside of me.

When I turned to her at last, she said, "Lizbeth . . ." Then her voice broke and tears spilled out of her eyes. She sunk to the bed and I sat down beside her, looking at her, deadly afraid to ask what was the matter.

"Tell me quick," I made myself say. "Is it Melissa? If it is, don't try to spare me, Delilah. Just say it! Oh, God, it is Melissa, isn't it?"

"It her and Daisy and Miz Ama, too," Delilah choked out, crying all the harder. "They got the typhoid. They had it for days only Miz Ama wouldn't let me say nothin'. The soldiers brung it. It hit hard and fast. Oh, Lizbeth, Daisy . . . Daisy died last night."

I sat looking at her, so stunned and heartsick I couldn't say a word. Died. That beautiful little girl dead. I put my head in my hands, feeling so sick in my stomach I almost threw up. Daisy dead. Those laughing eyes with all the mischief spilling out of them, closed forever. Dead! And Beulah . . . oh, *God*, poor Beulah!

"And . . . and Melissa's got it, too?" I said, forcing myself to take down my hands from my face and put them in my lap. They were shaking so bad I could hardly hold one with the other. "Delilah! You've got to tell me quick. Is . . . is Melissa going to . . . is she going to die, too?"

"She real sick," Delilah said, reluctant-like. "That why we decide you got to be told. But I don't think her so bad like Daisy. And not so sick like . . . like Miz Ama. . . . Oh, Lizbeth, Miz Ama, she . . ."

I grabbed hold of Delilah and buried my head on her shoulder. Felt her fist hammering my back. Felt my own fingers digging into her hair and pulling hard. Felt her tears drenching the shoulder of my dress, but my own eyes were dry and burning. I was too sick and scared to find any relief in crying. Ama, I thought, feeling the grief pumping through me like my own blood. Ama's going to die on me. I know it. I can feel it.

"Oh, don't let Ama die," I whispered to Delilah, my fingers digging into her flesh and knowing in that moment that Ama was my mother. Not taken Mama's place, but actually become my mother. More than Mama ever had. "Oh, God, Delilah, do something, please don't let Ama die, please!"

"Nothin' gonna stop her if she make up her mind to go. She one stubborn woman," Delilah whispered back.

She sat there on the bed holding onto me and letting my fingers claw her like it didn't even hurt. I envied her the way the tears poured down her cheeks, while I listened to her sob out the story of how Beulah had screamed and screamed and cried and wouldn't let nobody take Daisy away from her. How she cried out that she couldn't stand it, that she wouldn't let nobody take her away and put her down in the ground all by herself. Down at the bottom of a hole with dirt on top of her, all alone. How she'd begged Daisy not to be dead, to please breathe for her so they wouldn't take her away from her. Finally, it was Ama getting up out of her own sickbed that managed to get Daisy away from Beulah. She'd took the poor little body in her arms and washed her face and combed and brushed her hair in the little braid that Ama'd always liked to put into Daisy's thick hair.

"Miz Ama promise Beulah she be goin' soon to where Daisy go. And she take care of her, she say. She even say she be bury in the same hole with Daisy. That so she be near and Daisy won't have nothin' to fear. Oh, Lizbeth, we lost Daisy. We gonna lose Miz Ama for sure." Delilah sobbed, trying to wipe the tears away and them coming faster by the minute.

"Time's up!" Frank Wright hollered from behind the curtain, and I wasn't surprised to see how fast Delilah got to her feet.

I'd envied her before for her tears. Now I envied her for being able to run from the jail, back to try to wrestle Ama and

Melissa from death, while I could only sit here, trying not to scream.

Earlier, Cole had left to try to contact the rail to see what happened to a box of books he'd had sent from Richmond; then he had some telegrams to send. After that, he said, he had to meet with a committee of men who were going to decide some particulars about the courthouse. When he come hurrying back, surprised to find the front door still unlocked, he saw an empty jail with Frank and the men gone wandering out to the street, and me alone in my cell, laying face down on my bed. The blanket that usually covered the cell was on the floor, kicked aside.

"Elizabeth, what's wrong?" he said, sounding uneasy, and I forced myself to sit up. My body seemed wore out. I sagged back against the wall like I'd aged forty years since he last saw me.

I said, "It's little Daisy, Cole. Beulah's daughter. She died last night."

He looked like the wind was knocked out of him. After a minute of standing there without a word, he said he remembered her as a baby, a little laughing-eyed, chubby thing that was always into everything. Had to be pulled out of one thing, just to get into something else. When he heard about Ama and Melissa, he said, "Come here," and reached through the bars for me. I went to him and fell into his arms with the bars hard between our bodies, not even looking toward the back door to see if the sheriff was on his way back from eating over at Miss Margaret's. I held onto him, not hearing a word he was murmuring to me, just feeling his arms 'round me, hearing the soothing sound of his voice going on and on, feeling the weight of Ama's cameo 'round my neck, and finally I heard a harsh sound, something like a hoarse scream, coming out of my mouth, then there were a handful of tears. Another scream, then there were more, then relief beyond any words as a flood of tears come spurting out of my eyes onto Cole's coat.

"There now," he said, his hand pressing me closer against

him, the bars harder against my cheek. And I could tell by his voice that he was crying, too.

Later that night, laying alone in the eerie light of jail, with just one lantern lit and hanging by the door, sending long mean shadows over the floor, I imagined Daisy laying buried in that hole. Wide-awake dreams of her and Ama and Melissa swam all over the room. Daisy laughing. Melissa and her with their hands joined together tripping over the lawn looking for bugs under rocks. Ama in her sunbonnet, her face brown and healthy and smiling at me. Daisy dead. Melissa sick and calling for me and I couldn't get to her. Ama about to die without saying good-bye to me. Me locked up in this room that was something like a grave itself.

Except, in graves you can't see and you can't hear. And tonight, now that the rain had stopped, the street out beyond my high little window was noisier than I'd ever heard it. Music somewhere. Someone faraway playing a fiddle. And, yes, somebody else blowing a harmonica. Music that tried to be glad and ended up sounding more melancholy than a dirge. Men talking. Somebody shouting. A chorus of other voices, like cheering. And then the music and the voices stopped and a sudden hush fell over the world outside my window. A faint warning tickled my ear, because it was my ear that first realized something out there was different, more evil than usual.

Then from far up the block, I heard what sounded like a whole bunch of people moving along together. Not talking out loud, but whispering together. Headed toward the jail? Or toward one of the shants or maybe the hospital tents?

All of a sudden I wished I hadn't talked Cole into going to Symphony Oaks tonight to visit Ama. It had seemed so important to me that he go, and he'd seemed all tore up about it hisself. Wanting to go to Ama, and wanting to stay with me at the same time. But if only I hadn't told him to spend the night. I couldn't breathe right. Something that tasted bitter as gall pushed itself up in my throat.

By the time the doorknob turned, I was pushing against the wall and shaking, but when the door swung open, I froze. I caught a glimpse of a bunch of dark faces crowding into the jail. Faces I almost knew, even without seeing them clear. Faces that were part of my past. People I knew as friends of my parents. People I'd passed in the streets without knowing their names but knew all the same because they lived in my town.

When the first man moved, the whole group moved. Bertha Long's husband, Wade. Good old Wade, Papa used to call him. Good as they come. Earl Simpson, fat and evil. I wondered if Mattie had any idea he was here. Ferris Greenwood, the worm at the center of the rot. And Fat Charlie Greenwood. I hadn't known that Fat Charlie was in town, he must of just come back. Behind Fat Charlie was Wilbert Barr whose dog Angel had all the beautiful hound pups. We'd got Chip from him. Then there was Merl Smith, so tall the whole town called him Goliath. Goliath Smith run a cattle auction business. He could pick up two calves at one time, one under each arm. There were several men I didn't know, even by sight. Were they from Frisbin or just refugees, bribed by food or tobacco?

They come toward me like one person, the floorboards creaking. They even seemed to breathe as one person. A monster with about ten heads. All the separate heads of the monster were looking at me, all had the same idea inside their one big brain. And then I saw that Goliath Smith had a rope in his hand. As if there could be any doubt what they were there for, a man behind Goliath took a pistol out of his holster. He pushed and the crowd moved closer, creeping across the floor like a bunch of cats, and something inside me froze.

The man with the gun was Frank Wright. My heart pumping hard, I put my hand over Ama's cameo and watched Frank open the desk drawer and fish the key out. A lynching party, and the deputy hisself part of it. That must mean the sheriff knew about it. He'd gone out earlier and hadn't come back yet. That left just me against a mob of men. As Frank Wright fitted the key in the cell lock, I screamed.

After that, everything happened fast. The cell door flew

287

open and Ferris Greenwood lunged through with Fat Charlie right behind him. The two of them fell over me like an avalanche and jerked me away from the wall so hard that I hit the floor screaming.

"Get her, boys," Ferris whispered.

I felt huge arms lift me, and right away I knew Goliath Smith had hold of me. Ramming my head against his chest, I felt the air go out of my lungs like I'd collided with a wall. Somebody giggled and I caught a glimpse of Fat Charlie, both hands across his laughing mouth.

"Let me go," I kept hollering, looking from one man to the next, trying to find a spark of compassion, a flicker of mercy, but there wasn't nothing.

Wade Long picked up both my legs. When I kicked him as hard as I could, Frank Wright stuck his pistol under his belt and grabbed hold of my left leg and Wade Long grabbed the right, me screaming louder than ever as they started to carry me outside.

A hand came 'round Goliath's chest. It covered my mouth and nose and tasted of tobacco and sweat. I bit it hard as I could and heard Ferris's voice say, "Jesus God, the whore bit me!"

"Let's get her out of here fast before Ben gets back," Frank Wright said, sounding rushed and uneasy.

So Ben doesn't know! I thought, and somehow that gave me the strength to reach out one last desperate time and get my hands 'round the bars as they tried to carry me out the cell door. With them prying my fingers off the bars, pulling on my legs and arms, me kicking hard as I could, all at once I heard a door slam. Expecting to see the sheriff, I twisted my head to see tiny Miss Margaret standing by the back door looking at us down the barrel of a rifle.

"Oh, hell," Goliath Smith groaned, and there was a rustling among the men, an uneasy stirring. Wade Long scratched his ear, all of a sudden looking like a chicken-stealer. Frank Wright crouched down behind Goliath, like he was trying to make hisself invisible.

"I see you back there, Frank Wright!" Miss Margaret

snapped out. "Get your ornery hide out here. Well, come on! Are you a man or a coward?"

"I got a right to do what I'm gonna do," Frank Wright whined as he sort of slunk by me out the cell door.

"I ought to slap you right in the face!" Miss Margaret shot back. "All the rest of you, let go that girl and get out here! I said, Get out here, and I don't mean tomorrow!"

"Like men are goin' to listen to a midget woman," Ferris said, and Fat Charlie giggled again.

"Don't call Miss Margaret a midget," Wilbert Barr said. Wilbert were one of the men who hadn't come inside my cell. He'd been standing 'round by the circle railing, waiting, and he looked kind of fidgety.

"If she ain't a midget, what happened to 'er?" Ferris said.

"There ain't no cause to be rude," Goliath Smith said. "She's a nice little woman. Makes the best gravy in the world."

"Don't you nice-little-woman me, Goliath Smith!" Miss Margaret snapped. "Now you just set that gal on her feet."

"I don't like the feel of this here thing, Frank," Wade Long said in a low voice.

"I didn't plan it," Frank Wright said, as if all of a sudden he wished he was anyplace else but standing in front of my jail cell with a pistol stuck under his belt. "I went along to be one of the boys, but it ain't my idea. Hell, it's me with the most to lose. When Ben hears about this . . ."

"Just a minute, just a minute!" Ferris shrieked out, as he saw Goliath Smith let me slide out of his arms. "You ain't gonna let this short old woman boss you 'round! No, now wait!"

But all of a sudden I was on my feet, standing there hanging onto the bars of my cell with tears sliding out of my eyes and the taste of Ferris's fingers on my tongue. And the men were edging out of my cell and toward the sheriff's desk, looking sheepish as a bunch of boys in trouble with their mama. Miss Margaret glared back at them down the length of the rifle. It looked bigger than she was.

"Just what were they up to, Miss Margaret?" a deep voice drawled in the darkness by the open front door, and all at once

Ben Oates was there, stepping out of the shadows into the light of the hanging lantern. He had a rifle too, and his face looked as mean as any I'd seen that night. Meaner. Add to that, he was a tall man and just looking at him, you had a feeling he'd put a rifle hole in your chest without half a thought about it.

"What does it look like?" Miss Margaret said, lowering her rifle a notch.

The sheriff's eyes were on Frank Wright like he was looking at a warm pile of cow manure. "That gun under your belt's jail property, Frank," Ben Oates said. "I'll have it on my desk. That and your badge."

"Oh, hell, Ben, I never meant—"

"And don't think you'll get your job back, neither. After tonight, you're just a outlaw to me."

Frank put the gun on the desk. Then, looking ready to cry, he pulled off his badge and put it beside the gun.

There were a murmur of voices as several of the men tried to make their peace with Ben Oates, but he waved them toward the door with his rifle, shooing them out same as he'd of done to a flock of pesky critters. And they were going, heads hung down. Ferris and Fat Charlie went too, but stomping their way out, cussing at the other men who they said let them down.

"You oughta be locked up," Ben Oates told them as the men filed past him out the door. "Hell, *you* oughta be the ones lynched! How'd you like that? Go on, go on, I got no room here to lock up half the town."

He closed the door against Goliath Smith, the last of them, and turned to where I stood with my head against the bars, Miss Margaret hovering 'round me and whispering, "Don't worry, honey, they won't be back. Probably wouldn't of done nothin' nohow, bunch of babies."

But after that night, I was never left alone in my cell again. The sheriff slept on a mattress on the floor beside his desk with his rifle beside him. I'd listen to him snore and I'd think, Isn't that funny, Ben Oates sort of feels like a close friend now. You never know who's going to turn out to be a friend, you just never know. Sometimes while he laid there asleep, I'd get up and stand on my bed and stare up through the hole that served me as a window. The sky was at its blackest those fall nights and the stars and the moon were no more than faraway glimmers. Daisy's up there somewhere, I'd think. Running and playing in some dark place behind the moon. But Ama wasn't there yet. She was still in the world of the living, hanging on by a thread of stubbornness.

"She remind me of a traveler," Delilah said. "Somebody don't want to go till they water the garden, wash they clothe. I think she worry herself 'bout your trial, Lizbeth."

Cole nodded. "She said that very sort of thing to me. Lying there on her pillow looking like she was ready to drift through the pearly gates. Then she spews off about thirty clear-witted ideas about legal defense. A few interesting angles I may have missed." He turned to me. "Elizabeth, maybe if you could send her a note to reassure her that you'll be fine . . ."

"No. No letter, not a word from me. I want her to worry her head off about me," I said. "Maybe she'll be so worried she won't die at all. And, Delilah, you're *sure* Melissa's better?"

"Real fine," Delilah said. "She in Miz Ama room hour at a time. Miz Ama tell her thing. That li'l gal come out, look like she know a secret. She make her own marker for Daisy grave. Stick it in the ground next to the other. Say some day when she got children, she tell them all 'bout Daisy and make them tell they children 'bout her too. She don't want her to be forgot. She a baby. I don't know how she think such thing."

"Delilah? You never mention Beulah. . . ."

She and Cole looked at each other. After a minute Delilah said, "Beulah gone for a while. Never mind now. You can't think of her now. First come the trial."

Twenty-five

$\mathcal{B}$ut in the darkest, quietest part of the long days that followed, it wasn't only the trial I worried about. It was the future.

When I first come to jail, I knew what freedom I was losing. What life I'd go back to if I ever got the chance. All that had changed now, and in my heart, I knew that Cole stood between me and the life I'd left behind at Symphony Oaks. Just like I knew that love was one kind of word when it come to Tom, and another kind of word when it come to Cole. The first was like loving the earth that you walk on and the second was like loving the lightning that lights up the sky and sets your heart to trembling.

I was supposed to be engaged to the first . . . but what if I couldn't live without the second? Because once the lightning has come and your heart has trembled, how can you settle down and live in peace with the good solid earth?

The guilt of wondering was the worst. I locked it inside my heart and felt it swell every day until I was near exploding. And the words "faithless woman" never left me for long. Sometimes I hoped I'd stay in jail forever, because I knew when I got out there'd be two men standing in front of me, and only one to choose.

"Well, anyways," Delilah said, walking beside me through light snow, wrapped in Ama's dark cloak and looking like a blackbird, her hands fluttering to her face, now reddened some by the cold air, "I got to be gettin' home. Miz Ama not so good today. . . . Jinny be needin' me."

The sheriff walked behind us a ways with two men, all with shotguns hung over the crooks of their arms. I be needing exercise, he'd said matter-of-fact-like. Also protection.

"What do you mean, not doing so good?" I said, breath hot and steamy against the chill.

"Oh, she failin' some," Delilah said. "I was with her most all night." She looked so tired she seemed about ready to drop.

Though it was only October, snow had begun falling two days ago, and now the whole of Frisbin was covered except the fringe of hills, hollows, and ditches farther south. The fields and woodlands were deep in white, and the town looked like a charcoal drawing in a storybook.

"Is she eating anything?" I said. "Is she hot? Does she know you?"

"She know everthin'," Delilah said. "Don't eat, burn up, but she know everthin'. She know court day comin'. Want me to go to court, tell her everthin' that happen. I say black can't go to court, them throw me out. She say, Let them throw you out. Have the guts to go there. Then I say this no time to get them more mad at Lizbeth than they already be. She say, Oh, that right. This not the right time. You right, Delilah. She pat me on the arm. Jinny say to tell you she be here, not for Miz Ama. One thing, though . . ." Delilah stopped talking and looked down at her hands.

"Yes?" I said, expecting to hear something more about Ama.

"Tom say he like to come to court. Sort of represent us, since we can't be there ourself. Represent him, too. He love you like us do. All one big family, seem to me."

I waited till she finally looked up at me; then I smiled at her and said, "You tell Tom to come to court. It'd feel real nice to have him there."

She nodded at that and we walked on, hearing the men's footsteps behind us crunching in the snow, a few cuss words that hung heavy on the damp gray air, then something about soldiers being holed up. And Burnside. Always Burnside, lately.

All September, the eyes of the North and the South had turned to Knoxville, and now General Burnside finally held it in his hands as a prize for the North. We read in the papers that the Knoxville people celebrated, for though we were all Tennessee folks, them in Knoxville were Union to the core. Maybe, I thought, there might be a woman in Knoxville whose husband was a rebel. If so, I wished I could write to her, for I thought us two might have something to say to each other past our politics.

Anyhow, it was back and forth all the time whether Burnside was going to stay in Knoxville or move on to Chattanooga, and the other thing 'round our parts was . . . why was there no more fighting in our hills? The war seemed at a strange kind of standstill, even like I was at a standstill.

One of the military problems were mules and horses. So many animals had been lost to mud and to war, there weren't near enough to pull the artillery and the supply wagons. One of the main problems as I saw it was that same lack of common sense that had troubled Frisbin from the very beginning of the war. Only to me, the lack of common sense seemed a darn sight worse than needing horses and mules.

And Abe Lincoln didn't take to being stalled no more than me. He called Rosecrans "confused and stunned like a duck hit on the head." When I read that in Cole's newspaper, I thought President Lincoln could of been talking about me, not a famous general.

"You know, I been thinkin'," Delilah said, and her face was flushed under her dark loose hair and her eyes flickered with light as she gave me a quick little glance, walking beside me, so close our shoulders touched.

"Thinking about what?" I said.

"Well, I can't get you and Cole MacPherson out my mind. You know what, I think that man got somethin' for you. He never take his eye off you, and while he lookin', them eye on fire."

I said, very serious-like, "I'm an engaged woman, Delilah."

"Not when he lookin', you ain't!"

"Hush, now!" I said, turning to see if the sheriff and the other men were listening in on our conversation. But they were intent now, talking 'mongst theirselves.

"Um, um, um!" Delilah said. "Ain't you somethin' to see."

"Please, Delilah." I took hold of her arm sudden-like. "Don't tell anybody that or they'll think . . ."

"Everbody know," she said. "They have to be blind not to know. Even Miz Ama know, and she back home in her bed. Say she right worry 'bout you. What 'bout Tom? she say. Tell you the truth, that what worry me, too. He such a good man and all."

But I was still back on Delilah saying that everybody knew. What if Tom knew? But he couldn't. Still, all of a sudden I was having trouble breathing. "What about Tom?" I whispered.

Delilah said in a low unhappy voice that Cole and Tom had met the night after Daisy died. When Cole had gone to Symphony Oaks to visit Ama.

"I not sure what they say to each other," she said. "But I know they say somethin'. I seen 'em in the hallway, just cuttin' they eye at each other. Ain't no doubt, Lizbeth, they know what happen in your heart."

Her voice died away, and after a while I felt her hand on mine, patting me out of sympathy. Me with two men, her with none. Something was wrong about that, I thought. And every second bringing me down lower.

Then we were moving again, chilled from standing still. The sun was blotted out now by the thick gray on the horizon, and the wind picked up. Behind us the sound of footsteps. Ahead the creek that was near froze over, steeped in mist, thick and cold, swirling, and over all the gabble of wild ducks.

By nightfall the whole valley would be glazed white and crystal and the air smoked and tangy from the stoves and open fires where women would gather 'round the kettles with long wood paddles, children screaming, and now and then the distant howl-call of geese, men sitting in a blind somewhere, rifles aimed high, anxious to put a decent supper on the table.

"I wonder if us humans didn't make a big mistake," I said after a long silence. "All that pairing off. And having and holding. Two monkeys go off together, I don't think the other monkey that weren't chose thinks nothing about it. He just waits 'round for another woman monkey."

"With human, you downright *judge* for what you choose," Delilah said. "Even by people that shouldn't have nothin' to say. Say, 'How *dare* her choose him?' 'How *dare* him choose her?' Forget white choose the black, that bring down all hell on you head. And, oh, Lordy, if you want to change you mind 'bout who you choose! Why, you guilty as murder then! Sorry 'bout usin' that for the example," she added, remembering what brought me to jail.

All of a sudden I faced her. "Delilah, you know lately I've been thinking so much about Lucie."

"I think 'bout her near ever time I see Ben." She nodded. "Funny thing. She alive, none of this happen. She still be marry to Tom, they have two youngun. He never think 'bout you, I reckon. Or if he did, he wouldn't say nothin'. Just stay marry. If he speak to you, then *that* be the sin. You see how sin change?"

"Though in the case of women," I said, "you can love an acre of them. Nobody accuses you of nothing. I love Ama. I love you and Jinny and Melissa. I still love Daisy, even though she's gone. And Beulah who don't love me back. I love Lucie too. There's even a part of me that still loves my family."

"You can love all the relatives you want, course."

"But with men, you can only love one," I said. "Love more than one, you're a sinner. Why, you even feel like you're a sinner if you love more than one in secret."

Delilah nodded, then lifted her head and studied the sky curious-like. In a moment she turned to face me, her fine dark features outlined against charred gray tree branches and her eyes in shadows. "How you see love anyhow? Why you 'speck we got to choose just the one, Lizbeth?"

Time went by. And the world and the snow drifted in slow white silence on the wind while Delilah kept her eyes on me and waited. Then I heard myself say, "I think it's kind of like where to live, Delilah. You ever hear 'bout some of those ladies that move west? They can never be happy, 'cause they can't give their hearts to the land they live on. They don't see theirselves there. The tree in their yard can swing and sway for all its might, yet they just go on dreaming about that old shade tree back east. You got to see yourself on the land. And you got to see yourself with a man. You got to have the courage to put all your dreams in one place. Best thing is, when the land and the man are together. If I stay with Tom, I'll call the land we live on home. If I go with Cole, I'll love him enough to make his home my home."

"Lord, Lizbeth, which one you gon' choose?"

Just then I saw a black bird, a big crow. It swooped down on the other side of the tree and got something in its beak and flew up again with it. Something dead, for crows eat what's dead. In these days of war, the earth was covered with dead things. Good for the crows. Not so good for people who want to get back to living their lives.

"I don't know," I said to Delilah in a hushed voice. "I really don't know."

When Cole come for me early on that first trial day, I was already in my plain black dress, something that I had made last week, because Cole had decided to show me as a woman in mourning. Damaged by the war like so many others in this town had been. That was how he said it. I had Ama's cameo for strength, though Cole was afraid some might notice it and envy it, a decent pair of boots to walk through the light snow, and a dark cloak, patched over and stained, from my own wardrobe, that Cole said would show my poverty. He was dressed in gray, a silk cravat at his throat, his dark hair combed just so, and a kind of sheen about him.

"Are you all right, Elizabeth?" "Are you all right, Cole?" We both said it at the same time, and both of us tried to laugh and neither of us could. He come over and took my hands and kissed them. My hands were ice cold and I wondered if he could feel my pulse jumping against his lips. Trial day. But was it really a trial, or did everybody already know the verdict? Did we really have a chance, or were we just pretending, like children playing a game?

Miss Margaret showed up in a neat dark plaid dress and a shawl with a red clasp and said she'd decided to go to court. When the sheriff said he wasn't sure that women belonged in court, she said, "If Elizabeth can go to court, so can I. I don't give ten cents for what anybody thinks of me nohow."

"So let's go," the sheriff said.

Cole and me went out the door first, and it seemed to me we almost glided along through the light snow that come drifting out of the sky. People come from everywhere to see us walk the distance between the jail and the new shant just down the street from the ruins of the courthouse, and we could hear them murmuring to each other as we passed. We could of been walking toward the church for our wedding, with everybody staring at us and saying what a handsome couple. Miss Margaret plodded along beside the sheriff. He wore his gun on the outside of his coat so that everybody could see it. I guess they made the wedding party.

"Don't look at anybody; keep your eyes down," Cole said in a low voice as us four walked. He carried a satchel in his hand and walked at a steady careful pace, not too fast, not too slow. "Don't smile, don't frown. Don't take my arm. Head lowered just a little. That's it. Nod to me a little while I'm talking to you. Act like we're discussing the case."

We found a crowd 'round the door of the new courthouse, a plain building of rough planks, and when Cole swept open the door and nodded me inside, we saw a packed room in front of us. Almost all men, but sure enough there were several women wedged in between them, sitting on the low pine benches that must of been made with court in mind. I caught a glimpse of Mattie Simpson, her hair slicked back tighter than ever, sitting between Earl and Wilbert Barr. Bertha Long was alongside Wade and dressed in a dress so mended it looked like a rag, and

298

Gillian Brian was there, looking like she was dressed for a party, taffeta petticoats so full she took up more than her share of the bench. No Mrs. Reverend Harper, though. Probably she hadn't thought court a proper place for a reverend's wife. At least, I didn't see her in the sidelong peeks I stole, walking down the aisle toward a small table at the front right-hand side of the court that faced a podium and two rows of chairs that were for the jury. Cole and I sat at the table, and Miss Margaret and the sheriff just behind us in two of the four chairs behind the table.

And Tom was in the front row. He was sitting just behind the sheriff, and when I turned to look at him, he raised his hand to me and nodded without smiling. He looked as tense as me. Worried. But he looked handsome in his dark suit and cravat and all of a sudden I remembered the books he read, the education he'd got at fine schools. His face was as tan in winter as summer and he was a head taller than anybody near him. I saw Gillian Brian's eyes on him.

Another table spread over with papers and books was to our left. An elegant stout man with a bushy mustache that dipped down from his mouth and then climbed up both sides of his face to join with his hairline over top of his ears sat there with two other men.

"That's Gilmore Watts," Cole said in a low voice, opening his satchel and arranging papers over our table. "The prosecutor." As I turned to look at Mr. Watts, I saw Ferris and Fat Charlie sitting just behind the prosecutor's table. If they were washed or groomed for court, you couldn't tell it. Their beards were shabby, their hair was long and oily, and their Confederate uniforms were so patched and stained and mismatched, they looked shabbier than any clothes in the room.

"All rise," said a voice that I couldn't recognize at first; then I saw Abner Wilcox to one side of the podium, wearing his church clothes and his funeral face. "Court's in session, Judge Milton Early's presiding."

Everybody in the room stood up, and a few seconds later Judge Early come striding into court through a back side door, hopping into his seat at the podium with the same energy he might of used to jump onto a horse. He smashed a gavel onto a block, and the whole court jumped.

"Go ahead, everybody, sit down and make yourselves comfortable," the judge said, casual as ever. "We've got a long morning. First business is to choose a jury."

"Breathe!" Cole said, turning to me with a grin that showed me he felt right at home. Court was court to him, it seemed, whether it was in a fine building or in nothing more than a shant, thrown up in a week, the nails sticking out everywhere, the wood raw and unwashed. As I drew a long strangled breath, he said, "The judge is right. Choosing a jury may take the whole day. Or a lot longer than that, even. How in bloody hell am I going to find a jury in this town? I love you," he added in a low whisper, his eyes back on his papers.

Choosing a jury turned out to be as hard as Cole expected. To begin with, neither side wanted anybody who knew me or my family, which eliminated a fair amount of the citizens of Frisbin right there. Then over half the men who were called up as prospects had to admit they had a strong prejudice against Yankees of any shape or form, even women. Especially women who were the wives of Yankee soldiers. Most of the others who didn't admit to no prejudice were lying, as Cole would find out quick enough with a few questions like "If your son were to marry a woman of Yankee sentiment, would you allow her into your home?" or "If you were on trial, would you trust the verdict of a Yankee court?" The second question brought a rolling laugh from the court, especially when the man said, "Good God Amighty, no!"

For his part, Gilmore Watts didn't seem to want young, unmarried men on the jury. Without looking at me, Cole wrote on the paper in front of him "He knows they'll be attracted to you!" He also didn't seem to favor family men who had daughters my age. Cole wrote, "He's afraid they'll be thinking of their own daughters."

We ended up with mainly farmers on the jury, pig farmers without pigs, and dairy farmers without cows, and tobacco and corn farmers without crops. We also had a man schoolteacher who'd only lived in town three years and a man who'd raised thoroughbred horses before the army took them. The schoolteacher hadn't lost nothing much to war—he and his young wife had boarded over a store in town—and though the horse breeder had lost his horses, he hadn't lost his farmhouse, that he said looked more like a barn than a house. He'd been spared because the Yankees, not the Confederates, had taken his animals, and they were so happy to get them, they hadn't felt in the mood to destroy his place. The only man on the jury that I knew by sight was Simon Bell, the blacksmith. As a child, I'd often seen him working over a horse, his iron in the fire, his hammer ringing as he fitted a shoe to a horse's foot. Everybody were interested in Simon Bell's burns, terrible things, but he never paid no attention to any of them, not even a fresh burn. He said burns were part of being a smith and it was said that Simon Bell could hold a decent conversation with one arm in the fire, if need be. That I knew Simon and he didn't know of me were not so odd. I'd been one of a pack of children that used to kneel alongside the wall of his shop, watching him work. Still, somehow I was glad that Simon was part of my jury. And Cole liked Simon Bell because, he said, Bell knew what it was to suffer.

After a full day of choosing a jury, Cole felt we'd done very well, but who was to read the heart of a jury until the word come out of their own mouths? "Guilty." Or "not guilty." Or a hung jury, which Cole said would probably set me as free as a "not guilty" verdict. In these days, who would bother to set up a retrial, especially when the sheriff clearly needed his jail back and needed to be cut loose to do his job for all the people, not one?

What I needed was to hear "not guilty."

"Listen to me, my darling," Cole said to me that night, with his hand flat against the bars of my cell, "two words aren't going to put your relationship with this town back together again, you know."

It was six o'clock now and the sheriff was outside talking to some men. Any minute he'd be coming to shut the door on Cole. Every night was like the same pattern on a quilt done over and over again. After Cole left, Miss Margaret would come back alone with warm water and I would go to the outhouse and come back into a dark and quiet jail to have my bath. The sheriff would stretch his legs with a walk, always keeping the jail in sight, and after my bath, Miss Margaret would sit inside my cell with her sewing. Trouble was, with the dark come a kind of dread.

"I'm not expecting to feel part of the town again," I said.

"Then what *are* you expecting to feel?" Cole said, his fingers stroking the bars.

I sat there on my bed a minute, asking myself the same question. Then all of a sudden I knew. "I guess I'm expecting . . . I guess I'm hoping to feel . . . not guilty," I said. "Isn't that funny, Cole? I mean everything in my head tells me that even though I killed a man, I'm not guilty. Not *that* guilty, anyhow. And all the people I respect and love the most tell me I'm not guilty. But I feel guilt just pouring into me everytime I look into the town's faces. Sometimes when I'm sleeping here, I'll wake up real sudden and I know I've been having some terrible dream that I can't quite remember. And somehow I know it's about *them*. And maybe my folks were part of it. Maybe Mama was in that dream. And there'll be this terrible lump inside of me, just as hard as a rock and bitter as gall. It's guilt, Cole. I feel like it'll be there my whole life . . . unless maybe they say I'm not . . ."

Cole's face was very gentle. "Honey, I'm an attorney. Verdicts aren't always reliable. And even if this whole town all stood up and screamed 'Not guilty' at the top of their lungs, I don't think it would help as much as you might think."

"Don't mind me, Cole," I said, trying to smile because I could see he was worried about me. That he didn't want to leave me, and yet the sheriff had just come inside. Ben was standing by the door, impatient to get started on his walk, his hand on the doorknob. "I get crazy at night because I get worried about Ama. The sick always get sicker at night. Folks die at night. You know that." I got up and walked to the bars. Even with the sheriff standing there, I reached out and put my hand on Cole's

302

and his eyes sparked at me, reminding me that even a hung jury could put the two of us together.

"I tell you the truth," Miss Margaret told me after Cole had gone, when she was changing the sheets on my bed, fussing 'round cleaning my cell, "nobody lives who don't feel guilty."

"Not you!" I said, thinking of her blameless life.

"Well, now," she said, "I've always done the best I knew how. I've worked hard as I could and I took care of my mama after my papa died. But I have felt my share of guilt. Seems like almost anythin' can set it off. Lord, it's hard to forgive yourself for leavin' the soda out of the biscuits. That goes to show we're born guilty, and I suppose it all goes back to the original sin." The words fell from her mouth as rock-solid as the rest of her, and you could tell she bore her own guilt as comfortable as she endured the pain in her hands.

"Would you ever be able to forgive yourself for killing a man, Miss Margaret?"

This was as close as I'd come to telling her I'd really killed Hank Greenwood. She'd never asked me and I'd never told her. Now, looking into her wise eyes, I knew she'd known all along.

"Sometimes," she said in her slow way, "and under certain circumstances, you understand, I believe it might be easier to forgive yourself for murder than for most anythin' else."

"So you think that no matter what, my plea—not guilty— you think it's all right?"

Without a second's pause to think about it, she said, "If I'd been there, I'd of blowed his head off first chance I got and never thought twice about it."

"You really would?"

"Hell, yes," she said.

The moon come through the window, sliding across the walls, touching Miss Margaret's twisted hands as she patted my pillow. Like always, her face was peaceful.

"Miss Margaret, would you . . . would you please pray for Ama? If God will listen to anybody, I'm sure it's you."

"Well, now, I'll pray," she said, still working, "but . . . what if she does die? Would it be so tragic? Everybody got to die sometime. The way I figure it, if you love the place you live and if you get buried in the ground you love . . . you don't go so far, do you?"

It's people like Miss Margaret who ought to do the praying at funerals. She knew about matters of the spirit like the truth was written on the palm of her hand. When you was with her, you had a feeling there wasn't no fear in her heart or dark places inside her head. I laid back on my bed and watched her take her sewing out of her burlap bag and felt the tight knot inside me start to loosen.

"I love you, Miss Margaret," I said.

"I love you, too," she said.

Twenty-six

The trial to me was like unraveling a sock trying to find out how it was made, only in the unraveling, you lost the sock. Because in everything the prosecutor, Mr. Gilmore Watts, said, I couldn't find a speck of me. He said I'd committed willful and deliberate murder. He said I'd nagged Joe into Federal service for the steady Yankee paycheck, and said he intended to prove that I was the Yankee sympathizer, not Joe.

In fact, he said, I'd washed my hands of Confederates, including my own family, by the time my husband left for the war. Why, I'd never even visited my mother, nor so much as sent a letter home, since the war began!

He went on to describe me as a passionate Yankee partisan. A woman so stingy with my supplies that I shot a Confederate soldier in the back rather than part with a sack of food for the army of the Confederate States. Supplies, he added, that had been requisitioned from every citizen in the room. In his voice was moral outrage, for Mr. Watts was a lawyer from Chattanooga, a man who'd lost everything and was now living in one of our town shants.

"Cole," I said, "I just recognized Mary Crocker in back. Joe's mother, I mean. She's with Pauline, that's her only daughter."

"Pauline's on the prosecution's witness list," Cole said, "though I hadn't much felt like mentioning it to you."

Mary and Pauline Crocker were both dressed in their good clothes. I recognized Pauline's dress from Joe's and my wedding service. It felt strange to see them alive. When they'd dropped out of my world after Joe left and hadn't even showed up to see him buried, I'm imagined somehow that all the Crockers were either dead or gone. Maybe shame had driven them away, I'd thought on days when the silence of my cabin almost made me scream. Their dark heads were tilted toward each other now; their shoulders touched. They were so quiet listening to Mr. Watts droning on, they could of quit breathing.

And another thing, Mr. Watts said, scratching his finger 'longside the bushy line of his beard and adding that he hated to mention it, but he'd been informed that the court was to be subjected to claims of advances made by the Greenwoods. If so, the jury was to remember that I'd shot Hank Greenwood in the back. He said he would produce Hank Greenwood's gun that had been found beside my bed, that he would offer the jury an examination of the chamber of that gun, showing that two bullets had been discharged.

One of these bullets, he continued, was the bullet that had been fired at my husband when my husband had threatened Mr. Greenwood's life. The other bullet, or at least a duplicate to those bullets still remaining in the chamber of Hank Greenwood's gun, had been found in the decomposed body of Mr. Greenwood. He had two witnesses in court, Mr. Greenwood's surviving brothers, who were also distinguished soldiers serving in the army of the Confederate States, who would testify that not only had my husband taken a shot at Mr. Greenwood, but that I had produced a small pistol and held it at his head, all the while threatening to end Mr. Greenwood's life. They would further bear witness that when they left my premises, I was still holding this pistol over their brother, and this was, in fact, the last time they had seen their brother alive.

Furthermore! Mr. Watts exclaimed, startling the whole room, there was direct evidence that I had attempted to clean away Hank Greenwood's blood! Fortunately for the Greenwoods, and unfortunately for me, I had cleaned the floor with

306

a rush of water that not only cleaned Mr. Greenwood's blood from the floorboards, but left standing streams of water lodged between the boards. I had also inadvertently cleaned some of my husband's blood. He intended to produce the sheriff's log of the scene of the crime. The sheriff's own words would indicate his surprise at finding so little blood for such a catastrophic wound as Mr. Crocker had suffered.

In addition, despite all my cleaning, I had missed a pool of blood that had been found between the far wall and the crib that my baby had allegedly slept in that night, a pool of blood totally isolated from the blood of my husband and further isolated by a clean and soaking floor. This blood, Mr. Watts insisted, waving his finger at the jury, this, along with Hank Greenwood's gun and gunbelt, is all the evidence you need to know that Mr. Greenwood died on the Crocker floor that desperate night. That his gun remained by the lady's bedside was proof positive that he never left the Crocker cabin, for what man, especially what *soldier,* leaves a strange cabin without his gun? That lonely pool of blood, he said, his voice as sad as wailing, moaning wind through a chimney, is all the proof you need to know that he *didn't* leave. At least, not alive . . .

From time to time as Mr. Watts spoke, I'd sneak glances at all the people I knew sitting 'round me in the courtroom. There were a few ragged souls I didn't know, probably refugees after a roof over their heads for a few hours, but none of the Nigroes still left in Frisbin. Sure enough, the room were as white inside as the land outside. As Mr. Watts spoke on, telling the jury how I'd deliberately lied to Ferris Greenwood when he'd come back looking for Hank that night, how I'd dragged the body out the door and dug a shallow grave in a marshy spot of land, I could see the land as it had looked that night. Gray, not white. I could remember Ama and Beulah and me standing out there digging, the rain falling over us as we worked, and all of a sudden I thought of Symphony Oaks.

I felt my mind grab at the image of it. White, beautiful, with its porches and its long green lawn and the oaks shading it at every turn. The great chimneys, the handsome woodwork, the huge fires that burnt in its grates. Ama had said "Home is where we start from. Where the root of the spirit digs in so deep, it can never be uprooted without killing the soul." She was right. My life had started at Symphony Oaks. I had worked its fields, polished its dark furniture, cooked and served food from its huge kitchen. Heard Ama's footsteps on the stairs, sat beside her in the parlor while all us women sewed, our tongues as busy as our needles. Even when I was alone, the house seemed full of people, seen and unseen. If it had burned, I would of mourned its death, for it was alive.

Sitting there in the court, I could see myself on the green lawn, feel the breezes blowing down through the leaves of the trees, fanning my hair, feel the sun warm on my shoulder as it filtered down through the leafy branches. Those beautiful tall oak trees, still standing, I thought, and heard Mr. Watts say that had it not been for the unseasonable rains that had fallen that summer and again in the fall, who was to know whether Hank Greenwood's body would ever have been discovered. But God had sent the rains, and God himself had freed Hank Greenwood's body from its swampy grave! By these acts, we could divine God's intentions and we could clearly see the side on which God had aligned himself!

Mr. Watts took a long breath and faced the jury head-on, leaning over the jury rail, his eyes raking first one man then another. One last thing, he said, his voice angry, biting as a whip that cuts through the air. After shooting Mr. Greenwood, after cleaning the blood, after disposing of Mr. Greenwood's body, I had enough audacity left that same night to take my pack of lies to the sheriff and, far from saving me, that act alone might be the very action that would end in hanging me!

He made a short bow to the judge and said he was finished with his opening argument.

He'd been so long-winded that it was near noon when the judge brought his gavel down and called a meal break. Our little parade of people went down the aisle with our heads held high and the people stayed in their seats and watched us go, same as they'd of taken time to watch a wagon train full of low-moral women pass through town.

"Ain't it amazin'?" Gillian Brian said to somebody. "Simply amazin', ain't it?"

"A man don't attack a woman with his back," somebody else said. "You're right on that one."

"Depends on how the woman looks," another man put in, and the whole crowd laughed.

Our people went back to the jail to eat the food that Delilah had promised to bring every day of the trial. We sat together at a board laid across sawboards, Delilah and Tom on one side and me and Cole across from them, with the sheriff and Miss Margaret facing each other a long way across the makeshift table.

"Well," the sheriff said, tearing off a hunk of bread and passing it to Tom, "that Watts fellow would bore the horns off a bull, if you ask me. Don't appear to me he can much get to a jury."

"You'd be surprised what he can do," Cole said. "At the end of all those words, you find yourself walking into a house that Gilmore Watts built."

"What's that supposed to mean?" Tom asked, frowning.

Cole lifted his eyebrows and glanced across the table, as if surprised to notice that Tom was sitting there. Then all of a sudden they two were staring at each other with ice in their eyes.

"It means," Cole said, "that a jury finds itself believing what Gilmore Watts tells it to believe. He doesn't care if he bores you into a coma. Just so long as you find yourself thinking his way. It's a well-known fact that most of his juries end up giving him the verdict."

Tom let his eyes wander back to his plate, but somehow he could feel Cole turn to look at me like he was looking at a woman that was his, his desire for me wrote across his face like a banner.

"Don't worry, Tom," I blurted out, not able to choke back the words. "Cole knows what to do. . . ."

Tom's eyes raised and he looked direct at me for the first time since he'd raised his hand to me in court. "I'm sure he does," he said, his eyes sad but still searching, trying to find something he couldn't see. "I'm sure Mr. MacPherson's a very persuasive man when he wants to be."

Then a smile was on his lips and he offered it to me like a present, warm and open like the day he'd proposed marriage to me, and for a few seconds, even with Cole beside me, his shoulder touching mine, it was like Tom and I had left the room together, gone to someplace where there were just us and no decisions to make. I could feel the quiet strength in him, the caring, the quality in him that had made him go from the university back to his land. The peace that could be mine if I lived by the side of such a man. The certainty of us looking down the road with one vision, for Tom and I saw life the same, loved the same, and worked the same.

Then in the loud wash of quiet, I felt Cole stir beside me. Felt him ease his shoulder away from mine. "You think Watts is long-winded," he said, "wait until you hear me!"

But when court took up again that afternoon, Cole was on his feet for less than twenty minutes. He reminded the jury that the burden of proof was on the prosecution. That I was innocent until proved otherwise and that, indeed, there was no proof.

"This is a very simple case," he told the jury, standing before them. "You don't need to be a genius to understand this case. This is a case of words. It's the word of three murderers, thieves, and rapists against the word of a young widow and mother. They murdered her husband in the most brutal fashion imaginable, as we will prove to you through testimony, and they raped her in the presence of her husband and child. As their only explanation for what brought them to Elizabeth and Joe Crocker's home that night, they offer you the excuse that they were out requisitioning supplies for the army."

Cole leaned over the raw oak rail that separated him from the two rows of men, who seemed to be listening hard, never

310

taking their eyes off him. Raw-faced men who'd lived their lives in the sun and wind. And, sitting in the back row, the pale brown-haired schoolteacher beside the bald blacksmith with the scars, Simon Bell, who'd been chose foreman of the jury.

"Don't let yourselves be so gullible as to swallow that lie!" he told them, talking man to man. "Not here in this court, where you are being called on to believe only the sanest possibilities, the most *rational* basic beliefs. No, here today in this court, you will not believe that, when the Greenwoods made that trip to that godforsaken spot on that lonesome hill surrounded by those barren gray fields, they were requisitioning anything! There wasn't anything to requisition! Anyone with an eye, with a grain of intelligence, would have taken one look at that terrible place and known *there wasn't anything there!*

"And to get there, the Greenwoods had to ride right past the Taylor spread with its orchards, its crops, its big farmhouse . . . only to make their way up an overgrown path that led to . . . to what? A hovel! They bypassed the Taylor spread to get to a hovel? Why? What on earth would lead them past a prosperous farm and up that dark stubby hill that night, to knock on the poorest door in Frisbin? Unless they knew a Yankee was up there . . . unless they were looking for a little of what these kind of men call *fun!*" Cole stood there nodding for a few seconds; sweat popped out on his forehead, but he never budged an inch from the jury rail. And when he started talking again, it was like there was nobody else in the room or in the world but him and the jury.

"The gun was beside her bed because Hank Greenwood took it off to rape her. The floor was wet because she tried to clean up her husband's blood before her daughter woke up and saw it. They're basing a case on a half-washed floor. Because a woman only had enough strength left in her to wash half the floor before she broke. They're basing a case on what she said to a drunk, murdering rapist who came back looking for his drunk, murdering rapist brother. When, in fact, she told him the truth: Hank Greenwood had already raped her and left!"

There was more, but all of a sudden I couldn't hear Cole.

311

There was a roaring inside my head, a dizziness something next to sickness. It wasn't that the lie had come out so easy as it had, Cole speaking in the same frank way, meeting every eye, his breathing even. It wasn't the confidential little nod he gave to Simon Bell. It wasn't anything except . . .

My God, he'd added another rape. He'd added a lie to the lie. Or could he have misunderstood me? But I must of gone over it more than a dozen times. Only Ferris had raped me. Then when Hank had started toward me, when he was *going* to rape me, that's when Melissa had started crying.

I heard Cole's voice raised now, ringing with truth and conviction, and I knew he'd done it all for me. And half of me was stunned with the gift. But all of me was staggered by the lie. I saw myself sitting in Ben Oates's jailhouse that night, telling the lies that Ama had told me to tell. I could see the cold sweat draining down my neck. Cole was sweating, too. But lying with more passion than when he'd spoke the truth.

"They will tell you they have a case. . . . There is no case! They're looking you in the face and lying to you! The only man who died in that cabin that night was Joe Crocker, and yet it's the Greenwoods who say they want revenge. Elizabeth Crocker is not asking for revenge. She is not asking you for friendship. She's merely asking you to believe her. In the name of God, believe her! *She did not kill Hank Greenwood!* Thank you." He nodded, first to the jury, then to the judge, a slow courteous motion that gave sharp contrast to the way he whipped 'round to face Gilmore Watts.

"We invite you," he said in a ringing voice that stung, "to call your first witness!"

"Mr. Watts," Judge Early said from his high seat, "are you ready with your case? Good. Call your first witness. I hope somebody remembered a Bible."

Bertha Long carried her tattered skirts into the witness chair to say my mother and sisters were living in an old storage shack on our property now that their house was burnt down. They were hungry and cold and didn't know what on earth they were going to do. Without looking at me, Bertha said my

312

mother was real grieved that I hadn't bothered to visit her. She said that in looking back, she'd realized there was always something kind of different about me. As a friend of our family for many years, she'd been 'round me a good deal, and even when I was a child, there was always something about me that was out for myself. Never willing to share with the others. Always proud about my good looks.

"I'd appreciate it," Cole said, without getting up, "if this witness could be asked to refrain from stomping all over my client's character. This is a *child's* behavior she's remembering, Judge."

"Though I don't know," the judge said. "From the child grows the woman. Still, Bertha, I think we've covered her younger years."

"Can we get to the point, Your Honor?" Cole said. "If this witness is here to indicate prejudice against the South, she can surely—"

"Mr. MacPherson is right," the judge interrupted. "Move on, Mr. Watts. And be merciful. If you can say it in ten words, don't use four hundred."

Mr. Watts nodded, but moved on slow anyhow until he finally got to the heart of Bertha's testimony. My longtime Yankee sympathy. My Confederate hatred.

When it was his turn to question Bertha, Cole spent some time asking about her son in the war and her house that had burnt down and her life that had changed. He asked Bertha if she didn't hate the Yankees that had burnt her down. He asked Bertha if she'd ever mentioned any of her bad feelings about me until after Joe had left for the war, and if so, who had she told. He said he'd like to call those people to the stand to make sure they remembered what she'd said so long ago. He held the word *long* on his tongue for a minute, dragging it out.

Some folks make good liars. Bertha didn't. The longer Cole questioned her, the redder her face got and the more riled up she got about hating Yankees. Also, when Cole mentioned the oath she swore to God, she tried to hedge, probably to save her soul. When Cole asked Bertha if my mother had ever really said she wanted to see me, she said not in so many words, but she could tell. When he asked her if Mama ever mentioned my name, Bertha said that in her opinion, Mama was just too grieved to. When Cole asked her if, in fact, my mama hadn't told Bertha many times that she was never to mention my name in her presence, Bertha looked at him a minute, then burst out in tears. "Well, would you want to hear her name if she was *your* daughter and had shamed your name all over town?"

The next witness was one of the Louden boys, who'd been raised next door to us. I'd hardly known any of the Loudens except by sight and a wave now and then, and I wondered what on earth Boyd Louden could find to talk about. But all of a sudden there he was on the stand, the grown man who used to be a dirty child, and talking about how I used to go out of my way to make eyes at him and always trying to get him to pay attention to me. Suggesting, without really coming out and saying it, that he'd always kind of thought of me as the hussy next door.

When Cole stood facing Boyd, his voice full of cold rage, asking him wasn't it true that the Allens never had associated with the Loudens, Boyd smirked and said, "Too highfalutin, but the gals always had ideas."

" 'Gals'? Or just 'gal'?"

"Well, they all had their eyes out."

"*All* the Allen girls? Or just Elizabeth?"

" 'Specially her. Everybody callin' her the prettiest gal in the county and she lookin' to pull us over in the hayloft, if she had her way."

"When was this?"

Boyd's eyes spun away from where they'd been leering at me as I sat there, clutching my cloak 'round me in the half-freezing room. "When was what?" he said.

"When was it that Elizabeth tried to pull you into the hayloft?"

"I didn't say she did, I said she wanted to."

Cole turned to the judge. "Your Honor, I ask that the jury be instructed to disregard this witness's entire testimony. He's been imagining things. He's got a regular novel up in his head of things that he wished happened that never did."

I was in something of a daze. Boyd's words, then even Cole's, started to sound like so much mumble. Judge Early looked like some crazy kind of a bird, craggy head and all, his wrinkled neck twisting as he leaned over to say something to Boyd. By the time the judge finally opened his mouth, that looked something like a beak, I was in a boil. What started out as a jumping lump of indigestion inside my stomach grew bigger and bigger and I could feel my whole belly swell with it, like I was pregnant and getting ready to give birth right there in court. *What are you doing to me?* I screamed to the room, but the words were trapped inside that churning mess inside my stomach, and the sweat started popping out all over my body. I threw off my cloak but the sweat come harder and my hands were shaking, then my whole body was shaking, and my brain screaming harder and harder.

I felt myself turn in my seat, turn to look at the people that were snickering behind me. Look at them, I thought. Look at them talking behind their hands. Feel them. Feel them hating me. Almost groaning, I put my head against one shaking fist and dragged my body back to the table in front of me. Then I took hold of the edge of the table and hung on. In another minute I'd be on my feet screaming. I'd have my nails ripping down Gillian's silly face. I'd get my fingers 'round Bertha Long's throat. Traitor! You're a damned traitor! All of you! Traitors! If only I had some kind of weapon. A gun or something. If I had a gun in my hands, I'd just turn and start shooting. If I had a saber, I'd run it through Goliath Smith's belly. Cole was wrong, I thought, gripping onto the table hard as my wet shaking fingers could hold on. Something didn't break in me that night when the Greenwoods came. Something's breaking now! Right now! And I can't hold back no longer. But I have to hold on! I must hold on or they'll win! I don't care if I die, I just don't want them to beat me! Bastards! Bitches! Oh, God, help me. If ever day battled night, it was right then. With a roaring in my ears and my body wetter and wetter and so scalding hot, I wanted to throw off every stitch of clothes and run naked through the court, grabbing onto hair and ripping skin as I ran.

I could see that naked wild me so plain that I was sure she was there, just as sure as I was that my fingernails were scarring the table from digging into it. Both things were really happening. The real me managing to sit there and hold onto that table, the other actual rioting the court.

And all the while the people filing up from their seats to take the stand, smiling like they had a mouthful of warm marmalade. Telling tales about me, but it didn't matter no more because I couldn't hear them. I felt Cole's arm pressing mine, felt him bend over me. But I was gasping for air like a dying fish and I could hardly hear what he whispered into my ear.

He had to repeat it, holding my arm tight. "Hold on," he said. "It's almost over, almost over, honey."

"If only I was you, Cole," I managed to whisper back. "If only I could fight with words, then maybe I wouldn't feel like I needed to bash heads!"

I saw the startled look he sent back at me, the way he grew still, and all of a sudden I knew that was exact how he felt. That he was a lawyer because he couldn't sit still for injustice no more than me. That it was the choice he'd made. Words rather than fists. I felt myself steady at the idea. Felt my shoulder relax against Cole's as I started to understand him in a way I never had before and to understand another woman inside of me, someone that stood so deep inside me that she was all in shadows. Somebody who wished she could speak for herself, rather than let others do the talking. And I saw that Cole was looking at me, neither of us hardly noticing as another witness stalked off the stand.

In the square space of thirty minutes—or had it taken years?—I'd grown from a woman without a tongue, somebody who'd been longing for home, longing to be delivered from harm . . . to somebody who longed to deliver herself. If I could, I'd tell Cole to sit down, to let me take over my own case.

Sitting there beside him, taking long deep breaths, I watched the judge bring down his gavel, ending the day's session, and in a daze I got up and started down the aisle before any of my people were even on their feet. I caught a glimpse of Tom's face, puzzled and worried, felt Miss Margaret's arm through mine as she hurried up beside me and the sheriff pushed up close behind us. At the door, I turned to look behind me and saw Cole trailing us with his satchel, a strange look on his face. He was a little further away than usual and his eyes didn't search the crowd as though he felt responsible to protect me from anybody and everybody at one time. It was Tom behind him, carrying a box filled with books and papers, that was rushing. His eyes that were roving the room.

"Tom Higgins!" somebody hissed. "Takin' up with the Yankees! Your pa must be downright ashamed of you!"

"Think so?" I heard Tom say, as though he really didn't care. "If he's ashamed now, he hasn't seen anything yet!"

I felt fierce proud of us all. Tom, from a Confederate town and a veteran of the Confederate army, daring to love a Yankee. Miss Margaret with her arm through mine, her small brave back to the world she'd lived in her whole life. The sheriff with his hand on his gun, ready to take on the whole room. Cole striding along in his elegant clothes, saying he loved me, when he could be in Richmond right now, romancing the most beautiful belle in the city. And a woman who looked like me walking out of the mist in my head. Hair like mine, nose like mine, figure like mine. But determined 'round the mouth. A new something in the eyes. I could see myself walking toward myself.

And then, just when we reached the cold dim light of a dying afternoon, just as I was gulping cold air, watching gray snow clouds that made the day feel like night, I caught a blur of Delilah running straight down the middle of the street toward us, her hands lifting her skirts high, her mouth opened in a screaming hole as she called my name.

Oh, my God, I thought, and before she said a word, the truth of what was happening sank in me like a stone and I knew that Ama was dying.

Twenty-seven

By the time we got to Symphony Oaks, the storm clouds had brought on early night and there was a lamp burning in the front window. I stepped over the doorsill into the front hall and felt the house wrap 'round me as if it knew I'd come home. The others crowded in behind me and we fell into the hush of people listening for the sound of life when you know that death is in the very air you breathe. Delilah by Tom, her hand on the stair railing. The sheriff waiting by the door. On either side of me were Miss Margaret and Cole. A second later a door opened upstairs and I caught sight of Jinny standing by the upstairs banister.

"Thank the Lord y'all come," she said, her eyes finding me, and weeping the quiet way somebody weeps who's been at it for a long time.

"Where's . . . where's Melissa, Jinny?" I said, trying to keep my voice from shaking.

"She sleep."

"Now? This early? She isn't sick again . . . ?"

"No'm. She lose track of night and day. Spend most of last night with Miz Ama. Up till four o'clock in the mornin'. She sleep now for two hour. Just wore out. Oh, you got to come fast, sugar. Not much time left now."

But I could hardly make myself walk toward the stairs and all of a sudden I knew why. It was because of the image of Ama

318

I'd been keeping alive. Tan and strong as a workhorse. Likely to live past a hundred. After she got sick, I'd started carrying that other picture of her in my mind and making myself believe that Ama was strong enough to beat death itself. But now another time had come, and I knew with a sickening sureness that the minute I walked up those stairs and into her room, I'd have to believe something else.

"Go ahead, Elizabeth, Ama wouldn't like going without seeing you," I heard Cole say behind me. I felt his hand on my shoulder, pushing me toward the stairs, and I took a stumbling step forward. It was like trying to walk in a dream and no matter how hard you try, you find yourself in the same place.

"I can't," I whispered. "I can't go up there."

"We'll all go together," Tom said in a steady voice. He was all of a sudden beside me, his fingers under my arm.

Only the sheriff stayed in the hall, his hand on the stair rail, looking up, while the rest of us moved slow up the steps. In a few seconds I'd be seeing Ama again.

At the door, the others drawed back, and Delilah said, "You go on, Lizbeth. She want to see you for a long time now. She need to see you."

Jinny nodded and stood back from the half-opened door, tears still running down her cheeks, her lifting her apron to dry them.

I'd expected a dark room but as I passed through the door, I saw there were a half-dozen lamps lit, and a thought crossed my mind that maybe Jinny'd thought death comes in the dark. Maybe the light would keep the Grim Reaper from Ama's bedside. The air was clean, sweet-smelling. The rosewood vanity glowed, the rich carpet were smooth and soft under my feet. The huge four-poster bed seemed to of grown even bigger. Ama's face on the pillow was white, not tan, and her arms outside the blanket seemed thin as they rested peaceful on both sides of her quiet body. She was so still that for a minute I thought she was already dead and I couldn't bear to look at her.

"Don't be afraid, my dear," Ama said in a very clear voice. "It's just a body wearing out."

I saw that her eyes were open and they were Ama's eyes from old, just as full of mischief as ever, just as full of witchcraft as I'd ever seen. Though I'd told myself a dozen times that it was my turn to be strong for Ama, just like she'd been strong for me so many times, I felt myself start to cry. The tears come flooding down both cheeks and I fell to my knees beside her bed. Taking her hand in mine like a child goes to its mother, I let the hot tears flood from my eyes, felt her sigh as she tried to turn toward me, then finally managed it. I felt her other hand on my bent head, patting and smoothing my hair.

"Come on, come on," she said. "How's the trial going?"

I dried my eyes on my skirt and looked at her. "Ama, who cares at a time like this how the damned trial's going?"

"I do," she said. "It's a heap more interesting, for instance, than Bible-verse reading. My dear, is the judge pleased at finally getting a trial? I used to tell him he could hardly call himself a judge without at least one trial to his name."

Somehow, I found myself sitting there, looking into her bright interested face and telling her all the details of the trial, even how quick the shant had gone up during the last week and how Ned Baxter had got a pine splinter in his bottom from sitting on the unsanded bench and how freezing-cold air blew in 'round the windows and under the doors. There was a wild hope stirring in me that everyone was wrong and Ama was going to live after all. Even if her body were so very thin and still, there was energy in her eyes. And could a person lay there and talk so lively if she was going to die? Could she? Why, there was even a flush of pink over her cheeks.

I smiled and reached out to put my hand against her face, then pulled it away with a gasp. Ama was ice cold. Touching her was like laying your hand against a rock that had been laying all day in the snow.

"Elizabeth, did they tell you about little Daisy?" Ama whispered, her eyes never leaving my face.

The smile had died from my lips. Now I felt myself shudder as I nodded.

"I have this theory," she said.

"You always have a theory," I told her.

"I think Daisy needs me," she said. "She must be very afraid. She's so tiny. She's not used to being away from us. Why, it must be dreadful for her. Almost like being lost. Do you know that at night, if I listen very closely, I can almost hear her calling me?"

"What about God?" I said. "Can't he comfort her and leave you here?"

"I can't trust *God* with her," Ama said. "She doesn't know him. Anyhow, I want to go to her, and that's where I'm going. After I'm gone, you'll know we're together and you won't be worried about either of us. The point is . . . are *you* going to be all right? Wherever I am, whatever it's like to be dead, I won't rest contented unless I know you're down here being as magnificent and powerful as I know you were destined to be. And when I say *down here,* don't take me at my word. I have a feeling it's not a matter of down or up, but more or less a parallel situation. I believe that heaven and earth are something like shadows of each other. They're two planes of existence that are so close they almost touch at times. It's at those times that you get a creepy-crawly feeling down your spine. Or you turn around all of a sudden and you *know* you're not alone in the room though you can't see a soul. From now on, when that happens to you, I promise you, it'll be me. I'll be right there in the room with you, close enough so that we can talk, like we're doing now. Only you'll hear my voice inside your head, that's all."

By now, I didn't have any hope in me. I knew Ama had made up her mind to die and that nothing could stop her. Almost to myself, I said, "Life confuses me, Ama. It seems to push at me. It's like I don't have any power to decide *anything* that happens to me. You don't know how I long to be in charge. But life won't give me a chance. Like right now, it's taking you away from me. And it took Daisy."

"It rid you of Joe." Ama's eyes gleamed. "Now I know that's a terrible thing to say, but he wasn't any good to himself or you. If you ask me, life did you a favor on that one."

"What's life doing to me now, Ama?"

"Why, it's courting you, girl," she said in her gentlest voice without an ounce of mocking. "Don't you know? Don't you feel it?"

"Right now," I said, "men are not exactly on my mind, Ama!"

"Who said anything about a man!" she exclaimed with something close to astonishment. "I mean *life,* girl! *Life's* courting you!"

"How's that?" I murmured, patient with her, believing she was starting to hallucinate. "By taking me to jail . . . to trial . . . ?"

But she was dragging herself up on her pillows, her whole body quivering with excitement. "No! No! You don't understand. Life's *happening* to you! It's not passing you by. Life's proposing to you . . . saying, Elizabeth, will you take the bad with the good? Will you stand where you are and fight for the right as you know it? Will you take the road of responsibility and be a woman? Will you look this town in the eye and be strong enough to rise before them?" Her cold fingers were plucking at my sleeve. Her breath was raspy, but sustaining to her.

"Ama, please. You must lay down. You must."

"Or what?" she said. "Or I'll die?" Her teeth bared in a death-mask laugh.

My eyes wandered 'round the room and I could feel her watching me every second, her eyes big as soup spoons. "Why does it have to be so hard?" I said, my voice dull and flat.

"Elizabeth," she whispered, "at least things are happening to make you think, to figure things out. Do you know there's people in the world who never live at all? They sit in their houses and nothing ever happens to them. They're cowards! They think the same way, they never ask themselves any questions they can't answer and before they know it, they're on their deathbeds and *then* they're full of fear and trembling. Am *I* full of fear and trembling? Do you know why I'm not? Because I got married to life a long time ago. I've lived. If I hadn't, I'd be moaning and

322

screaming and begging not to die. Look at me! *No, really look at me!* Have I ever lied to you? It's how you live that makes dying either terrible or all right. Remember Moses? The boy Gray? They're a part of you now. I'm a part of you now. Wherever you go, whatever you do, I'll be there. Somebody will say something and you'll tell them, That reminds me of something my friend told me. . . ."

". . . my mother told me," I said.

"Yes, I am your mother. You're my child. Delilah is my other child, and Jinny and Beulah are my sisters. Melissa and Daisy are my grandchildren and I have the major . . ." All of a sudden, her strength seemed to fail her and she collapsed back on her pillows. "Elizabeth, will you remember what I've said about life? Will you take the bad along with the good and know that both are life's gifts?"

"I'll try."

"No. Don't just try, Elizabeth. Promise me."

"I promise. Ama, about Beulah, do you know . . ."

"I know that she's family in her heart," Ama said, closing her eyes. "She just doesn't realize it yet. Someday she will."

"Someday," I said, believing her.

"You remember what I said, now. This is your time to live. This is your time to be whatever you're going to be. Don't forget, my dear. Don't ever forget."

Ama's hand rested in mine. The room grew very quiet. I thought I heard the door swing open. When I looked, I saw Jinny, her eyes huge in her face, and Delilah, her face wet with tears, over her shoulder. Cole and Tom were standing further back, looking troubled and grieved. Only Miss Margaret stood peaceful, at home in this room of death.

Then a little voice spoke up in back of them all, and they turned as a child in a long white nightdress come walking between them. "It's all right," she said in such a calm mature way that it took me a minute to realize it was Melissa coming into the room and heading for me. She come straight up to me and crawled into my lap and put her cheek against mine, like she'd done even when she was a baby. "It's all right," she said again, patting me. "It's all right, Mama. It's just that Miz Ama's dyin' now. She woke me up and told me so, so I come to say good-bye."

I looked down at Ama. She hadn't stirred, and her head was pushed back on her pillow. Her mouth was just a little open and she was smiling. Every breath she drew took a little longer, come a little more soft. The others who had waited at the door crept closer and knelt down 'round her bed. I had hold of one hand and Jinny the other. Delilah and Cole were on one side of her bed with Jinny, and Melissa and Tom were with me. Miss Margaret wet a rag and pressed it to Ama's temples, her throat, for she'd turned feverish. During the next quiet hour, we talked to her. We told her how much we loved her. You could hear the oaks whispering outside the windows. That's the way Ama died.

Twenty-eight

O Heavenly Father,
Take the body,
Take the spirit to your bosom,
Bless the memories,
Bless her departure.
This we pray,
O Heavenly Father.

We'd sat up all night with Ama's body, then had a service at first light beside Daisy's grave. Then the men took turns digging Ama's grave. While Cole dug, Tom come to stand beside me, brushing the dirt from his hands, his eyes going to the hills. The sound of war was up there this morning, reminding us that soon the Yankees would be back. That soon the floodgates of Tennessee would open wide and the South would be brought to its knees, along with every man, woman, and child by the wayside.

I reached out and touched Tom's hand and said we'd have to send word to the major about Ama. He studied my fingers that rested on his strong tan wrist. The major, he said finally, had died eleven days ago in prison, but he hadn't had the heart to tell Ama.

There were no words from me then. No way to tell Tom how I felt. I could only stand beside him, held by the warmth of his hand under mine, remembering the night Ama had told me of meeting the major. Fresh out of the university, she'd said. I was a young belle . . . can you imagine me a belle? I was. And trying to fall in love with a couple of young men who claimed to be in love with me. The major came into my life like the north wind. He swept everything else away. Those two young men never had a chance. Nobody had a chance. I would have married him if he was poor, black, my father's worst enemy. Though none of that was true. My mother approved of his family. My father couldn't have liked him more if he'd been his own son.

I squeezed Tom's hand sudden-like. "You did right not to tell Ama, Tom. You did right."

He looked up at me and half-smiled. "Did you ever feel like Ama knew everything anyhow?"

Before I could answer that I knew just what he meant, Old Man Higgins was there, wandering 'round, asking why there wasn't no food. Why couldn't we buy a cow from somebody and get some milk? Where was his gun? He didn't know nothing that was going on. It wasn't only that he was deaf as a stone, which he was now, or that he couldn't see well, which he couldn't. He didn't have a perception of people either. He kept calling Cole Tom, and the sheriff a damned Yankee.

He'd been picking at his clothes all morning, taking off one thing then the other, until now he had hardly a stitch of clothes on. Somehow he'd taken off his shoes, too, and were barefoot, making a pitiful sight, his cragged face covered with dry skin that flaked as he yelled, pieces of him falling into the snow.

Finally the sheriff said it were time we got back, the trial would be starting soon. Tom nodded, put his father gently aside, and took the shovel from Cole. He'd decided to stay and finish the digging. When we rode out of the yard in Ama's wagon, I could see him standing there, the spade in his hands, digging Ama's grave deeper and deeper, the wet snow falling over him, him working alone out in the cold without a thought to weather. He was going to dig right into Daisy's grave, the way Ama'd wanted, so's the two graves would be one.

Later, as Miss Margaret and I followed Cole down the courthouse aisle, her arm tight 'round my waist, me a sleepwalker, her steering me along, it come to me how many more women there were in court today, and so, less men. Either the women had taken their husbands' seats on the pine benches or had got to the courtroom before the men who had sat there yesterday. The second thing I noticed was the way everybody looked at me now that the word had gone out that Ama was dead. Up till that very moment, Ama Hadley had stood between me and them. Even with her sick at home, they'd known she was on my side, known she was tougher than them, more determined than them. It was only now, with Ama gone from me, falling away like a knight's armor tore from his body, that I realized she'd been protecting me all along, even laying in her bed. Now everything was different.

"We'll get through this," Cole said, turning to me as we took our seats.

"Yes, I know. I promised Ama. . . ." I shivered and Miss Margaret put her wool muff in my lap.

"Tuck your hands in here," she whispered, "and you'll soon feel warm as hot toast. There, didn't I tell you? Looky there, you've stopped shaking already!"

The first witness of the morning was Joe's sister, Pauline. She told how I'd chased Joe until he finally married me. Through Cole's objections, one after the other, and the judge's peppering back "Character!" "State of mind!" "Prejudice against the Confederacy!" "Pertinent background!" she droned on and on while the snow that had started early this morning turned to mush that sloshed down on the thin roof and blew wet patterns against the windows.

Pauline pressed a stained white handkerchief under her puffy eyes and said Joe used to be a loyal Southerner until he married me. She'd heard me many a time saying how my sympa-

327

thies were with the North and how much pay the Yankee soldiers sent home to their families. She told the court that I'd acted uppity about the Crocker house Nigroes and once I'd even tried to take the mop away from Savannah and do the floor myself.

Through the haze that had closed 'round me since Ama died, the pain, the memories that were worse than any headache, I stared at thin pale little Pauline Crocker, with the mop of dark hair straggling down out of her hat, and I remembered Savannah in the Crockers' kitchen with her big pregnant belly, bent over the mop and groaning. Saying the baby was coming. And Mary Crocker, Joe's mama, saying "Savannah, finish the floor, then you can go on out back and tend to yourself."

Looking at Pauline, I realized the Crockers had always been strangers. After Joe had left, they'd never come to see me once, and as time had gone by, it was like they'd disappeared from the earth. After a while, I couldn't even remember what they looked like. Now all of a sudden, I could see Mary Crocker sitting in her chair in her home with her sewing all 'round her, staring at everyone, even her own children and husband, with those eyes. Black almost, with something evil brewing in them. And Pauline always over in the corner or sneaking up on you with that sly look that made you think she'd caught you out at some mischief.

"It was Liz Ann that made Joe go enlist for the North all right," Pauline said in the witness chair. "My brother Ed told me so at the time."

"Did *Joe* tell you?" Cole asked her on cross-examination.

"He told Ed."

"But did Joe tell *you*?"

Pauline drew a long breath and stared at somebody sitting far back in the court, and I knew without looking over my shoulder that she was checking with Mary Crocker.

"Yes, he did," Pauline said, still squinting out over the court. "Joe said she begged him into it. And o' course, we'd heard all them things she said about likin' the Yankees."

"Pauline," Cole said, trying to make her look at him. "Are

328

you sure . . . are you absolutely *sure* . . . that Elizabeth was a Union partisan in those early days?"

"What? Oh, yes. She was a Yankee from the first." Pauline sounded out of breath, and spoke so fast she sounded like she was rattling away.

"Who are you looking at in the courtroom?" Cole shot out, and I knew his patience was slipping.

As Pauline stared past Cole, squinting out in the crowd, he turned 'round to stare with her.

"I asked you who's out there! Who's telling you what to say?"

"Objection, Your Honor," Gilmore Watts said, jumping to his feet. "That has no relevance to the witness's answers."

"It does if she's being spoon-fed the answers to my questions!" Cole snapped.

"You have no proof of that," Mr. Watts said, clicking his tongue at Cole. "Your Honor, Mr. MacPherson's influencing the jury. I will ask you for a reprimand and instructions as to how he's to act. It seems the counsel is more than a little confused as to proper technique in cross-examination! I'd expected more from a lawyer coming out of Richmond."

"I don't even understand what this witness is doing in the box!" Cole said, holding onto the last shreds of his temper. "Your Honor, please, for the last time, what is Miss Crocker's *purpose* here beyond prejudicing the jury against my client?"

"I'm allowing the prosecution to develop background, state of mind, possible motive!" the judge shot back. "And I must have told you twenty times, young man, I want all this objecting to stop. This is my court and you're being downright rude. If this were my living room, I'd show you right out the door! Now you listen to me . . ."

As the judge tore into Cole, I turned my back on the witness chair and looked for Mary Crocker. Sure enough, there she was, sitting toward the back door. She was staring right at me, black eyes stewing in more hate than I'd ever seen in any one person. And in that one look, I knew the shame of the Crocker family, and why they hadn't come to see Joe buried.

"Liz Ann plays up to men and the whole town knows it!" Pauline Crocker said all at once in a raised voice. She was either answering a question, or just saying what she wanted in the same way somebody puts a needle to a festering boil and lets the poison fly. "She makes them cotton to her. Everybody knows that. No wonder them men done what they done to her. It was her asking for it!" she half yelled.

But only part of me was listening. The other part was with Ama. By this time she would be laying in the bottom of the hole, covered over, her wood coffin beside Daisy's. Tom would be standing there, his head bowed over his spade, or he'd be helping Delilah pack the wagon to bring our noon meal. The house would be listening for Ama's footfall. The oaks would be as crazy with sorrow as they were at dawn, their bare limbs whipping over our heads, scratching together and moaning like they were part of the funeral party.

Ama's with Daisy and the major now, I thought. Where she wants to be. And maybe part of her was right next to me, close as my own shadow. For that's what she'd compared the other world to. A shadow.

As the morning wore on, Pauline left the stand, and the owner of the general store got up to tell how prosperous I'd been during the first part of the war. Yes, he said to Cole's question. That would have been more or less the beginning of the war. Only thing he remembered for sure was that I hadn't tried to charge nothing like most folks he knew. Probably that was because the Yankee soldiers were well paid. God knew, they had warm clothes and boots. He'd hated having to take Yankee money. On the other hand, he wouldn't of let me have so much as a measure of salt without paying.

"Perhaps that was why she never tried to charge anything," Cole said, waving the witness away.

After the shopkeeper come the sheriff, the first witness who could do me any real harm, if the jury was to go on evidence alone. By this time Ben Oates was a friend, and I knew he hadn't been looking forward to taking the witness chair. It was too late to do anything else, though; his report was already part of the evidence. Dwarfing the chair, his long legs crossed at the ankles, he gave testimony as to my appearance that night, telling in a sympathetic way that I'd looked done in, that my daughter was asleep on my arm, that I'd insisted on telling him about the rape, that anybody could see I was upset and near collapse.

Then Mr. Watts led him through his written report about how he'd gone in person the next morning to inspect our cabin and found the floor mopped clean except for the one area 'round Joe's body. Except for that spot, the rest of the floor was not only clean but wet and there were traces of blood between the floorboards and one puddle of blood behind my daughter's crib.

"But who's to say the moppin' come after the shootin'?" the sheriff said, the words coming out of his mouth so fast that Gilmore Watts didn't have a chance to object. "She could of mopped up before the Greenwoods got there. And the reason the front room wasn't mopped was because she hadn't got 'round to it yet. And if the cabin was only half mopped—maybe her strength plumb gave out!" As Mr. Watts stared at him, Ben Oates smiled. "You see, I've had some time to think the whole thing out."

Mr. Watts took a minute to think, staring down at the notes in his hand. After several minutes of standing there very still, looking half asleep on his feet, he said, "Tell me this, Sheriff Oates, was that floor carefully mopped? Was it mopped so's Mr. Crocker's blood remained in its rightful place?"

Cole had been over that question with Ben, so I knew what he'd say even before he cleared his throat and shrugged. "How could I know something like that?"

"But you're an expert in this area, aren't you?"

"Objection," Cole said, getting up. "The witness himself denies his competency in making this kind of judgment."

Judge Early's jaw worked. "He may deny it all he wants, counselor, but in this town, he's our authority."

"And he has stated the room was selectively cleaned—here," Gilmore Watts said, pointing at the copy of Ben's report he held in his hand.

"Come on, Ben, stop being so ornery and answer the question," the Judge complained, and added, "What's wrong with you today, anyhow?"

"She's probably been making eyes at him, too!" a woman's voice cried out.

As the court rocked with laughter, I turned to look for Gillian Brian, thinking it was her voice. For a minute, all I saw was men, bent double, punching each other, almost hooting, and then I saw Mattie Simpson, not laughing, her fingers pressed to her eyes, her shoulders shaking. Two seats away, Mrs. Reverend Harper had a grim look. She was wearing black, and her arms were folded tight across her breast, like she was hugging herself. Josephine Steedman with her chin in her hand. Bertha Long, chewing her lip. A dozen other women, most bending forward, listening hard. Then I realized that except for Gillian Brian, the women weren't smiling, weren't screaming and poking each other like the men. Instead, they were staring hard at Ben Oates and keeping their own thoughts.

Up front, the sheriff and Gilmore Watts were still deep into that mopped room, Mr. Watts trying to make Ben admit somebody'd cleaned one part of the room and at the same time deliberately left Joe's body laying in blood. Ben was still slipping in all the little explanations and possibilities he'd worked out with Cole. Maybe you do wash a floor at night, especially if your baby has a training accident. Maybe the floor would still of been wet the next morning, if the floor had been mopped in the early evening. It was a damp night, no sun or heat to help dry the wood. Gilmore Watts kept telling Ben to just answer the questions without explanations, but here the judge's habit of letting his witnesses say fairly much what they wanted worked for our side. The judge told Gilmore Watts that Ben Oates could do all the explaining he wanted.

"Was that room selectively sanitized or not?" Gilmore

Watts asked, standing very close to Ben and leaning into the little space between them.

"What the hell's that mean?" Ben growled.

"It means that you know as well as I do that the lady tried to clean around her husband's body! She tried to clean up the blood that was shed by another body, even while she left her husband's body and blood where it was. Only problem with that"—the prosecutor smiled—"is that she got a little too zealous. She cleaned up too much of the blood. She also used too much water, didn't she? She left water between the boards in the floor, and some blood, too. Didn't she, Mr. Oates?"

"Well, if she did start to mop up after her husband got shot, maybe the blood between the floorboard was Mr. Crocker's," Ben said.

"Did it look as if she were mopping up after Mr. Crocker?"

"Well . . ."

"Or was she washing an entirely different part of the floor?"

The sheriff sighed. "I will allow," he said, after a minute of frowning over the question, "that it looked that way, but—"

"Thank you," the prosecutor said in a quick satisfied way before Ben could think of any more explanations. "Now I'd like to direct your attention to the part of your report where you mention a puddle of blood found behind the crib that the Crockers' daughter slept in that night."

The sheriff took the clipped papers that the prosecutor passed him and looked down at the report.

"Is that your report?"

"Yep."

"Those your words, written in your own hand?"

"I said so, didn't I?"

"Then just go ahead, read what you wrote." Gilmore Watts rested his arm on the bar before the witness chair and waited.

"Just that part you underlined . . . ? Just a minute . . . all right." Ben held the paper closer and started to read. " 'After I examined the floor and saw it was wet, I noticed something like half blood, half water, between the floorboards. About half a minute later, I also noticed a small puddle of blood between the crib at the far end of the room and the wall behind it. It was unconnected to the body of Mr. Crocker in any way. In fact, somebody looked to of washed the floor between his body and this other puddle of blood. Question—is this puddle Mr. Crocker's blood? Question—was somebody else wounded in some way? Something's not right.' "

By the time Mr. Watts took back the report, people were whispering and he was smiling into both bushy sideburns. "Sheriff Oates, what did you think when the Greenwoods came to tell you their brother Hank had disappeared? Before you answer, bear in mind you cover this in a later report, written after your interview with the Greenwoods."

"Well," Ben Oates said in a slow way, looking at his feet, "at first I didn't connect it with what had happened to Mr. Crocker. But then Ferris Greenwood mentioned that him and his brothers had been in a ruckus at the Crockers' place, so I thought—"

"What kind of ruckus?"

"Ferris told me they were on a raidin' party and the Crockers threatened their lives when they tried to requisition goods."

"And what did you think after that?" Gilmore Watts asked, tapping his finger against the report in his hand.

"Listen here," Ben Oates said. "No matter what I thought at the time, and no matter what I wrote in my notes, there was no *evidence* that puddle of blood was Hank Greenwood's blood. What you read was just me thinkin' things out on paper, the way I sometimes do."

"But you did write that you believed it to be Hank Greenwood's blood?"

"There's no way in the world," Cole said in a tired voice, not moving from where he sat, "that Sheriff Oates could have known whose blood it was."

The judge looked at Ben. "I'll trust him," he said. "Ben, answer the question."

Still Ben didn't answer, and Mr. Watts held out the report again. "You want to read what you wrote after you interviewed the Greenwoods?"

Ben Oates shook his head.

"I'll ask you one more time," Gilmore Watts said. "Did you write in your report that you believed that puddle of blood to be Hank Greenwood's blood?"

"You read the report," Ben Oates said. "You know I did. But, like Mr. MacPherson pointed out, there's no way I could—"

"Thank you." Mr. Watts smiled. "That's all I need on that. Now . . ."

He moved on to Ben's second interview with me, the one with me and Ama over tea at Symphony Oaks. Me saying the lights were off because I'd run out of fuel when there was a lamp more than half full of kerosene. The story I'd invented about Melissa's wetting the floor and me upsetting the bucket. Cole had told me this would probably be brought out because it looked like obvious lying and would suggest I'd tried to cover up the crime.

"Her story could of been true," Ben said without batting an eyelash.

"What about the lamp?"

"She could of forgot. She was terrible rattled."

"Come now," Mr. Watts said, stroking his beard. "It's obvious there's something wrong about that kerosene lamp, isn't there? Isn't it obvious she turned out the lamp because she didn't want Hank's brothers coming in and finding his body? Isn't it also obvious she mopped up Hank Greenwood's blood? And later claimed to be mopping up after the baby? Isn't it obvious, Sheriff, that there's a link between Hank Greenwood's death and the puddle of blood and the washed floor—"

"Objection, Your Honor!" Cole said for about the fifth time, the judge waving him down at every turn. Now he was on his feet, talking through the judge's orders to sit down. "Nothing's obvious!" he said. "Neither Mr. Watts, nor the sheriff, nor, for that matter, *anybody* who wasn't in the room that night can be certain there's any link between Hank Greenwood's death and that wet floor. In fact, the only thing we *know* is that Mr. Crocker was murdered by the Greenwoods. Mrs. Crocker reported the crime; the Greenwoods don't deny it. The only questionable issue is what happened to Hank Greenwood. Mrs. Crocker claims he left her cabin about an hour after his brothers left, while—''

Ferris Greenwood stood up and yelled, "Hank never left no cabin! The Yankee whore murdered him in cold blood!"

"Just like them Yanks are doin' to our boys. Murderin' them!" somebody else yelled.

I turned, but couldn't see who it was. The courtroom erupted again. It was worse than before. Much of it I couldn't make out. Hoots, hisses, and grunts. They wanted to see somebody get hurt. It was out of control.

By the time the judge gaveled the room back to order, it was time for noon recess. Cole had to push the people back from me as we made our way up the aisle. "Yankee whore!" rang out like "Hello there!"

All of a sudden the courthouse door was flung open and slammed hard against the wall, and I looked over Miss Margaret's shoulder through swimming eyes, expecting to see the sheriff standing there. Instead, it was Ferris Greenwood, looking nasty at seeing Cole and me so close together, yelling and screaming about the slut widow being at it again.

Then Cole let go of me and started toward Ferris, both hands rolled into hard fists. I heard Cole use the word "scum." Saw Ferris's crooked teeth as he grinned and reached down under his coat.

"Cole, no!" I begged, but he didn't pay no attention, just kept going. I saw Ferris's gun under his coat and his hand on the butt and I screamed, "Don't you get yourself killed on me, too! Cole, he's wearing a gun! Come back here, oh, God, come back here!"

A second later a shot rang out, and I screamed again and closed my eyes. When I opened them a second later, expecting to see Cole laying dead on the floor in front of me, the sheriff was standing there. Hardly able to believe that somehow Cole was still alive, I followed the direction of Ben Oates's pointed gun and saw that he'd aimed a clean shot through the wall and that Ferris's gun was only halfway out of the holster.

Everybody drew back then, pushing and shoving, as the sheriff stepped forward and took a long hard look at Ferris. "That'll be the last time for somethin' like that," he said. "And I mean the last."

Ferris let his gun fall back in his holster, but he jerked his thumb at Cole. "The son of a bitch attacked me," he whined.

"This is my town," the sheriff said, stepping in front of Cole, who'd lunged at Ferris again. "My law." The sheriff had a look about him that I'd seen before. When he was doing his job, he seemed to carry a sense of having the Office of Sheriff behind him. It made him more like a posse than like one man. "Any guns drawed in this place, there'll be almighty hell to pay," he said, his face inches away from Ferris's. "You understand how it works?"

"You better understand how *I* work," Ferris said, not budging. "I do pretty much like I want to. Ain't nobody, includin' no sheriff, that bosses me 'round. 'Specially when the other man does the attackin'. I'll shoot him dead and never think nothin' about it. Don't matter shit to me what you say, Ben."

That quick, I saw the sheriff's whole body change. Saw his back get stiff, his head kind of swivel 'round on his neck. Saw him shift his weight. Right up to that second, he hadn't really made it clear to the townfolk whose side he was on, though I'd known for a long time. But now all of a sudden he was ready to make a stand.

"Your pa's a friend of mine, Ferris," Ben Oates said in a slow voice, his gun still in his hand. "But he raised you boys without a woman and you ain't amounted to spit. No, don't talk back to me, you ain't got a word to say that interests me. Just git out of this courtroom."

"You ain't sidin' up with Yankees, Ben."

"I ain't sidin' up with the likes of you, either, Ferris. Now I said git!"

337

It was the gun, not the words, that finally made Ferris amble through the door, trying to act like he was leaving on his own muster. But he said he wasn't the only one sick to death of Yankee-lovers, and we'd all see what was what soon enough.

"What did he mean by that?" Cole asked after Ferris had left.

"Just blowin' hot air," the sheriff said. "That's all, just blowin' smoke."

But when we come back to the courtroom that afternoon, there was a nasty surprise waiting for us. I saw her the minute I stepped through the door. A dark-skinned woman sitting at the prosecution table side by side with Gilmore Watts, a woman so thin and crazy-looking that for a minute I didn't recognize her. I looked and looked again, thinking I must be seeing wrong.

Surely, if Beulah had come back . . . But she was back, I was certain of it. Oh, God, the hollow look in her eyes, like pain had carved out her insides. Her skin paler than before, the rich color faded to almost a light tan. She looked like . . . like me when I'd thought about killing Melissa before she starved. Like a mother who'd lost her child.

"Your Honor," Gilmore Watts said when the court come to order, "we've had a witness come forward unexpectedly . . ."

The rest was a roar in my ears. A witness? Who can . . . ? He can't mean *Beulah*? I thought. Then the trial fell away like silly child play. And in a second I read my own verdict in Beulah's eyes. What she knew was going to hang me the minute it passed through her lips. I could imagine her saying the words. Knew the rough way the truth would spill out of her, as though every word had been rinsed in a glass of water to get rid of any trace of kindness.

"What in the name of God . . ." Cole began, wearing the only true blank look I ever saw on him. Mr. Watts was standing, saying something over the loud fuss people were making about a Nigro being in their court. Men stood on benches, hooted and cussed.

338

Cole started to rise, but I held onto his arm. "She didn't want to be there that night, Cole," I said. "It's something to do with a Nigro risking herself for the whites. With Beulah, everything comes down to the white."

"Good Lord, you mean she'd have you hanged for it?"

It took five minutes to quiet the court. Finally, the judge banged order and frowned at Mr. Watts. "A nigger to testify in a white man's court . . . ?" he muttered. "I might have expected something like this from the other side, Mr. Watts, but frankly, you surprise me."

"This nigger woman's an ex-slave, Judge," Mr. Watts said, smoothing his beard. "She was cook for Mrs. Ama Hadley and . . ."

Cole couldn't stay seated any longer, and jumped to his feet. In the gray light of the courtroom, his face was pale as snow. He knew as well as me what Beulah had to say. It was plenty to hang me.

"Your Honor," he said, with heat, "there's no mention of this woman on Mr. Watts's witness sheet. Why is she being sprung on us? I haven't had a chance to think about my own line of questioning. I'm totally unprepared. Besides, as you yourself have said, it's certainly the exception to every rule to bring a black woman into a Southern court. Add to that, she's actually indicating her intention to testify against a white woman. . . . No, Your Honor, I don't think this is proper procedure."

I heard the strain in Cole's voice and I knew he didn't like using this argument no more than I liked hearing him use it. But he was desperate. Though I didn't like it none, I understood.

The judge was in deep thought, and he took his time in answering either man. Finally, he said, "Well, I'm certainly not concerned about her not being on the witness sheet. And if the witness has just stepped forth, both sides are equally unprepared." He looked at Cole. "Counselor, it seems to me if you just ask good honest questions, the line of questioning will take care of itself. What does concern me is bringing in this nigger woman to testify against a white woman. I don't like it much."

"Mrs. Crocker is a Yankee, as Your Honor knows," Mr.

Watts said, giving the judge a look. "Presumably, her sentiments are in favor of treating Nigroes on an equal basis. Probably wouldn't mind sending her children to school with them." That brought a laugh, and he waited a minute before finishing. "I'm sure Mrs. Crocker won't have any objections to us bringing in a member of the darky race."

"Well, it's true enough that Mrs. Crocker's a Yankee," the judge said.

"Tennessee is a seceded state," Cole objected. "You have to go by Southern precedent, no matter what side of the war her husband fought on."

"We're a new union," the judge said. "There isn't much precedent. Anyhow, Confederate or Yankee, I'd like to hear all the evidence I can get on this matter." His head turned toward the jury box, where all the jurors had been hanging onto every word. "I do believe I'm going to let this nigger woman testify," he said. "But just you remember that a darky tends to lie and that by and large, niggers are a shiftless undependable race. You can never be sure of their motives. I hope I don't find this wench's been paid off." He gave Cole a suspicious look. "She better not all of a sudden start giving testimony for your side, Mr. MacPherson, or I'm going to be powerful suspicious."

"Oh, fine," Cole said, throwing his arms up. "You'll believe her if she denounces my client, but if she says anything positive about her, you'll be inclined to think we bought her testimony. For God's sake, can't you see—"

"Quiet," the judge said. "I've heard all I need to hear from you. We'll go ahead and hear the nigger woman. No, not another word, I've decided."

I could see Cole lose his temper before the words were even out of his mouth, before his fist hit the table. "I've had about all I can stand," he snapped, "of this biased one-man hangman's court. No wonder you've never had trials. They're superfluous. They're ridiculous. You're going to do as you want, no matter what. You don't even have a court stenographer. You know why? Because you don't want any written record of this non-

340

sense! But don't think you're going to get away with this! So help me, I'll take this matter to the Supreme Court, I'll—"

Judge Early leaned toward him. "There isn't any Supreme Court in the South, counselor. Have you forgotten?"

Before Cole could answer I stood up beside him and said, "Judge!"

The whole court looked at me and I heard Cole whisper, "Please, Elizabeth, not now. This isn't the time."

The judge looked from me to Cole and back. "Go ahead, Mrs. Crocker," he said, and relaxed in his chair. "Speak your mind."

I saw Beulah's head turn and I knew she was finally looking at me, but that was a second or two before I stopped seeing or hearing altogether. The only thing I knew was that an odd sort of rippling was sweeping over the courtroom, something that raised goosebumps and gave me a chill down my spine. Ama's here, I thought, and so close that she's liable to have her hand on my arm this minute, laughing that laugh of hers with her head thrown back and her eyes closed. I squinted through the dim room. *Ama?* I looked for her at the windows, at the doors, in the shadows on the walls. She wasn't there, and all of a sudden I remembered what she'd said about God being part of the air you breathe. And I opened up my mouth and breathed in Ama.

"Well, Mrs. Crocker, you have the court's *undivided* attention," said a voice from miles away.

"Judge," I said, hearing Ama's voice coming out of my mouth, "I'm sorry to interrupt, but you're wrong about what you said. About shiftless and undependable and likely to lie and all. I have to tell you that Beulah . . . well, Beulah's not lazy and she's not stupid, either. She's downright smart. And a hard worker and as brave as any person I ever met. And she's honest, too. Her only problem, if it is a problem, is not liking the white much, but can you blame her for that? What white likes her? Excepting for me and Ama Hadley, she never had a white friend. She's been whipped by the whites, had relatives killed by overseers, and been kept ignorant down on the plantation when she wanted to read and write more than anybody in this court. And her daughter died because of a disease brought by the white. But hate the whites or not, nobody could buy her testimony if they were to offer her a hundred dollars. That's all I have to say, sir."

"Just a minute," the judge said, not stirring in his big chair. "If she's your friend . . . what—"

I knew what he was going to ask—everybody in court must of known. What had brought her to testify against me, if I was one of the only two white friends she'd ever had. And with a sharp *ping* in my stomach, I knew the answer. My head turned to Beulah and she stood up beside Mr. Watts's chair, silent, black, thin. She was always tall, but now she looked like a skinny giant of a woman with her eyes glistening, her jaw lifted high.

"I think I know why she's here," I said, my eyes fixed steady on hers. "It's because . . . because Daisy died and Melissa Sue didn't. Is that why, Beulah?" I said, and I saw her chin drop, saw the huge tears that rolled down her cheeks. My own eyes were dry. No more tears, though God knew I wanted Daisy back, too. And Beulah back, and Ama back. And the old life back. Those long slow days, with Joe at the war and me there at Symphony Oaks with the women.

"Let's put the darky on the stand, Your Honor, and hear what she has to say!" Gilmore Watts said, with a sharp jerk of his chin toward Beulah. But she didn't seem to hear him. She was drying her eyes on a white handkerchief, locked away in a misery so deep she could of been twenty feet under the ground.

The judge brought his gavel down hard and the court came to a hush. "Take the stand, Beulah, there's a good girl. Nobody's going to hurt you here." Abner Wilcox came toward the witness chair with the Bible under his arm, but the judge waved him away. "No earthly use to swear in a darky," he said. "They don't understand."

I would of sworn that Beulah would never stand to be treated like this, but all her power to resist went into bearing her grief, and at the look of her, letting herself be led up to the stand like a child, I felt my knees give on me and I fell back into my chair.

Cole took hold of my hand quick. "Elizabeth, whatever you do, don't speak out again. Just let her talk. After Watts is done with her, I'll—"

"No, I want you to let her be," I said. "Don't tear her apart worse than she already is."

Cole had always been so careful about touching me in court, or even looking at me. When he did look, his eyes were usually cool. Now he'd lost his own control. His eyes were full of the worst fears and I felt his hand on mine under the table, felt it tighten.

"Do you know what *evidence* is?" Gilmore Watts was asking Beulah. "Do you know that word? It means if a cat eats a pitcher of cream, there might be cream on his whiskers. The cream is evidence. . . . Do you understand? Beulah? You hear me, now?"

She sat like stone, only her jaw working from side to side. Her eyes were dry now, but her face was still damp. It was like thousands of tears had soaked into her skin and nothing could dry them away. But she was calm as the dead, sitting there staring at nothing.

"Come now, if you don't talk, you'll make a fool of yourself. You wouldn't want that, would you? You take pride in being one of the smart ones, don't you, Beulah? There's not many darkies with brains like yours, are there?"

She moved then and her eyes saw him. But she said nothing.

"Now you listen to me, Beulah," he said. "Something brought you here. You told me you knew enough to—" He stopped short of saying "hang the defendant" and stared up at the judge, who was leaning well over the side of his stand, chewing on a piece of unlit cigar. "She said she could tell me everything I needed to know about what happened to Hank Greenwood, Judge."

"Well, then, for God's sake, Beulah, tell us," the judge snapped. "Come on, don't make us sit here and wait on you."

343

Still she sat there, keeping her thoughts to herself, and Gilmore Watts kept after her, practically yelling at her to speak, with the judge chiming in.

"Did Mrs. Crocker tell you anything about Hank Greenwood?"

Beulah's eyes were on me now and I nodded at her. Go ahead and speak, I tried to tell her. Make it easy on yourself. Say whatever you have to say. I understand. Maybe I would of hated you too, if Melissa had died and Daisy had lived. Who knows how insane a mother can get if her child dies?

Beulah opened her mouth and said, "No. She never told me nothin'."

Gilmore Watts sighed with relief that she was finally talking. "Well, then, did she tell you anything about the other Greenwoods?"

"She say them men rape her. Say they kill her husband, that all."

"Wait a minute!" Gilmore Watts said, and I could see the idea hit him square between the eyes like a blow from God's fist. "You were there that night, weren't you?" he almost yelled, his eyes boring into Beulah's. "You helped mop the floor, didn't you? You helped carry Hank Greenwood's body to the wagon, helped her dig the grave, helped to cover him over! Didn't you? *Didn't you!*"

By that time the people were squawking and the judge was gaveling and Gilmore Watts was so excited, the sweat was pouring out of his whiskers. His hands flew ever which way and his energy was fair bouncing off the walls. In the sudden silence that come over the room, he and everybody else turned to Beulah. Her eyes had that chill to them. Enough to make you reach for your coat. And she was squared off to face Gilmore Watts and everybody else. They'd never seen that arrogance of hers, but I knew it well enough. I'd been scorched enough times by it.

"You came here because you were with Elizabeth Crocker at that cabin that night, weren't you?"

344

She blinked at him, her eyelids flickering over those cold tombs she had for eyes. "What night?" she said.

"Don't pull this, woman!" Gilmore Watts said, putting both hands on the side rail by the witness chair and looming over Beulah with all his learning and all his puffy whiteness.

"What I pull?" Beulah said. "I just a poor ignorant nigger. Can't pull nothin' on the white. Y'all too smart."

"You want to be whipped? Is that what you want?" Gilmore Watts screamed. "You want fifty lashes with a lead-tipped whip?"

Beulah lowered her head and took a few seconds to think, then raised her chin, looked Gilmore Watts square in the eye, and smiled. "I been dyin' for that," she said soft-like. "Been too long since I got a good switch to my hide. Nothin' like it. I do believe it help the blood circulation."

He seemed to leap at her then, got halfway over the witness rail, her just sitting there with that smile on her face, when the sheriff was on top of him, pulling him away from the witness chair, with Abner Wilcox sort of fluttering 'round in the background, making fists out of his hands. Like Abner had ever had a fight in his life.

Not that Gilmore Watts put up any kind of resistance. He'd just got carried away for a minute, probably because he wasn't used to a black woman sassing him. Once he remembered he was in court, he calmed right down, even kind of mumbled a red-faced apology to the judge and then he demanded that something be done to get the impertinent black wench to talk. Everybody could tell she'd been there that night with me, and only thing left was to make her admit it—then we'd know all the truth there was to know.

Trouble was, nothing could move Beulah, not Gilmore Watts or the judge. Not threats or wheedling. I could of told them that. Once she'd made up her mind to something, that was that. Twenty minutes later, they were beat and she was heading up the aisle with a sassy look 'round her mouth. When she passed me, I stood up and whispered, "Beulah?"

345

She stopped and turned to look at me. Up front of the court, she'd been strong, calm. Up close, she looked exhausted and wild. Her lips moved. "Miz Ama dead?"

"She . . . she's with Daisy," I managed to say. "Same grave. She wanted you to know she's with her. She'll take care of her. Daisy won't be scared."

She nodded. "That help, maybe. I don't know. I sane one minute, gone the next. Nothin' help for long. Maybe I live to find Henry, maybe I already dead and don't know."

"I love you, Beulah," I said, knowing that I wasn't never going to see her again.

Those crazy eyes of hers narrowed as she stared at me. She sighed. A long tired sound. "And . . . and I don't hate you no more, neither," she said.

A minute later she was gone.

Twenty-nine

The courtroom might of vanished when Beulah shut the door that day. Seemed like she took all reality, all my belief in life with her. Like anybody overcome by misery, I felt everything outside me melt away. Only the pain was real. And to me, sitting there trapped in my seat, while Ferris and Charlie Greenwood took the witness chair, yelling something about killing a slew of chickens and hogs that night at the cabin—oh, yes, and Joe, too, a matter of self-defense—it seemed like all creation were losing the force to speak to me anymore. Even Ferris's voice seemed not much louder than a moth's wings flapping against a glass candle holder.

"Oh, Ama," I whispered, "I've forgot what you wanted from me."

Maybe an hour passed. I sat and stared at my hands and seemed to hear a hundred little noises pressing against the outside of the building. Probably children. Throwing something against the side of the courthouse. A creature running across the roof, tap-tap-tap. The creaking of the door as someone peered in and then closed it again. All these sounds were louder to me, more important, than the voices of Charlie and Ferris Greenwood, Mr. Watts's last two witnesses.

A strange light started drifting in from the window. Maybe people had crowded 'round the courthouse. Cole got up every now and then to say something, but if he looked at me, I didn't notice.

Finally, a man I didn't know come into the court and slipped a package on our table. Cole had been sitting slumped in his chair. For the first time, he seemed to find energy. As he opened the package, I glanced at Tom sitting behind me. He nodded, smiled—trying to say, I guess, that everything was going to be all right.

When Ferris Greenwood left the stand, taunting me as he walked by, trying to make me react, Mr. Watts turned to the judge and said he considered his case closed.

Then there were a few minutes' pause while Cole took his watch from his vest pocket and checked the hour. Simon Bell, foreman of the jury, stood up to stretch, and I wondered if the verdict was already set down. Wondered if Mr. Bell had accepted five dollars and a bottle of homemade brew for his guilty vote, when all at once Mrs. Reverend Harper stood up, clutching her ragged black shawl 'round her shoulders.

"Can I say something, Judge?" she asked from where she was standing.

Both lawyers started to object, and nobody, including me, had any idea what she was going to say, but the judge said, "You come right up here and speak your heart out. Never mind them. They're just lawyers."

"I don't want to sit in that fool chair," Mrs. Reverend said. "And, anyhow, I don't have much to say."

Judge Early grinned and stuck a little stub of a cigar in the side of his mouth. "Go ahead and talk then, you good woman, you. If you're comfortable where you are, I'm easy about it."

Abner Wilcox hurried over and said something about swearing her in.

"A minister's wife doesn't have to be sworn in," the judge said. "If anybody lives in fear of the Lord, it's a preacher's wife."

Mrs. Reverend drew a long breath, her face turning bright red. "All I have to say, Your Honor, is that Liz Ann attended a sewing benefit for our soldiers. It was at my house. And I don't recall her saying nothing bad about the Cause. If anybody said anything bad about it, it was Ama Hadley."

"You mean Mrs. Crocker's friend?" Gilmore Watts said right away.

"Yes," Mrs. Reverend said. "But then, Ama was always a little different . . . and you have to remember she helped everybody in this town. If you needed anything, and most of us did, sooner or later, you went to Ama Hadley. What she said was one thing. What she did was something different. I just wanted to say out of fairness that we may not like Liz Ann much on account of her war sympathies, but it's not like she was born and raised in the North. In fact, her folks come from Georgia. Let's see, the older children were born in Flintstone. I believe Liz Ann was the second Allen to be born in this town. Am I right, Mattie?"

"The third," Mattie Simpson said. "Jessie Lee and Buddy was the first two born here. I slapped their bottoms myself."

"Fact is," Mrs. Reverend said, looking out over the room, "that though her folks weren't from these parts, we've all known Liz Ann since she was the size of a grasshopper. My husband baptized her. I never knew her to be a liar. If she said them men did what she's claiming they did—"

"Objection to any opinion, Judge!" Gilmore Watts boomed.

"Oh, hush!" Mrs. Reverend snapped, looking down her nose at him. "If Liz Ann said she was outraged, I believe her. I certainly don't believe that Greenwood story about hogs and chickens. I know folks in this town that rode up there out of curiosity. She and Joe were poor as field mice. If it weren't for Ama Hadley, they'd've starved. That's all I have to say."

I saw some set faces, some mean looks, but I saw a few heads nodding. It hit me that a verdict takes place in separate hearts. To some, you're guilty. To others, you're innocent.

And then I heard Cole saying I should take the witness chair; I felt his hand under my arm, helping me out of my chair. We'd gone over what I was to say so often that I'd memorized it, but as I walked up there, I couldn't remember a word. I put my hand on the Bible, I sat down in the chair, and I thought, This is where Beulah sat. This is where Ferris Greenwood sat. This is where Pauline Crocker sat. And everybody swore to tell the truth and the stories were all different. Why should anybody believe anybody? I could certainly understand why they wouldn't believe me.

Cole took up a place right beside the chair, his foot on the step, his eyes calm on my face, and he said, "Just tell the jury what happened, Elizabeth."

I looked past his face and saw two rows of serious men. Men who'd been wiped out by a war that didn't have nothing to do with them. These weren't plantation owners—they'd been duped by the plantation owners, just like Ama said. They were like the rest of the poor South . . . fired up by the rich man's passions. They sat there staring at me, patched and dirty and needing to get this trial over so's they could go back out and try to rebuild their houses and barns and take care of their families and I knew they were in a hurry though they couldn't say so. That every day, every hour, were important to them.

I heard myself telling my story for the last time. About Joe leaving for the war and Melissa almost starving. How Mama and the girls wouldn't take us. About Ama saving us. I looked right at Mary Crocker when I told how come Joe'd signed for the North and how he'd come back from the War a pitiful, beaten man. I said about the Greenwoods coming. How Hank had shot Joe and how Ferris had raped me. I saw Mattie with her hands over her face and Mrs. Reverend Harper with her handkerchief pressed under her eyes and Mary Brian biting her lip. I told them about Ferris and Charlie and Cecil leaving and Hank saying he was going to see if there was anything left in the bottle. Then I stopped.

"Go on, Elizabeth," Cole said. "Did he rape you then?" The answer was in his eyes. He'd taught me what to say.

I took a long deep breath and thought about Ama. *Life was calling, and I had to be ready to answer.* And some of those talks we used to have at Symphony Oaks. Trying to figure out the mysteries of life. If a man with a gun breaks into your house and

350

tries to murder you, is it all right to kill him? Is it just your own life that's sacred, or all life? If a man hates you, do you hate him back? Or is he part of you? If your family disowns you and won't ever look on your face again, are they still your family? When people lie about you, do you lie back just as hard? Or do you tell the truth just for the sake of the truth? Now, right there on the witness stand, I knew how dead people must feel facing St. Peter. You probably wished you'd tried harder to figure everything out earlier. And now, caught between two answers just like the dead caught between heaven and hell, I wished the same thing. All those days back at Symphony Oaks, working out under the sun without a thought in my head. When the truth was probably pouring over me like hot lava. *All* those looks from Beulah that were like a road leading to a new me, if I'd just tried a little harder to understand. All those cold nights laying in the jail clinging so hard to a story I'd memorized. Holding onto a life raft instead of learning how to swim. And everybody could tell how needy I was the whole time. Else why the people all lined up to save me? . . . O, God, give me the courage to quit begging you and everybody else for salvation. Give me the courage of love, even in the face of hate. Give me the courage of truth, even facing liars. Give me the courage to save myself.

I looked 'round the court and saw all the faces, the eyes. Mattie and Mrs. Reverend. Miss Margaret. Tom and the sheriff, their faces long and worried. The room was so quiet everybody might of stopped breathing.

"No, Hank didn't rape me," I said in that quiet, and saw the look on Cole's face. "Only Ferris. Hank was going to, but—"

"Elizabeth," Cole said in a quiet voice, but I was looking at my people.

"I can't tell you any lies," I told them. "Hank Greenwood never left my house. I killed him."

The room exploded. I heard the yell that come out of Ferris Greenwood's mouth as the judge brought down his gavel. I felt Cole there beside me, steady and sure. As rooted as the tree I knew Tom to be. His head kept nodding, even though his eyes were kind of dazed. His lips moved. All right, he was saying, without making a sound. If that's the way you want it. Let it be. Let it be.

When the place settled down, I said, "Maybe when there's a war, everybody turns into a soldier. Just like so long as there's color, everybody tries to divide up into black and white. And maybe when you lose your homes and your families, you have to hate somebody. I can understand that. I may not be a Confederate, but I know what it means to lose everything." I looked at Ferris Greenwood and I told him that in a way, him and his brothers had actually done Joe a service when they killed him. And I told him and Charlie how and why I'd killed Hank. About Melissa screaming so hard and not being able to get her arms from 'round my neck. Of strapping her to me and riding through a night so black you couldn't see your hand in front of your face. Of sliding down a wet hill and digging a hole. Of the dreams I'd had ever since. The waiting for somebody to knock on my door.

Cole took a moment. Then he said, "Do you expect mercy?"

I shook my head. "No."

"Then why do you speak now?"

"Because it's the truth."

"All right," Cole said finally. His eyes were doubtful, his hair sweated to his scalp. "I think that's all."

The next half hour was Gilmore Watts and me. When he'd cock his head at me and try to make me out a liar, I'd tell the truth. It all come out of my mouth the way it should. You can't get tangled in the truth. You can't get mixed up.

"That's the way it was," I said. "And nothing can make me say any different."

And when there wasn't no more to say, Gilmore Watts went back to his chair and I went back to mine. I didn't know who'd won. I thought to myself, Life isn't about losing or winning. It's about being who you are.

"Judge, I'd like to call the sheriff back for just two or three questions, if you don't mind," Cole said. "It won't take long."

When the sheriff was in the chair, Cole asked him whether he'd examined Hank Greenwood's body.

"Yes. Not too much left of it," Ben said.

"How did you identify it?"

"Mainly clothes. And Hank's chipped tooth."

"The prosecution is making a lot of the bullet wound in Mr. Greenwood's back, Sheriff. Are you sure he really took that bullet in his back?"

"Both his spine and the back of his shirt could tell you that," Ben said.

"What kind of shot was it?"

"A big revolver of some sort. Same type as Hank's own gun."

"Could it have been a small handgun? Something that a woman might own?"

"Nope, we're talkin' about a substantial firearm."

"Are you absolutely positive about that?"

"I know guns. I saw the bullet. It was a revolver, but a large one without doubt."

Judge Early leaned down over his stand. "What point are you making, counselor? Mrs. Crocker has already admitted to shooting Hank Greenwood."

"The point I'm making, Judge," Cole came back, "concerns the *way* she shot him. Mr. Greenwood's brothers would have it that their last glimpse of their brother was of him held captive under a small revolver held by Elizabeth Crocker. Her story is entirely different and, if valid, would constitute justifiable homicide. Accordingly, at this time, I would like to change Elizabeth Crocker's plea to self-defense." Voices rose, but Cole spoke on. "The nature of Hank Greenwood's wound substantiates her version of how it happened. There were two bullets shot from Hank Greenwood's gun. The first went through the roof of Joe Crocker's mouth. The second bullet killed Hank Greenwood."

Gilmore Watts got up, smiling. "That's fine with me, Your

Honor. I'm only too glad the defense has stopped lying. Mrs. Crocker held her own revolver on Hank Greenwood, made him take his revolver off, then shot him with his own gun."

The judge stirred at that and frowned down. "Sounds a terrible awkward business to me," he observed. "Why not use her own gun if it's right there in her hand?"

"Because," Cole put in, "there was no other gun. Hank Greenwood removed his revolver with the full intention of committing rape. Ferris Greenwood had already outraged Mrs. Crocker. Hank Greenwood had stated his intention of following suit, and he took off his gunbelt and laid it on the chair beside her bed. It was when her daughter started crying that Mrs. Crocker shot him—"

"In the back!" Gilmore Watts reminded the court.

"Because the man was a madman: He had already killed her husband and he was starting toward her daughter!"

"Mr. MacPherson, the Greenwoods were there for one reason only," Mr. Watts said. "To requisition goods for the Confederate army. They weren't murderers, they were soldiers. They haven't lied; only the defense has lied!"

"In that case, Your Honor," Cole said, "Sheriff Oates can step down. I'd like to recall Ferris Greenwood."

While Ferris stomped up to the witness chair, eyeing me as he went, Cole lifted papers with military stamps on them from the open package on our table and started making checkmarks here and there. It was an evil look Ferris had given me, gloating and cold.

He was seated but still staring at me hard when the judge said, "Remember, Mr. Greenwood, you're still under oath." Ferris half raised his hand, and Cole straightened beside me and went forward.

"Mr. Greenwood!" Cole said, circling him. "All this must be . . . very disrupting in the life of a soldier. Wouldn't you say?"

Ferris's eyes half closed in a squint. "Yeah," he said.

"Hard to get away from camp, I guess."

"Yeah."

Cole put his thumbs in his vest pockets and seemed to mull

354

something over in his head. He was taking his time now, almost like all of a sudden he'd started to enjoy hisself. "Well, tell me, if you would," he said, "how it works. Do they give you some sort of official leave?"

Ferris chewed his lip and thought about it.

"Or is this kind of an unofficial leave?"

"Well, that's the way of the day," Ferris said. "Hell, half the army disappears come plantin' time. When this is settled, I'll go on back to my unit. Won't nobody care. At least I'm servin' my country. And I ain't one of them deserters that goes off and lives in the mountains just so's he don't have to fight!"

"That's truth!" some man's voice agreed, and the judge looked down and said, "Quiet out there!"

Cole walked back to our table and picked up paper and pen. "What unit are you in, anyhow?" he asked, ready to make the note.

Ferris scratched under his beard. "Up in the Cumberlands."

"Which regiment, though?"

"Rather not say." Ferris grinned. "Not till I get a chance to sign back in on the rolls."

A few of the men laughed, but when I looked over my shoulder, I noticed the women were mostly frowning.

"Whether you'd rather say or not," Cole told him, "I want to know. Which regiment are you in?"

Ferris moved 'round some in his seat, then said, "First Tennessee."

"And you say Hank was with the Morgan Raiders?"

"Yeah, we was proud of that."

"Your other two brothers—what units are they with?"

Ferris's face darkened. "What does that have to do with her murderin' Hank?"

Judge Early's face leaned down over the witness chair. "Answer the man's questions and don't ask him any. He's the solicitor."

Ferris chewed on his lip awhile, then said, "I don't remember what their units are. You'll have to ask 'em yourself."

355

The judge looked out over the benches and found Fat Charlie. "For the record, Charles Greenwood, give me your unit." When Fat Charlie sat with his hat in his hands and looked at the floor, the judge frowned. "It's just a formality," he said, sounding impatient. "Give the man your unit and let him make his note."

Fat Charlie half opened his mouth, but Ferris jumped in first. "He's nothin' to say. We're soldiers in the Confederate army. That should be enough!"

It hadn't seemed an important question. Now all at once you could hear feet shuffling, see necks craning all over, as everybody tried to get a look at Fat Charlie, who was scrunched down in his seat.

Cole smiled. "For the time being, Judge, let's forget Charles Greenwood. There'll be time enough for him later on. For now, let's stick to Ferris Greenwood." Ferris twisted some in his chair, and Cole swung 'round to face him again. "By the way, Mr. Greenwood, have you seen much action?"

"Some. I've killed me a few Yanks."

"Which battles?"

"Up in the hills."

"Where, exactly?"

Ferris looked at the judge, and the judge stared back at him. "Well, Liberty Gap and all."

"Why don't you describe that battle for us? The units involved, field leaders . . . just the details as you remember them."

"Hell, who knows about details?" Ferris said. "I was up there shootin', runnin' here, there, everywhere, that's all. Hidin' in trenches . . ."

Cole's eyebrows lifted. "You mean on foot?"

"Yeah."

"Weren't you mounted when you raided the Crockers?"

"Well, yeah."

"Which came first? Liberty Gap or the Crocker raid?"

"Oh, let me see . . . Liberty Gap, I believe."

"Was that *the* battle of Liberty Gap? The one we all know of?"

"Sure."

Cole seemed puzzled. He put his hand to his head. "Didn't the battle of Liberty Gap take place in June? Over two months after you raided the Crockers?"

Ferris scratched under his beard and thought. He'd stopped being smug a long time ago. "Well," he said after considerable thought, "maybe I got it backwards."

"That roan you ride. Isn't it the same horse you were riding at the time of your brother's death? Before you answer: A wagonload of women, as well as Tom Higgins, saw you on that horse two days after you and your brothers murdered Joe Crocker and raped Elizabeth Crocker."

Ferris was so busy thinking about the horse, he didn't pay attention to murder or rape. "All right," he said finally. "I guess it's the same horse."

"But for a stretch of time after that night and before coming back to town, you were in the battle of Liberty Gap without your horse? What happened to him? Was he injured?"

"Stone in the forehoof," Ferris grunted. "He couldn't be rode for a while."

"Where did you keep him while you were away fighting?"

Sweat had started to gather at the corners of Ferris's eyes and along the ridges in his neck. "I left him home with Pa. At Murfreesboro. Tell you the truth, I just picked him up 'bout a month ago when I was home visitin'."

Paper snapped in Cole's hand as he held a letter and envelope high and I got a glimpse of the crudest printing I ever saw, full of ink blotches and dirty smudges.

"I submit this letter as evidence, Judge. It's from Cecil Greenwood, Senior. He writes that he hasn't seen any of his boys for close to a year. If necessary, we can put this trial on hold and I can bring him in to testify."

"What does a horse have to do with anything?" Gilmore Watts said, giving Cole the evil eye. "What does it prove?"

"More lying," Cole said, his voice heavy on the word. "If you look at what the Greenwoods have said after putting their hands on the Bible, it's a long spiderweb, spun with lies. A lady's handgun, horses, requisitions—"

"We was requisitionin' and you can't prove nothin' else!" Ferris yelled from his chair.

"Let's see about that," Cole said, taking a stroll toward the witness chair. When he got closer, he stopped to take a hard look at Ferris, sort of like a doctor examining a sickly specimen of a human. Then, as he'd done so often, he put his foot on the step leading to the witness chair and leaned in. "I've been wondering," he said, "how you get to be on a raiding party. Is that a prime job, raiding? Or do you volunteer? Or what, exactly?"

"Me, I volunteered," Ferris said. "I guess some was appointed."

"Without any specific plan?" Cole said. "Was there, for instance, a list of towns known to be sympathetic to the Southern cause?"

"Yep. There was a list. We knew Frisbin was rebel."

"Rebel? You're a Confederate and you call a Southern town *rebel*?"

"It was Confederate."

"Were these supplies to go back to your regiment—the First Tennessee, I believe you said?"

"That's right."

"What about the units of your fellow raiders . . . beg pardon, your fellow requisitioners? Were their units to go hungry? How do four brothers who are in different military units get assigned to the same detail?"

"Your Honor," Gilmore Watts said, "I don't understand where this whole line of questioning is leading. We're here to talk about a specific murder, not the workings of an entire army. We're civilians; what do we know about the workings of an army?"

Cole swung 'round to face him. "Then you think these questions were better addressed to the military?"

"Exactly."

In a flash Cole was at the table, his hand sweeping up the folder with the military stamp on the cover. "I had some questions about the Greenwoods from the very beginning. The most obvious question was what four brothers from different units were doing in the same supply unit. On the surface, it seemed improbable. Because of that one improbability, I troubled myself to have a lengthy telegraph correspondence with some acquaintances I have in Richmond. Only this afternoon, I received a packet of information, which I wish to enter into evidence in the trial at this time."

"What sort of information?" Gilmore Watts said. If he looked uneasy, Ferris looked worse, his face growing redder by the minute. His eyes went from Cole to Mr. Watts and back, over and over again, his mouth opening and closing like a gasping trout flopping 'round in a fisherman's boat.

Judge Early took the folder from Cole and opened it, his eyes skimming over the pages as he turned them. Seeming to find a place with his finger, he frowned at Ferris, then flipped the page, found another place, and reached for a pen. He marked it, then went on and found two other places, then looked up.

"What's in that folder?" Gilmore Watts yelped, hurrying up to the judge's stand.

Without waiting for Cole to explain, Judge Early glared down at Ferris. "I read here that you and your brothers were never in the military," he snapped. "Only one of you ever enlisted, and that was Hank. He deserted the Raiders after six weeks of service, when he was caught using confiscated military supplies for his own use."

In a sudden roar of voices, the judge slammed his gavel onto his block of wood. "Keep quiet," he bellowed, "I'm trying to think!"

"While you're thinking, Your Honor," Cole said, waving papers, "here are some letters that were in the same packet. I also wish to offer them into evidence. They're from over a dozen farmers near Murfreesboro, where the Greenwoods lived before the war. As I told you, their father still lives there, and has been trying to maintain a farm although he's near starvation. The letters state that the Greenwoods were found to be looting neighborhoods while calling themselves Confederates. Probably, they got the idea from Hank. In his brief stint as a Morgan Raider, he apparently fell in love with plundering. Liked it so well that he even stole from the army. He and his brothers dressed themselves as soldiers and went out to steal whatever they could get in the name of the Confederate army. Your Honor, it's obvious that these Greenwoods are thieves, traitors to the cause they pretend to honor. And it's equally obvious that they're the kind of men who would shoot a man in cold blood and insult his wife. I move for dismissal at this time!"

Then, like in slow motion, I saw Gilmore Watts waving his arms, saying something to the judge, and the judge nodding. I heard Cole almost shouting, his voice hoarse, and I saw Ferris Greenwood looking at me, his face all pinched together. And then a sudden terrible quiet swept over the room.

"No," Judge Early said to Cole. "No, it's not going to be all that easy. After all this trouble, this verdict is going to be put to the jury."

Thirty

The closing arguments were short, Gilmore Watts and Cole ramming at each other like wounded bulls. People argued out loud in the courtroom, and the judge had to gavel order a dozen times. Then, like I were in a trance, I watched the jury of men stand and leave the room, Simon Bell leading the way. When the back door closed behind them, we were left with an uneasy ripple that spread through the whole room.

At first, people tended to watch the back door. Then, as the minutes crawled by, some of the more restless men headed outdoors. A few women drifted over to our table and touched me on the shoulder. Their eyes were watchful. Soft and wary, all at the same time. Mrs. Reverend sat next to Miss Margaret and I heard their voices murmuring above the idle chatter of the room. Over their shoulders, a man was looking at me, making noises—"Aunk, aunk"—with something fierce in his eyes. Saliva hung like molasses in his beard.

Tom came from the front door, where he'd been leaning against the wall, and pushed the man away, but the "Aunk, aunk" sound kept coming until Ben Oates come over to settle him down. A few women shouted at the man, "Aunk yourself!"

"Perhaps we shouldn't wait it out here," Cole said. "Juries can take hours, even days."

I looked 'round the room. At every sound, even a cough, everyone would turn to the back door. I could see faces change, some dreading, some anticipating, some just excited. My blood quickened and my throat was tight.

"I'll be all right," I said. "The rest of you can go." And I saw the look that went from Cole to Tom, as neither man moved.

Twenty minutes passed then, not more. First thing I heard was heavy footsteps in the back. Then the door opening. The judge, who had been at the front door smoking his cigar and talking to some of the men, come running down the aisle with the cigar still stuck between his teeth. He hopped on the judging stand and started hammering.

"Sit down, everybody! Sit down, for God's sake! Jury's coming! Jury's coming!"

My people were still at my table. Miss Margaret and the sheriff. Tom. And, of course, Cole, his face going dead white when he heard all those feet marching through the back door. I looked back and saw people leaning forward on their benches, and I thought: You never know what people are really thinking. The folks in this town have their own way of looking at things. Mattie and Mrs. Reverend had come 'round. But most folks probably wouldn't never accept me, no matter what the verdict was. Like the man making the aunk, aunk noises, whoever he was, and Deputy Frank Wright and the two men telling Nigro stories in the jail that night. And the Crockers and . . . even my own family. They'd been in the habit of hating me too long. They'd forgot about feeling anything other than hate.

And what if I was found guilty? Would this town wait for all those appeals Cole talked about? Or would they just take me out back and string me up? I saw the sheriff touch his gun and wondered if he was thinking the same thing.

Quiet hung heavy on the air as the jury come filing into their two rows, Simon Bell up front after spending the whole trial in the back. The horse breeder stood beside him. Then two farmers, the schoolteacher . . . Trying to read their faces was impossible. They were all looking at the floor except Simon Bell. His head was up and I imagined I read my fate on his broad face, in his unblinking eyes.

"Stand up," Cole whispered, and I was somehow on my feet, with Cole beside me. Then all of a sudden Tom stood up too, taking his place on my other side. Then Miss Margaret and the sheriff. All standing. Waiting with me. Then across the room Mattie hauled herself up, then Mrs. Reverend and several other women. Josephine Steedman. Even Gillian Brian. Then a few men got up, Goliath Smith's head towering over the room. Until half the room were standing and the other half sitting.

The judge's gavel fell and the courtroom seemed to freeze 'round me.

In the quiet I could hear an odd sound, something like a loud thumping, and I thought it was like the room had a heart and the heart had started beating. I saw Simon Bell get to his feet. Saw his eyes were on me, those clear eyes, unclouded even by the pain of his blacksmith's fire that I remembered from my childhood.

"Well, in the name of Jesus, go ahead, Simon!" the judge barked, the veins standing out on his neck. His face had sweat on it and he swabbed it away with a huge white handkerchief.

Simon Bell looked at me a moment longer, eyes staring hard, as if trying to tell me something. I saw him stand a little straighter, like all of a sudden his wide shoulders had been freed of a weight. Then he said, "Your Honor, we find the lady not guilty!"

He said something else, but the roar of the courtroom drowned him out, and in the crush of people that swarmed our table, my people were first to hug me. In different ways, I owed my life to all of them. Including the two men who put their arms 'round me, each one hugging me. Each one trying to read his own fate in my eyes.

"A lot of spunk," the judge was saying to Ben Oates, holding his cigar at arm's length. A loop of spittle woggled from its underside. "Yes, sir. For a woman, she's got a lot of spunk," he said as Tom and Cole began escorting me from the court-room.

People shoved, tried to get closer to me. I heard more than saw the front door of the courthouse thrown open. Ferris and

363

Fat Charlie glowered at me as I passed. I heard sobbing noises. Jeers. People calling my name.

But the voice I'd always remember, the voice that rang out above the rest, was Miss Margaret's. As I hesitated at the door I heard her say: "Go home now, child. Go on. You're free."

And then I was outside, the cold air stinging my face, and I wasn't afraid no more.

Thirty-one

Seems to me that a person's life is made out of long stretches of time that don't mean nothing, and a few days here and there that do.

I didn't know why I would think of Moses now. Maybe because I seemed to be following him down a long, winding road. It rained the night I met him, and since then the rains had fallen hard and steady, worse than any rains ever known in the state. Moses and me, we had run along the valley, hiding in the shadows of the mountains, on nights too black to see the moon. While the soldiers fought the war, we fought our little battles. And I lived to tell about it and Moses didn't.

But the details don't matter. Just like the lamp in your hand don't matter, only the oil it burns on. If there's a record being kept somewhere, it's of the silence you find in the noise of the battle, the sight you find through the cloud of smoke. Your hand against a warm piece of soil as it crumbles through your fingers. The cry of your child in the night, that stops as you hold it to your breast. For Ama, it was the wind in the oaks. For Beulah, it was finding her own voice. For Jinny, it was love, and for Delilah, it was waiting patient while youth slipped by. For Cole, it was the truth of the law. For Tom, it was the truth in the land. And Joe didn't find his.

But for me, I guess, it was being worthy. Maybe it come from feeling unworthy for so long. Or maybe from knowing in my heart that if you're not worthy, you've got nothing. Nothing is real. Your friends are there because of what you've pretended to be. Your daughter loves you only while she needs you. Your husband picks you out because of how you look or how you keep house and never loves you at all. And the worst is the picture you keep locked inside. The kind of image that keeps a pretty woman on the run all day to the looking glass, afraid that the picture's sneaked out of the box.

For Moses, there weren't the same questions about worth. He knew who he was on the night he ran. From the moment he took off, it wasn't hisself he doubted, only those of us who crossed his path. It's here we come to our differences, yet, after all, they weren't so great. A runner is a runner. A seeker is a seeker. And the beginning of the journey is at least as important as the end, it appears to me. At least, to my own way of thinking, you have to have a fair amazing idea if it sets you rolling under a fence owned by a man like Mr. Jackson. Or confessing to murder in a hangman's court. For once you confess to murder or roll under that fence, you do not deny any longer your true self. After that, you run in search of a truth that is so private only you can read the handwriting on the wall. You do what you do and you do it without regret.

I found Tom in his chair, an open book across his chest, his legs crossed. He was so still that for a second I thought he was sleeping, but right away his head turned toward me and his eyes were open. Like always, I was caught by those eyes, so kind, so wise, and I could no more look away than stop breathing. I dropped to my knees in front of his chair and he smiled at me.

"That chair you're sitting in," I said. "I love to see you sitting in it. I used to sit in my cell, and along about seven, I'd think: Maybe Tom's sitting in his chair now, and I'd picture you here like this and it would bring me peace. I care about you so much." I reached out to take his hands in mine. "I love how tough your hands are," I told him. "I love seeing you striding across a field with your head up. I love all the work you've done for us, without never a thought for yourself or a word of complaint about how hard it was to do the work of five men, or even more. I love how you are with your son and with my daughter. I love how gentle you treat your father, though he's the meanest old cuss I ever saw."

He laughed some at that, but his eyes were serious as I'd ever seen them as his hands tightened 'round mine.

"Why are you telling me this?" he said in his quiet way.

"Because," I said, my eyes never leaving his, "I don't want you to ever think it will be easy for me to leave you, Tom. Right now, my heart feels heavy as iron. It aches. See, I never wanted to leave you, not any of you. You're my family. This is my home. Ama's in every room of this house. And this land . . . I dreamed of living on this land with you forever. But . . ."

"You don't have to say any more," he said, reaching out to smooth my hair. Then he pulled me up and held me against him. I could hear his slow steady heart beating. I felt sad enough to die.

"Poor little bird," he said. "You've fought so hard for your wings, and now you're afraid to fly."

"I don't want to fly," I said, feeling the tears push up in my eyes. But I blinked them away. "Tom, it's not . . . it isn't *just* Cole, you know. It's like God whispered in my ear. He told me, Elizabeth Ann, I dragged you a country mile toward a new you. . . . Now you got to walk on for a spell on your own muster." I pulled back some, so's he could see my face. "I've been *changing*, Tom. I think maybe this war's going to change all of us. Not all at once, but a little at a time. You know how Ama used to drag Jinny and Delilah into white folks' conversations? Set them down in the parlor with her company? That was Ama's way of changing things just a little bit. . . . Do you understand what I'm saying, Tom?"

Something flickered in his eyes and he nodded. In that second, though he hadn't said a word, I felt sure as if he'd told me that he was thinking of his father and the way Old Man Higgins treated black people.

"What I think is, Tom, that it may be high time for some new blood in that closed Virginia society!"

He smiled at that, then laid his head top of mine, and I

could feel him sigh. After a few minutes, he pushed me away. Something like pushing that bird he'd called me out of its nest. Then he got up, crossed the room, and stopped at the door, his head only inches shorter than the tall arch over him.

"I'd best be checking on Ben," he said. "Elizabeth, I'm here. That's all I'm saying to you. I'm here like the land is here. And I'll do everything that can be done under the sun to keep the house here. If you need me, just look behind you and I'll be standing there close as your own shadow."

"I won't need to look behind me, Tom," I whispered. "I'll be carrying you with me—all of you—wherever I go."

But he never heard me. He was gone. I could picture him on his way to Ben's room. See him walk into the dim light of the one candle that always burned alongside Ben's bed until he slept. I could see Ben laying there, his face flushed from the day's excitement. Not so thin no more. His eyes behind his closed lids were Tom's eyes.

"Oh, Ben! I'm sorry. I'm truly sorry."

"I'll take care of him for you," said a low voice from the door Tom had left open, and somehow I wasn't surprised when Delilah stepped out of the dark. She come toward me, her eyes glistening, her skirt rippling against the floor. Then she was standing in front of me, putting her arms 'round my shoulders, her cheek against mine.

"I'd recognize you anywhere, even if I was blind and deaf," I told her, holding her. "We're so close that we could . . . well, we could almost be the same person, you and me."

"And one of us stay," she whispered against my ear. "And one go."

"It's funny, isn't it," I said. "I always thought you'd be the one going, Delilah."

"The boy," she breathed. "Way thing be, Ben almost like mine. That the way I see it, anyhow. Like I said, I look after him, Lizbeth. Truth be, it not just for you. It what I want for my own self, or else . . . well, I wouldn't do it," she finished, and I could feel her shrug.

"Delilah? Will you . . . ?" What I wanted to say—and I

don't know where it come from, just all of a sudden it were there—was, *Will you look after both of them?* I didn't say it, leastways I was fair certain I didn't, but anyhow she answered me.

"I will," she said, never taking her arms from 'round me.

Time passed and shadows pressed 'round us, but we never stirred. We were as close to being one woman as it was possible to be. And one of us was staying and one was going.

I found Cole in the back acre, where I knew he'd be though he'd never said a word of us meeting and neither had I. He was leaning against the same tree he'd leaned on so long ago. For a long time neither of us said nothing, and I could hear him breathing, see his shoulders rise and fall as if he had to struggle some to catch his breath.

"I suppose I'm a coward," he said after a while, and though his words were low, they carried easy on the cold crisp air. The bare trees were iced over and a film of frost laid over the ground. Even the air seemed to sparkle as Cole and I stared at each other.

"Strange, isn't it," he went on when I didn't say anything. "I've never been afraid of anything. Never tried much to please anybody. Fairly well told Richmond society to go to hell years ago. Hung around in the worst neighborhoods visiting the downtrodden masses I liked to call my clients. I had a few threats on my life. . . . Once I stuck my finger down the barrel of a loaded revolver. But I was afraid to face you. I was afraid that I'd read you wrong . . . or that you'd changed your mind . . . or perhaps I was just afraid I'd made you up. That when I'd look at you as if you were really for me . . . just the instant I'd start to believe in us . . . you'd vanish right before my eyes." Then finally he come to me, his collar open against the night air, the crunch of ice sounding under his heels.

I reached out to take the hand he held out as if he didn't dare touch me first, and the minute I touched him, I felt the breath go out of me, my heart pick up speed.

Yes, I thought, holding onto his hand. Yes, I do want to fly.

The next second his arms went 'round me and his warm mouth was on mine and I felt him shaking, felt both of us shaking as his lips moved onto my cheek, my throat.

"God, I love you, Elizabeth," he said, lifting his head to look in my eyes when he said it. "Are you real? And if you are . . . can you really walk away from all this? From Tom? Can you do all that to go with me? Tell me!" His hands closed on my arms and he shook me a little. "For God's sake, *tell me!*"

"I love you, Cole, and I'll go with you anywhere," I said, and I saw the tight look of fear leave his face. Felt his heart racing as he pulled me back into his arms. Time passed or stood still. Who knew, who cared how long we stood there. There was no time with Cole's arms 'round me, his lips open on mine. There wasn't even a world. Only Cole and me, trying to get closer and closer, and when he finally pulled away to whisper, "Why in God's name would you choose me?" it wasn't hard to find the answer. It was the same answer I'd found once before in court.

"Because anything else would be a lie," I said, my voice steady and sure.

"No regrets? Are you absolutely sure?"

"The only regrets would of been the other choice," I told him. "I'd of been missing you my whole life."

He searched my eyes, looking for doubt, and finally he smiled. "I don't know what kind of father I'll be. But I love every hair on your head, so I'll worship the hell out of your daughter. Still, I don't know the first thing about it."

"I don't know anything about Richmond, either," I laughed. "So I guess we'll both have our hands full."

But standing there under the icy trees, hands locked, warm, staring into each other's eyes, we would of dared far more. I would of followed him anywhere. Chose him over all the world if he'd been poor, or black, or had only an hour left to live. That he felt the same was in his eyes. The feeling in him ran deep. As deep as the silence in the hills.

*   *   *

Cole and I were married a month after the trial. Our people were with us and Reverend Harper, home from the war, said the words that joined us. We took the train to Richmond that same night; I sat beside Cole, watching Melissa sleep on his shoulder, his dark head bent over her, his hand against her back.

One way or the other, I knew we'd get by. There isn't much to need but air to breathe. Food and water. Sleep. Shelter. You need to see yourself as part of something bigger than yourself alone. Beyond that, there's choices. There's the middle of the journey, so much harder to see than the beginning or the end.

"We can still turn around and go back," Cole said in a low voice, his hand moving to pat Melissa as she stirred in her sleep. "Can't you see me as a lawyer in Frisbin? I could take a lot of pleasure in being the bane of the judge's life."

I only smiled. I had come to peace with my decision. For while others clung to the old ways, I had married the lightning in the sky. Loved it and let it light up my life and gone where it would take me, knowing that, like Ama, I wasn't afraid of change. From farther back in the car, I heard the soldiers who'd been arguing for the last hour grow quiet, and Cole and I turned to each other, his free hand finding mine. Somewhere out there, the world was still at war. There was the white hating the black, the black hating the white, the Yankee and the rebel blasting each other with whatever weapons were at hand. The war was such a part of us, it seemed likely to last forever. Meantime, there was a house in Richmond waiting for me. A new language to learn. A closed society just waiting to be pried open.

I had made my choice, I believe, the way Ama would of made it. In reverence for love. In consideration of truth as I had come to understand it . . . that every day of life is a new celebration. That running free is worth every risk.

And yes. Ama, like Moses, would of understood, and approved.

37 21 34 5 3 7 23 210